CHLOE ZHIVAGO'S R
MARRIAGE AND M

# CHLOE ZHIVAGO'S RECIPE FOR MARRIAGE AND MISCHIEF

A NOVEL

## Olivia Lichtenstein

BALLANTINE BOOKS

NEW YORK

*Chloe Zhivago's Recipe for Marriage and Mischief* is a work of fiction. Names, characters, places, and incidents are the products of the author's imagination or are used fictitiously. Any resemblance to actual events, locales, or persons, living or dead, is entirely coincidental.

Copyright © 2007 by Olivia Lichtenstein

All rights reserved.

Published in the United States by Ballantine Books, an imprint of The Random House Publishing Group, a division of Random House, Inc., New York.

BALLANTINE and colophon are registered trademarks of Random House, Inc.

Originally published in Great Britain as *Mrs. Zhivago of Queen's Park* by the Orion Publishing Group, London.

Grateful acknowledgment is made to the following for permission to reprint previously published material:
John Gregory Brown: Excerpt from *Decorations in a Ruined Cemetery*, copyright © 1993 by John Gregory Brown. Used by permission of John Gregory Brown.
David Higham Associates: Excerpt from "Les Sylphides (Novelette II)" from *Collected Poems* by Louise MacNeice (Faber and Faber, London, 2002). Used by permission of David Higham Associates.
P&P Songs Ltd.: Excerpt from "Raindrops Keep Falling on My Head," words and music by Burt Bacharach and Hal David, copyright © 1969 by Hidden Valley Music. Used by permission of P&P Songs Ltd.
Warner Bros. Inc.: Excerpt from "It Had to Be You," words by Gus Kahn and music by Isham Jones, copyright © 1924 (Renewed) by Warner Bros. Inc. Rights for the extended renewal term in the U.S.A controlled by Gilbert Keyes Music and Bantam Music Publishing Co., and administered by The Songwriters Guild of America. Canadian rights controlled by Warner Bros. Inc. All rights reserved. Used by permission of Warner Bros. Inc.

ISBN 978-0-345-49575-4

Library of Congress Cataloging-in-Publication Data
Lichtenstein, Olivia.
Chloe Zhivago's Recipe for Marriage and Mischief: a novel / by Olivia Lichtenstein.
p. cm.
ISBN 978-0-345-49575-4 (alk. paper)
1. Women psychotherapists—England—London—Fiction. 2. London (England)—Fiction. 3. Married people—Fiction. 4. Adultery—Fiction. 5. Psychological fiction.
I. Title.
PR6112.I25M77 2007
823'.92—dc22          2006049889

Printed in the United States of America on acid-free paper

www.ballantinebooks.com

1 3 5 7 9 8 6 4 2

First Edition

*Designed by Stephanie Huntwork*

FOR MY FATHER, EDWIN
MARCH 1923—MARCH 2004

*So they were married*
*To be the more together*
*And found they were never again so much together,*
*Divided by the morning tea,*
*By the evening paper,*
*By children and tradesmen's bills.*

—LOUIS MACNEICE, "Les Sylphides (Novelette II)"


*Marriage may be compared to a cage:*
*the birds outside despair to get in*
*and those within despair to get out.*

—MICHEL DE MONTAIGNE, *Essays*


*Happy families are all alike;*
*every unhappy family is unhappy in its own way.*

—LEO TOLSTOY, *Anna Karenina*

# Chloe Zhivago's Recipe for Marriage and Mischief

*Chloe Zhivago, age thirteen, carefully folded a sheet of writing paper with psychedelic swirls in various shades of pink. On it she and her best friend, Ruthie Zimmer, had written,* To Help the Work of Future Historians and Archaeologists: This box contains important clues to the lives of two girls in the 1970s. *They placed the letter in a tartan biscuit tin that contained a plum-colored Biba lipstick, a copy of* Jackie *magazine, odd pieces of broken jewelry, letters they had written to each other, and a contract of eternal friendship signed in their blood. Once they had taped the tin shut, they dug a deep hole at the bottom of Chloe's garden and buried the box in the earth. The two girls stood solemnly in front of the freshly turned earth, their heads bowed as they mourned a future that would, one day, no longer contain them. Later, they sat indoors, watching the rain fall and having a race with two raindrops that were running down the windowpane: one was Chloe's, the other Ruthie's. "What are you going to do when you grow up?" Ruthie asked Chloe. "Get a good job, fall in love, have children, and live happily ever after," Chloe answered. This is it, then, the bit that came after* happily ever after.

*Chapter 1*

I'd been fine when I got up that morning. Quite chirpy really. Not even irritated when I couldn't find the kettle because my husband, Greg, had hidden it. It's the very things that so charm you about a man when you first meet him that subsequently cause you such intense exasperation. Greg's uncle had got Alzheimer's when he was thirty-two and, as a result, Greg had developed a pathological fear of his memory deteriorating and had set himself little memory tests from an early age. "The brain's a muscle just like any other and needs exercising," he'd say. Absolutely fine for him, but irritating for the rest of us who don't feel that remembering where you hid the kettle from yourself is a major and necessary triumph in the muscle-taut memory stakes. But that morning I remember whistling as I hunted for it and giving an exultant and good-humored cheer when I finally unearthed it in the drum of the washing machine.

Greg remained oblivious. He was sitting at the kitchen table scratching out yet another furious letter in his illegible doctor's handwriting with the quill pen I had jokingly given him some years before with which to write his many letters of complaint. (I was surprised that he didn't write on parchment, use a wax seal, and get a liveried footman to deliver his missives by hand.) This current letter was to the council about a parking fine.

"Ha, Chloe, listen to this," he said. "I'm demanding a reply from the councillor himself." He stood up, held the letter as far from himself as his arm would reach (vanity forbade the use of reading glasses and concomitant recognition of middle age), cleared his throat, and, using the special voice he reserved for officialdom, read: "Upon examining the legislation, I am astonished to learn that the London Borough of Brent, or its agents, appears to be attempting to extort money from me in an unlawful manner. Please find enclosed an extract of the Bill of Rights Act 1689, enacted and formally entered into Statute following the Declaration of Rights 1689. I draw your attention to the following section: 'That all grants and promises of fines and forfeitures of particular persons before conviction are illegal and void.'"

He looked up at me, delighted with himself, like a dog that has brought a far-flung stick back in record time to lay at his master's feet. He reached for a slice of toast, which he spread carefully with a thin layer of cholesterol-busting Benecol.

"What does that mean? That they can't enforce parking fines at all without convicting you of a crime?"

"Precisely," he said, giving a smug little smile as he left the room. "First you have to be found guilty in a court."

Leo, our fifteen-year-old son, made a lightning kitchen raid before my eyes, during the course of which he successfully snatched a chocolate bar from a tin that was supposed to be hidden in a top cupboard, swigged orange juice from a carton in the fridge, and left before anyone could shout at him. Bea, the Czech au pair, gave a characteristic scowl at the space he had briefly occupied before shrugging and returning to her careful task of assembling a platter of exotic fruits that I had bought specifically for that night's supper. I said nothing, assuming it was for my twelve-year-old daughter, Kitty, who had recently announced that she was on a health kick and, as every parent knows, nothing and no one should stand in the way of any child who voluntarily eats fresh fruits and vegetables.

Just then Kitty came in, carrying a plate of half-finished instant mashed potato.

"I've got a tummy ache," she said.

"I'm not surprised, eating that processed rubbish," I answered unsympathetically. "What happened to the new health regime?"

I realized then that the exotic fruit platter must be intended for none other than Bea's own stomach; sure enough, Bea settled herself comfortably at the table while I tried not to watch as, delicately, with a knife and fork, she ate slice after slice of expensive mango, papaya, and guava. The sun was shining and I was determined to preserve my good mood. So with only the merest tightening of the jaw, I emptied the dishwasher and brushed Kitty's hair. Really, everything was fine until I saw my third patient of the day.

I'm a psychotherapist, and our Queen's Park house has a separate basement flat where I see my patients. "Most people put their nice harmless old mothers at the bottom of their houses, instead of using the space for a bunch of self-pitying whiners who bore on about their problems," says Greg. The idea that Greg is able to put the words *nice* and *harmless* anywhere near the word *mother* is, in the light of his own female parent, frankly risible. Moreover, my "self-pitying whiners" helped see him through the last few years of medical school. But, being a GP, he doesn't really have much patience for any sort of illness, and especially not for ones that have no obvious physical characteristics. The notion that people can feel better and happier by talking to a trained therapist causes him to roll his eyes in exasperated disbelief. "Why don't they just talk to their friends instead of to a complete stranger like you?" We discuss my work as little as possible.

That morning, I'd said goodbye to Furious Frank, who has a little anger management problem we've been working on, and was enjoying the ten minutes between patients by looking out the window and watching feet crunch autumn leaves as they passed. Summer was over, but I didn't feel my usual desolation in the face of the impending season of mists.

The doorbell rang with a familiar nagging insistence. It was Gloomy Gina, who has been coming to see me for five years.

("Do you think they know about the names you give them?" my friend Ruthie recently asked me. "Of course not," I'd answered. "You're the only other person who knows. It's just my gallows humor, an affectionate shorthand for differentiating between them." I hadn't always been so cynical. At twenty-eight, I'd been the youngest person to qualify at the British Association of Psychotherapists and had always been dedicated to my work. Just lately, though, the gloss seemed to have faded and I often felt I was only going through the motions.)

Gina is rarely able to see the good side of a person or a situation and makes me feel like Pollyanna in comparison. She'd been much happier recently, as she was soon to marry and hadn't yet found much wrong with Jim, her fiancé, although, God knows, she'd tried. By her standards, she'd been positively jubilant for the past three months. That day, however, her pretty face had a pre-Jim look about it. Something was up.

"I've been thinking," she began. Always a bad start with Gina. "This is it. I'll never sleep with another man again. I'll never know that excitement and mystery of discovering someone for the first time, of having that first kiss, of waking up together full of the wonder of newness."

I wanted to say, Don't be silly, he could die, you might get divorced, you could have an affair, but I didn't. Instead, I suddenly realized, Oh, my God, I've never thought of marriage like that. In that instant, like a painful and unexpected blow to the head, the seed of betrayal took root in my own breast.

I'm afraid I barely listened to anything Gina said for the rest of that session. I even felt a twinge of guilt when I took her check, but only the slightest twinge; after all, she gets her money's worth with all her after-hours phone calls and midnight panic attacks. Instead, I sat there nodding absently and staring at the wall behind her. The streaky, bubbling smears of the earth's oozings that were rising damply up my basement wall mirrored my mood of growing unease perfectly. The day, which only moments before had felt bright and full of promise, now felt cloudy and damp. The sun had gone in.

Never again to feel the first kiss of a new lover? What was that e.e. cummings poem, something about liking your body when it's with someone else's, the thrill of "under me you so quite new"? I've always rather loved e.e., initially because he died the day and year I was born, September 3, 1962, which for an adolescent is a spooky coincidence, full of mystical significance. I felt we must have had an unique spiritual connection. For a while, I even thought that as his soul left his body at 1:15 A.M., the time of his death, it flew directly into mine as I opened my mouth to take my first breath at 3:23 A.M. Just over two hours seemed about the right amount of time for a soul to travel from the East Coast of the United States to Chalk Farm in London. Mainly I admired him because he was naughty enough to ignore capitals and muck around with grammar, something I was never able to get away with at my "grammar" school. I tried it, obviously, in my "the soul of e.e. cummings lives on in me and I'm going to be the world's greatest living poetess" phase. But Miss Titworth, our English teacher, was a stickler for punctuation. She even made us verbally punctuate our spoken English. "Miss Titworth comma please may I be excused question mark." This was the source of hours of witty schoolgirl repartee over crafty cigarettes in the cloakroom. "Miss Titworth comma how much are your tits worth question mark."

But now, sitting in my consulting room, all I could think was, *Is this it question mark.* Forever and ever, the same-old same-old? After Gina left, I went upstairs and straight to the fridge, gloomily surveying the contents and grazing on pieces of cheese and cold meat like a sheep with attention deficit disorder. I needed something to fill the gaping abyss of the bleak unchanging future I faced. Of course, I should know better, food isn't love and all that, but just as all dentists don't have perfect teeth, neither do all psychotherapists have perfect psyches.

Kitty came in and caught me guiltily sucking Philadelphia cream cheese from an index finger that had clearly scooped it directly from the tub and drinking orange juice straight from the carton.

Both my children have been taught that these two crimes carry a custodial sentence. "You're always bloody telling us not to do that," she protested.

"You weren't meant to see me and don't say bloody," I responded feebly. "Anyhow, why aren't you at school?" She did that sighing-and-rolling-eyes thing I thought was only supposed to happen after puberty, when you are suddenly struck by the overwhelming stupidity of your parents. She was still meant to be at the stage where I could do no wrong and her adoration was unequivocal.

"I told you I had a tummy ache this morning," she said accusingly, "but you *made* me go to school and I was sick, so Bea had to come and pick me up." Bea had been rather pointedly and not altogether silently hovering outside the kitchen door; now she came in and shot me a reproachful look.

"Thank you, Bea. Did you tell Dad you had a tummy ache?" I asked, deftly trying to pass the buck. "I mean, he *is* a doctor."

"Mum, you know you have to have your head actually hanging off your body before Daddy will take any notice at all."

"Poor baby." I took Kitty in my arms and held her.

I loved being a mother from the first moment I held my babies. Even now, I often lull myself to sleep at night by replaying their births like a treasured movie in my head. I loved the sweet milky smell of them and wore them close to my heart on my breast like a precious brooch for as long as they were small enough. I loved that part of them at the nape of the neck where you had to bury your nose in to kiss; I still do. I loved stuffing whole tiny newborn feet into my mouth. Kitty continues to let me nibble on her limbs and cover her with kisses, and Leo is unusually accommodating for a fifteen-year-old as long as no one else is watching. I tease them both by telling them I long ago made them sign contracts in which they undertook to suffer my kisses and cuddles irrespective of their age and in perpetuity.

I'm a respecter of contracts. Call me old-fashioned, but I'd meant it seventeen years ago when I had made my wedding vows to Mr. Grumpy, their father, promising to forsake all others and be faithful to him as long as we both shall live. I've had the odd little dalliance, a few stolen kisses, but never seriously contemplated infidelity.

Recently, though, I'd found myself flirting with my only single male friends who are dyed-in-the-wool homosexuals.

"What's wrong with us girls?" I bleat occasionally.

"You're just not—well, furry enough."

"We can be if we don't wax our legs and upper lips," I protest.

But now, with Gina's words on the finality of never sleeping with another man ever again ringing in my head, I felt as though I were gasping for air. What was I to do? Was Greg the only man I would ever have sex with? But could I really imagine having a lover? I'd rather assumed that you weren't allowed to take your clothes off in front of a stranger once you were over forty. Wasn't it actually against the law on the grounds of common decency? It's fine for your husband to see you naked if absolutely necessary. After all, the less-than-taut post-childbirth body is his fault, so there's a kind of perverse pleasure to be gained in parading it in front of him, the very act a silent scream of *Look what you've done to my body, you bastard*. But someone new, that would be—well, the word *impossible* springs to mind.

Y̶ou find me interesting, don't you?" Ruthie asked me later, as we reclined like Romans on her sofa and ate lunch.

" 'Course, or we wouldn't be celebrating our thirty-second year as friends. Why?" I asked, as I popped the last bite of a lox and cream cheese bagel into my mouth.

"It's just that whenever I say anything to him, Richard sighs and closes his eyes."

"Ah, HHATT," I pronounced sagely.

This is our shorthand; it makes text messaging much faster and allows us to tell each other how we're feeling without fear of prying eyes. It came about after I'd had a particularly bad fight with Greg, when he had spent an entire weekend shouting at the children and me. I tapped out my message—MY HUSBAND IS A PRICK—but I sent it to Greg instead of to Ruthie. When I realized what I'd done, my heart raced and I felt like a child caught poking her tongue out at the teacher. I had to bluff it out by sending Greg another one: ONLY JOKING, DARLING, WHAT DO YOU WANT FOR SUPPER? Luckily, I pulled it off. After that, acronyms seemed a safer route, hence HHATT: Hating Husband All The Time.

Ruthie yawned and stretched. That's how I always think of her, yawning and stretching in a smudged, sleepy sort of way, like a cat rousing itself briefly to change position in front of the fire. At work she's all sharp pressed businesslike efficiency, but I know her secret; she's always longing to go and have a little lie-down. She has a beautiful heart-shaped face, a Marilyn Monroe body, and liquid brown eyes. When she was younger, boys wanted to stab each other to win her affections. Irresistibly, she is unconscious of her allure and wears it as comfortably and absentmindedly as a favorite and slightly grubby bathrobe.

We met our first day at grammar school, when we were initially nudged into friendship by being seated at adjoining desks. Our surnames began with the same letter, Chloe Zhivago and Ruthie Zimmer. (Hers used to be Zimmerman, but the border guards found it unnecessarily long and dropped a syllable somewhere along the route when her father walked from Germany to England to escape the Nazis.) Ruthie was a better Jew than I and knew stuff. For, in spite of the fact that I'm a psychotherapist, make fantastic chicken soup, and do all that soul-food business, I'm fundamentally ignorant about Judaism. It's not surprising, really. I remember asking Dad once what the Hanukkah candles signified, and he looked at me with bemusement and said, "Do you know, darling, I have absolutely no idea."

"What sort of a Jewish father are you?" I asked.

"A very bad one"—he smiled—"but I can carry a tune." (My father, Bertie, composes musicals for the West End stage.)

Mum would have known but pretended not to; after marrying Dad she rejected her religious upbringing, and the only holiday we celebrated was Christmas. So I'd gone off to ask Ruthie. Apparently, thousands of years ago in Jerusalem, oil was needed for the candelabrum in the Temple. This was supposed to burn throughout the night, every night, but there was only enough oil for one day. Inexplicably, however, it burned for eight. So they declared an eight-day festival to commemorate it. It's a bit like the loaves and the fishes feeding the multitude. Every religion needs its miracles. We used to joke that it was also like the miracle of Stevie Brick, who when we were fifteen managed to kiss—get off with—four of us in the same evening at three different parties.

Anyhow, since then I have always consulted Ruthie on matters Jewish when the need arises. We made each other into the sisters neither of us had, vowing to live as close to each other as possible and have our children at the same time, and had succeeded in doing both. Ruthie was just the other side of Queen's Park, and we could have communicated by semaphore from our roofs if either of us had the ability or the inclination. Instead, we phoned and texted constantly and bumped into each other often in the course of going about our local business, quite apart from our many scheduled meetings. Her children, Atlas and Sephy (Persephone), were best friends with Leo and Kitty and the same ages. Her husband, Richard, was a classicist. Ruthie felt—since he had had so little say in so much of their life—it would have been churlish of her to begrudge his naming the children. Atlas was a small fine-boned child. You couldn't imagine anyone less physically capable of bearing on his shoulders the pillars that kept heaven and earth apart, but he did have the air of someone who wore the weight of the world heavily. Like his Greek counterpart, he was passionately interested in physics and astronomy and spent his evenings perched dangerously on the rooftop of their house, often with Leo, peering through a telescope and pointing out the stars and the planets. (Ruthie's Jewish-mother instincts were in conflict: on the one hand, joy at having a son who pursued knowledge; on the other, anxiety that he might fall to his death in his quest for it. The solution? A sturdy iron railing that circumvented the roof installed at considerable expense.) For her part, Sephy was an unlikely Queen of the Underworld. She was a joyful fairy princess of a child, just like my Kitty, and when they both left the room it felt as lonely and barren as if they'd returned to Hades, heralding the onset of winter. In choosing your child's name, to some extent you can help choose their destiny and decide their personality. That's why I'd gone for strong names like Leo and Katherine, the names of former emperors and empresses. No one was going to push my kids around.

"When did you last have sex?" I asked Ruthie.

"With Richard? Don't be disgusting, he's my husband."

"I know what you mean." I munched on a hot green pepper, enjoying the way it made my eyes smart. "We haven't done it for so long that the very notion of bumping and grinding in the marital bed feels inappropriate and obscene. Thank God we both had so much sex before marriage; there's bugger all after."

"Do you think it was like that for our mothers? Maybe the fact that they saved themselves meant they had lots as married women?" Ruthie reached for an olive and nibbled at it; she'd hardly eaten a thing. "Perhaps we should just ditch the husbands and set up a lesbian commune," she suggested.

"In principle, that's an excellent idea. One slight hitch: We're not actually lesbians."

"I know," said Ruthie regretfully. "Pity. How about a commune, with a separate wired-off area for men? We could go and play with them when the fancy took us."

"A men pen?" I mused. "Actually," I said, Gina's words still ringing in my ears, "I was thinking I might take a lover, purely for reasons of weight loss; you know how new sex makes the pounds drop off." I pinched at more than an inch around my midriff.

"No one could blame either of us for having an affair. No woman can be expected to live a life with so little sex, it's a human rights issue, really," Ruthie said, as she dipped the tip of a finger into a bowl of hummus. "The real problem is that the only sex there is after marriage is with other people." She looked at me appraisingly and added, "If you do have an affair, though, make sure you remember the Rule."

Ruthie is the editor of *Smart Magazine, Beauty and Brains for Today's Woman* and frequently uses me under a variety of pseudonyms for her case studies. She has written or edited articles on virtually every subject imaginable and is the font of all knowledge. I studied her. She was dressed in her professional uniform: Issey Miyake; she never wore anything else for work. (His clothes, made up of thousands of little knife-edged pleats, always make me feel rather nervous. Does someone have to sit there folding and folding like a lunatic in Bedlam with obsessive-compulsive disorder?)

"What rule, O wise and pleated one?" I asked.

*"Never have an affair with anyone who has less to lose by its disclosure than you do."*

Very clever and absolutely obvious, if you stop to think about it. It was all I could do to prevent myself from surreptitiously jotting it down like an over-zealous student.

"You'll have to have an affair for both of us," she added. "I could never let anyone other than Richard see my untidy, ever-increasing middle-aged breasts."

I looked at her breasts; they did seem bigger.

"You know how ears and noses never stop growing?" she went on. "Well, my breasts are just the same. They don't seem to know when to call it a day."

"At least you *have* breasts. Mine never really started growing, and now they're like small empty socks."

Ruthie laughed. "Go on—you were always the adventurous one— and then I can have an affair vicariously."

"As usual, I have to do all the work. Things really haven't changed much since the days you used to copy my Latin homework."

"I know, darling, you've always been so much better than me at actually *doing* things; I just write about other people doing them."

We both laughed, knowing the important and equal nature of the symbiosis that bound us.

"Did you know that seventy percent of men and thirty percent of women commit adultery?" Ruthie said.

"It's about time women caught up, then," I commented wryly.

I hadn't really meant it, the "Shed Those Unwanted Pounds the Fun Way: Shag-a-Man-Who-Isn't-Your-Husband Diet." I'd just wanted to roll the words around my tongue, taste the idea, and say it out loud. It had felt like so long since I'd had any fun; life was full of being a wife, a mother, and a psychotherapist, and here I was suddenly in my forties with no time to feel carefree and full of joy. I could see why the forties were the Decade of Divorce; everyone was bolting in terror in a last bid for freedom from the drudgery of responsibility and obligation. As I was leaving Ruthie's, I nearly collided with a woman who was dragging a crying toddler and pushing a howling baby in a pram. When I looked closer, I saw that tears were trickling down the mother's weary face too. That love-and-marriage, horse-and-carriage song started playing ironically in my head. It was now one of those drizzly gray London days when the damp snacks greedily on your bones and you think you'll never ever see the sun again. I felt depression nudging at my gut like a wet cat rubbing itself insidiously against chilly bare legs.

By the time I'd walked home, I was feeling increasingly rueful about my life. What had happened to the flurry of passion and whole weekends in bed that Greg and I had once shared? I asked Greg when he came back from work. He was looking for some chocolate he'd hidden from himself.

"Don't be silly. That honeymoon period can't last forever; you'd never get anything done."

"But don't you miss it, darling? Don't you wish we were still like that?"

"No. There's too much to do: kids, work, books to read, films to watch. Ah, here it is." He beamed with satisfaction as he pulled a chocolate bar from behind one of the many recipe books that looked about to tumble from their overstuffed shelf. "Want some?" (He willfully refused to discuss his diet's strange bedfellows of Benecol and chocolate.)

"Why not?" I answered bitterly, thinking, *I can always burn the calories off adulterously.*

Greg went off to the living room, greeting Leo with a cheerful "Yo, Rasta man, I and I have learned our lesson with the weed." This arose from the small matter of a confiscated matchbox full of grass that Greg had found as he was trying to reclaim stolen designer boxers from his son's wardrobe. Greg is no stranger to the weed; he'd sniffed it ostentatiously and said, "Looks like good gear, might have to smoke it myself." Ever since, we'd had the Rasta joke, amusing initially, but we were ten days in and it was wearing thin.

Leo shuffled into the kitchen, almost visibly cocooned in the cloud of disgruntlement that had become his constant companion over the past two years. A bizarre physical change overcomes boys on their thirteenth birthday. Overnight their heads, which they previously had no trouble supporting, become too heavy for their necks, and their speech, once clear, becomes indistinct. That once upright, chatty, and articulate son becomes a slouching mumbler.

"Have you done your homework, darling?" I asked.

"Mmmf, mrumf," he answered.

"Pardon?"

"Yes, yes, whatever," he enunciated, with exaggerated clarity.

I threw the last of the chocolate bar away; the self-loathing that accompanied every mouthful was too much to bear. Besides, perhaps I should at least try diet and exercise before resorting to adultery. I decided to flirt with Greg and seduce him. That's what you're meant to do; that's what I always tell my patients anyhow. Rediscover each other, put the romance back in the marriage, go out on dates together, make time to talk and enjoy each other. Who's to say a relationship with another man would be any different? After the honeymoon of the first two years, it would probably settle into what I had now. Was it worth the lies, the deceit, and the risk to everyone's happiness for a couple of years of good sex? (Although, in my case, it didn't even have to be good; just some sex would do.)

I could hear the television in the living room and, through the doorway, saw Greg slumped on the sofa, his mouth slightly open as he watched the weather forecast with an intensity more usually seen on the face of a hungry infant at its mother's breast. I took off all my clothes and undulated sinuously in front of him to see if he would notice. He waved me aside before pointing at the television. "Very nice, darling, but, you know, the weather. . . ." It is his favorite program, but still. At that point the telephone rang. It was one of Greg's regular patients, Mrs. Meagan, or Me Again, as she is known from the frequency of her calls. God knows how she'd managed to get hold of our unlisted number; I think Mr. Meagan works for British Telecom or the police or is a thief or something. Normally I field these calls; Greg hates ill people at the best of times and hypochondriacs are his bêtest of noirs. But this time, after my bitter rejection, I said sweetly, "Yes, Mrs. Meagan, of course, he's right here" and, wearing only my high heels, harrumphed out of the room, nearly colliding with Leo as he slouched up the stairs. He took one look at me, shuddered, and said very clearly, "Urgh, naked parent! That's like really bad for my psycho-sexual development, Mum."

I spent the rest of the evening sulkily sewing a felt elephant badly for something or other that Kitty was doing at school while she told me all about Henry the Sixth and his eight wives or Henry the Eighth and his six wives—*yes, yes, whatever.* Is this my life? Whatever happened to me and how did I get here?

# Chapter 2

## GRANDPA NEEMAN'S
## RECIPE FOR A HAPPY MARRIAGE

. . . . . . . . . . . . . . . . . . .

*8 ounces love*

*8 ounces humor*

*8 ounces sexual attraction*

*16 ounces admiration and respect for each other*

*16 ounces intellectual parity*

*1 small pinch in-laws (unless to your taste,*
*    in which case add more)*

*1 reasonable budget*

*A generous dash of teamwork*

*4 teaspoons readiness to admit fault*

*8 ounces quick and easy apology*

*8 ounces each confidence and encouragement*

*1 large (or several small) interests or hobbies in common*

*8 ounces delight in each other*

*Separate bathrooms (budget permitting)*

Sift together ingredients, removing any lumps of jealousy, accounting of wrongs, grudge bearing, point scoring, temper, or accusation. Stir in frequent helpings of healthy and satisfying marital sex. Pour into generous servings of love, and bake over many years in the steady warmth of affection, mutual respect, and desire.

That night I had my recurring contact lens anxiety dream. It comes in various forms; this version was the one where I tried to insert an enormous contact lens into my eye. It was simply too big and wouldn't go in, but I kept trying. I was confused: I wear these lenses every day; why did they no longer fit? The contact lens in question had extra flaps on the side, like those sanitary napkins with wings that you're meant to tuck round your knickers. The flappy bits were supposed to fit onto the white of your eyeball, but try as I might I couldn't get them in. It was a relief to wake up. I glanced over at Greg, who was snoring less gently than he imagines next to me. What did it mean? I always examine dreams; it's the Jungian in me. They make us think about our lives and are the way our subconscious talks to us. Mine was clearly telling me I was anxious. Was it also trying to say that Greg didn't fit me anymore? Maybe he had, day after day for seventeen years, but now he no longer did? A few hours before, when we'd got into bed, I'd rubbed my foot up and down Greg's calf, our marital Morse code to signal the desire for sex. I knew he was still awake, but he'd deepened his breathing to pretend he was already asleep, grunted, and turned over with his back to me, leaving a lonely ocean of white sheet between our two bodies. His lack of response couldn't help but make me feel unloved and unlovely.

It was 4 A.M. It's always 4 A.M. when I wake up anxious and alert in a sleeping house. I got out of bed, went into Kitty's room, and sat in the chintz-covered nursing chair that she insists on keeping by her bed. I love to watch her sleep. Asleep she looks like a baby again, her features soft and contented, her arm carelessly flung across her chest, her long dark lashes sweeping damply across her cheek, and her mouth slightly open. She has a particularly beautiful mouth, full and red, ripe like succulent fruit and full of the promise of the sensual young woman she is soon to become. I wanted to kiss her but resisted and, instead, laid a hand gently on her to feel the rise and fall of her chest. When she and Leo were babies, I used to put a finger under their noses to check that they were still breathing. Sometimes their infant breath was too soft to detect and I would accidentally wake them with my fearful prodding. I remembered all those times I would sit in this same chair in the middle of the night, breast-feeding first Leo and then, a few years later, Kitty. I used to feel I was the only person awake in the world and was at pains to be silent and keep my babies from crying so we wouldn't wake Greg. He would be in a terrible ill humor all day if he didn't get enough sleep at night.

Now Kitty stirred and said mysteriously, "Four chestnuts and a badger's tail." Everyone in this house talks when asleep except me. Greg especially is given to loud biblical pronouncements that wake me up. Is he dreaming he is Jesus? This is his biggest fear, that he will suddenly see the light. He's made me promise to shoot him if he is born again and gets religion.

I made my way downstairs. In response, the house creaked, groaned, and turned over in its sleep. I looked around me, at my life, the clutter of it. Coats in a jumble in the hall, shoes scattered on the stairs. Fetching and carrying, that was what life amounted to: picking something up from one place and putting it in another, then later picking it up from there and putting it somewhere else. Every available surface was full of *stuff*. Items seemed to mate with each other and reproduce at a terrifying rate. Odd socks gathered in gangs and had parties with empty coffee cups, carelessly discarded items of clothing, and endless pieces of paper. Sometimes the clutter threatened to overwhelm me. What if I just walked out the door and never returned? Drove to the airport, took the first plane to somewhere, and started a whole new life? Occasionally, I liked to examine this idea, roll it round in my head and taste it before rejecting it, because I could never seriously contemplate it. The thought of leaving Leo and Kitty behind literally made me feel ill, physically ill, a dull nauseating ache in the core of my being.

When I was a child my father would bring me hot milk after a bad dream or if I couldn't sleep. He would sit with me while I drank it, stroking my forehead and smoothing my eyebrows with his thumb. He'd sing me his latest song, one he was still writing that no one else had yet heard. Sometimes it would be just a phrase or two and he'd sing it over and over, more and more softly, until I fell asleep. I loved those Daddy-and-Chloe nights when he made the world safe for me. These days the only time I ever drink milk is in the middle of the night. I heated some now and curled up, hugging it to me on the sofa as I tried to examine my unease. I must have dozed because the kitsch clock my brother Sammy had given us sounded six times, a small pink pig snorting its way out of the hatch where a cuckoo should be. I picked up the phone and dialed.

"Daddy?"

"Who is this, please?"

"Which other woman calls you Daddy?"

"We won't go into that now." He laughed.

"It's Chloe," I said, playing along.

"It's true, I used to have a daughter called Chloe, but I haven't heard from her for a very long time."

"I spoke to you three days ago."

"Three days multiplied by a Jewish father is three months, as you well know."

"Are you awake?"

"I am now."

He was anyway; I knew he would be. He's always up and at his piano by six.

"Hold on, darling," he said. "I just have to get the birds out of my head and onto paper before they fly away."

My father has songs in his head the way the rest of us have thoughts. When I was little, I used to imagine that his head was full of birds and that when he opened his mouth they flew out singing. Then he had to capture them, and I was certain that when he did he glued them down on paper, because the little black notes he inked onto his manuscript pad looked just like tiny blackbirds perching on telegraph wires. When the birds were ready to come out, Dad would get agitated and didn't like to talk until he'd got them all neatly stuck down. So I held on patiently for a few minutes.

"There, all done. What gets you up so early, Chloe?"

"Thinking. Dad, do you think you can be happily married to one person for the rest of your life?"

I listened to the clock tick in the quiet early morning and waited for him to answer.

"I think relationships change like everything else. There were times when I thought I couldn't stand another minute with your mother; then, the week after, I'd feel that life would be impossible without her. Sometimes you're happy, sometimes not. Lust is instant, but love takes a long time to grow. Mark Twain said, 'No man or woman really knows what perfect love is until they have been married a quarter of a century.' Maybe you haven't been married long enough."

Among all the things I loved my father for, and there were many, I loved his ability to encapsulate the issue at hand with a quotation; he had one for every occasion.

"Aren't you happy, darling?" he asked.

"It's not so much that, Dad, it's just that everything seems to have settled into this monotonous continuum. As though everything that's exciting has already happened and now it'll just be the same forever and ever and there's nothing left to look forward to."

I could hear the petulant child in my voice, but it in no way weakened the intensity of my feelings.

"It's your age, Chlo. You know, you've married the man and had the kids and now what? I remember feeling it in my forties too."

"What did you do?"

There was a long pause. I looked out of the window at the blue dawn light. It was raining, and I could hear the swish of wet tires on asphalt as cars passed with increasing frequency. The world was rubbing its eyes and coming to life. A new day. But how new would it be and how much would it be merely a repetition of the old day that was yesterday?

I waited. Dad cleared his throat on the other end of the phone.

"Well, Chlo, I wouldn't recommend it, but I had an affair."

I paused. A half-forgotten memory rose unbidden. The phone ringing, a stream of angry words, the phone being slammed down, my father's face ashen, my mother's red-eyed and tearful, shouting in hoarse whispers from behind closed doors. My father away suddenly for a few days, "visiting one of his shows in Leeds." I must have been about twelve, uncomprehending but aware that divorce was, if not in the cards, at least under discussion. With the egocentricity of a child, all I could think was *Will I be allowed to live with my daddy?*

"God, did Mum know?"

"Only later," Dad said. "Let me wait till I see you and I'll explain."

My mother was the youngest of four, the much-wanted, pampered only daughter who came, just as hope was almost lost, after three brothers. They were so pleased to have a girl in the family, a daughter, that they always called her Girlie. Actually, that's all anyone ever called her; all they were allowed to call her. Her real name was Gertrude, Gertrude Neeman. "It makes me sound like a plump matron with thick ankles," she complained. She was a beautiful child who, as family lore had it, emerged from the womb with abundant dark curls and long dancer's legs. She started dancing as soon as she could walk and won a scholarship to the Royal Ballet School at the age of eight. Her parents, who came from generations of learned Talmudic Jews, her father a rabbi, her mother a teacher, could tolerate the dancing when it was classical and qualified as "art." They found it less easy to cope when she left the Royal Ballet and leaped to the freedom of the West End stage's "racy musicals." And their horror knew no bounds when she fell in love with and married my father, who was ten years older than her and composed the very musicals that had lured her from her true artistic purpose. The fact that his parents were in the *shmotte* business (they had a dress shop) was yet another black mark against him.

"We are book Jews. That our daughter should marry a money Jew? Pah!" they said.

"At least he is actually Jewish," Girlie retorted.

They turned pale. A week later, they were back to patting her cheek and telling her how beautiful she was. She was their miracle, their gift from God; how could they stay angry with a face like that?

Girlie was a rare and quixotic creature, and everyone always told me how lucky I was that she was my mother. But she wasn't terribly motherly, not a "sit down and let me give you something to eat, my darling" sort of mother, and at an early age our roles had become blurred and confused, so that by the time I was a teenager I seemed to be the responsible adult and she the moody, tyrannical, and depressive child. I would come home from school, turn my key in the door, and sniff the air apprehensively. I could tell by some subtle odor whether or not all was well in my mother's world and therefore in mine. All families have their own smell, a subliminal aroma that speaks of familiarity but not necessarily of contentment. I could sniff out my mother's ill humor or distress at twenty paces. She would lie in her bed in the darkness, her voice a lifeless monotone, while I tiptoed around the house, fearful of making matters worse, and tried to dispel her mood by tempting her with food or drink. All my offerings would be rebuffed. "I suppose you want me to get fat," she would say. "That's what you want, isn't it, a fat, mummy sort of mother?" She was probably right; I did want a mummy sort of mother, not the unpredictable and disappointed woman who was hiding in the dark. Her mood could change in an instant. If the doorbell rang, she would hurry out of bed, put on her makeup, and make her entrance, ready to perform and to dazzle, her former misery forgotten in her delight at unexpected guests. It was as if she had ceased to exist away from the glare of the spotlight. Her dancing days long over, friends and acquaintances were now her audience. Without them, she withered; her family was not enough to sustain her.

This neediness certainly put me off show business and turned me firmly to books. I'd inherited my mother's dancer's legs but not the desire to show them (or any other part of me) off, and observing Girlie in the grip of her dark moods made me vow never to fall prey to depression. It became something of a phobia. The vain hope that I could become mistress of my own mind kicked rather than pushed me toward psychotherapy.

I made my way back to bed. Through the window, I could see the Pigeon Lady in the yellow glow of a nearby streetlamp. She was, as usual, surrounded by pigeons. Sometimes she talked to them as though to close friends; occasionally she appeared to quarrel with them. It was as though the birds had said something particularly offensive and she had to persuade them of their error. Again and again she would rush at them, shouting and admonishing, shopping bags and wild gray hair flying and her coat pulled tightly around her tall thin body. This time, two of the birds remained impervious to her cries. They stood side by side on the pavement, one seeming to shield the other with its wing as they pecked at the ground companionably. A third pigeon whooshed between them, pushing them apart. It seemed to me that this was what I had done to my parents: By being my father's favorite, I had destroyed their unity and wrenched them asunder. I remembered all those nights I had left my brother Sammy alone in our room and crept into our parents' bed, forcing my determined way into the middle. I would dig my small heels into my mother's thighs and push her a little farther away so I could take my rightful place next to my father. Then I would rest my victorious head on his chest.

I loved the smell of him, his expensive Givenchy cologne that was made especially for him in a little place just off the Place de la Concorde in Paris, where he went twice a year, also to buy his socks: thin, black, and made of silk. My father has always been a dandy, immaculately dressed whatever the occasion. He carries a spare tie in his pocket at all times, in case the worst should happen—a stain on the one he is wearing. I wasn't surprised to learn that he had had an affair; he was too charming, too ebullient, and too affectionate to be contained by a marriage. I suppose somewhere I must have known it and read the currents of the tension that flowed between him and my mother. After a few days, he returned from "Leeds," and normal family life was resumed. My mother felt, I think, that in any case, he had betrayed her long before by falling so deeply in love with me, his little girl. But then, she had my brother.

Over the next few days, I couldn't stop thinking about Dad's affair and what it might be like to have one myself. When Greg wasn't at work, he was spending much of his time writing furious letters to the council and scouring the Internet for legal precedents that would support his newly declared war on parking fines. The rest of the time, he was on the phone to his new friends: fellow parking-fine warriors. There was a nationwide network of them with their own Website, bonded like brothers by their common purpose.

"It's all very well fining people who obstruct the road or park in resident permit areas," Greg said, at the end of a long exposition over dinner one night, "but now they're doing it purely for revenue and they must be punished." He had no other topic of conversation, and the children and I gave him a wide berth. We could only hope he would tire of it eventually.

The universe seemed to be screaming adultery at me. When one afternoon a patient canceled and I treated myself to some illicit afternoon television, the theme of the Jerry Springer show was "My Partner's a Cheater." There they all were, black, white, fat, thin, cheating away to their hearts' content and looking rather smug about it. Jerry summed up the program sanctimoniously. "The person you really cheat is yourself. What sort of relationship is it if you're not being honest?"

"An exciting one," I said aloud, as I threw down the remote control in disgust and left the room. Everywhere I looked I saw lovers walking along streets, their bodies as close together as possible, kissing on street corners and holding each other's faces lovingly. Women's magazines in the newsagent's round the corner assaulted me with their adulterous headlines: FALLING IN LOVE WITH A MAN WHO ISN'T YOUR

HUSBAND; MY HUSBAND AND MY LOVER BOTH LIVE WITH ME; MY AFFAIR BROUGHT US CLOSER. On the street outside our house, the Pigeon Lady shouted incongruously at me, "Go find yourself a fancy man why don't you? You're all the same." I found myself looking at men again, really looking in an up-for-it sort of way, and some of them started looking back. The invisibility pill I had unwittingly swallowed with my fortieth birthday seemed, temporarily at least, to have lost its power.

# Chapter 3

# SARIPUTRA'S CACTUS SALSA

. . . . . . . . . . . . . . . . . .

*1 (24-ounce) can Italian peeled plum tomatoes*
*2 (16-ounce) cans marinated cactus (or fresh if you can find it)*
*2 pounds fresh tomatoes*
*2 large red onions*
*1–2 bunches spring onions*
*1 bunch fresh coriander*
*4 small hot red or green chilies*
*Juice of 3 lemons*
*6–8 cloves of garlic, crushed*
*1 teaspoon salt*
*1 teaspoon freshly ground black pepper*
*3 tablespoons olive oil*

Open can of tomatoes and mash in a large bowl. Dice strained cactus, fresh tomatoes, red onions, and spring onions and add to mashed tomatoes. Finely chop coriander leaves and chilies and add, along with the juice of the lemons and the garlic, salt, pepper, and olive oil. Mix together and leave to mature for a few hours.

Serve with fish, chicken, or meat or blend briefly to make a finer mixture and use as a dip for tortilla chips.

I thought *happily ever after* would be more satisfying than this, didn't you?" Ruthie said. We were in one of our habitual haunts, the café in Queen's Park. She looked tired and seemed to have a perpetual cold these days. When I asked her what the matter was, she said that work was getting her down.

"Mmm," I said. "But maybe, just maybe, it *is* possible to have a different life. You know, a life full of love and passion, to talk and have someone listen, to stroke and be stroked, to have someone gaze into your eyes and tell you they love you, to look in their eyes and find everything you need."

"Oh, Chlo, you're a hopeless romantic," Ruthie said, pushing her food around her plate like an anorexic pretending to eat. "By the way," she said suddenly. "Happy Birthday."

I looked at her in confusion. "It's not my birthday."

"I know. It's just that Lou hasn't spoken to me for weeks because I forgot her birthday, so now I'm wishing everyone happy birthday whenever I talk to them; that way they won't get cross when I forget on the day. Anyway," she went on, "Lou's got other things to worry about now since she and James split up."

I was horrified. Lou and James had been together for twenty years; they'd married before the rest of us and had had children as quickly as they could, four of them, one after the other: boy, girl, boy, girl. They actually liked each other, laughed at each other's jokes, and talked—real proper conversations, not mere business meetings about whose turn it was to call the plumber or get the car fixed. Lou's hand was always fluttering affectionately around James, smoothing his hair, tracing the curve of his jaw. James noticed what Lou wore and liked to shop with her, pulling the clothes he knew would suit her off the racks and holding them up against her. We always joked that he was a gay man trapped in a straight man's body. They were the standard-bearers for the rest of us: Mr. and Mrs. Happily Married, living proof that it was possible to live happily ever after. Their union was essential to the ecology of everyone else's relationships. How could they split up? They had always seemed to stand together in marital harmony like two strong oak trees flourishing under the same sun, their roots intertwined beneath the ground, their presence untroubled by the passing of years. There'd been the odd creak or metaphorical shedding of a small branch, but no one could have imagined this would lead to a felling of the tree itself. Until now.

"What? How? When?" The words tumbled out of me. "I can't believe you haven't told me about this."

"I forgot . . . like birthdays. They're having a trial separation. They feel they've been taking each other for granted and need to start dating again or something."

"If *they* can't stay together, what hope is there for the rest of us?" I muttered.

"True," said Ruthie, "but you never know what goes on behind closed doors. I always thought all that lovey-dovey stuff in public was a bit suspicious; you know, a sign that nothing much was actually going on between their sheets."

"Nothing much is going on between our respective sheets, but we're still with our husbands," I said.

"Did you know that lack of sex is actually grounds for divorce?"

"But we're nice Jewish girls who will do all we can to keep the family together, remember?" I said.

"Of course, but if we were religious and really were in celibate marriages we could go to the rabbi, who might well sanction a divorce. Jews are big on sex and intimacy; the Torah actually obligates the husband to meet the sexual needs of his wife. Some texts even suggest that a man must bring his wife to orgasm first."

"Very clever people, Jews, I've always said so." I finished my coffee and was silent for a few moments; something she'd said was bothering me. "Just hold it right there," I said. "What's all this *if we really were in celibate marriages* stuff? Ruthie, have you been having sex with your husband?" I asked sternly.

"Not really," Ruthie answered. "You know, just the normal twice a month thing."

"That is positively rampant in my book."

Ruthie looked at me.

"Two hundred and forty-five days," I said.

"What do you mean?"

"Since Greg and I had sex: two hundred and forty-five days. It was a drunken shag last New Year's Eve. I think that means I'm officially a virgin again."

"I can't believe you haven't told me this before."

"I couldn't bring myself to say it."

"Have you talked to him?"

"I've tried, but he says everything's fine; we're both busy and just going through a bit of a no-sex phase. It's no big deal as far as he's concerned."

"At what point does a phase become a permanent state of being?" Ruthie looked at me as if I were a recently discovered example of a rare species. "It'd make a good feature. 'Women in Celibate Marriages Speak Out.'"

"Cheers. Well, you know where to come for copy." I looked at my watch. "Christ, on that bombshell, I must dash."

I hadn't realized Ruthie's definition of no sex was sex twice a month. Her shock at my revelation made me realize Greg and I really did have a problem. That's what happens sometimes when you say things out loud.

I only just made it back in time for my three o'clock. Gentleman Joe is American and used to be a stripper with the Chippendales—"Before they were all gay," he repeatedly assured me. Gentleman Joe was his stage name and after he'd come clean about his colorful past, three years into therapy, I could never think of him as anything else. He was gorgeous: olive skin, floppy black hair, eyebrows like luxurious furry caterpillars, and lashes so long and heavy it was a wonder that he could keep his eyes open at all. He had commitment issues and a deep and abiding disappointment in the female species; he couldn't get a single one of them to commit to him and become his wife. Joe was a serial fiancé; his brides-to-be always ditched him as soon as they came within sniffing distance of the altar. "What is it with these British broads?" he complained. "They all cheat, every single one of them. You think you're in an exclusive relationship, and then off they go with some chap who went to school with their brother."

"Have you considered dating another nationality, a fellow American perhaps?" I suggested.

"Nah. American women are too needy."

*Pot, kettle, black,* I thought. "Hmm, you know, Joe, perhaps you should just stop looking for marriage and it will happen all on its own. Do you think you might be attracted to women who are unavailable to you?"

He was an anomaly, the exception that makes the rule, a Jewish man who wanted to settle down, but then he was forty-four and his Chippendale heyday had been in the eighties. Stripping: What kind of job was that for a nice Jewish boy?


I've never really been able to have a serious relationship with a Jewish man. I must have an inbuilt incest taboo about it: Jewish men are too much like family.

I knew they'd send food back in restaurants, answer a question with a question, and secretly lust over icy blond shiksas, and we'd wind up more interested in eating cake and chatting in bed than having wild tempestuous sex. I did have a Jewish boyfriend once; the sex was even quite tempestuous until the day we were doing it in front of a mirror and simultaneously realized how similar our reflections were. It felt like I was going out with my brother, and much as I love Sammy I have no desire to sleep with him.

Sammy is two years younger than I and lives in a tepee in the Alpujarras in Spain. He's got a Buddhist name now, Sariputra, which means Child of a Spring Nightingale. We call him Sari, which if you mumble it, sounds pretty much like Sammy. That keeps everyone happy. He used to be a musician and was on the road to success in an R & B band, but

then our mother died and after we'd numbly buried her ashes in my garden and planted a cherry tree above them, Sammy ran away to North
Carolina to live with the Cherokee Indians. "It's a matriarchal society,"
he said, before he left. He was grief-stricken. We all were; we felt
betrayed, bereft, and bewildered. Mum didn't like getting older, and at
fifty-five she'd simply decided not to. She'd gone to sleep and never
woken up. No one knew what caused her death; the postmortem didn't
reveal anything. She might just as well have said, *Right, well, I'm off. I've had
enough of you all.* (I couldn't help feeling she'd done it on purpose, just to
be the center of attention once again. Not so much making an entrance,
which she so used to relish, as an exit.) Sammy lived the Cherokee life
for five years and wouldn't talk to me or to Dad. As a matter of fact, he
wouldn't talk to anyone. "Peace may be found in silence," he finally
explained, when he set up his tepee in Spain, embraced Buddhism, and
got back in touch. "I seek to walk a gentle path on this planet."

"Yes, and a bloody uncomfortable one too," I'd retorted, as I'd
hugged him fiercely, feeling that my heart would burst with pain and
joy. Secretly, I love his tepee, the woody smoky smell and the simplicity of his existence. Over the years it's become a sort of haven for me,
a place to which I can escape and taste a different life. I go at least four
times a year, usually with the children and sometimes with Greg.
Sammy's cut six windows into the canvas walls, complete with glass
panes and wooden frames, an innovation he's immensely proud of.
"No native American thought of that, did he?" When we were children, we insisted on sharing a room and would lie in our beds in the
morning looking through the skylight at the clouds. We called it Animals in the Sky. One of us would make out the shape of an animal and
the other had to find it.

"Unicorn," Sammy had said, as we lay on a mountaintop on my last
trip to Spain, lazily dipping tortilla chips into cactus salsa, his trademark dish.

"Are mythical creatures allowed?" I'd asked, competitively scouring
the sparse puffballs above.

"Is that a sensible question to ask a man who lives in a tepee?" I'd hugged him, inhaling the sheer brotherliness of him and loving how his sense of irony about himself was still intact. Kitty and Leo play Animals in the Sky too and call Sammy "Uncle Bonkers." He takes them trekking through the mountains and tells them about the grandmother they never knew.

Mum died twelve years ago, and I'm still furious with her for leaving me with a three-year-old, a swollen pregnant belly, and no mother to help me. Greg's mother doesn't count. We don't see her often enough, and when we do we wish we hadn't. Most children go through a phase of worrying about whether they were adopted: Greg used to hope that he was. He felt he'd turned up in the wrong family, an uninvited guest at a party that was not to his taste. He looked nothing like his brothers and sisters and had nothing in common with any of them. They were all fair-haired and brown-eyed; his hair was jet black and his eyes blue. They were Irish Methodists, and no alcohol was allowed in the house except for Baileys, which for some reason had been declared nonalcoholic and was drunk by the crate load at family gatherings. Aunts and uncles would grow flushed and fulsome, and emotional renditions of "Danny Boy" would swell the air. These were Greg's few happy childhood memories. His father, the one person approaching an ally in this family of strangers, had long since relinquished his own membership when Greg was eight by going to America—ostensibly to see if it was a suitable place for them to move. He was never heard from again, and his face was painstakingly excised from all early family photographs, which were displayed prominently on every available surface. Greg remembers his mother sitting night after night snipping away at a pile of photographs with a pair of sharp nail scissors. He managed to rescue a few of his father's severed heads when she wasn't looking and has kept them in his wallet to this day— his only memento. No one was allowed to mention his name, and life was neatly divided into two sections: B.E. (Before the Event) and A.E. (After the Event). Edie, his mother, had spent the years A.E. with an expression of distaste, as though there were a bad smell permanently under her nose. When Leo was born, Greg had said, with all the relief of a drowning man who has found dry land, "At last I've got a family that I like."

I felt tired. Sometimes my patients drained me. Usually it was when I wasn't feeling robust and was unable to keep their lives from seeping into mine. I went upstairs and found Greg bustling about in the kitchen, peering inside drawers and cupboards, slamming doors and growing more and more exasperated. His hair was standing on end like a toilet brush, and he was wearing Kitty's flamenco apron in vivid red with yellow spots. It suited him. With his right hand he was miming the action of the object he sought, an incantation to abracadabra the item into being.

"Soup ladle?" I guessed correctly. "Top left-hand drawer, unless you have hidden it from yourself."

"Taste," he said, proffering hot soup. "Hmm. Well, mmm?" He nodded impatiently.

"Delicious, darling, but—"

"But what? What, it's perfect!"

Greg has spent all the years of our marriage in self-declared chicken soup combat with me, an unspoken challenge that by the time the marriage ends, whether by divorce or one of our deaths, he will have emerged the chicken soup victor. He's a good cook—it's one of the reasons I married him—and has his own repertoire but is obsessed with the need to prove that you don't have to be Jewish to make Jewish Chicken Soup. His soup is good, near perfect even, but less authentic and aromatic than my own, and he hasn't quite mastered the correct consistency of the *knaydlach*, the dumplings.

As a Jew, I am genetically programmed to respond to news of friends' or relatives' misfortunes by going straight to the kitchen and making soup. This gene can, it turns out, be transferred by marriage. This is what Jewish women do to their non-Jewish husbands: irrevocably and osmotically we turn them into Jews. If Dad's not feeling well, Greg is now as likely as I am to hurry round with chicken soup, Jewish penicillin, the known cure for all ills from heartache to cancer. This latest challenge meant that I would have to make defensive chicken soup as soon as I could, to take up the gauntlet he had flung before me and prove, once again, my supremacy in this realm.

"I can't do it tonight," I said irritably. "I'm going to FF's thing; aren't you coming?"

Greg shuddered. "I would rather eat a stew of poisonous snakes. I'm going to watch telly in bed and read up on the Road Traffic Act of 1991." He nodded toward his steaming pan of soup. "I win, then."

"Your misanthropy is becoming an illness. I'll make my soup tomorrow, and we will settle this once and for all by putting both our soups to the test of a wider audience."

"Fine. Let the public decide whose soup is the best," he said.

I flounced out of the kitchen. I'm a great fan of flouncing, and Kitty and I practice together to see who can look the haughtiest as we toss our heads, turn on our heels, and exit rooms. Kitty, who had come in and heard the last of this, was standing by the fridge. She discreetly gave me the thumbs-up as I whisked past her. (She can already shrivel a teenage boy at twenty paces with her narrow-eyed contemptuous glance and barely audible snort of displeasure.) I winked and beckoned with a slight inclination of my head for her to follow me.

"Help me dress," I said.

She took the stairs two at a time. If she's my dolly, I too am hers, and she likes to lay prospective outfits out on the floor for me so we can see how they look. Blouses, skirts or trousers, tights and shoes, belts, bracelets, and scarves; bodiless and spread-eagled on the carpet, they remind me of the cut-out outfits that used to be printed on the back of the comic book, Bunty, the ones with paper tabs, that bent around your cardboard Bunty to transform her from workaday to party girl.

My Famous Friend Lizzie, known to all as FF, was having a party to celebrate the publication of her latest book, *Celibacy: Learning to Love the*

*Essence of Self.* She'd somehow managed to make celibacy seem cool instead of the guilty secret it was for me, but then that was because she wasn't actually married at the moment. I peered despairingly into my closet, which offered only two choices: reassuring cardigan shrink clothes, or outmoded fuck-me wear, with a few obligatory grungy T-shirts and jogging bottoms in between. It took Kitty longer than usual to find something that she and I agreed on: a short black skirt, red shirt casually unbuttoned to reveal cleavage (such as it was), black jacket, and red high heels. By the time I'd showered, moisturized (different creams for different body parts; it's a wonder one manages to leave the house at all), and done my makeup, I was running late.

Greg was in the living room doing embarrassing dancing to *Top of the Pops* while Kitty and Leo cringed on a sofa. "One of the great pleasures of being a parent," Greg always said, "is being able to take revenge for the embarrassments of your own childhood." Air guitar, pointless pointing, ill-coordinated movements, little leaps, and contorted facial expressions all contributed to his exquisite version of parental torture. The children were beside themselves. I joined in with hip gyrations for their added mortification and kissed Greg goodbye. As ever, he patted me heartily on the back.

"I'm not a horse," I said.

He proffered a hen's bottom of a mouth for a kiss.

"Nor am I your maiden aunt."

I opened the front door, breathed in the chill night air, and felt freedom course through my veins, as a prisoner must, allowed out on leave for good behavior.

# Chapter 4

## RECIPE FOR TROUBLE

*1 part sexually neglected woman*
*1 part dissatisfied, questing, exotic man*
*2 parts need for adventure*
*1 dash all-done-up and out-on-their-own*
*3 drops heady scent of desire*

Mix together and wait for results. . . . Stand well back. (Can sometimes explode.)

Famous Friend's party was in full flow by the time I got there. It was in one of those trendy Soho media joints, the kind of place where the queue for the loo is longer than the queue at the bar, owing to people's urgent need repeatedly to powder their noses. (I've never understood the lure of cocaine. I tried it a couple of times and felt that I was snorting anxiety and depression in powder form. Since I have more than enough of both, it seemed a pointless exercise.) I was already on the sartorial spiral of shame as I walked through the door, tugging at my too-short skirt, trying to hide my lack of cleavage, and generally feeling all wrong and far too Eighties. Why is it that we all get stuck in some sort of time warp of our youth, our "hottest" moment, frozen in a time that has become for us forever synonymous with looking sexy?

London's literati were draped about, chattering, drinking, and inhaling faux workingman's fodder of tiny fish and chips and sausages. FF's book was everywhere, and she herself was unmissable in a bright red shift dress with NO ENTRY signs embroidered in white over the breast and genital areas. Suddenly I felt rather better about my own attire. FF has an uncanny knack of capturing the zeitgeist, which, coupled with the best contact book in London and great personal beauty, had catapulted her to fame with her first book, *How to Be a Geisha*, published just as the post-feminist era was dawning. She'd been at school with Ruthie and me, and our friendship, although fundamentally warm, was shot through with a certain amount of envy, like the letters in a stick of rock candy. Ruthie had phoned me earlier and said she wasn't feeling generous enough to play the part of fawning acolyte; she was a bit sleepy and dying to lie down with a book. Could I do it for both of us? She'd owe me one. "You owe me about twenty," I had retorted, but she'd already sent loud smacking kisses down the phone and was gone. I had sent her a text, saying if she didn't come I would terminate the contract of eternal friendship we had signed in blood and buried in the garden thirty years before.

FF swooped like an exotic red bird to air-kiss me. "Hello, darling. I want you to meet Brian; he's got such an interesting relationship with his father."

That's the trouble with being a psychotherapist, everyone you meet wants their pound of flesh, an instant slot-machine-pouring-cash kind of answer to all their troubles. In the days when Greg still came with me to parties, we had a secret game: How Much Could You Have Earned This Evening? Many of those we encountered would either ask him for medical advice or me for psychological guidance. We would convene in a corner of the room, after having gone the first round.

"I'm up to five hundred guineas," Greg would mutter. "You see that woman over there? She's having fertility problems and thinks her husband has a low sperm count, but he won't go to be tested."

"See the chap to the left of her?" I might have countered, "He's full of rage because his mother wouldn't make him pancakes for breakfast when he was five."

It's not so much fun now that Greg has eschewed the human race; I have to do the therapy anyhow, but without the thrill of the game. I braced myself and turned to Brian, trying to look interested as he told me how his father never once told him he loved him in all the time he was growing up. He had rather a cute Hugh Grant haircut, though. Sexual abstinence and thoughts of adultery had mixed a heady cocktail, and my hormones seemed to have taken on a life of their own. To my horror, I realized that my long dormant flirting muscles were twitching into life.

"And then, when I was six," Brian was saying.

I stifled a yawn as I recognized that we were about to travel the entire road of his psychological development year by year, each imagined slight, each moment of rejection, every nook and cranny, no stone unturned. No amount of cuteness could help sustain my interest under these circumstances. I looked past him and saw that Ruthie had just arrived. I surreptitiously SOS'd her with my eyes. She waved gaily, made strangling signs with her hands, and moved away. She was punishing me for making her come at all.

"I can't remember his ever taking me to the park to kick a ball,"

Brian said. Over his left shoulder, a tall striking man with exquisite cheekbones came into focus.

"Who's that?" I hissed at FF, who had just joined us. Cheekbones was now staring intently at me.

"Oh, that's Ivan."

"Shagmeister?"

"Don't think so. From what I hear, just married to a rather plain publisher called Becky."

"Hmm." I glanced over covertly.

So far everything seemed in accordance with Ruthie's Rule. What was happening to me? I was starting to feel like Tintin's dog Snowy, who, when faced with a choice between good and evil, has a bad black dog on one shoulder and an angelic white one on the other. The black dog urges him on to acts of perfidy; the white points him toward the path of righteousness. My black dog was clearly in the ascendant. I found myself returning Ivan's gaze with fluttery under-the-eyelashes glances; it seems this flirting business is as unforgettable as riding a bike. Within moments, he was by my side, thrusting a card into my hand.

"Here is my phone number," he said. "I am Ivan." He pronounced it *Eevan*. "You must phone me. I never usually do this, but I have to get to know you."

I laughed politely as I offered my hand. (Why is it that the charming ice-cube tinkling laugh of one's youth seems to become a deep-throated witch's cackle as one grows older?)

"You may call me Vanya for short and, when we are better friends, Vanka," he continued.

I hooted unbecomingly.

"Yes, yes, I know this is very funny in English."

I blushed.

"No," he said, so vehemently that I jumped. "I don't trust you to phone. Give me your number."

"Shall we have a round of conversation before I do?" I suggested coquettishly.

He was from St. Petersburg and looked like a count straight out of a

Tolstoy novel: tall, dark, and with those chiseled high cheekbones that bring the Russian steppe to mind. He was really right up my Strasse—or, rather, the Strasse I used to inhabit in my single days.

"You know, when I left Russia, it was still Soviet times. I wanted so much to leave and finally I got out. All those years I felt like a bird in a cage, flapping my wings futilely, eager for the freedom of flight. Then when I got here, suddenly there was no cage, but I discovered I could no longer fly. My wings had been clipped."

"I'm married with two children: Leo, fifteen, and Kitty, twelve," I blurted out.

"I also am married." His smile was a little sad at its edges. "But, you know, sometimes. . . ."

"Yes, I know." And I did. Sometimes. . . . He was terribly alluring, with a tiny twinge of something tragic about him, a little residue perhaps of the brutality of Soviet rule. I felt weak and destabilized by a barely remembered sensation. It was the steady pulse of sexual desire, an altogether unfamiliar emotion after so many years of holy matrimony. What was it about him that touched me so, my own need to *feel* again? The sense of a man's interest in me? A rare feeling of being looked properly in the eyes and listened to? I couldn't stop staring at his hands. They were the hands of a pianist or a surgeon, long tapering fingers, combining strength with delicacy. As I spoke, he tilted his head to one side, his beautiful hands held as though in prayer, the fingers interlocking, except for the index fingers, which he held against his lips like a small church steeple. I imagined those hands stroking my face, moving down to my body. The cuffs of his shirt fell back slightly to reveal black-haired forearms. I wondered about the hair on the rest of his body and blushed for imagining him naked so quickly. His mouth was full, his eyes a piercing blue. My favorite combination: dark hair and blue eyes. Just like Greg. Oh, God.

I gave him my number. How could I not, after the bird-and-wings story? All of a sudden I wanted to leave. I felt dizzy with possibility and scared too. I grabbed my coat and was making my exit when FF stopped me, waving tickets under my nose.

"Tickets to *Frou-Frou*, darling, it's soon to be the hottest late-night show in town." She is the queen of the freebie and, from the age of fourteen, could wangle free passes to pop concerts, even when people like The Who or Reggie (Elton John to you and me) were playing. Now that she's rich and successful in her own right, she still likes nothing better than a freebie.

"No, thanks, FF, I'm off."

"Come on, it'll be fun, and afterward we can go to the First Night party; my name's on the door."

"Of course it is," I said, and moved away quickly before she could bend me to her will. She has an extraordinary ability to make people do what she wants.

I looked around and saw that Boring Brian had Ruthie *pinned and wriggling* up against a wall. She looked panic-stricken.

"We have to go," I said, taking her arm, smiling briefly at Brian, and leading her to the safety of the door.

"I love you," she whispered, "always have and always will. I won't have a word said against you, not by anyone, ever."

"Yes, well, you don't deserve me. I'm a much nicer person than you. You didn't help me out earlier; next time you're on your own."

I was pleased she hadn't noticed me talking to Ivan. I wanted to keep our meeting to myself for now. Speaking about it would have meant recognizing the beginning of something, and at this point I wasn't prepared to do that, even to myself.

Once home, I walked through the silent sleeping house. A shadowy figure made me jump. It was Leo.

"Grumph a fiver, yeah, like, wanna, you know, with the guys tomorra."

Which is adolescent-speak for "Could I possibly have five pounds, Mother? The chaps and I want to go out tomorrow night." Filled with guilt at the adulterous thoughts simmering in my head, I paid the parental toll. Then I removed my makeup—I always do because it is a truth universally acknowledged that you will burn in the fires of hell if you don't—and crept into bed beside my snoring husband.

"And they came forth in their multitudes and lo! the antibiotics were shared between them," he muttered in his sleep. Bizarrely, so used am I to sharing all news and views with him, I had to restrain myself from waking Greg to tell him my latest delicious bit of gossip: that I'd just met a wonderful and exotic man.

I woke up with a sense of excitement and luxuriated in memories of the night before, parceling them out for myself like a child might an illicit bar of chocolate eaten just before dinner. My sense of well-being was quickly diminished by the harsh reality that is the school day routine. Bea was moving around the kitchen in that irritatingly lan- guorous way she has in the morning when everyone needs to *hurry*. I stumbled in, blindly feeling for the kettle.

"Greg, kettle," I snapped.

"Voilà!" He beamed, producing it with a flourish from the top of the fridge like a rabbit from a hat.

"Could you perhaps exercise your memory on the things that only you require rather than items that are for collective use and save us the fucking Tommy Cooper act in the morning?" I snapped.

"Mummy!" Kitty scolded, from behind a cereal box.

I squinted at the clock on the wall. "Give it a rest, Kitty. The swear- ing police don't report for bloody duty by seven-forty-five A.M."

Kitty pushed her head far enough over the edge of the cereal box to roll her eyes. "Someone's a bit grumpy this morning. Did you get drunk last night?"

"I see the drinking police are here too," I muttered. "Actually, I had one glass of champagne and I have a witness prepared to testify under oath."

Bea was smiling. This was as unusual a sight as watching an ortho- dox Jew set up a picnic table beside the Wailing Wall and tuck into a plate of pork sausages.

"You all right, Bea?" I asked.

"Yes, yes, today I am very happy. My friend Zuzi she come today from Czech Republic. Is OK she staying with me in my room for few days until she find job?" Bea held my eyes in that age-old unblinking glare of the warrior au pair. It was a look known to and feared by all working mothers. Louder than words, it said, *You say yes to whatever I want or I'm out of here, and you, lady, are fucked.* I know defeat when I see it.

"Yes, Bea, of course. A little bit more warning would have been nice, and it mustn't be for too long."

"Well, that's telling her," Greg whispered into my ear as he pushed past.

"Is Leo up?" I asked.

"I wake him five time already," said Bea. "Seven o'clock, ten past seven, twenty past seven, half past seven—"

"Thanks, Bea, I'm getting the picture. Could you wake him for the sixth time? That generally seems to be the one that works."

I pushed my way through the barricade of cereal boxes that Kitty had built around herself. She's entering that excessively self-conscious stage associated with the first surges of estrogen and doesn't like any-one to watch her while she eats. I brushed her hair, trying to work my way through the knots as gently as I could.

"Ow!" she squealed predictably. "You're doing that on purpose. You're just trying to hurt me."

"You're right, that's why I endured nine months of pregnancy and agonizingly painful childbirth, just to get my own back by brushing your hair."

A disgruntled crouching shape shuffled into the kitchen, grunting and snuffling its way to the fridge. Leo was up at last.

"Morning, darling," I said.

"*What?*" snapped Leo, as if I'd interrupted him.

"I can't find any clean socks," Greg shouted from upstairs.

"Marvelous, now I'm the bloody sock curator too," I said.

I hate mornings, the whole getting up, getting everyone else up, getting them ready for school, getting myself ready. . . . My mobile phone bleeped.

"Now what?" I muttered. "Will no one leave me alone?" I snatched it up and opened the message. I AM THINKING ABOUT YOU. YOU ARE VERY BEAUTIFUL. IVAN.

It was a beautiful day. The sky was a crisp autumnal blue, the trees were alive with pinks, reds, and browns, leaves were falling gently in the breeze, and the horse chestnuts lay on the pavement gleaming like jewels, their hedgehog casings flung aside like picnickers' discarded sandwich wrappers. I picked one up and felt its hard smoothness under my thumb and remembered those early mornings of my childhood when I'd hurry to be first in the park to collect the day's new crop. I'd felt full of possibility then as I did again today. The pigeon lady interrupted my thoughts. "Very pleased with yourself today, Mrs. Madam, aren't you?" Well, yes, as a matter of fact I was, rather. I hurried to the café to meet Ruthie for a quick coffee before my first patient.

"Bloody hell, you look good," she said, when she saw me. "You are positively glowing. So who was that man last night?"

"Which man?" I said coyly.

"They look quite good up there against the blue sky, don't they?"

"What does?"

"The pigs on horseback, flying. For God's sake, Chlo, you might just as well have FUCK ME tattooed on your forehead."

"That bad?"

She nodded. "Now come on, give."

So I told her about Ivan. I felt like a swooning Shakespearean maiden in love for the first time. The mere uttering of the loved one's name made my face flush warmly. I had no appetite for my croissant and sipped peakily at my cappuccino like a child with a fever.

"For God's sake be careful, Chlo," said Ruthie. "You've got a lot to lose."

"I haven't done anything yet. I haven't even answered his text message. Look, I know this is all classic midlife-crisis stuff. Woman in her forties needs to prove she's still attractive; it's not all over; there's life in the old girl yet. But, it's nice to have met someone who finds me interesting and beautiful."

"Well, just because he does, it doesn't mean you have to sleep with him. You should work out why you're not sleeping with your husband instead."

"You should be the therapist, Ruthie."

"All those books, all that analyzing? No, thanks. Anyhow, I only care about my friends and family. I have no need to heal the world like you do."

"So what should I do?"

"Nothing. Just do nothing."

"You're right."

Walking back home, I texted him: I LIKED MEETING YOU TOO. I sent it and immediately wished I hadn't. How articulate. *I liked meeting you too.* I was out of practice. I didn't know how to do this anymore. I wasn't even quite sure what *this* was.

FF was waiting outside my door with her daughter, Jessie. Me and Mini Me, identically dressed in long skirts and tight little tops that accentuated their perfect breasts, tiny waists, and flat stomachs. But the long skirts hid a secret: heavy legs and thick ankles, burgeoning in Jessie's case, well established in FF's. This was her secret flaw, her area of less-than-perfection. She hid it well, but we girls who had been to school with her used secretly to call her *Tree trunks* and offer silent thanks to some unseen deity who had given her this cross to bear. It allowed us to look a little more charitably upon her absurd beauty. She easily escaped the miniskirt by taking the hippie route of long skirt and billowing flared trousers and then quickly embraced feminism, not so much for its ideology, but for its fashion. Doc Martens and dungarees hide a multitude of sins.

Jessie never looked very happy, her face a somewhat off-center copy of her mother's. Looking at them together was like doing a test to identify what makes one thing beautiful and another plain. Jessie had the seeds of beauty within her, but not yet the talent or temperament to make them flower. Now and then, a rare smile would bring her face to life, but this just seemed to highlight her troubled nature. I recognized the look on her face—it had been mine once—it was the look of a child forced into the roles of *friend* and *confidante* at too early an age; the look of a little girl who longs merely to be a daughter, with all the requisite coziness and nurture. At thirteen, Jessie already had a sense of the overwhelming burdens of the world, a place of sorrow, double-dealing, and thwarted expectation. We had an understanding, Jessie and I. My role was to feed her, spoil her, ask her all about school and her friends, and never tell her how I was or what I was doing.

"There you are, darling," said FF. "We've been waiting ages. I rang the bell and heard giggles, but no one answered."

"That's odd." I peered through the letterbox and saw an unknown suitcase in the hall. Muffled sounds came from the living room. I rang the bell.

"Haven't you got a key, Chloe? It *is* your house." Jessie looked at me quizzically.

"Yes, of course, quite right, my house, I live here." This Ivan business had got me all mixed up. I fumbled around in my handbag. Ruthie had told me once that three percent of a woman's life is spent with her hands in a bag trying to locate a ringing phone, a set of keys, or some other piece of essential equipment. Those accumulated minutes would probably add up to extra weeks that could be spent far more profitably—weeks that could be devoted to wonderful illicit sex with a glorious new lover, for example.

"You all right, Chlo?" said FF, looking at me curiously.

"Keys, yes, here they are," I said brightly, as I opened the door, tripped, and fell over the suitcase in the hall.

"Didn't you hear the doorbell?" I asked Bea crossly, as she emerged from the living room, looking oddly flushed.

"No, I was talking with my Zuzi. We have so many things to talk about." I had never seen Bea look so happy in the two years she had been with us. Her heavy-featured face, characterized by an almost permanent scowl, had lightened and looked contented. A pretty redhead appeared at her side.

"Ah," I said, "you must be Zuzi and this must be your case?" I rubbed my shin ruefully.

"Thank you for to allow me to come to live in your house," Zuzi said, wrinkling a small freckled nose in a manner that someone had clearly once told her was adorable. I threw a look of alarm at Bea, who stared back at me impassively. I reassured myself that this was a mere linguistic error; "stay for a couple of days" and "live" were no doubt served by the same verb in Czech. I took FF and Jessie off to the kitchen.

"I met someone last night after you'd gone," FF said excitedly, once we were settled at the kitchen table, a cup of builder's tea in my hand and fennel tea in hers—very good for lymphatic drainage, apparently.

"Jeremy, Jeremy, Jeremy. I never realized what a lovely name that is. He's a fabulous shag."

It all became clear. FF had scored and then rushed over to tell me all about it.

"Jessie," I warned, indicating Jessie's presence with a tilt of the head.

"Oh, don't worry, darling, Jessie and I are the bestest of best, I tell her everything. We're bosom buds, aren't we, darling?"

Jessie assented wearily.

"Sweetheart, go upstairs and see if you can find a book or something in Kitty's room. Too boring for you here with us," I said.

"I've got some of my own here," Jessie said, tapping the heavy bag she'd eased onto her shoulder. Jessie's visits were frequent, and each time she came she seemed to leave more of her things in the spare room.

I turned to FF. "What happened to *Celibacy: Learning to Love the Essence of Self?*"

"Don't you see, it's because I love myself that I can now love another," said FF. "Well, maybe not love, but certainly fuck the arse off."

She's always had this habit of giving too much sexual information. The face of an angel and the mouth of a fishwife. I'm told it can be very alluring to men, that old mother-in-the-kitchen whore-in-the-bedroom stuff. But here she was being a whore in my kitchen. The detail was just a bit off-putting, a little too close to a gynecologist's textbook and not the kind of stuff you want to know about a friend.

For the next hour, I was subjected to a blow-by-blow (yes, indeed) account of their night of passion. It was enough to put a girl off sex, which, given my current febrile state, was no bad thing.

"His penis is absolutely splendid," she was saying, "about this long"—she measured out an improbable length with her two hands—"and nice and thick. I really hate those long thin ones, don't you?"

"I can't remember," I said. "I can barely remember what a penis looks like, much less what it's for."

"Anyhow," she continued, "it's given me the idea for my next book: *Back in the Saddle: Embracing Your Sexuality.* Fabulous, don't you think?"

FF was very serious about her work and approached it with the solemnity of an Oxbridge don on the brink of some new scientific discovery. I doubt whether Crick and Watson were as pleased with themselves when they discovered the double helix as she is when writing one of her self-help books. Her books were her very own DNA, each one a new and vital piece of the jigsaw puzzle that formed her picture of what it meant to be a human being—more specifically, what it meant to be her in all her wondrousness. But it was all her own made up nonsense, with no scientific, sociological, or psychotherapeutic basis. She hadn't spent years in therapy as I had when I was training, years of reading Freud and Jung and delving into my own psyche and those of others.

Now she was flushed with excitement at the brilliance of her new project and, when excited, she had this annoying habit of jiggling her leg up and down as she talked, which always made me want to smack her and send her to her room. As always, I wondered why I put up with FF and her self-centered nonsense. We were bound by the past, by shared history and my sense of loyalty, by my credo of "once a friend, always a friend," and to be honest I enjoyed the patina of glamour I acquired through association with this famous, beautiful, and somewhat absurd woman. There was something seductive about being in the presence of beauty; some Keatsian truth that compelled you to sit and stare in the belief that you would be warmed and aesthetically enriched. Not all beauty has this effect. FF's ex, Jessie's father, was an absurdly handsome actor who had changed his name from Eric to

Helvetica, believing it to be the name of a handsome Greek god. He and FF had bathed in the pool of their reflected beauty, like Narcissus. (Now, *he* was Greek.) Eric/Helvetica was very good in the role of lovesick swain but not up to the demands of the part of dutiful husband and father. I felt sure that if I were to ask him what he did for a living, he would reply, "I am handsome," perhaps with a look of surprise that he should be expected to do more. He was *professionally* handsome. I've never found the type attractive. There's something oddly asexual about male perfection, too mannequin-like; in fact, you wouldn't be surprised to find a mound of pink plastic where the genitals of a perfectly handsome man should be. In any event, Eric, or Swissy, as we somewhat unkindly called him, wasn't around long. He collected beautiful women like trophies and, had he been a barbarian, would doubtless have exhibited them like the stags' heads found on the walls of hunting lodges. FF had tired of him just as fast, although the marriage was fruitful, giving birth as it did both to Jessie and to FF's first book, *How to Be a Geisha; The Fundaments and Principles of a Successful Marriage*, which told us all how to be the perfect wife. Always make his dinner and never refuse him a blow job was pretty much what it boiled down to, but FF somehow managed to make it last three hundred and fifty pages with pictures. It was a publishing sensation, and now she could do no wrong. "See," she had said, when the book came out, "not just pretty, clever too." That was her Achilles heel, the fear that she was nothing more than just a pretty face.

"So just as I was about to come, he stuck his finger up my bum. I had the most amazing orgasm," she went on. Out of the corner of my eye, I saw Greg on the kitchen threshold. On hearing the O-word, he grimaced, executed a sort of midair soundless pirouette, and crept away backward, his hands held out in mute supplication, entreating me not to give him away. Poor thing, he'd just popped back from the surgery hoping for a spot of lunch. A minute later, my phone bleeped TEXT ME WHEN COAST IS CLEAR. Greg is squeamish about hearing the details of the sexual exploits of others.

"You know how I only really like one-night stands?"

"When you're not being celibate, you mean?"

"Yes." The irony escaped her. "Well, last night was so good, I think I might have to shag Jeremy again, although not exclusively, obviously. I've got a bit of catching up to do." She paused, gave an exaggerated sigh of contentment, and said, "Oh, Chlo, I so love it here in your kitchen, you and me together, sharing everything just as we've always done. Isn't it lovely that we'll always be friends? I don't know what I'd do without you. And Jessie adores you too."

It was always the same. Just as you thought you couldn't take another moment of it, FF would bathe you in her golden light and make you feel special and wanted—and trapped in a friendship with no hope of escape.

Once she'd gone, I felt deflated. Her sexual adventure had somehow tainted any thought of one of my own, and the prospect of an affair with Ivan now felt faintly distasteful. I sat at the table and stared at a sticky patch of jam left over from breakfast. A fly had found this treat and set about spitting all over it in that nasty flylike way. It was soon joined by another, who, shunning the delicacy, jumped on top of the first fly. The birds and the bees and the frickin' fli-eeze. Two flies fucking. It reminded me of that silly schoolboy joke about a Native American boy who wants to know why his sister is called Running Deer. His father explains that the custom is to name a new baby after the first thing you see after its birth. "Why do you ask, Two Dogs Fucking?" You know the one? Fucking hilarious. Yes, my mood was clearly ruined.

"I suppose she's forgotten me again," said Jessie, who'd just come into the room.

"No, angel, of course not," I lied swiftly. "She's gone to get you some clothes so you can stay the night. Why aren't you at school anyhow?"

"Mum was too busy shagging to wake me up, so by the time we all got up it was really late and there didn't seem much point. I don't need any clothes; I've got enough in my room—I mean, the *spare* room— here."

It was lucky really that FF had stopped at one child. Lucky for me mainly; Jessie stayed over so often she was fast becoming my third child. I loved her, so I didn't mind. For her part, FF couldn't bear to repeat the trauma of childbirth, which had been far, far worse for her than for anyone else in the history of womankind. Naturally her periods were terrible too; they'd always been absolute agony and had usually necessitated a day off school. This is the kind of woman who gives the rest of us a bad name.

I left the room to phone FF discreetly and tell her to bring some clothes over for Jessie without revealing that she had, in the glow of newly sated sexual passion, in fact forgotten her. I bumped into a shadowy figure lurking in the stairwell.

"Has she gone?" Greg hissed, doing a bad imitation of an East End villain hiding from the law.

"Yes, just a few minutes ago."

"I'm starving and I've got to get back to the surgery. Bugger. Where did she go?"

"To have her pubic hair shaved in the shape of a heart for the delectation of her new lover."

"A bit old hat," he commented. "Mary Quant did that in the sixties for her husband."

Greg is a mine of extraordinary trivia—although it's not really that astonishing, since it's yet another way he flexes the memory muscle. It's quite useful, especially when you're struggling to remember who had a hit, say, with 1-2-3 (Len Barry in 1965).

"Name of Quant's husband?" I shot out.

"Alexander Plunkett-Green," he answered.

"I'll make you a sandwich to take with you," I said admiringly.


Greg had gone back to the surgery, a chicken, avocado, and tomato sandwich in hand (olive oil but no butter—bad for his cholesterol); I'd put FF in the picture about her motherly duties, and Jessie was reading to Janet the cat. Kitty had chosen the cat's name; she'd wanted her to have a proper name, not a silly cat name that no human being would answer to. So she was Janet, not Spoofie or Paws or Fifi, but Janet

Zhivago McTernan (she had both my surname and Greg's, just like the children), and she had a complicated human psychological disorder to match her name. Janet was anorexic, and it was all we could do to make her eat enough food to stay alive. On the few occasions she did eat, she would gorge herself on massive portions of food and then be found quietly throwing it all up in a discreet corner of the garden. Mike the vet, a frequent visitor to the house, had made Janet his special case study, and his latest theory was that since Janet thought she was a teenage girl, she should be treated like one. So Jessie was reading *Fat Is a Feminist Issue* to her while Janet lay on her lap taking surreptitious glances at herself in the small mirror beside them. What did she see reflected? An image disfigured by her dysmorphia into a cat of gargantuan proportions or the small rather too-thin cat that she actually was?

I felt vaguely depressed, the elation of the early morning soured by subsequent events. I looked at myself in the mirror and saw a tired-looking middle-aged woman staring back. Who was she? I didn't recognize her at all; I'd been looking for the face of a young girl. That's what happens. One minute you're young, juicy, full of sexual power, with your life ahead of you; the next, you're sliding inexorably into old age, your flesh loosening like the elastic on a pair of old school gym knickers.

I heard a sort of mewling noise coming from upstairs and went to investigate. The sounds led me to Bea's door, and I peeked in to see her head bobbing enthusiastically in between Zuzi's parted thighs like a cat lapping at a bowl of milk. Well, not our cat obviously, but any normal cat. A memory flashed: me at the age of eleven. I had been woken by a bad dream and had crept to my parents' room for comfort. As I neared their door, I heard strange breathing noises and, peeking in, saw them spread-eagled across the bed. I had stood in the doorway rocking silently with horrified and embarrassed laughter. I did the same now and tiptoed away. Everyone, it seemed, was at it except me. My phone bleeped, and the words winking at me sent a treacherous jolt of pleasure through me: I AM THINKING ONLY ABOUT YOU AND ABOUT HOW I MUST SEE YOU AGAIN. IVAN.

# Chapter 5

## CHLOE ZHIVAGO'S JEWISH PENICILLIN

### THE ULTIMATE CHICKEN SOUP WITH DUMPLINGS

*Serves 6–8*

FOR THE STOCK

*1 fresh stewing chicken*

*1 stick celery*

*1 peeled carrot*

*2 bay leaves*

*4 black peppercorns*

*1 onion, peeled and quartered*

*1 handful fresh parsley*

Place all ingredients in a large pot and cover with cold water. Bring to a boil, then reduce heat and simmer for two and a half hours.

Remove the chicken to a platter, strain the broth, and discard the vegetables. Allow broth to cool and skim off fat. I find the stock can be a bit watery so, for extra oomph, add a few teaspoons of Telma chicken stock (it comes in powdered form).

When chicken has cooled enough to handle, remove skin and tear meat from bone. Discard bones and reserve chicken meat.

Set stock on low heat and prepare Grandma Bella's Knaydlach (dumplings).

FOR THE KNAYDLACH

*1 egg*

*2 tablespoons secret ingredient*

*6 tablespoons soup stock*

*¾ cup medium matzo meal*

*3 tablespoons ground almonds*

*1 tablespoon chopped parsley or coriander*

*Salt and pepper to taste*

Beat the egg into a mixing bowl; add and whisk in the secret ingredient. As you whisk, add the soup stock, matzo meal, ground almonds, parsley or coriander, and salt and pepper. You should have a firm but malleable mixture. Leave it to chill in the fridge for at least an hour. Then roll into small balls (makes 15 walnut-sized balls).

Add Knaydlach balls to your stock with:

*2 peeled and sliced carrots*

*1 washed and sliced leek*

*Reserved boiled chicken*

*Salt and pepper to taste*

Simmer on low heat for 40 minutes. Serve with a sprinkle of fresh parsley. Proven to cure guilt, remorse, and all major illnesses.

reg was intensely amused by my account of the lesbotic antics of the au pair. In fact, he was positively titillated by it, but then nothing excites men more than the prospect of a little girl-on-girl action.

"It's all very well," I said, "but she's settled in, put a framed photo of her dog next to her side of the bed, and shows no signs of leaving."

"What kind of dog, a big licky sort of one?"

"Don't be disgusting."

"Who exactly was doing what to whom again?" he asked.

"For God's sake."

I was making chicken soup. Dad was coming for supper, and Sammy had tepeed into town. Greg had insisted that this was the perfect occasion for the Chicken Soup Tournament. Both his and my soup would be served, and the winner would be declared by independent arbitration after blind tasting. He had been adding secret ingredients to his soup, his body hunched over the brew, much like a child shielding his homework to stop the person sitting next to him from copying. I made a sticker that read TOP SECRET and put it on Greg's pot while he was happily engrossed in his weekly task of examining all the use-by dates on everything in the larder, hurling offending expirees into the rubbish bin in a long arching throw that would have done justice to Michael Jordan.

I hadn't answered Ivan's text yet. I felt poised at a crossroads, in need of a wise man to point me in the right direction. Of course, it didn't take a biblical stranger with long flowing hair and silver beard to tell me what was right. But I felt so bored with my life, with my job, with myself; so in need of a big adventure and painfully aware that this might be my last chance for one. Knowing how lucky you are compared with others doesn't stop you from aching for something more. In addition, it seemed a bit rude not to answer Ivan at all. PERHAPS WE'LL MEET AT ANOTHER OF LIZZIE'S PARTIES IN THE FUTURE. There, polite and friendly and not suggesting intimate meetings à deux. I was just about to send it when the devil entered my body and made my fingers tap out I CAN'T STOP THINKING ABOUT YOU AND WOULD LIKE TO SEE YOU TOO.

"You didn't tell me that Lou and James had split up," said Greg.

I jumped, my finger springing guiltily off the SEND button. "Forgot. Who told you?"

"I bumped into James in the park with a young woman he introduced as his girlfriend."

So much for trial separation.

"What, MAN LEAVES WIFE FOR YOUNGER WOMAN? Gosh, I don't think I've ever heard of that before," I said. (I'm prepared to admit that the sarcasm was a bit rich from someone who'd just sent the twenty-first-century equivalent of a billet-doux to an admirer.)

"Funny, I thought those two were so happy," Greg said.

"What about us, are we happy?"

"Mmm, 'course we are. Now where did I put the teabags?" He stood with his eyes closed, like a game show contestant trying to recall the prizes on a conveyor belt in order to win them. "Of course, in the mop bucket." Looking very pleased with himself, he went to retrieve them. Endearing, I grant you, but just the tiniest bit irritating after seventeen years.

Bea and Zuzi came into the kitchen, bathed head to toe in post-coital glow.

"We will be staying for the supper and the chicken soup examination," Bea announced. "Then I will to take my Zuzi to a club in the London."

I shrugged agreement halfheartedly. While my long years in therapy had taught me that I had boundary issues, I still hadn't learned how to deal with them. Professionally, I more or less kept my boundaries clearly demarcated, but personally they were about as effective as a chastity belt with a broken lock.

"Righto," said Greg to Bea, "the more the merrier. I need a few non-partisan testers, you know, people who aren't actually Chloe's blood relatives with a vested interest in her winning."

Kitty, who was off school again with a cold, was sitting in a corner with Janet, trying to coax her to eat.

"Leo and I are just as much your blood relatives as Mummy's," she said.

"You do know what *blind* testing means?" I said irritably. "No one will actually know whose soup is whose."

Kitty got up, pirouetted to the cutlery drawer, and started laying the table. She had inherited Girlie's showing-off gene. Simple acts are transformed into showstoppers; face washing and teeth brushing become a small ballet about a beautiful young princess who wakes up, prettily rubbing her eyes, stretches, and goes about her ablutions. The miming and the dancing often supersede the activity in hand, so Kitty often performs the tasks themselves in a perfunctory manner.

Just the other day I had watched her dancing in a ballet school show, tears running down my cheeks; not just a delicate moistening of the eyes but great shuddering sobs shook me. I've always been like this, watching my children perform, and can never understand how other mothers remain dry-eyed. Leo as third shepherd from the left in the school nativity play age five was, for me, a six-tissue experience. There's something about watching your child onstage, separate from you, that I find unbearably moving. Watching Kitty perform, I wept at her talent, lost in admiration and wonder at her ability to do something that I couldn't. Although each of us is an individual, we are also the sum of the individuals who have preceded us, the solution to the equation formed by our ancestry. Kitty was a culmination of the dancing talent in the family; it had taken generations to hone the art so it would find full and complete expression in her. How proud my mother would have been to see Kitty dance. As I watched I could see flashes of my mother in her, in the tilt of the head and the sweep of an arm.

*Battement frappé, pas de bourré*, Kitty mouthed, as she danced the setting of the table.

"So Zuzi, how's the job hunting going?" I asked, in the bright tones of someone pretending complete indifference to the answer to her question.

"Is good. I have found the job in restaurant."

"Excellent. Do they give you a room too?"

"No, I prefer to stay here with my Bea. She say this make her happy, and if she happy then also you happy and your family happy." She smiled and, throwing Bea a coquettish glance, added, "And I too, of course, happy."

Bea looked me in the eye unflinchingly, daring me to say something. "Which one you prefer, smiling Bea or crying Bea?" she asked, smiling exaggeratedly and then pulling her mouth down into a cartoon of misery. She looked different; her mono-brow was gone, neatly plucked to extinction, doubtless due to the affectionate ministrations of Zuzi. She had also taken to wearing a tie, a nod perhaps to her role as the male in this relationship. (Why did some lesbians need to pretend to be men, and why did their partners need them to? If Zuzi wanted a man, there were any number who would surely have been willing.) The tie looked familiar; it was one I had bought Leo for his birthday. My boundary fence had not merely been vaulted, it was lying in pieces.

"Well, we'll see," I muttered, beaten, "just for a little while, then."

Across the room, Greg raised his eyebrows at me and wiggled his tongue lewdly. "I'm off to get changed for evening surgery. See you later; don't touch my soup." I followed him upstairs, tripping over a solitary shoe lying in silent reproach. Its partner, long lost, had been hidden somewhere by Greg. He had unique feet; the little toe of each permanently hitched a ride on top of the fourth as though too lazy to take part in the standing and walking business itself. As a child, Greg had been embarrassed about this minor deformity and had developed a shoe habit to compensate. He was Queen's Park's answer to Imelda: the owner of fifty-one pairs of shoes, all in mint condition, bought in charity shops throughout the land. "My dead men's shoes," he called them cheerfully. I found it odd that he was prepared to walk in other men's shoes and felt haunted by the stories those shoes could tell. Leo, who had inherited his father's feet (it was a boy thing apparently), was wholly unconcerned about his affliction.

As soon as Greg had gone, I checked my mobile to see whether Ivan had replied, but my inbox was empty. "It's probably for the best," I reasoned. "I must pull myself together. I'm a grown career woman, a mother, and a wife." Scrolling through my phone, I noticed I hadn't sent my message to Ivan after all; Greg's talk of Lou and James had interrupted me just as I was about to press the button. As my finger hovered uncertainly above my fate, the phone began to ring.

"Hello," I said, too eagerly.

"Darling, Lizzie here," said the brusque self-assured voice.

"Oh, hi." Disappointment overwhelmed me.

"You all right, angel? You sound like you've taken a job as receptionist in an undertaker's. Are you chicken-souping tonight?" She bulldozed on without waiting for an answer, as to my well-being or otherwise. "I thought I'd come and join you; my nutritionist says it provides the correct fuel mix for my body." What was she, a fucking car? "'Bout eight, but I can't stay too long; I've got to go on somewhere after, private art celeb thingy."

I tried to tell her it was a family supper, not a free-for-all, but for some reason it's impossible to say *no* to FF. The word starts to form; the tongue gets ready to do its job on the roof of the mouth behind the teeth, and then, before you know it, as though you have been overtaken by an irresistible force, it relaxes across the back molars and the word *yes* pops out. I comfort myself with the thought that in bygone times she would have been burned at the stake as a witch for her ability to bend people to her will.

"OK, sweetie, must dash, there'll be two of us." She hung up. *She* was the one who had rung *me*, but her haste always left me feeling rebuffed, as if I were somehow detaining her from a more important task.

It was 3:50 P.M. I suddenly remembered my last appointment of the day. "Fuck, God's Gift!" I rushed down to the basement and got there just before the doorbell rang. No time to text Ivan. This was officially A Good Thing. Enough of this nonsense. So you saw some guy at a party, so he liked you, so you liked him. (Not only was I thinking like a fifteen-year-old, my syntax had become teenage too. Whatever.) I smoothed down my hair, caught it in a scrunchie, appeased my residual-food-particle-in-teeth phobia by quickly grimacing in the mirror, and opened the door to my patient.

God's Gift swaggered in, holding my hand and looking me in the eye just that little bit too long. I had thought this was classic transference— shrink-as-object-of-desire stuff—until I got to know him better and realized he thought everyone he met was dying to fuck him. It's true that he was exceptionally handsome and equally true that no one realized this more than he did. He came in through the narrow hallway and passed the mirror, into whose loving gaze he briefly lost himself while sucking in his stomach. Flicking at an imaginary bit of fluff on his immaculate suit, he worked his lips in his own odd, slightly camp way. It was as if he was barely able to restrain himself from puckering up and covering his own body in kisses or self-inflicted love bites. God's Gift ran a television production company, made famous less by the quality of the programs it produced than by the young, long-limbed, full-mouthed girls it employed: blow-up porn dolls made flesh. The only other man working there apart from God's Gift was his PA, Baz.

"I can't have girls working too closely with me," God's Gift had told me early on. "They fall in love and the whole thing gets messy. Mind you, between you and me, I think Baz has a bit of a thing for me too."

"But I thought he was dating a supermodel," I'd protested.

"Well," God's Gift had said, leaning forward conspiratorially, "there's something in the way he looks at me."

God's Gift came to therapy less to discover and understand himself than to "understand what it is about me that makes women fall for me. I want to learn to deal with it better and break fewer hearts." His real problem was self-delusion; he had little more than a nodding acquaintance with reality.

"So," I said, as I settled into an armchair by the window and he seated himself opposite me in another, "what's been happening with you this week?"

"Same old story," he said with a heavy sigh. "There's a new girl in the office, and she's been giving me the come-on all week."

"What exactly has she said to you?"

"First day, she told me she liked my shirt. Next day, she asked me if she could get me a coffee. Classic symptoms." He shook his head as though in sorrow at the irresistible pull of his sexual magnetism.

"Is it possible that she just liked your shirt? And that as a new employee she thought it appropriate to offer you coffee?" I reasoned.

God's Gift sat back, held both hands up, tilted his head back slightly, and raised his eyebrows as if to say, Who can resist this? Certainly he was good-looking and he dressed well, but he did nothing for me. He had an irritating habit of twitching his jacket collar up with his fingers. Leaning forward, he did so now while shaking his head in sorrow. "Please don't take this the wrong way, but you're a woman."

I bit my tongue to stop myself from shouting out, Thanks for the breaking news, pal, and here I've spent the last forty-odd years thinking I was a man. Instead, I nodded silently, inviting him to tell me more.

"You see," he continued, "men know when women like them. They just do, and God knows I should know."

I was feeling quite pleased I hadn't texted Ivan back. God's Gift was putting me off the whole damn sex; he was condensed man, poisoned by testosterone and turned into a parody. Nor was his self-love as harmless as it might seem; he harassed the girls who worked for him, convinced that they invited his attentions, and then coerced them into acquiescence. However handsome, he was in his forties and therefore invisible to most twenty-year-old girls, but with their toes just barely on the first rung of the precarious TV ladder they were ill-equipped to rebuff his advances. I was trying to help him, but the cure for both his delusion and his habit of sexual harassment was, it seemed, still some way off.

I was running late, and I still had to make my *knaydlach*, the matzo balls for my soup. I couldn't make them while Greg was watching. This was my secret ingredient, the lethal weapon in my Jewish cookery armory. It all boiled down to this one essential constituent. To make matzo balls with the right consistency, fluffy and chewy at the same time, you needed *shmaltz*. I kept mine in a jar hidden at the back of the fridge. Greg would pick it up from time to time, asking what an old jar of fat was doing cluttering up the fridge, little realizing that this was the very obstacle that lay between him and chicken soup supremacy. *Shmaltz* is rendered chicken fat. You boil the fat to sizzle away any old bits of chicken still hanging about and then you strain the chicken fat through muslin to remove the remaining dark particles. Once you have mined this liquid gold, you fold it into the matzo meal mixture in the time-honored tradition of Eastern European Jews for ultimate dumpling perfection. The matzo balls, correctly made, then infuse the soup itself with its particular flavor. What non-Jew can be expected to know or understand this? It's the sort of thing you have to learn at a grandmother's knee, as I did at mine.

Grandma Bella, my father's mother, was born in Vilnius, the capital of Lithuania. She had come to England as a young girl in the summer of 1917, as the revolution fired its opening shots in nearby Russia. She brought with her her elderly parents (she had been a late addition to the family), a Yiddish-English dictionary, and a jar of *shmaltz*. Somehow they made their way through war-torn Europe, and thereafter, in gratitude for their safe passage and to add flavor to food eaten away from home, she always carried this talisman in her handbag. Her sturdy brown gladstone bag with two handles and a zip across its worn belly was an Aladdin's cave of treasure to a small child: a lipstick in its own ornate golden holder complete with small mirror; jeweled powder compacts; hair combs; faded sepia family photographs of white-bearded serious-faced men and full-bosomed demure matrons, and, finally, carefully wrapped in a plastic bag to avoid spillage, a jar of *shmaltz*, which she would whip out and open; then, using the small bone-handled knife she always carried with her, she would slather the golden fat onto a piece of bread and push bite-sized pieces into my small child's mouth.

She looked just as a grandmother should, which was comforting to a child whose mother didn't look much like a mother. Small, plump, soft, and white-haired, she had that prettiness that some elderly women retain, a fond memory of their youthful selves etched nostalgically onto their features; age had not dimmed her astonishingly turquoise eyes. *Bella mit die shayne oigen*—Bella with the beautiful eyes—was her nickname. My father had inherited those eyes. They were also her legacy to me, although mine were a little less bright than the original, as though they had faded through replication.

Her plumpness irritated her but she couldn't resist the foods that caused it. In a vain attempt to counteract their effect on her waistline, she would eat each mouthful with a face twisted into an expression of distaste, as if to inform both the world and herself that there was no pleasure to be gained from it. I remember her spooning potato salad, wet with mayonnaise and gleaming with the emerald of its salted cucumber, into her mouth and wrinkling her nose in apparent revulsion. As she helped herself to another portion, seemingly against her will, she would shake her head and tut-tut her disgust.

When I turned thirteen, the age when Jewish boys become men, she took me by the hand, saying, "It's time." We marked my important rite of passage into womanhood in her kitchen, where she taught me the art of chicken soup with *knaydlach* while telling me stories of her life "back home" and how she'd met Grandpa at English classes for Jewish immigrants in a small library in London's East End. (He'd arrived in London a month before her from Oryol in Russia.)

I felt the pleasurable texture of the matzo meal against my fingertips and could hear Grandma Bella's soft voice in my ear. "Gentle, gentle, make like you crumble autumn leaves with your fingers, not like you pack a snowball."

Yo, motherfucker, you my bitch, you my 'ho." I was jolted from my reverie; Leo was home. He sauntered into the kitchen, singing along to his iPod.

"Leo," I admonished.

"Yo, Mamma." He shook a hand, balled into a fist, index and little fingers extended, and grabbed his crotch with his other hand. A hip-hop king in school clothing. I was about to remind him that he was not black and did not in fact live in a New York ghetto when I had a vision of myself at his age, with bright pink hair, wearing a tattered ballgown from the 1890s. Since the advent of the Great God iPod, conversation with Leo had become increasingly difficult. Extraterrestrials, visiting earth for the first time, would be forgiven for assuming that humans were connected to some power source by means of the white earplugs with long white wires snaking their way to a batterylike device in their pockets. Those of us without the trailing wires were perhaps the masters and mistresses of these slave iPodians. Through their wires, we controlled their actions and issued instructions to them. Although it didn't seem to be working now, as I tried to tell Leo to change and wash.

He shook his head and shouted, "I can't hear you!"

I unplugged him. "You don't have to shout. Supper's in an hour. Grandpa and Uncle Bonkers are coming."

"Cool," he said. "Fuck you, man, fuck you."

"Pardon?" But it was no use, he was plugged in again and making his way out of the room on the balls of his feet, with a funny little half hop between each step.

The house was alive with the sounds of early evening: the TV blaring, the children arguing, Bea giggling with her Zuzi, and Greg shouting on the phone about something to someone who had made him angry.

"No," I could hear him say, "I'm afraid I can't bring it in next week. It will be too late. . . . Why? Because by that time I will have picked the computer up and smashed it through the window, and it will be lying in the middle of the road, where it will have been run over by passing cars and shattered into a thousand small pieces, making it rather difficult for me to deliver to you, that's why."

He slammed the phone into its cradle. I waited. He came down stairs and held the broken and now useless phone out to me. Wordlessly I took it from him, opened a cupboard, and handed him a new one. We were stocked up for the next few months or so; there were five new phones in the cupboard. It had become a contest between us to see who could spend the least money on them; Greg was winning with a 50-pence phone bought on eBay. His emotional temperature could be measured in telephones. The best we'd ever had was a one-phone year, the worst, a twenty-niner. That was the year Leo was born, when Greg, struggling to come to terms with fatherhood, was sleep-deprived and overwhelmed by responsibility. Me? I just turned my rage at his unreasonable behavior inward, where it roared and crackled like a dragon that has set itself on fire by chasing its own tail. Home, sweet home. I went off to have a bath before the soup kitchen opened.

# Chapter 6

## GREG McTERNAN'S WILD MUSHROOM RISOTTO AND SALADE FRISÉE AUX LARDONS

### *Serves 4*

. . . . . . . . . . . . . . . . . . .

1 large onion, chopped

6 tablespoons olive oil

2 cloves garlic, minced

2 cups arborio rice

1 cup dry white wine

7–8 cups hot chicken or vegetable stock (use the mushroom water to
    make up stock)

2 ounces dried porcini mushrooms soaked for 30 minutes in a cup of
    warm water. Strain and reserve the water; dry and chop the
    mushrooms.

4 cups assorted fresh wild mushrooms (shiitake, oyster, portabello),
    cleaned and roughly chopped

1 ounce unsalted butter

1 cup grated Parmesan cheese

¼ cup chopped flat parsley

Salt and pepper

In a large heavy-based saucepan, sauté the chopped onion in
the olive oil. When it begins to brown, add garlic and rice and
stir until the rice is coated. Add white wine and, stirring all the
while, cook until absorbed.

Now add the hot chicken or vegetable stock, one ladle at a time, stirring every few minutes until the liquid is absorbed. After about 15 minutes, add the chopped porcini mushrooms. When the rice is al dente and all the stock has been added, throw in the fresh wild mushrooms.

After a few more minutes, remove from heat, add the butter, the Parmesan cheese, the chopped parsley, and the salt and pepper. The cooking process takes about half an hour; the trick is to ensure that the mixture remains wet and creamy.

FOR THE SALAD
*1 head frisée lettuce*
*1 cup lardons (or* jamón serrano*)*
*3 tablespoons olive oil*
*Juice of ½ a lemon*
*Pepper to taste*

Wash frisée lettuce and tear into small pieces in a bowl. In a frying pan, cook the lardons, small pieces of thick-cut bacon, often sold already diced. (Or use small chunks of Spanish *jamón serrano* when available.) When browned, add this meat and its juices to the frisée. Dress with olive oil, fresh lemon juice, and pepper (the lardons add enough salt) and serve.

Somebody get that!" I yelled. The doorbell rang again. "Bugger, I'll get it myself."

Greg was responsible for the rest of the evening meal and was in the kitchen making his mushroom risotto and salad. I'd fallen asleep in the bath and hurried to the door, skin wrinkled by over-immersion, a towel wrapped around still-wet hair, another around my body, both colored that off-putting gray symptomatic of the washing techniques of the careless au pair. I opened the door to FF. A man was standing next to her; he had his back to me and was pointing his key at a car parked in the street outside and pushing a button to check that he'd locked it. There was something familiar about the angle of his head. I greeted them. He turned around. It was Ivan.

My astonishment and pleasure at seeing him on my threshold were quickly replaced by horror at my appearance and the question, *What the fuck is he doing with FF?* This last I only just managed to stop myself from uttering out loud. And why did FF have to be fifteen minutes early for the first time in her life? I'd said eight o'clock. My heart was beating so fast I was surprised it didn't leap out of my throat to lie throbbing pinkly on the floor between us as I said, "Come in, come in," in a chummy, expansive way. "Go on down to the kitchen, I'll just be a sec."

*Typical,* I raged, as I flung clothes out of my wardrobe. *FF must have known I liked him, and now she's back in the saddle she's nabbed him. It's always the same; that's exactly what she did with Matt Salmon in 1975.* Then I remembered two things: One, I was married; two, my husband was actually on the premises and probably shaking hands and making polite conversation with Ivan right now. Three, I was no longer in the third form. (Yes, yes, I know that's three things.) At the back of the cupboard I found a little black dress I thought Bea had lost: a stalwart, dependable Lycra friend who pulled me in and pushed me out in all the right places. I sprayed Vivienne Westwood's Boudoir into the air and walked through the mist (a little trick my mother taught me), ran a comb through my hair, mascara-ed my eyes, glossed my lips, prepared my mirror face, nodded grudging acceptance at my reflection, and made my way with unseemly haste downstairs to the kitchen.

En route, I opened the door to Sammy and Dad, who had been ringing the bell unnoticed for some time. Sammy, newly arrived from Spain and here to stay for a while, was holding a *pata negra* (dry-cured ham, particularly delicious to secular Jews who enjoy pork more than most Christians) strapped to a *jamonera* (the wooden rack invented by Spaniards for holding a pork leg in just the right position for easy slicing). He was brandishing a scary-looking knife like a pirate.

"Acorn-fed. Delicious," he announced. "Got it in Seville."

"How do you do," my father said, proffering his hand. "I'm your father."

I kissed him. "Aren't you the man I spoke to this morning? You could phone me yourself sometimes too, you know."

"Don't want to pester you, darling." He looked at Sammy and me together and beamed. "What wonderful children I have."

In the kitchen, we found the assembled company seated solemnly at the table. Dad, Sammy, and I joined them. There were the four of us, Bea and Zuzi, Dad and Sammy, FF and Ivan, and Nick the vet, who wanted to see whether eating with us could inform his treatment of Janet. I loved having everyone around the table, eating my food; my compulsion to feed people is the most Jewish thing about me. Kitty had been put in charge of organizing the tasting. In front of each person were two bowls labeled A and B and two spoons. Beside each bowl was a piece of paper and a pencil and, in the center of the table, a ballot box—Leo's piggy bank in a former life. Kitty had dressed the table with small furry yellow chicks, former Easter cake adornments she had found lying forgotten in a drawer. Greg stood at the head like a conductor on the brink of an overture. At his signal, we each picked up a spoon and drank first from Bowl A and then from Bowl B.

"Are we allowed to taste them again?" asked Dad, keen to offer a reasoned empirical response to the experiment in hand.

"Yes," said Greg. "Just make sure you use the correct spoon with the correct bowl."

Matzo balls were rolled around tongues, soup was sucked from spoons, considering and exploratory noises were made, lips were licked, and votes were cast. Ivan didn't seem at all surprised by the bizarre ritual. He caught my eye, glanced sideways at FF, and shrugged apologetically. I was struck once again by how attractive he was and had to struggle to remain calm.

Kitty had appointed herself ballot keeper, and she now danced the extraction of the tightly folded pieces of paper from the piggy bank, fluttering each piece expressively through the air before laboriously smoothing it out on the table.

"For God's sake, Kitty, you don't have to make everything such a drama," Leo complained. "Stop doing your bloody ballet and just count the bloody things."

Undeterred, Kitty laid the ballot papers out on the table in a row. Each bore a single letter: B. Greg tried to laugh it off, but I could tell he was really quite upset.

"Why, why?" he muttered, his hand covering his face in despair. Dad patted him on the back in a there-there sort of fashion. I tried to kiss him.

"I don't want your pity," he said, in that brave, jokey tone people use when they're not really joking. He held his hand up to ward me off, his eyes drawn to something on the floor. I followed his gaze to find that salt had been ground further into his humiliating wound. A smaller Bowl A and Bowl B had been laid out for Janet the cat. Bowl B was empty, Bowl A untouched.

"Well, at least we now know that Janet will eat chicken soup," I said brightly, trying to gloss over his public defeat.

Nick was writing furiously in a notebook, his pointy beard bobbing up and down in excitement. "She needs to be treated as one of the family," he was saying. "She needs to eat what you eat with you."

"Eureka!" I said.

As I was serving the next course, which, in an attempt to appease his humiliation, I took pains to point out had been prepared by Greg, I saw Greg stuffing one of my matzo balls into a specimen jar from the surgery. The cat's problems may have been improving, but Greg had been driven to the limits of his endurance. Only science could save him now; he had obviously decided to send a sample to the lab to solve the mystery once and for all.

"Let me help," said Ivan, leaving the table and coming to join me by the oven. He lowered his voice. "I'm so sorry, Chloe, I didn't know we were coming to your house. I didn't want to come out with FF at all, but for some reason she persuaded me."

"She's a witch," I said. "She bends you to her will."

"Yes, that's exactly what it felt like, but it seemed too ridiculous to say. Anyhow, I don't want to embarrass you in your own home, but I would very much like to see you again." His hand started on a journey toward my face. He looked at it in surprise and drew it back like a child caught stealing from his mother's purse. "On our own," he added quietly.

"Where's your wife?"

"She's gone away for a week or two." He shrugged. "We need a little break, some time to think."

Hmm, trial separation, how did this square with the Rule? I'd have to check with Ruthie.

He scribbled something on a piece of paper and gave it to me. "You have to work this out," he said enigmatically.

*Tvoi sup-chudo, kak i ty. Ponedel'nik v shest' chasov, 23 Potter Lein*

"What is it," I asked, "a riddle?"

"Find someone who speaks Russian. They will help you." He smiled, and our eyes held each other's faces as though memorizing their contours. For a moment, he stood just a little too close. He smelled heavenly, of soap and of some other scent, all his own and yet somehow familiar to me. Everyone has his or her own odor with the power to attract or repel, just as families have their own smell. Our *eau familiale* hit you as you walked through the door and was notable by its absence when we'd been away and someone else had been staying in our house. Leo had always had particularly well-developed olfactory powers; he could name the owner of any item merely by sniffing it. Out of the corner of my eye, I saw him doing it now as he picked up a scarf that had fallen on the floor, sniffed it, and silently hung it over the back of Dad's chair.

I sat down at the table next to Ivan. "Mm, this is delicious risotto," I said.

Everyone made appreciative noises and praised Greg on his culinary skills.

"Don't patronize me," he said, still smarting from his earlier defeat.

I could feel the heat from Ivan's body beside me. Our surroundings seemed blurred, the sound of everyone's voices excitedly chatting and laughing little more than a distant rumble. Ivan's hands stood out in sharp relief as they went about the business of eating, and then his lips, teeth, and tongue came into sharp focus as he chewed. I wanted to kiss him and feel his mouth on my face, his hands on my body.

"Chloe, Chloe." A familiar voice was calling me as though from a great distance, and then a face gradually came into focus beside me. Greg was looking at me quizzically. "I have to make a house call. Bloody Mrs. Meagan; she thinks she's having a heart attack. She's been in to the surgery three times this week. I'm sure it's nothing, but her husband is very insistent."

"Fine, OK then, yes indeed." I snapped back to reality from the warmth of my unfaithful imaginings.

"We must go too, Chlo, darling," said FF. She stood, smoothing her hands down her body. Her chemically enhanced blond hair was caught up into an instant face-lift in the form of a tight high ponytail that somehow succeeded in looking more chic than chav. "Come on, Ivan."

Ivan began to remonstrate—"No, I think I will stay—" and then he stood, meekly pulled on his coat, and followed her out, a lamb to the slaughter.

Sammy and the kids had abandoned us for the television upstairs, Bea and Zuzi had giggled their way into the night, and Nick the vet had said his goodbyes, muttering "astonishing, truly astonishing" as he went. Dad was humming, his hands moving in silent conversation with himself as they often did and his feet tapping to the music that played continuously inside his head.

"Tell me about the affair, Dad."

He sighed, poured us each another glass of wine, and turned to face me.

"You remember Jürgen Geber." It was a statement, not a question.

J ürgen Geber had been a part of our mythology for as long as I could remember. The story of how he and Dad met was a family fable that Sammy and I begged Dad to repeat at every opportunity.

In 1943, Dad had joined the army. Only sixteen, he changed the birth date on his passport, forged his father's signature, and—leaving a note explaining his actions—crept from his parents' sleeping house one night to join the Fifth Armored Division for training. A year later, he found himself in Italy, the radio operator of an armored tank. (He said Morse code was a music all of its own, and he picked it up very quickly.) It was July 15, and the sky was blue and cloudless. Dad and his five tank mates were lying on their backs in a wood near Sienna, a welcome lull in their life as soldiers. They were enjoying a few moments of the careless relaxation that young men deserve, smoking and exchanging stories of their lives back home, the girls they had known and loved, and the ones they hoped still to meet. Bonded by their common purpose, they would never have met in civilian life, far less become friends. Jimmy, Bertie's closest tank mate, was a bricklayer from Croydon whose idea of a joke was to raise his leg like a dog and fart as loud as he could. The fact that he could sing like Frank Sinatra and had an irrepressibly cheerful nature had endeared him to Bertie, and the two of them would sing and dance sequences from *Las Vegas Nights* to amuse the others.

The afternoon was made even more magical by the normality lent to the scene by the buzzing and humming of myriad insects. It seemed they too had laid down their arms, for they were not bothering the men but were quietly going about their business of supping nectar from one sparse wildflower to the next. One of the men got up, walked a few yards from the others, unbuttoned his fly, and peed in a great stream that arched over his companions and landed just the other side of them. The others applauded his skill. Bathed by the sun's warmth, lulled by the hypnotic buzzing of insects, and drugged by the smell of the sun-scorched earth, they soon slept, all but Bertie, who stood and stretched, enjoying the freedom of movement after being confined in a tank for so long. Then he wandered off into the woods, the nature of his business requiring privacy for a man of his fastidious disposition. He squatted above the dry earth, feeling the soft warm breeze on his naked haunches. When he'd finished, he walked farther into the woods, relishing this rare privacy after months in the company of rowdy soldiers.

Lost in thought, his head was, as always, full of the music that rushed in to take the place of quietness and solitude. He must have walked for quite some time; the sky was growing dark and he realized he had reached that Hansel and Gretel moment of no return. Tiring, he sat under a tree for a few moments to order the melodies that were taking shape in his head and decide on his next course of action. He must have fallen asleep, as the next thing he felt was the ice of a rifle's nuzzle against the back of his head.

"I remember thinking quite clearly: So this is how it ends for me, before it's barely begun. I felt a sort of distant sorrow, as if I were watching someone else, rather than myself."

Turning his head slowly, he met the eyes of a German soldier around his own age. The terror in his eyes matched Bertie's. Both young men were trembling; the German's finger shook on the trigger. His eyes never leaving Bertie's face, he muttered over and over, like an incantation, *"Der Sohn einer Mutter,"* before finally flinging his gun aside and bursting into tears. "We were little boys, two little boys, frightened, alone, and far from home," Bertie used to tell us. He took his own rifle and ceremoniously placed it next to the German's. He held out his hand and introduced himself as if they were meeting at a cocktail party.

"Private Bertie Zhivago, Fifth Armored Division."

"Jürgen Geber, Second Division, German army." The German shook Bertie's hand politely.

Using Bertie's broken Yiddish and Jürgen's schoolboy English, they took their first steps on a journey of kinship that was to last until Jürgen's untimely death in 1973.

"I couldn't kill you," Geber said, as they sat shoulder to shoulder in the shade of a tree, sharing a cigarette. "All I could think was that, like me, you were a mother's son, *Der Sohn einer Mutter;* it would have been like killing myself. I could see my mother's face when I left for the war. She held me close and I felt how small she was, how fragile, as if I could snap her with a hug. She looked at me intently as though she were taking a photograph of my face with her eyes."

Physically, they were strangely alike, short and well-built with dark, wavy hair and blue eyes. Jürgen had become detached from his regiment as he took cover from enemy fire. For the next two days, the two of them hid together in the forest. They survived on rabbits, which they shot and skinned inexpertly before cooking them over an open fire of their making. Lying back after these charred and somewhat furry feasts, they shared their stories.

"I didn't want to join the army, I was forced to," said Jürgen. "What is this impulse to die for your country, whatever it stands for? Nationalism is a bad thing, it teaches you to hate and then it teaches you that hatred is a good thing. They tell us lies about Jews and compare them to rats and show us pictures of rats being exterminated. You tell me you are a Jew, but I see you are a man like me. We are all people in this world, people with hope and fear, people who want to give love and to receive it. Those who led us into this war are villains, but they do not wear their villainy on their faces, they hide it in their hearts and minds and take it out to use to their advantage when they choose."

The similarity in thought of the two young men made a nonsense of war. Bertie could just as easily have been born Jürgen and Jürgen, Bertie. What throw of the dice determined who they were and where they lived? Those two days in the forest changed their lives forever; it taught them to look for the truth and commonality in their fellowman and to think for themselves. Too frightened to commit each other's addresses to paper, lest they be found and accused of spying or collaboration, Bertie composed a little song for each of them to memorize. They parted company on the evening of their second day together. Bertie heard later that Jürgen had shot himself in the leg in order to get invalided out of the war. After several months in a military hospital, he was sent back home. For his part, Bertie took another day to find his way back to his tank. He had left his mates dozing peaceably; he found them frozen forever in the still of that July afternoon, shot dead as they slept.

How must it feel for a seventeen-year-old to find the dead bodies of his young companions? Bertie felt terrible guilt that he had been spared, coupled with incredulity that the trivial need to perform a bodily function had saved his own life. He sat on a rock and wept. Then, realizing his own possible danger, the instinct for self-preservation took over. He made his way to the tank and radioed for help. He realized that Jürgen's regiment had probably been responsible for the death of his friends and was struck by the bitter irony of fate, which holds each of us in its teasing grasp. Then he collected the few personal effects of each of his comrades, determined to deliver them to their relatives when and if he got home. And as he waited for assistance, sitting behind the tank, out of view of his friends' dead bodies, he sang quietly to himself:

> *Jürgen with an umlaut,*
> *Geber with a G,*
> *Lives on Friedrichstrasse*
> *In Apartment C,*
> *Building number eighty*
> *In Berlin, Germany.*

Safely home at the war's conclusion, Jürgen and Bertie stayed in contact and traced the trajectory of each other's lives with letters and photographs. But they never met again, both fearful of destroying the magical quality of those two days together. Jürgen became a painter and managed to escape from his home in East Berlin to the west of the city just days before the wall went up in 1961. Bertie became a composer. As children, Sammy and I had sung "Jürgen with an umlaut, Geber with a G" the way other children sang "Twinkle, Twinkle, Little Star."

Dad leaned toward me and took my hand. "Now let me tell you the rest of that story," he said. I must have looked surprised because Dad patted my hand soothingly and smiled. He told me how, in the autumn of 1973, Jürgen's widow, Helga, had traveled to London with the sad news of Jürgen's death from cancer and to give Dad one of Jürgen's paintings. It was of a young man in uniform, lying asleep beneath a tree: Bertie as Jürgen had first seen him all those years ago in that Italian forest, astonishing in its detail and verisimilitude. I knew the picture well; it hung on the wall in Dad's study, next to a photograph of Sammy and me wearing the bright shining faces of well-loved children. Dad was drawn to Helga as though to the young man he had once been in that forest far from home, and they quickly became lovers. United by grief, they recaptured their youth and kept Jürgen alive in their urgent lovemaking. Helga was Jewish; Jürgen had joked to Bertie that this had been his way of making amends for the misdeeds of his countrymen. The gesture of defiance, while alienating his relatives, was no hardship, for Helga was a beauty. When Dad met her, she was a tall redhead in her early forties; with her full bosom and generous lips she reminded him of Rita Hayworth. Her English was perfect, with that slight precision and clipping of the vowels that betrayed her native tongue.

"We meet in Paris four times a year," Dad said.

"Still?"

"Yes, still. For the past thirty years. I love her. Loving Jürgen's widow is my way of thanking him for saving my life all those years ago. *Geber* means *to give*, you know. Without Jürgen's giving there'd be no me, no you, no Sammy."

"And Mum?"

Dad got up and walked to the window, looking out into the darkness of the garden. He sighed, his warm breath leaving a mist against the window's cold glass, and ran a hand through his hair. It was still thick and wavy but had been faded white by the passing of the years. This is what aging does; it bleeds the color from you, softening and blurring your edges until you fade away and disappear altogether.

"She found out. I'm afraid I was so caught up in Helga I wasn't very discreet. It caused her terrible pain, and I swore to give Helga up. I tried, but I couldn't. Your mum believed I had, formally forgave me, and took her revenge by having her own affair. Tit-for-tat was always your mother's way. I can't say I blame her."

My own recent turmoil felt trite. Here I was, wanting to shag some bloke I'd met at a party, and here was Dad, bubbling in a cauldron of life, love, honor, and death. His life felt epic, mine mundane.

I was touched by his story and saw my father as children rarely do, as an individual, a man with memories that did not include me, a person in his own right with his own life and secrets. The appreciation of his separateness from me somehow made me feel even closer to him.

"Why don't you and Helga live together now?" I asked.

"We have our own lives in our own countries," said Dad, "but, more than that, we don't want to tarnish our time together with the details of day-to-day life. It suits us this way. The writer Helen Rowland said, 'After a few years of marriage, a man can look right at a woman without seeing her and a woman can see right through a man without looking at him.' I never want that to happen with Helga and me."

We heard the front door opening above and Greg's voice as he returned from his house call.

"I must go," said Dad, kissing me as he always did, once on the lips, once on the nose, and once on the forehead. I quickly parceled leftovers in Tupperware for him to take home. I hated to think of him cooking and eating alone and, now that I knew about him and Helga,

I found myself wishing that they lived together. He took my hand and held it in both of his.

"Just because he wants you doesn't mean you have to give yourself to him," he said.

I flushed, realizing he was talking about Ivan and wondering whether it had been that obvious to everyone.

"That's pretty much what Ruthie said."

"Smart girl, that Ruthie, I've always said so."

# Chapter 7

## Mutton Dressed as Lamb

..................

*1 woman over age forty*
*1 wallet full of cash and/or credit cards*
*1 part Top Shop*
*1 part Mango*
*1 part Zara*
*1 dash each Accessorize and cosmetics*

Mix woman with Top Shop, Mango, and Zara. Allow selection of age-inappropriate apparel. Decorate with costume jewelry from Accessorize and paint with cosmetics. When ready, steal furtive and insecure glances in mirrors, shop windows, and the eyes of those you meet (especially men).

Banging noises woke me early the following morning and, exploring the source, I found Sammy noisily hammering tent pegs into the garden lawn. His hair fell in untidy curls over his face and he looked invigorated by the exertion.

"Too stuffy in the house," he said. "I couldn't sleep with the central heating. OK if Kitty, Leo, and I sleep here for a few days?"

I patted his shoulder, went back inside, and wearily started clearing up the devastation that had been the previous night's meal. Among the crumpled-up ballot papers I found Ivan's riddle. I'd carelessly left it lying on the table; clearly I had a thing or two to learn about duplicity. My resolution to forget all about him, made as I had fallen asleep the night before, was quickly discarded as I racked my brains to think of someone who spoke Russian.

Later, between patients, I almost collided with the Pigeon Lady as I turned out of the front path into the street. "Watch this one, ladies," she told the pigeons that hopped and flapped around her feet, "she's heading for trouble." She held out her hand to me. I took it; it was surprisingly soft, white and delicate. She pulled me toward her and studied my face closely. "Just as I thought," she murmured enigmatically. She turned and, in a flurry of wings and footsteps, she and the birds made their way briskly down the street. I felt unnerved and strangely exposed and stood watching long after she and her entourage had disappeared from sight.

"Of course, the delicatessen!" I remembered the Volga, a Russian shop on nearby Salusbury Road. I cut through the park. The playground was empty save for a mother and her small twin boys, one of whom she was pushing dispiritedly on a swing as she said, "Just one more, Charlie, we really have to go home." Then she called wearily to the other, on the slide, "I *am* watching, Freddie, really I am." A drunk sat alone on a bench, a can of beer in hand; eyes closed, he was swaying to the beat of a tune only he could hear. Most of the trees were bare now and swaying skeletally under the gray sky, the flesh stripped from their bones by the cold. I pulled my coat around me more tightly. As I passed Ruthie's house, her front door opened and a young man in leathers bounded down the front steps. I caught a brief glimpse of her as she closed the door. The man answered a ringing mobile. I heard him say, "Be there in five," and he jumped on a motorbike and sped off down the road. Ruthie sometimes worked from home, but rarely on a Friday. Perhaps she was ill.

I'd never actually been into the Volga before, although I'd peered curiously through its windows a few times. It was only a few doors from our friend Abe Green's Jewish diner, where we went quite often, particularly on the nights when his brother Herbie's band was playing. The Volga was small and dim, with one of those bells that give a merry little tinkle as you open the door. I walked up and down its few aisles, examining the unfamiliar tins and jars with their Cyrillic writing. There were old-fashioned hand-wrapped chocolates with pictures of squirrels, loaves of heavy dark aromatic bread, a freezer full of dumplings that looked like wonton, and neatly stacked bottles of vodka.

*"Chem ia mogu vam pomoch'?"* said an unsmiling man in his fifties from a corner of the shop. He sat on a stool, a strange-looking cardboard tube of a cigarette hanging from his lips in front of shelves untidily stacked with Russian videos and newspapers.

"I'm sorry, I don't speak Russian."

"How I can help you?"

I showed him my piece of paper. He smiled and the sun came out: most of his teeth were gold. He was younger than I'd first thought, nearer to my own age, although he wore the face of a harder life. Taking his cigarette from his lips, he plucked a flake of escaped tobacco from his lips, came closer to me, and nudged me in the ribs. *"Nu-ka, devushka,"* he said. "Well, well."

"What does it say?" I asked, at once nervous that Ivan had written something too intimate for the eyes of a stranger.

*"Your soup is a miracle, and so are you. Monday, 6 o'clock, 23 Potter Lane."* He looked at me intently, his eyes moving from the ring on my left hand to my face. It seemed to me that he grasped the situation in its entirety.

"Life is short," he said softly. I flushed but was saved from the need to reply by the beeping of my mobile phone. A single word glowed at me: WELL? It was Ivan. I thanked the shopkeeper and backed out of the shop. My heart was beating with excitement and, without allowing myself time to think, I texted back: CODE CRACKED. SEE YOU THERE. The die was cast.

Ruthie wasn't answering her house phone or her mobile, so I rang her doorbell on my way home. She didn't answer that either. It was odd and not at all like her; we made a point of being able to contact each other at any time. I felt uneasy, but since I had to hurry back for Gloomy Gina, I resolved to track Ruthie down later.

Gina, it seemed, was feeling better about her impending nuptials. "It's all fine. I mean, I really love him, and it's not as if I haven't slept with enough men. They're all the same anyhow. Well, Jim's not, obviously, he's better than the rest. I mean I love him. And that's all you need, right? Love is all you need."

Clearly, she had stepped inside a Beatles song. But then, that's what happens when you're in love; every song is pregnant with meaning, every cliché startles you with the sharpness of its truth. Greg and I had had two songs: Chaka Khan's "Feel for You" and Stevie Wonder's "I Just Called to Say I Love You." Slushy, I know, but they were two big hits of 1984, the year we met. I wondered what Ivan's and my song might be, "Duplicity"? Then I lost myself in thoughts of what to wear for our meeting on Monday. I looked at Gina, admiring her gypsy skirt, which she wore with a turtleneck sweater, wide leather belt, and cowboy boots. It was a good look; maybe she'd lend me something. I opened my mouth to ask her and only just caught myself in time. I was her shrink, for God's sake, not her bloody girlfriend. I was losing my grip. I've always taken pride in my job and done it well. I even have a waiting list of people keen to come under my care. I was shaken by the recent dilatory nature of my "shrinking." Perhaps I needed to take a few weeks off.

I said as much to Greg later, after we'd tucked Kitty, Leo, and Sammy up in their freezing tent and were enjoying the barely remembered comfort of a living room with the television tuned to a channel of our own choice.

"Nah, you're all right, Chlo. You're better when you're working," he said dismissively.

I searched for the words to tell him of my restlessness and longing for something more without giving my secret away. I also wanted to ask him why he no longer touched me. But before I could speak, he started telling me how Mrs. Meagan had been perfectly healthy when he'd been to see her the night before.

"She's fucking bonkers, if you ask me. I think I'd better refer her to one of your lot. Well, to a proper one—you know, a psychiatrist."

It really annoyed me when he did that, rubbishing psychotherapy by only recognizing psychiatry.

"Psychiatrists are medically trained doctors," he said, as he did all too often, with the exaggerated patience of a man used to explaining things simply to small children. "There is concrete evidence that drugs cure people, but it's far less certain that just sitting and talking to them does."

"And so I killed him, Your Honor," I muttered, preparing my defense at the trial for his murder as I stomped furiously off to bed. It would be Greg's fault if I did have an affair with Ivan; he would have driven me to it. Before I went to sleep, I sent Ruthie a text: WHERE AND HOW ARE YOU? COFFEE IN PARK AT 11? HUSBAND IS KING CUNT OF CUNTSVILLE. I was too furious to observe the need for acronyms.

Kitty and Leo must have come in from the cold sometime in the night; I found them asleep in Kitty's bed in the morning, curled around each other, two orphaned puppies seeking comfort. I was still angry with Greg. *I know what our song is now,* I thought as I emptied the linen basket and put the washing machine on, "After the Love Has Gone." In silent fury, I ate four pieces of toast and Marmite. "Get out of the kitchen!" I shouted out loud, to stop myself from eating any more, and went to the basement to see my two Saturday-morning "earlies."

Piqued by Greg's disparaging dismissal of my chosen profession, I forced myself to concentrate.

Furious Frank was my first patient. He apologized for being late and explained it was because he had to finish writing his letters of complaint to various government bodies in time for the first post. I was struck by how like Greg he was and how odd it was that I'd never noticed before. He'd been keeping an anger diary, and today I found myself nodding in agreement with some of the things that made him really furious: automated choices on telephone answering lines; absurd railway pricing systems where return fares are cheaper than singles; motorists who idle in the middle lane of motorways. I couldn't help feeling he was right: Sometimes white-hot rage is the only response.


Ruthie was queuing up for coffee when I got to the café. She looked tired. She had dark circles under her eyes, her hair was lank, and she was wearing a hideous pair of fluorescent green tracksuit bottoms with a purple sweatshirt. I pointedly pulled a pair of sunglasses out of my bag and put them on. She laughed.

"Croissant, Chlo?" I shook my head as though she'd just offered me hemlock. I had fifty-four hours until I was due to meet Ivan, and after my early morning toast fiasco I'd resolved to fast until then to ensure maximum svelteness.

We made our way to the only free table. Next to us sat a father with the same twin boys I had seen in the park the day before. They were dipping sticky fingers first into a sugar bowl, then into the mug of hot chocolate in front of them, before licking their fingers and wiping them on each other's faces, hair, and clothes. Simultaneously, they banged their spoons loudly on the table. The noise the spoons made clearly did not satisfy their auditory requirements, so they were actually shouting "Bang, bang, bang" at the tops of their voices. "Freddie, Charlie, stop it!" their father said, swatting at them ineffectually, as one might at a troublesome fly, with his copy of the *Financial Times*, in the pages of which he quickly lost himself once again. He caught my eye and shrugged as if to say, Kids, eh? But what a great guy I am, taking them out for my wife. No doubt he was giving her a lie-in, in that self-consciously generous way peculiar to the breadwinning man with the stay-at-home spouse.

This is what happens when you have children: on your arrival home from the hospital with your precious bundle clasped fearfully to your bosom, you find that someone in your absence has erected a giant scoreboard in your house. All the things that you and your partner used to do unthinkingly are carefully entered onto the board: who last made a cup of tea for whom, who put on the duvet cover, who changed the most nappies, who went shopping for food, who emptied the dishwasher. Constant reference is made to the entries in this imaginary ledger ("I did bath time five times last week"). Although women keep score just as assiduously as men, men also demand recognition and praise for everything they do because they do it *for women*. "I'm putting the rubbish out for you"; "Look, I've raked all the leaves in the garden for you." Thus without doubt the man at the next table—"I take the children out every Saturday morning for you"—never mind the fact that his wife is at home with them every single day, that very same tired-looking woman who yesterday had listlessly been pushing one of them on the swing in the playground just as she had done on countless other yesterdays and would do for as many tomorrows.

"Ruthie, you don't look your best. Are you OK?" I asked her.

"Just fed up with work. I seem to spend all my time sorting out everyone's problems. I feel like a mother bird pushing chewed-up food into their greedy little insatiable beaks. People can't do anything for themselves these days. And then, if I'm not doing that, I'm trapped in pointless meetings where time stands still. I might as well be working for Shell or in a biscuit factory or something; I never seem to do any of the fun creative stuff anymore."

"That's what happens when you've been around awhile," I said. "You move into management, which is pretty much the same whatever the job."

"I'm just so tired of it all," said Ruthie, blowing her nose. "Meetings with pompous people who like the sound of their own voices and start off their sentences with *This may sound a bit wacky, but what about if we. . . .* Or phrases like *Let's do some blue sky thinking.* Then some little popsy with a name like Wendee, spelled with an unnecessary number of *E*s, pipes up with some trite comment in her little-girl voice and all the men look at her as if she were Einstein, when really you know they're wondering how they can fuck her without their wives finding out." She pulled her hair back wearily, shaped it into a bun, and stuck a plastic knife through it to keep it in place. "Maybe I should just chuck it all in and go freelance. The trouble is, I don't think I could be bothered to go around interviewing some bloody Z-lister who's famous for having tits that fall out of designer frocks. I'm really not sure I care about magazines at all anymore."

That was the trouble with growing up. You spent all those years scrambling up the ladder, only to find you didn't much like the view when you reached the top. You were left with three choices: stay up there and admire it anyway, slide down the big snake back to the bottom, or find another ladder to climb.

"One last whine and then I promise I'll stop," Ruthie went on. "I'm also suffering badly from HHATT. Everything about Richard is driving me mad: the way he clears his throat pompously before talking, the way he doesn't look at me when I say something to him, the way he never listens to me, and the way he takes out his floss to clean his teeth just as *The News at Ten* comes on." She looked at me brightly. "There, kvetching over."

(*Kvetch* is a particularly useful little Yiddish word meaning to gripe or complain. I'm not entirely sure how anyone manages to get through life without it. Ruthie and I had long ago built a virtual kvetchatorium, giving us carte blanche to vomit out our complaints at any time of the day or night, the beauty of the kvetchatorium being that it was always open.)

On the other side of us a man and a woman our age were holding hands across the table. He was feeding her with little pieces of croissant as they giggled at some shared intimacy.

"Look at those two," I whispered. "Do you think they're married?"

"Oh, yes," Ruthie said, and paused. "Just not to each other." She licked the froth from the rim of her cup, and added, "So, when is *your* secret assignation?"

I kept my eyes down, busying myself by mopping up spilt coffee with a bedraggled-looking tissue selected from the many that festered in my handbag.

"It's written all over you," she said smugly.

"Monday." It was futile to deny it, she knew me too well. "What shall I wear?"

"Your period knickers, so you don't fuck him on the first date."

I must have looked shocked because she added, "Don't look so guilty. You don't have to have a husband that beats you to justify your interest in another man. A total absence of sex is reason enough. Just be careful and discreet."

I was saved from further discussion by Sephy and Kitty, coming through the door in a blast of cold air and eager anticipation. Weeks ago, I had promised to take them shopping.

"Distant elephant," I muttered to Ruthie, as I went to my fate. (Elephants look very small on the distant horizon; it's only when they're close that you realize just how big and overwhelming they are. I'm always saying yes to things that are weeks away, lacking the imagination to believe that the appointed day will ever dawn.)

O migod, it was, like, so fun."

"She's, like, such a bitch, she asked Molly and Anna to her party like right in front of me."

Kitty and Sephy were twittering in the backseat of the car, each sentence ending on a rising cadence. Too much American TV. Was it still acceptable for parents to wash their children's mouths out with soap and water, I wondered, or, if not, perhaps to bang their heads together?

We rode the escalator down into what was, for them, girlie heaven and for me the fiery depths of hell. Top Shop on a Saturday afternoon; what was I thinking? I was in the worst kind of furious ill humor, the type when you have only yourself to blame. I left the girls to it and slumped in the café with yet another coffee and a paper I was meant to be writing on Understanding Adolescents for *Psychotherapy Today*. Every now and then, Sephy and Kitty would come and twirl their girlish bodies in front of me in this outfit or that. Looking past them, I spotted the same skirt Gina had been wearing. If she could do it, so could I. She was only a few years younger than I—well, fifteen actually. Defiantly, I gathered the ingredients of Gina's outfit from various corners of the shop and went to try them on. A bored, gum-chewing girl stationed by the changing rooms looked me up and down. For a moment I thought she was going to call security and have me thrown off the premises for daring to try on clothes that were age-inappropriate.

She wore the lowest of hipster jeans and turned to reveal a fatly bulging bottom. Since when had builder's crack become so ubiquitously à la mode? I wanted to grab her by the belt hooks, pull her trousers up, and shout in her ear, *I can see your bum!* I studied myself in the mirror. I looked rather fabulously boho, without seeming too much like the sort of woman who keeps an abundance of cats and has old newspapers piled high in the attic.

"I fort she'd look a bit mutton in that lot, but it suits her, innit?" I heard the keeper of the changing room say to her colleague as she disentangled the chewing gum from her tongue piercing.

"I'm standing right here," I said, as I swept haughtily past them.

This Top Shop business was great fun; I lost myself in boots and belts, scarves and makeup. The girl at the till looked like she wanted to see my ID for proof that I was under twenty-one, but instead she smiled, put my purchases in a bag, and said, "Your daughter will love these." Sephy and Kitty were waiting impatiently by the door, their own retail appetites long sated. I'd hidden my Top Shop swag in another bag, away from Kitty's beady eye.

"Come on, Mum, we've been waiting for ages and we're really hungry."

"When I was a child, Kitty, parents did what they wanted and *children* had to fit in."

Kitty rolled her eyes.

"Don't do that," I said. "I used to spend ages sitting in cars while my mother finished her boring conversations with boring people on boring pavements, or else I'd be dragged out to tea with some of her boring friends (who had nothing for Sammy and me to play with while the grown-ups talked and talked). You and Leo never do anything you don't want to do. In fact, I spend most of my time doing the things *you* want."

"Like what?"

"Watching endless episodes of that crap reality TV show where couples scream and shout at each other."

"You mean *Bit of a Barney*? Come on, Mum, you love that show; you always want to see if they're going to hit each other. That doesn't count, what else?" said Kitty.

"Watching you and Leo play computer games that all seem to be about how many people's heads you can blast off with a range of increasingly lethal weapons in the shortest time possible. It's not fair. It's never been my turn to do what *I* want to do."

"Yeah, well, I was actually the one who suggested we go to Top Shop in the first place," said Kitty. This was, of course, the fatal flaw in my argument. We were doing what *she'd* planned.

"Time to go," I said, sweeping them out the door.

"Hold it right there," she said, "what's in the bag?"

Damn.

"Nothing much, a few bits and pieces. Hurry up, let's go." Luckily, at that moment, her attention was deflected by a young boy walking past.

"*Très* buffting," Kitty said, giving Seph a nudge.

I must have looked nonplussed.

"Buff—you know, fit," she explained.

"Ah, you mean what we in ancient times might have called *handsome*?" It was becoming clear to me that, despite my new clothes, I was an old, old woman.

# Chapter 8

## RUTHIE ZIMMER'S RECIPE FOR ADULTERY

1. Never have an affair with anyone who has less to lose by its disclosure than you do.
2. Never confess: If you can't do the time, don't do the crime.
3. Tell nobody: Your friend has a friend; don't tell him.
4. Never pay by credit card.
5. Never fall in love with your lover if you don't intend to leave your husband for him.
6. Deny and lie.
7. Make sure you're strong enough to bear the guilt of deception.
8. Do not leave any visible marks.
9. Only swallow the first time and then you never have to again, but they always think you might. (NB: refers to all relationships with men, not only adulterous ones.)
10. Never agree to a DNA test.

I woke up on Monday morning feeling a warm tingle of expectation, quickly followed by a warm trickle of blood. My period had started. Typical. Now I would have to wear period knickers after all, not the whisper of erotic lace I had planned in defiance of Ruthie's advice. Women's lives are measured by the state of their knickers. Periods, absence of periods, thrush, miscarriages: it's all there in our underwear waiting to trip us up. The power of the knicker was such that I even had a lucky pair, red satin bikinis with ribbons on the side. I felt that familiar dull ache in my lower abdomen and looked down to see the unwelcome curve of the bloated menstrual stomach. "Thanks, mate," I said, to the God I only believe in when things go wrong.

Kitty jumped guiltily away from her chest of drawers when I went into her room. "What are you hiding?" I asked.

"Nothing," she lied. She has yet to acquire the moody secretiveness that is nature's birthday present to every thirteen-year-old. At twelve, Kitty still wears her lies on her face as openly as someone on a hilltop communicating in semaphore.

I gave her my stern don't-hide-things-from-me look.

"I bought a bra." She broke down and confessed at once. Really, she'd be useless under torture.

It was small and pink with tiny red roses stitched around the cups. I looked at her narrow child's body with its flat chest and up at her little face; tears welled in her eyes as I took her in my arms.

"Don't be in such a rush, baby," I said.

"Everyone else has got one. I hate not having bosoms."

"I know, darling. I was the same. My first bra was a Lucky Check. We all had them; they were gingham and came in very small sizes. Mine was purple and white, a 28AA with a little triangular gap in the middle that you could slip a thumb in to pull it down."

We used to pull our bras down ostentatiously all the time, as much to advertise their presence as to stop them from slipping up to our necks, unfettered as they were by the presence of any actual breasts.

The seven stages of woman: bras, periods, exfoliation, sex, marriage, children, and the menopause. Followed by an eighth stage of course, that old showstopper, death.

I kissed Kitty, told her she could keep her bra, and took her to school. As usual, the other mothers by the school gate ignored me. I'm beginning to think there is some magical power that renders me quite literally invisible as soon as I set foot in the school grounds. Either that or I become the plump, plain girl in the playground whom no one wants to play with. I see all the other mothers laughing and chatting, cloistered in groups that allow no chink for my entry, calling to each other, "See you for coffee in our usual" or "Don't forget, Molly's coming to yours tonight." It's a club I am not a member of, but I haven't yet worked out why.

"You know how you like some people and you don't like others?" Ruthie said once when we were discussing the whole issue of other children's parents and why we felt so out of place with them. I nodded.

"Well, they hate us. Why they should and why they do, I don't know. They just do."

"But aren't we nice?"

"We're all right, but we're different. We have other stuff to worry about than whether little Jimmy's costume is ready or whether or not to make little Sophie wear an undershirt, since she seems to have a bit of a cough. We just do the parenting thing differently."

"You mean our benign neglect as opposed to their precious parenting?"

"Yes, I think it threatens them. Parenting is a competition. For them to be doing it all right, we have to be doing it all wrong."

I still wanted them to like me and kept looking for ways to ingratiate myself in an anxious, people-pleasing way. Perversely, to amuse myself, I also liked to count how many mothers could blank me at one go. This morning I had become so invisible that Molly's mother actually bumped into me in her efforts to walk through me. Anna's mother had involuntarily given me the beginnings of a smile, but it had barely lifted the corners of her mouth when she remembered herself and halted it before it could embark on the long cold journey toward her eyes.

On my way back home I saw Sammy chatting with the Pigeon Lady. They were sitting together on the stairs outside her basement flat as though they'd known each other for ages. Sammy has a talent for making friends, often with the most unlikely people. The railings were decorated with brightly colored rags and she sat as she always did, her legs apart like a statement to reveal the astonishing white-ness of her pants. Perhaps her madness had spared her from the stains of normal womanly life? The image of her remained in my mind like an accusation.

That Russkie Ivan's not really my type," FF said, when she phoned later. "He's more the sort of dago type you used to go for." Political correctness and FF were Johnny Foreigner to each other.

"What were you doing with him then, and what about Jeremy, Jeremy, Jeremy?"

"Jeremy's been out of town for a couple of days. A girl's got to eat."

"So you shagged him?" I asked, with affected casualness.

"Ivan? Nah, he's married, remember?" FF did not sleep with married men. It was her one rule, illogical in the light of her general bad behav-ior but one that I was grateful for under the circumstances. For, witch that she is, Ivan would have had no choice but to sleep with her if that is what she had decided.

"I'm seeing Jeremy tonight," she said. "We're going to a film pre-mière. By the way, Jessie's coming to stay with you for a few days, so can you ask Bea to pick her up with Kitty from school? I might stop by, later in the week. Got to run."

"I'll be holding my breath," I said, as I put the phone down.

I had one last thing to do before I went to meet Ivan, and that was to resolve which lie to tell. I didn't want to implicate any of my friends, so where could I say I was going at six o'clock on a Monday evening? I was in the bathroom putting the finishing touches to my makeup when Greg came in. I felt slim and sexy, if a little dizzy and faint from hunger.

"You look nice, Chloe," he said.

I threw myself onto the floor in an exaggerated faint.

"Ha ha, very funny," said Greg. "You see, I do look at you."

He lifted the toilet seat. I'd become so fed up with his and Leo's careless aim that I'd had a bull's-eye painted at the back of the bowl. Give a boy a target and he will have to aim for it; *pee-pee partout* had happily become a thing of the past in our house.

Leo came in to squeeze a pimple. "You look cool, Mum," the iPodian screamed in my ear.

"Very sexy skirt," said Zuzi, nodding approvingly as she checked her face in the bathroom mirror on her way out to work. Bea stood in the doorway and scowled at her jealously.

"Where did you get those clothes?" Kitty asked. "You got them at Top Shop, didn't you; that's what was in the bag. Honestly, you're not a teenager, you know. Dad, you can't let her go out like that."

"She looks very nice," said Greg.

"Where are you going, Mum?" asked Kitty suspiciously, her eyes locking with mine in the mirror from where she sat on the lid of the toilet.

"Anyone else want to come in here and join us?" I hedged.

Janet jumped up onto Kitty's lap and Sammy came in to sit on the edge of the tub, where he began eating a banana. The bathroom was filling up.

"I'm going to have a drink with the editor of *Psychotherapy Today* about an article I'm writing for them. I should be back by nine." There, it just popped out, ready-made, like a foil-wrapped lie from a box labeled LIES FOR EVERY OCCASION. It seemed I was naturally duplicitous after all.

I quickly did my Latin and English homework (it wasn't actually mine, but it might just as well have been), checked that Bea wouldn't forget to feed the children, and left. *Anyhow,* I reasoned as I walked to the tube, *I'm only having a drink with him. Just because a woman has a drink with a man doesn't mean she's having an affair.*

Raindrop was in his usual place outside the station, hawking *The Big Issue.* His unique selling point was that he sang while he sold, his tuneless voice belting out "Raindrops Keep Falling on My Head" whatever the weather. This was the extent of his repertoire. He winked recognition at me with his mournful brown eyes as I paid my guilt tax. "It won't be long till happiness steps up to greet me." Today he seemed to be singing just for me.

Potter Lane was a dark and narrow alleyway off Beak Street, the sort of place, you couldn't help feeling, that Jack the Ripper would have been proud to call home. I pushed open the heavy oak door of Number 23 and found myself in one of the many private drinking clubs that proliferate around Soho. This one had an air of faded elegance about it: sloping floors, shabby armchairs, and shelves lined with books. There were framed cartoons everywhere, hung haphazardly from floor to ceiling. Thinking I had arrived before him, I was just about to run to the Ladies for a last check when Ivan's head appeared round the side of a winged armchair in front of a roaring fire. He got up and came to greet me, taking my hand and pressing it to his lips with old world charm while looking me intently in the eyes.

"What a nice room. What is this place? I never knew it was here. Why are there all these cartoons? Can anyone come or do you have to be a member?" I was babbling. Ivan took a finger and placed it to my lips and drew me down onto a sofa. God, this man was sexy. I took a deep breath to compose myself.

"I'm nervous," I said simply.

"I know," he said. "Me too."

He was wearing a beautifully cut dark suit with a white T-shirt in place of a shirt and tie. His face was closely shaven, and for the first time I noticed a small scar that interrupted the passage of his left eyebrow. He pushed his dark hair back repeatedly with his right hand as he spoke. His hair was delicately frosted at the temples, time's way of gently tapping him on the shoulder. Leaning forward, he took a small package from the briefcase next to him and handed it to me. It was a Russian-English dictionary.

"To help you with future riddles," he said. We settled into the business of exchanging life stories, and I found myself indulging in that cute flirty stuff where you offer up anecdotes that illustrate how interesting and adorable you are, rather like a chef whetting a customer's appetite with an array of tantalizing amuse bouches.

"Then, when I was five," I heard myself saying, "I decided that I was the secret love child of royalty, abandoned on my parents' doorstep for them to raise. I used to lie awake at night waiting for my real parents to come and claim me."

Ivan was a cartoonist, which explained why we were sitting, as I now learned, on the overstuffed sofa of the London Cartoonists' Club. He had met his wife, Becky, when he was a postgraduate student in what used to be Leningrad and is now, once again, St. Petersburg. A student of Russian, she had come to study at the university for a year. Ivan used to contribute cartoons to the Soviet satirical magazine *Krokodil*, but he fell afoul of the system with a cartoon depicting Brezhnev as a dog on the end of a leash being pulled along by Margaret Thatcher. "I must have been mad to draw it, but I was becoming disillusioned with my country and no longer believed the lies they told us."

To avoid the inevitable reprisals, he quickly married Becky and made his escape.

"When I was growing up, I wasn't one of those Russians who dreamed of coming to the West," he explained. "I used to feel terrible pity for anyone who wasn't a Soviet citizen. I really believed that our country was the finest in the world. Now, of course, I understand why they made it so difficult for us to travel abroad: We would have seen immediately how hard our lives were by comparison and what lies we were being told." These days he drew cartoons for *The Times* and had met FF when she asked him to illustrate her book on celibacy.

He took my hand in his, his skin warm and exciting against my own.

"Chloe, I don't want to make your life difficult. Your children are still young, mine have left home." The terrain was growing more dangerous with each passing moment, and I almost expected a neon sign to flash DANGER! behind his head. I nodded and looked nervously at my watch. It was eight-thirty. I'd have to hurry to meet my nine o'clock curfew.

"Let's have dinner later this week?" Ivan suggested, helping me into my coat. I went to kiss him on the cheek and found instead his lips on mine. I lost myself in his mouth, and my whole body felt heated by his in the way a fire warms you when you've come in from the cold. It had been years since I'd felt like this, so eager for surrender and for physical intimacy, so aware how perfectly every cliché about attraction described my emotions. As we parted, I saw my desire reflected in his eyes. He pressed a piece of paper into my hand, with the squiggles that, while not yet understood, were becoming familiar,

*Ty mne ochen' i ochen' nravish'sia. Prikhodi ko mne na uzhin, v piatnitsu v vosem' chasov, 125 Sankt Peterburg Pleiz.*

I couldn't wait to get on the tube and use my new dictionary to decipher them, although it quickly proved hopeless. I'd have to go back to Volodya, my man in the Volga. I was no longer merely poised on the edge of a precipice; my toes were now dangling dangerously over it.

"And if this ain't love . . . why, why does it feel so good?" I hummed, as I made my way onto the platform. Then, in the way moods so often do, mine plummeted from elation to a feeling of flatness. In the carriage I saw a couple arguing in what sounded like Portuguese. Although I couldn't understand them, their bodies told the story well enough. She was shrunken into the corner of her seat away from him, while he leaned into her, pleading and asking for forgiveness. She stared through the window into the blackness outside, her eyes cold and unyielding. Her physical removal from him echoed the distance between them, which seemed to increase with the steady movement of the train. His voice grew louder as his pleas went unheeded, and at the next station he got out. Her eyes followed him, her neck craning forward for a final glimpse as we pulled away, and then she turned once more to the cold glass, where I could see the reflection of tears as they traveled down her cheeks. It starts with a kiss and ends with this.

I thought of how Greg and I first met. It was a rainy November night in 1984. I had recently been chucked by my university boyfriend, Geoff, after three years together, and was still at that stage of wanting to look at old photographs of the two of us as I held a damp tissue to my eyes and wallowed in self-pity and the intermittent alcoholism that so often attends lost love. In truth, I was suffering more from injured pride than a wounded heart; I had long grown bored, but the bastard had got in first and ended the relationship. My friends were tiring of my Ancient Mariner tale of woe, and FF, who was occasionally sleeping with a jazz saxophonist, had bossed me into going with her to Ronnie Scott's. I hated jazz, especially the free-form stuff that was being played that night, which sounded like the buzzing of a roomful of furious flies. I was making my way out of the hot, smoky room when I noticed Greg standing by the bar with a pint of beer, hair long and shaggy, jeans black and tight. He had long legs, a dimple in the middle of his left cheek, and a small muscular bottom. We'd started talking in that noisy, above-the-sound-of-the-music sort of way.

"I always thought I was the abandoned love child of royalty," I was shouting, when a passing waitress shushed us.

"Let's get out of here," said Greg, grabbing my hand and leading me into the cold street. We discovered that we both loved walking in the rain and we'd got soaked, pausing only to kiss in doorways until the need for privacy drove us back to his flat, where we made love all through the night.

"I've never felt such passion," he had said, lying beside me during a brief intermission. "I always hoped that one day I might."

He'd felt so right. I'd rested my head on his chest as if I had finally arrived home. We stayed in bed for a week, the curtains drawn, only escaping to the kitchen to hunt and gather the food that one or the other of us would bring back to bed on a tray.

Eventually, regretfully, we'd had to get up and take up the reins of our lives. I was doing my postgraduate training at the time and undergoing therapy with a Mr. Jolly, by name but not by nature. I'd first encountered him in early adolescence, when I was packed off to see him by my parents. It was the year that Grandma Bella died, and I had been having anxiety attacks and weeping hysterically every time my father left the house. On my first visit, Mr. Jolly sat me on a small chair in front of a small Formica table and laid out page after page of inkblots; I weighed my responses—"butterfly"; "monster with horns"; "two people kissing"—calculating how disturbed I wanted him to think I was. Later, I drew a picture of a rocket going to the moon. "Ah." He nodded wisely. "Daddy rocket going to Mummy moon to make babies." I remember thinking, but not saying, *No, you idiot, it's a rocket going to the moon. If Mum and Dad want to fuck, they can do it at home.* After this unpromising beginning to our relationship, it was something of an irony to find, all those years later, that he had been assigned to me when I began training as a psychotherapist.

"Just because something is familiar, it does not necessarily make it a good thing," he had said, when Greg and I were in the first flush, his voice rolling around his vowels as though he were savoring a boiled sweet. He peered irritatingly at me over small horn-rimmed spectacles, his highly polished shoes neatly side by side as if their spaces had been meticulously measured and marked out. *Mummy shoe and Daddy shoe lying next to each other to make babies,* I thought viciously. I decided I hated him. *He* was familiar and definitely not a good thing. So I sacked him and took up with Mrs. Kleinman, who suited me far better. Greg and I were married three years later.

Coming out of the station, I bumped into Lou. She was holding two bottles of wine, which she quickly hid in a bag when she caught sight of me. We'd spoken on the phone after her breakup with James, but this was the first time I'd actually seen her. In accordance with the rules governing the behavior of women who have just come out of a relationship, she had cut and radically restyled her hair.

"You think you've got it all and then you find you've got nothing," she said, twisting a ring round and round her little finger. "I feel like I've lost everything."

I don't know about everything, but she'd certainly lost weight, that was for sure. She looked fantastic—well, her body did; her face didn't look so good. Forget Atkins; the Separation Diet should be marketed as the world's most successful. For this reason alone, I felt tempted to rush home and tell Greg he was history.

"The worst of it is that it's such a bloody cliché. Maree even looks like me—or like I looked twenty years ago. I didn't know he'd met someone else. I thought we were just going to give each other some space," Lou continued. I hugged her, not knowing what to say.

"You *will* feel better, Lou," I said. "You just need time. Who knows, this may be nothing more than a blip."

"He's moved in with her and bought a motorbike. Arsehole. We had a life together, Chloe. It may not have been perfect, but it was ours."

"How are the kids?"

"Filled with fury." She shrugged. "Why did he have to ruin everything? Why couldn't he just have had his bit on the side and kept quiet about it?"

I left her outside the house that had once been her home and had now become her prison, chaining her to the past, each book, each picture, each coffee mug a reminder of the life she and James had shared, each of their four children a living embodiment of what their love had created.

T he thing is," Ruthie said sagely, when I met her for a quick lunch the following day, "people always feel an absurd need to confess, as if offloading their guilt and making it someone else's misery somehow makes everything all right. If you want to be unfaithful, shut up and live with the consequences. Never confess: If you can't do the time, don't do the crime."

We'd been discussing Lou and James.

"Is that Rule Number Two?" I asked.

She laughed. "Perhaps I should write a little handbook? Rule Two leads directly on to Rule Three."

"Which is?"

"*Tell nobody*. Actually there's a Jewish proverb that says it better: *Your friend has a friend; don't tell him.*"

"You don't count, do you? Not telling you something would be like not telling myself."

In fact, I hadn't told her much about my drink with Ivan. I was trying to be strong and resist him. It wasn't easy, I couldn't stop thinking about him, and his latest text had read I CAN'T WAIT TO HOLD YOU IN MY ARMS.

Greg had been in good humor when I'd come home the night before.

"I've snookered them," he'd said, waving a letter about parking fines in my face. "The council, they don't know what to do. They know the law's against them."

When we were in bed, I'd started trying to discuss our lack of a sex life and to have a proper conversation rather than the impersonal communication more common between business partners: *Have you spoken to the builder? Can you remember to phone the dentist?* But I quickly realized, by the change in his breathing, that he had fallen asleep. "And I sayeth unto you," he muttered, gave a loud snore, and fell silent.

# Chapter 9

## Volodya's Siberian Pel'meni

. . . . . . . . . . . . . . . . . .

*½ pound beef*
*½ pound pork*
*1 onion, chopped*
*2 cups flour*
*3 eggs*
*1 cup milk or water*
*½ teaspoon salt*
*1 tablespoon vegetable oil*

Grind beef and pork in food mixer. Add chopped onion, and salt and pepper to taste. (To make the mixture more tender and juicy, add a bit of milk.) Mix flour with eggs, milk, ½ teaspoon of salt, and oil until a soft dough forms. Knead on floured surface until dough is elastic.

Take some dough and make a "sausage" 1 inch in diameter. Divide into inch-thick slices. Roll out each slice to a thickness of ⅟₁₆ inch. Take a glass or a cup, about 2 inches in diameter, and cut rounds from the dough. Fill each round with 1 teaspoon of the meat mixture. Fold into half-moons. Pinch edges together and connect the opposite sides. *Pel'meni* can be cooked immediately or frozen for later use.

To cook, bring a large pot of salted water to a boil. Carefully drop *pel'meni* in and boil for 20 minutes, stirring occasionally.

Serve with butter, sour cream, or vinegar.

Volodya, my new friend who ran the Volga, had given up trying to teach me the Russian alphabet and was explaining how to make Siberian *pel'meni* instead. These were the beef-and-pork-filled wonton dumpling look-alikes I had seen in his freezer on my first visit.

"At our home in Tomsk," he said, "all the women get together and make hundreds of *pel'meni* at the end of summer. When I was a child, my mother used to lift me onto a chair, give me a steaming glass of tea and a spoonful of jam, and leave me while they worked. I would sit sipping my tea while I listened to their gossip and songs, faces flushed from their labor as they competed to see who could make the most. Then they would wrap them in paper and store them in the snow; our whole backyard was a freezer in winter. If you were hungry, you could just grab a handful, boil them in water, and eat them with sour cream or vinegar. Delicious. Here, take these home and try."

He wrapped a packet up for me and popped them into a string bag.

"Of course, they're better when you make them yourself."

"It's funny how every culture has a dumpling," I remarked.

"They're comforting and filling, aren't they? Soul food."

"Eating *can* be comforting," I said, remembering how Grandma Bella would pop delicious morsels in my mouth. "My daughter, Kitty, calls it *eating your feelings*."

I'd had a shock when I'd come into his shop earlier to find Volodya drinking tea with Bea and Zuzi, the three of them grouped round a small table at the back, arguing in their accented English.

"I didn't know you knew one another," I'd said, taken aback.

"We are working to improve Czech–Russian relations," Volodya said, smiling. "We do this by shouting at each other about the books we have read."

"This is our Club of the Books," Bea explained.

"Yes," said Volodya. "We are having a quarrel about *Anna Karenina*." He pointed a finger at Zuzi. "She says Anna deserved to die for betraying her husband, but I think people can become helpless in the face of passion, and everyone must take love where they can find it."

"You Russians, always so full of the hot head and the passion this and the passion that," Zuzi protested, her pretty face flushed with anger. "This passion, it hurt the other people."

I found myself joining in. "Anna Karenina's mistake was in not keeping her love for Vronsky a secret. She could have quietly had her affair without hurting anyone."

Volodya looked at me knowingly. "Anyway," he said, "we have finished that book, and now we start to read this one." He picked up the book on the table in front of him.

How appropriate; it was *Doctor Zhivago*.

"Surely you've all read that before?" I asked. When I was eighteen, I'd spent a summer immersed in the Russian classics, burning with a teenage compulsion to find the answers to life's big questions and to find my roots. For obvious reasons, *Doctor Zhivago* was first on my list.

"I haven't," said Volodya, "and they pretend that they haven't just like they pretend they don't understand Russian." He looked at them tauntingly and added, *"Na samom dele vy vse ponimaete."*

Bea and Zuzi scowled at him.

"What was that?" I asked.

"He say, *In fact, you understand everything,*" Zuzi explained, realizing as she said it that she'd rather proved his point. She made a small clicking sound of annoyance.

"Really, none of us have read the *Doctor Zhivago*," said Bea, "so please don't to tell us what happens." She took Zuzi's arm and they left. It was clear that Zuzi was firmly established, not only in my house but in the neighborhood.

"Have you got another note for me to translate?" Volodya asked, after they'd gone. "Don't worry," he added, seeing my worried expression, "I do not gossip."

"I'm sorry to ask you again, Volodya."

"Nonsense, we Russians like nothing better than a conspiracy." He looked at Ivan's note and laughed.

"What does it say?"

"*I like you very, very much. Supper at my house, 8 o'clock, Friday, 125 St. Petersburgh Place.* Watch out, Chloe. Russian men will do anything to get what they want, especially when it comes to love."

"I wonder what he'll cook," I mused. Then it occurred to me that dinner itself was hardly the point. If I went, I would sleep with him.

In a carpe-diem moment I texted Ivan, agreeing to dinner. With only two days to go, I had to get my preparations under way. My first stop was at Absolutely Gorgeous on the High Street for vigorous exfoliation. There were four or five other women sitting in the reception area, all in early middle age. We were fighting the good fight to preserve our waning beauty, but I wondered if that was the only reason we were there. The definition of a good husband used to be one who "left you alone," but what had once been a compliment had today become a complaint. Starved of physical affection, we had to resort to paying for massages and facials just so someone would touch us, knowing all the while what a poor substitute it was, because nothing can replace the intimacy of the touch of a man who truly desires you and whom you in turn desire. When spa treatments were no longer enough, the next step was to take a lover.

My beauty therapist had a strong South African accent and wore a tight white uniform with a badge on her left breast that announced her as JACQUEE. She had an irritating habit of saying, "Is it?" quite indiscriminately in response to everything I said.

"Could you do my eyebrows too?"

"Is it?"

I kept words to a minimum and nodded when she asked if I wanted the special bikini wax, without understanding that this meant a Brazilian. She wiped me down briskly, as a nappy-changing mother would a baby, poured hot wax over my most intimate parts, and tore off almost every last hair *down there*, leaving me with a mere landing strip down the center. "Is it?" I was too taken aback to scream with the pain and submitted silently to her further ministrations, eyebrow plucking, leg waxing, and the like. I felt like a chicken, plucked and ready for the pot. Thank God my skin had a day or two to vent its fiery redness and return to its usual winter yellow.

I was looking forward to a little lie-down to recover from the trauma but found FF and Jessie in the kitchen at home. FF opened the fridge, scoured the contents, and, without removing anything, closed the door and sat down. We all have a compulsive need to check one another's fridges; it's something we've been doing for the past thirty-odd years. In the early days, we would wolf down the contents with the abandon of young girls who were still growing. Now that we no longer wanted to grow, we took a small vicarious pleasure in simply feasting with our eyes.

"You look nice, darling," I said to Jessie, who had a new top and looked less haunted than usual.

"Never mind her, look at me," said FF, pushing Jessie aside to bring herself into my line of vision. "Don't I look fabulous? I've had the fat sucked out of my bum and put into my lips and cheeks."

Her mouth was pouted into an artificial O. It looked like the sort of mouth that would only be happy if it had a large penis positioned between its lips. But, I reasoned, this was probably the look she was after, now that she was so determinedly back in the saddle with Jeremy.

"Mmm, very good," I said dutifully. "But doesn't the fat sucking mean you're off games with Jeremy?"

"No, no," she answered, "they're very clever these days. I've got just two little incisions, one on each buttock, that I can easily cover with crotchless panties."

I was sorry I'd asked.

"I'm off to my room," said Jessie hastily. "I mean, upstairs," she corrected. The spare room might just as well be called hers. In the past week she'd spent most nights in it, and each time she came she carefully unpacked the bag she'd brought with her, so that the cupboards and drawers were now filled with her belongings. A few days before,

I'd found her and Sammy sitting on the bed bent over a color chart; he'd offered to repaint the room for her. They hadn't thought to ask if I minded, and it hadn't occurred to me that they should until sometime later. How could I expect others to observe my boundaries when I was barely aware of them myself?

FF droned on about cellular therapy, some new procedure she was considering where they grow your own cells in a lab and inject them back, returning you to the full glory of your former youth.

"You really must go to Rasa Rastumfari," FF was saying. "In fact, I'll buy you a session with him for your birthday. He's from Afghanistan and has a two-year waiting list."

"Why, will he move my fat around my body?" I feigned interest.

"He's the world's leading expert on colonic irrigation. Just absolutely the best. Once you've been to him, you're clean as a whistle inside and out; it's a crime not to have anal sex."

"Sounds like quite a good reason *not* to go to him," I said. "Anyway," I added, "it actually *was* a crime to have anal sex before 1967."

"You're such a prude," she said. Her eyes took on the dreamy cast of reminiscence. "Last night, Jeremy was just about to penetrate me when—"

I put my fingers in my ears and sang loudly to block out the intimate details. FF swatted me with her copy of *Celebrity Today*, which she had cleverly folded to ensure that I could see her full-page picture.

"You look different, Chloe. What have you done?" She appraised me curiously.

I flushed; even FF had noticed the glow of anticipated adultery that illuminated me. Fortunately, it didn't take long for her to bring the conversation back to herself.

I could hardly sleep that night; I was full of a child's excitement on the night before Christmas mingled with the adult's anxiety before I did wrong. I lay there, my own version of "Aquarius" playing on a loop in my head as Greg slept fitfully beside me.

*This is the dawning of the Day of Adultery,*
*The Day of Adultery.*

Sure enough, a few hours later the day dawned. I locked myself in the bathroom and carefully examined my bikini area. The redness had mostly subsided and I looked more or less normal, if a little bald. It was lucky my husband was so uninterested in my naked body; a more attentive man might have wondered what I was up to. I looked critically at my face and unscrewed a jar of eye cream (ounce for ounce the same price as gold). The top slipped from my fingers and onto the floor. As I scrabbled about for it on my hands and knees, I pulled various items from under a small cupboard: a runaway sock, three Biros, two balls of fluff, a button and . . . a box of GrayAway. The box's retro fifties design showed a red-lipsticked woman looking admiringly at a man with sleek black hair.

*Use GrayAway to restore your natural hair color and become the man you once were. This melanin substitution preparation will give you your youth back in one easy step: no gloves, no dyes, no bother. Stop Old Father Time dead in his tracks and feel young and in control again.*

I'd discovered Greg's secret. It seemed I wasn't the only one having a midlife crisis. Who would have thought that my no-nonsense husband would be unwilling to go gray? Was melanin the source of his potency and desire just as Samson's hair had been the source of *his* legendary strength? Was the loss of melanin the reason he'd lost interest in sex? I carefully put the box back where I had found it.

Later, as Greg had one new bright-red dead-man's shoe out the door on his way to the surgery, I told him I had an evening conference at the Royal College of Psychotherapists, the lie slipping out as smoothly as honey off a spoon. "I might be late," I added for good measure, quite awed by my own wickedness.

Furious Frank brought in a box of his correspondence with the gas board to justify why he'd punched the gasman when he'd visited the day before. It was a complicated but familiar tale of appointments made and missed and bills overpaid and not refunded.

"I have been driven beyond the limits of human endurance. Anyone else would have done the same," he said.

He was facing criminal charges for attempted assault, which only served to make him all the more furious.

Gentleman Joe spent most of his session in tears. "I just want to settle down with a nice woman and have children," he said. "Is that so much to ask?"

I felt so sorry for him I almost considered the ethics of setting him up with a single girlfriend who'd spent the last twenty years searching for and failing to find Mr. Right. I tried to suggest gently that it was better not to have too overt an agenda when it came to relationships; prospective partners could smell the heady fumes of desperation and ran from the odor as if from anthrax.

I was just about to go and get ready when Dad phoned to tell me there was going to be a gala evening at the Royal Albert Hall in his honor.

"That's fantastic, Dad. I'm so proud of you."

"It must be because they think I'm about to pop off," he said brightly.

I searched around fearfully for some wood to touch; I couldn't find any so I touched both hands to my head instead (in our family this had been decreed an appropriate wood substitute for the purposes of seeing off evil spirits and safeguarding good fortune). I hated it when Dad joked about death.

"Helga will be coming over. Maybe you and she can get to know each other a little?"

"I'd really like that, Dad. I can't believe you've kept her a secret for so long."

"What's happening with that Russian fellow?" he countered.

"Nothing," I lied.

"Ha, you can't fool me. According to Shakespeare, I'm a wise father."

"What do you mean?"

"He said, 'It is a wise father that knows his own child.' "

By way of answer, I sang him my version of "Aquarius."


I'd decided on jeans. I didn't want it to look like I was trying too hard. The fact that I had bought the jeans specially and that they had cost a shocking £150 is neither here nor there. What with the beautician's bill and all the new clothes, this adultery business was proving rather pricey. And I hadn't even done the adultery part yet. It would be stupid now not to get my money's worth, but I was still wrestling with my conscience. Should I or shouldn't I? I'd tried playing Ick-Ack-Ock with myself but quickly realized that your right hand does actually know if your left hand is planning to make an entrance as rock, paper, or scissors. (Greg and I usually did the best of five; if the stakes were really high, we'd been known to do the best of twenty-one. We made both major and minor decisions this way and had signed a declaration years ago that the outcome of Ick-Ack-Ock could never, under any circumstances, be contested. It was how we'd come to live in Queen's Park and have two children and even why Greg had once spent a week with only half a mustache.)

Kitty was at a friend's for tea, so I managed to leave the house without her scrutiny, although Sammy, who was sitting on the front wall looking at the night sky, watched me as I got into my car and gave a mock wolf whistle. St. Petersburgh Place is off Moscow Road in Bayswater. I thought it was very clever that Ivan had found a way to pretend he was still in Russia but wasn't sure I would have chosen to live in London Road in Moscow, even supposing one existed. But then, I'd always felt stateless and liked to think home was wherever I chose to hang my hat. After all, as long as you have your loved ones near you, it doesn't much matter where you are. I noticed that the former

Russian Orthodox Church on Moscow Road had been appropriated by the Greeks to become an Orthodox Greek Cathedral. It was Byzantium all over again. It was a wonder the street hadn't been renamed Athens Road.

All too quickly, I found myself at Ivan's dark-green front door. I could barely breathe; my heart was pounding, and it seemed likely I would be sick. Could anything that made one feel this bad possibly be a good thing? I ran back down the few steps to the street, begged a cigarette from a passing smoker, and walked back and forth outside his house while I smoked it. I'd given up when I was pregnant with Kitty, and the unfamiliar rush of nicotine went straight to my head. It felt like meeting an old friend after a long absence, but after a few more puffs I remembered that this friend was false. Grinding the stub into the pavement, I had to go and find a newsagent's to buy the mints that this fall from grace necessitated.

My mobile rang. It was Kitty; she'd just got home.

"I don't feel well, Mummy," she said, illness making an infant of her. "My head aches and I feel sick."

"Does your neck hurt? What about your eyes when you look at the light? Any rashes on your body?" The cloud of meningitis, which claimed lives with the stealth and silence of a professional hit man, hovered menacingly.

"No, that's all fine. But my tummy aches. When are you coming home?"

"Not till later. Where's Daddy? Let me talk to him; he'll look after you."

Greg promised he would be sympathetic and caring; in other words, he would treat Kitty like a daughter and not like a patient.

The green door rose once again between my future and me. I rang the bell. Ivan answered, barefoot and wearing a dressing gown. It was silk paisley, the sort you see in shops like Harrods and expect *gentlemen* to wear while reading the paper over a breakfast served to them by the butler. He had beautiful feet, unlike Greg's idiosyncratic trotters. I pulled my jacket around my body and felt shocked by his presumption. Couldn't he at least have started the evening fully dressed? We both knew the score here, but it might have been a little more polite to pretend that the outcome of our meeting had not been so fully resolved before it even began. I turned and ran. I could hear his voice calling after me.

"Wait, Chloe," and then his footsteps as he ran barefoot to catch up. "Why are you running away?"

"Dressing gown," I said, pointing.

"So? Did I run away when you answered the door to me wearing a towel?" He was hopping up and down to escape the freezing cold of the paving stones.

"That was different. I wasn't expecting you."

"Look, I'm sorry. I fell asleep after my bath. I intended to greet you fully dressed. Now will you come back in, sit down, and have a drink while I go and put my clothes on?"

Meekly, I followed him back into the house. He led me into a high-ceilinged living room where a bottle of vodka was chilling in an ice bucket. A large Persian carpet hung on one wall; other walls were lined with books and Ivan's cartoons. Heavy midnight-blue velvet curtains were drawn against the night, and a fire crackled in the grate. It was a scene set for seduction.

"You've done this before," I accused.

"I'm forty-nine, Chloe. This may shock you, but I'm not a virgin."

"Go on, go and get dressed." I shooed him away as he drew in close to me. When he'd gone, I felt lonely and wished I hadn't. I walked around the room, picking things up and putting them down, a dog turning round and round before it can settle. I hadn't expected to be especially interested in Becky. Her main function as far as I was concerned was simply to exist in order to fulfill the criterion of Rule One. Now I was overwhelmed by the need to know everything about her. Was she thinner than I, prettier, taller or shorter, older or younger? A photograph on the mantelpiece had some of the answers. I studiously avoided looking at the two teenagers in the picture and focused instead on the small woman who stared out at me. She had the appearance of someone whose good looks had been nothing more than the fleeting gift of youth. The passing of the years had faded any former bloom and left an ordinary-looking woman with a faint air of disappointment. Hair brown, eyes hazel, figure unremarkable. Next to her stood a slightly younger Ivan. By contrast, in that irritating way in which men improve with age, he was even more attractive today than he had been then, his lines adding character to his face and giving him that sexy lived-in look I found so irresistible.

I felt his hands on my shoulders as he turned me to face him. His outfit still retained a distinctly temporary air: stone-colored chinos, a T-shirt with Bob Dylan on the front, and no shoes. He handed me a shot glass of icy vodka and raised his own toward me in a toast.

"Let's drink Russian style. The first toast is to *znakomstvo*, to acquaintance, or in our case to getting to know each other better." He held my eyes with his in a way that made me feel he was touching my naked body with his own. "Here, take this." He handed me a small piece of black bread. "First drink the vodka, then sniff the bread hard before you eat it."

It had a pungent aroma that soothed the fire of the vodka and filled my senses with exhilarating warmth. Ivan had it sent over from Moscow. "You can buy it here, but they never get the flavor or the consistency quite right." We settled on a sofa in front of the fire.

"The next toast is *za krasivykh zhenshchin*, to beautiful women, and to one in particular: you."

He pushed my hair away from my face, and the way he looked at me made me blush like a girl on the brink of her first kiss. I could smell something delicious: He had clearly cooked dinner, but it was quite apparent that we would not be eating it. We were destined to feast hungrily on each other instead.

He touched me; his finger softly outlined the curve of my cheek and came to rest on my lips as though gently advising me to remain silent. He followed the contour of my mouth and lifted my chin as he bent to kiss me. I inhaled him, the exciting and unfamiliar smell of a man whose body I did not yet know. My heart pounded with a mixture of guilt, betrayal, and excitement. God, he smelled good: musky and male like forbidden fruit. His lips were soft and he kissed beautifully. (A bad kisser, I have found, nearly always equals a bad fuck. All too often in my misspent youth, I had continued the seemingly unbreakable line from bad kissing to bad fucking out of politeness: If you backed out after the kiss, you might be branded that worst of all things, a prick tease.) My whole body went into our kiss, arching into him, trying to get as close as possible. I wanted to burrow my way into his body. I love a man who knows how to undress a woman. No clumsy elbows in the eyes or hair caught in zips and buttons. Ivan whisked every stitch of clothing off me in moments. For the first time in seventeen years, I found myself completely and alarmingly naked in front of a man who was not my husband. Next, he slowly removed every item of the jewelry I wore as part of my daily armor: rings, bracelets, watch, earrings, even my delicate necklace—all had to come off.

"Jewelry represents the chains of the other men who have known you," he said, "and I want you for my own, unfettered by your past."

"How do you know I didn't buy it for myself?"

"Did you?"

"No."

I was too shy to meet his eyes as I started to undress him, my fingers shaking on his trouser buttons and then desire taking over as I felt his warm skin. He bent his head to my breast and I was lost, free-falling in pure sensation. I wrapped my body around his, the smoothness of my skin rubbing pleasurably against the hairy hardness of his. His mouth worked its way down my body. At last, all the noisy incessant voices inside my head fell silent as I gave myself up to sensation. I existed only in the moment, kissing and being kissed, whispering, touching and exploring the new territory of him with my hands, my skin, and my mouth. He laughed out loud as he came, and I tightened my legs around his waist, wanting to keep him inside me forever, and then we lay in each other's arms in that contented lazy afterglow that I had not experienced for so long.

Y ou're just as I imagined you would be," Ivan said, as he meticulously peeled an apple with a small bone-handled knife and fed me slivers. It reminded me of the one Grandma Bella used to spread *shmaltz* on bread. (He'd forgotten to turn the oven off and dinner had burnt hours before.)

"What do you mean?"

"Soft, silky, and sexy. I want to make love to you all night."

We must have dozed off, but no unruly sun came through the curtains to call on us; instead the deafening siren and blue lights of a police car startled me. I looked at my watch. It was 2 A.M. Ivan lay sleeping beside me. The fire was almost out, save for a few glowing embers, an echo of the flickering remnants of passion spent.

"The word for *passion* and the word for *suffering* have the same root in Russian," Ivan had told me earlier.

I hoped that the one did not necessarily follow the other, although if I didn't get home soon, some suffering looked likely. I gathered my clothes from where they had fallen, put them on, and made my way silently into the night, leaving a soft kiss on Ivan's sleeping shoulder. I was full of a voluptuous sense of my own being, full to the brim of having touched and been touched. The physical intimacy of my encounter with Ivan had opened something up in me and left me vulnerable. I realized how long I had kept myself separate and locked away, boiling around inside my own head, my body little more than my brain's vessel. I became aware of how hurt I was by Greg's physical neglect of me. *It's no surprise I've ended up in another man's bed,* I thought, justifying my behavior to myself. It was so much easier and less painful to lay the blame at someone else's door. I hurried to my car, got in, and quickly drove home.

I rehearsed excuses for my inexcusable lateness. I had met an old girlfriend, we had gone back to her place; talked for hours, and lost track of the time. Would that do? As I drove past, I could see the Pigeon Lady looking out of her window, a lamp illuminating her white face and long gray hair. She seemed to shake her head, and as I drove on she turned, drew the curtain, and faded from sight. I felt I was her naughty child, late arriving home, and she, my mother, anxiously waiting. My own house was in darkness, sleeping. I felt changed by the experience of infidelity, a stranger, as if I had forfeited my place here in this house kept warm by the lie of a happy family. I found Sammy sitting cross-legged, motionless and meditating on the living room floor, his eyes were closed, his breathing deep and steady. I sat opposite him and watched. He opened his eyes slowly and looked at me without saying anything. After a few moments, he got up quietly, took my hand, and led me off to the kitchen.

"Where have you been, Chlo?"

I started with the whole running-into-an-old-friend thing, but he wasn't buying it. He shook his head. "You see, that's why I've never married. I just don't think human beings can be monogamous. Not in our society anyway, it's the Hundredth Monkey Syndrome."

"What do you mean?"

"Well, you know how individual cells make up one human body?" I nodded. "We are also, each of us, individual cells in the body of humanity. So whatever we think or do individually affects all of us. You know this stuff, Chloe, it's what Jung calls collective consciousness, a oneness we're all part of."

"Yes, but I still don't see what it's got to do with monkeys or with monogamy."

"The Hundredth Monkey Syndrome is a spontaneous leap of collective consciousness that is achieved when a critical mass point is reached."

"Meaning?"

Sammy folded his legs under him and leaned toward me intently, his storyteller face close to mine.

"In the 1950s, there were these monkeys on a small island off the coast of Japan. For years they couldn't eat a certain type of sweet potato without getting sick; they were too sandy. Then one of the monkeys worked out that if you washed the potato before you ate it, it wouldn't make you ill. Before long, all the other monkeys on the island were

washing the potatoes. Soon, other monkeys from other islands around
the world who had no contact with the original potato-washing monkeys started doing the same thing. So the theory was that after the hundredth monkey on the original island began washing potatoes before
eating them, a critical mass was reached and the collective consciousness of monkeys everywhere was affected. In the same way, no one
respects their marriage vows anymore. It seems to me that once the
hundredth couple broke them and slept with people other than their
partners, it became inevitable that everyone else would do the same."

"Blimey, that's quite a theory."

"So you see, it really matters what every individual does because it
can affect the behavior of everyone everywhere. Gandhi said, 'You
must be the change you wish to see in the world.' I don't want to marry
because I'm not sure I would be capable of keeping my marriage vows."

"But surely the point is that if you married and were faithful and
others followed suit, you could reverse the trend. It could be the Hundredth Sammy Syndrome."

"Sari," he corrected me. He shook his head. "The trend away from
it seems too strong at the moment. Look at you, for example."

I blushed, ashamed that my transgression was so evident to
him. "Gandhi also said, 'Live as if you were to die tomorrow,'" I said
defensively.

"But you're looking for something in someone else, Chloe, a sense
of wholeness and completeness that you can only ever hope to find in
yourself."

First Ruthie, then Dad, now Sammy; everyone, it seemed, was a
bloody philosopher-cum-psychotherapist.

"Can't a girl just have a bit of fun?" I whined.

"This affects other people too, Chloe, not just you."

He was right, of course. That was the trouble with growing up, getting married, and having a family. You had a collective responsibility,
and everything you did had an effect on those around you. It didn't
take a hundred monkeys, just you on your own, monkeying around, to
do the damage. The even stranger thing was that knowing this was

true wasn't enough to stop me. I felt I'd been good and responsible for too long and couldn't wait to see Ivan again. I peeled a banana and ate it pointedly. Sammy laughed.

"You know that whatever you do, I'll always love you," he said.

"I know. Me too. Love you, I mean."

Sammy was chipping away at a small piece of wood with a knife. His Spanish tepee was full of the strange creatures he had fashioned from driftwood.

"What if you are happily married?" he said suddenly.

"What do you mean?"

"Well, what if this is what a happy marriage feels like." He held his arms open wide to embrace the kitchen, the house, my life. "You know, here you are seeking something better, discontented with your lot, and in fact you actually have what most people are looking for."

I shrugged. "Happiness is in the eye—and the I—of the beholder. It's such a subjective thing."

"True," he said, looking me up and down. "Tell you what, though: Objectively speaking, I can see it must have been great sex."

"It was. Lip-smackingly good."

He let himself out into the garden and made his way to the tent, his silhouette soon invisible in the darkness. I was tempted to join him, but the November air put me off. Instead, I showered as quietly as I could in the basement bathroom, to wash the wages of sin from my body before going upstairs, where I slipped like a viper into the marital nest. What would be the outcome of my actions? At that moment, I was simply too happy to care.

# Chapter 10

## Bea's Halupki
## Stuffed Cabbage Rolls

*Serves 4-6*

. . . . . . . . . . . . . . . . . . .

1 head cabbage
1¼ pounds minced beef or lamb
Salt and pepper
1 egg
1 teaspoon parsley
1 clove chopped garlic
½ cup chopped onions
½ cup cooked rice
2 cans chopped tomatoes
1 tablespoon sugar
1 tablespoon vinegar
1¾ cups water

Boil whole cabbage 10 to 15 minutes. Drain. Carefully remove the leaves from the head and set aside. Mix the meat, salt and pepper, egg, parsley, garlic, onion, and rice together. Make individual balls out of the meat mixture and fold them up in cabbage leaves like a parcel.

Line the bottom of a roasting pan with some cabbage leaves. Place cabbage rolls on top with the folded edges underneath. Mix together chopped tomatoes, sugar, vinegar, and water. Pour over cabbage rolls, cover, and cook in the oven at 325°F for 1½ hours.

God, but I felt fantastic the following morning. Not even guilt could spoil my delicious sense of inhabiting a body that had recently been put to the good use of loving. These legs, arms, lips, and hands—they'd done the stuff they were meant to do. At last, they seemed to say, you've remembered what we're for. For the first time in ages, I felt as if my body belonged to me. I wished I could do one of Kitty's beautiful princesses-in-love waking-up-and-stretching dances. Instead, I hummed "I Feel Pretty" as I made breakfast, and ignored the looks of astonishment my unusual early morning good cheer provoked.

"You've got a text message, Chloe," said Greg, picking up my mobile.

I only just managed to restrain myself from diving on him in a rugby tackle to get it. Affecting nonchalance instead, I said, "Pass it over, would you?" and slipped it into the safety of a pocket.

"What time did you get home last night?" Greg asked.

Bea, Zuzi, Kitty, Leo, and Greg all looked up at me expectantly. Sammy paused on the threshold on his way in from the garden, and Janet the cat waited, poised, one paw in the air, for my answer.

"One-ish," I lied.

"No, this is not right," said Bea. "I went to the kitchen at half past the one for to get me and my Zuzi a glass of the orange juice. You were not in the home at this time."

She and Zuzi exchanged a complicit glance and a giggle, as if reliving the activities that had given rise to their nocturnal thirst.

"Sorry, Torquemada, must have been sometime soon after," I said, as I went off to the basement, eager to escape the grand inquisitors that had taken up residence in my kitchen.


I'M MISSING YOU. Ivan's text message seemed to caress me. I wondered how people had ever managed to have affairs before the advent of mobile phones and the Internet. Both were so perfectly suited to the needs of clandestine relationships it was hard to imagine they had been invented for any other purpose. Information highway, big business, ha! It probably all went back to some guy who was good at computers playing away from home.

I studied my face in the mirror. My forehead looked like a wedding banner gone awry: JUST FUCKED, it seemed to say. I looked radiant; my eyes were bright, my cheeks rosy, and my mouth full and heavy with satisfaction. I'd come alive. I'd barely eaten for days and those stubborn seven pounds that had refused to leave my sides for years had simply melted away. Forget cellular therapy, all a girl needed was a good seeing to.

The sky had never seemed so blue nor had the birds ever sung so sweetly! Walking through the park after seeing my first patients, I saw Ruthie in the distance, standing under a tree and talking to that same young man in leather I'd seen coming out of her house just the other day. Why wasn't she at work? Something was going on; I'd have to subject her to ruthless cross-examination later. We were all going to a parents quiz night at Kitty and Sephy's school. This was the only event at school that Greg was prepared to attend. It was the perfect way for him to keep his memory on its metaphorical toes—all those trivia questions, all that general knowledge; had he managed to retain it or was incipient Alzheimer's waiting to erase all the answers, one by one, from his deteriorating brain? I'd caught him in the bath that morning, turning on the tap with his curious toes, as he thumbed a waterlogged copy of a book entitled *Do You Know All the Answers?* If he did, I couldn't help thinking, perhaps he wouldn't mind telling me what to do about Ivan and my life in general.

I wondered what it was that felt so unfamiliar in the kitchen that evening as I was getting ready to go out, and then I realized: It was the sight of Bea actually doing something that corresponded to her job description. She was busy making Halupki, a Czech stuffed-cabbage specialty, for the children's supper. Actually, it was more probably for Zuzi's supper, with the children thrown in as a hasty afterthought.

The children didn't much like it when Greg and I went out. Leo wasn't especially interested in interacting with us, but he liked to know that we were in the house and available should the mood take him, and Kitty still wanted to be put to bed. "It's your duty as a parent to look after me," she would say, "so it's your duty to put me to bed." It was hard to fault the logic, but I couldn't help feeling that I was caught in the vicelike grip of an expert manipulator, whose skill had been honed to perfection by many generations. On this occasion, we managed to slip out easily; Kitty was absorbed in choreographing the Dance of the Cabbage for Zuzi, and Leo had locked himself in the bathroom with the telephone. Although he had sworn Kitty to secrecy, she had nonetheless revealed to me that he had decided it was time he found a girlfriend. To this end, he was working his way alphabetically through all the girls in his class and phoning those he had short-listed, to interview them for the job.

Greg and I walked silently to the school. It had rained earlier, and the evening cold had turned the pavement to ice. I had to hold on to his arm to stop myself from slipping. We walked in perfect step, our feet even now synchronized in a way that the rest of our bodies no longer were. In spite of our physical proximity, I felt increasingly absent mentally. This is the real problem with adultery, I realized. It wasn't so much the act of sex with another but what it symbolized: the transference of intimacy with your husband to intimacy with someone else. That was why sex was so important to a relationship; it maintained closeness, a sense of belonging with and to each other. Without it, I'd sought and found it elsewhere.

I beat an all-time record: six mothers blanked me before I'd even made it into the school hall.

"Congratulations," said Ruthie, when I told her. "Hang on a minute," she added accusingly, drawing me into a quiet corner and scrutinizing me. "You've had sex."

I blushed.

"My God, what was it like?"

"Blissful," I said.

"I want full chapter and verse later."

The four of us had a table to ourselves. No one else, it seemed, wanted to be on our team. Quiz night was a serious business, and it looked like a few of the contestants had been in far more assiduous training than Greg. I could hear the people at the next table doing a warm-up; one was asking the others questions about the current government.

"They take this so seriously," I said, indicating the next table with a nod of my head, where the quizee was now actually standing and doing star jumps while shooting out staccato answers, as if this physical preparation would make him more adept at the task in hand. Ruthie whispered, "Some people will do anything to win."

"Too right," said Richard, lining up paper and pencils in front of us in his precise way.

I leaned forward conspiratorially. "Watch out for Cheating Charles; he wanders around the room eavesdropping on everyone else's answers so he can report back to his team."

"I hear he's taken lip-reading lessons since last year," said Greg.

The quiz began, and soon enough Ruthie and I grew bored and started writing each other notes and giggling just as we used to in physics class thirty years before. People at other tables were tutting and exchanging glances, so we tried to apply ourselves properly.

*Globe and Jerusalem are types of what?* Cheating Charles must have noted my smug expression, he watched me so closely. I wrote *artichoke* on a piece of paper and showed it to the others. The next question was a cinch for Richard: *Lending her name to a famous brand, who was the Greek Goddess of Victory?* In his excitement he said *Nike* out loud. I saw that Cheating Charles had an accomplice: a man at the other side of the room who, his eyes on Richard, signaled something to Charles like a bookie at a racetrack. We'd have to be more careful. Greg came into his own with the next two questions: *What license cost 37 pence when it was abolished in 1988?*—he laughed at the ease of it and scribbled *Dog license*—and *What is the meaning of the word Hypocaust?* A woman at the next table glanced at me and Ruthie and, covering her mouth with her hand, whispered loudly, "I know, I know, it's when Hitler killed all those Jews in the war."

Ruthie and I looked at each other in disbelief. "There was a survey done where they asked American schoolchildren if they knew what the Holocaust was, and about forty percent of them said it was a Jewish holiday," Ruthie said, loudly enough to be heard. "At least she knows what the Holocaust was, even if she thinks it's called a Hypocaust." (Greg knew the real answer: *underfloor heating.*)

I knew all the answers to the cookery questions, Ruthie had celebrities covered, and Greg and Richard took care of everything else. We won. Rivers of dislike flowed from all corners of the room, amassing into an ocean of swirling hatred on reaching our table. I got up to get the prize: a bottle of wine. Enemies notwithstanding, I did quite like winning after all.

Phil, the father of Kitty's former friend, Molly, was standing behind the trestle table. He looked me up and down. "He's a lucky man, that husband of yours, he'd better keep his eye on you." I smiled weakly. Clearly I was radiating pheromones that seemed to be affecting those around me. Phil was balding and overweight, with a curiously unlined red face. He wore a navy-blue blazer with gold buttons and a striped tie with insignia that denoted that he was the very important member of some very important club. On weekends, according to Kitty and Sephy, who'd been to Molly's house for a sleepover once, Phil—or Fractions, as he'd come to be known—set Molly and her brother, Fred, extra math homework. When they had completed it, he signed the sheets with the date and the time and marked them in red ink. Too many wrong answers meant no sweets on Sunday, the one day allocated for this special treat. Kitty and Sephy had been made to do the sheets too, since which time they had unsurprisingly refused further invitations. As a result, Molly had ganged up against them with Anna, another friend.

"Fractions can't take his eyes off you," said Ruthie, coming up behind me and nodding in Phil's direction.

"I know. Have I got a sign pinned to my back saying AVAILABLE FOR A BIT ON THE SIDE?"

Ruthie turned me round and nodded. "Yes, you have actually." She drew me into a corner. "So how was Ivan?"

"Delicious."

"I hope you used a condom," Ruthie said.

I didn't answer.

"Chloe, for God's sake, you don't know where he's been, apart from anything else."

"He withdrew," I lied.

"Yes, well, you know what they call people who use the withdrawal method, don't you?"

I stared at her blankly.

"Mummy and Daddy."

"Oh, ha-ha. I'm not worried about that; my menstrual cycle is so up the spout these days, I think I'm having an early menopause."

She looked at me sternly.

"OK, I promise, condoms from now on. I mean, if we do it again."

"You'll do it again, all right," said Ruthie, studying my face.

I examined hers in turn. She wasn't looking well.

"Have you got a cold?" I asked.

"No, some sort of allergy, I think. I'm just going to the loo, won't be a sec."

While she was gone, I sycophantically told Molly's mum I *loved* her outfit. It was that safe but pretty Monsoon look, favored by the slightly older woman. Still fashionable, but *appropriate* for a woman in her forties. Long maroon velvet skirt, matching V-neck jumper revealing the most discreet of cleavages, a coordinating scarf tied loosely around the neck, and maroon boots with a sensible heel. It was all a little too matchy-matchy. Her makeup was carefully applied but understated and her hair neatly cut and blow-dried. I looked down at my too-short denim skirt, cowboy boots, and torn denim jacket. My hand went up to the pencil that was holding my hair up in a messy bun. My lips were painted bright red, my eyes heavily mascara-ed, and I had a hole in my tights. Molly's mum mouthed a barely audible thank-you as she moved away quickly as though fearful of catching something. I watched her greet Anna's mum with an effusive "We're all having coffee at Janice's after school on Tuesday."

I could see Greg and Richard over by the hall stage, talking to Claire and Ian, the only other parents who spoke to us, because they, like us, were Johnny-no-mates. Near them, another group stood talking. One of the women was standing anxiously next to her husband. Every time she opened her mouth to speak, he would silence her either by saying, "You always get it wrong, let me tell it" or simply by holding up a hand to halt her and closing his eyes in irritation. With each rebuff, she seemed to shrink into herself, as though wishing she could become small enough finally to disappear forever to a place where she could be shushed no longer. Observing them, I couldn't help feeling that marriage can subsume individuality, particularly when one partner is more forceful than the other. An affair sets a couple apart and allows the adulterer to reclaim herself. My encounter with Ivan made me feel liberated from Greg, with my own identity intact, but part of me longed for the oneness of a marriage without a secret.

Ruthie, back from the loo, laughed when I recounted my vain attempts at acceptance by Molly's mum. She was evasive when I asked her about leather man, saying he was just a courier delivering something from work and she'd taken to working from home as often as she could. It was all perfectly plausible, but there was something about her manner that continued to trouble me, although I couldn't quite put my finger on it. She seemed unusually animated and chatty and, I noticed, was drinking rather a lot.

"God, it's boring here," she said, a little too loudly. "Let's go and have a drink somewhere else," and she walked over to Richard and Greg. "Come on, husbands, let's get out of here."

Neither Richard nor Greg turned around. The curious alchemy that rendered us invisible to other mothers seemed now to have extended itself to our own husbands.

"You see," said Ruthie, turning back to me, "he never listens to me, ever." I thought she was joking, but her tone struck an odd note. Richard must have heard it too; he turned toward her sharply, his expression a mixture of bemusement and concern.

"Why don't you ever bloody listen to me?" Ruthie asked, her voice rising to a shout. Other parents were looking over at us; like sharks that have smelled blood, they edged closer. Richard put his arm around her.

"I do, darling, you know I do," he said quietly. He looked around nervously and tried to lead her into the corner.

"I don't know what you think you're looking at." Ruthie yelled this at a woman whose head was craned eagerly forward. "Does your husband listen to you? Mine doesn't," she continued, without giving the woman time to answer. "When I come home from work he is buried in a book. He doesn't even lift his head to greet me or ask me how my day's been. If I told him I'd just been diagnosed with a terminal disease, he wouldn't hear." The woman quickly looked away in embarrassment, and the rest of the room went quiet. Richard and I swapped more concerned glances, and I put my arm around Ruthie and led her away. This time she didn't resist, just kept her head on my shoulder and cried quietly. Outside, we stood in the dark, concealed in a side doorway, and listened to voices calling goodbye and car engines starting. The beams of headlights swung past us as cars began slowly to file out, their tires crunching on the driveway's cold gravel.

"I just wish he'd listen and talk to me," Ruthie said quietly.

"Don't cry, darling, I'm here. What is it that has upset you so?" I asked.

I could see Richard and Greg standing in the main entrance, peering out into the darkness.

She shook her head. Her former animation had drained from her face, leaving her exhausted. For the first time, she looked her age; disappointment does that to you.

"I'm so tired, Chlo."

"Let's talk properly in the morning," I said. She nodded.

We stepped out and made our way back to our husbands. Richard came toward us, took Ruthie's arm, and walked her to their car.

"What was all that about?" Greg asked, as we walked home.

"I'm not quite sure. The loneliness of marriage, I think." I pressed myself against him and felt him check his reflex to move away.

"Why don't we ever have sex?" I asked quietly.

"What?" he said, pretending not to have heard me.

"Nothing," I said.

# Chapter 11

## GREG McTERNAN'S SUGAR-FREE APPLE HASH CAKE

. . . . . . . . . . . . . . . . .

2 cups all-purpose flour
1 teaspoon baking powder
1 teaspoon baking soda
1 pinch ground cinnamon
1 pinch ground nutmeg
1 pinch salt
2 eggs
½ ounce Splenda (or other sugar substitute)
12 ounces unsweetened applesauce
1 teaspoon vanilla extract
1 scant tablespoon grated hashish (or more, according to how stoned
    you want to be)
⅓ cup raisins

Preheat oven to 375°F. Spray an 8 × 4–inch loaf pan with cooking spray. Sift together flour, baking powder, baking soda, cinnamon, nutmeg, and salt. Set aside. Beat the eggs until light and incorporate the Splenda (or other sugar substitute). Add applesauce, vanilla, and hashish, followed by the flour mixture, and beat until smooth. Fold in raisins. Pour batter into loaf pan.

    Bake at 375°F for about an hour, or until a toothpick inserted into cake comes out clean.

Next day, over coffee in the park café, Ruthie said, "We'll talk about my behavior last night in a minute. First I want to hear all about Ivan. You *are* going to see him again, aren't you?"

"God, yes, it was too delicious not to do again." I looked at her; she seemed more like herself.

"Be careful," she said. "You're a married woman with a family."

"Do you think anyone is really happily married, Ruthie?"

"Depends on what you mean by *happily*," she said.

"If this is what it's meant to be like, then that's OK, I accept it. But if it is possible to have a really happy marriage—you know, a rapturous walking-barefoot-on-the-sands sort of marriage—then that's the one I want. I can't tolerate the thought that someone is having that sort of marriage and that someone is not me."

Ruthie put her hand on my arm, like a mother comforting an unreasonable child. She looked tired. "I'd be happy if my husband just noticed me now and then." We sat in silence for a few moments.

"It might be better to be married to someone who was away a lot," I said, thinking of Dad and Helga's relationship. "That's the best marriage, one with an absent husband. That way you don't feel sorry for yourself for not having a husband, but you don't actually need to put up with the inconvenience of having one in the house."

"We should have married men in the armed forces," Ruthie agreed. "Do you remember what Ron wrote in the copy of *One Hundred Years of Solitude* he gave me for my eighteenth birthday?"

I nodded. We had spent years trying and failing to make it our mantra. Ron was Ruthie's first proper love, ten years older and wiser than us. He had written, *If one were to look on life as a simple gift, one would perhaps be less exacting.*

"Who is that courier, really?" I asked, returning to the subject of the mystery man in leather. Instinct told me he was the key to everything.

Ruthie looked up at me. "His name is Carlos."

"Where's he from?"

"Clapham."

"No, I mean, where are his deliveries from?" Things crashed loudly into place. "Colombia?" I asked. How could I not have realized this sooner?

"Look, I started doing a bit of coke with some of the girls in the office to alleviate the mind-numbing tedium of the workplace. It's no big deal. Anyhow, the Ancient Egyptians used to take it."

"What are you talking about?"

"Some Russian forensic scientist found traces of cocaine in Egyptian mummies a few years ago, so clearly they weren't averse to a little recreational drug use."

"Aren't Russians clever," I said dreamily.

"Like the Ancient Egyptians, I've developed a bit of a taste for it, that's all."

But it wasn't really all. She seemed grateful for the opportunity finally to confess and told me how the odd line at an office party had become almost a gram a day, starting at eight-thirty in the morning with a get-myself-to-work line, followed by a keep-myself-going-till-coffee-time line, and so on throughout the day until bedtime.

"For God's sake, Ruthie," I said, "you're not meant to have a drug problem in your forties. You're meant to have one in your teens or your early twenties. I mean, I know you were always a late developer, but this is ridiculous. If you're not careful, your nose will fall off."

"I know, I know. But I seem to have created my own *Valley of the Dolls* situation. I take coke to pep myself up and escape from the dreary boredom of my life; then I'm so hyped up I can't sleep, so I have to take Xanax to calm myself down. Anyhow," she went on, "how about all those women in the fifties and sixties who were addicted to Valium? I'm merely continuing the noble tradition of midlife neurosis and associated drug or alcohol addiction."

"Yes," I said, "but the point about them was that they were dying from boredom because they were at home all day and couldn't find fulfillment in work. We're meant to be *having it all*."

"So why does it so often feel like we're not having anything?"

I couldn't answer that, so I held out my hand to confiscate her drugs instead.

"I haven't got any," she said, turning out her pockets.

"I'll be watching you," I warned.

I felt destabilized by Ruthie's revelation, as if the ground were shifting ever farther beneath my feet. Although I was the therapist, Ruthie had always been the one who held me steady and anchored me. I offered to go to Narcotics Anonymous with her.

"These places aren't taboo any longer," I assured her. "Anyone who's anyone is a member of AA or NA these days. In fact, you'd be giving me the perfect excuse to go; I've been feeling rather left out."

"That's the trouble," said Ruthie. "We'd probably bump into everyone we know, which makes a bit of a nonsense of the *anonymous* part."

Still, I knew I'd have to find a way to help her; I loved her too much to let her carry on like this.

As I walked back home, I texted Ivan; CAN WE DO MORE KISSING SOON?

CAN YOU TALK? he answered.

YES.

He rang me straight back. I blushed when I heard his voice, my mind full of images from our time together. His dark head busy between my thighs; the gasps of pleasure that had escaped my lips. What intimate things we had done and how little we still knew each other; pleasure threaded with embarrassment shivered up and down my spine.

"*Chudo,*" he whispered.

"What does that mean?"

"Miracle. It's my name for you."

"Oh, yes, that was in the first riddle. I thought my soup was the *chudo.*"

"You too. Don't you remember? *Tvoi sup-chudo, kak i ty.*"

"You're rather miraculous yourself," I said coyly. I couldn't wait to see him again.

We fell silent. What was supposed to happen next? Our initial curiosity about each other satisfied, should we now quietly return to our respective partners?

"I'm getting hard just talking to you," said Ivan.

Quietly returning to respective partners was clearly not on the agenda. Ivan gave good dirty talk. Some of it was in Russian and therefore incomprehensible—but strangely exciting nonetheless. I love men who talk dirty, nicely dirty, dirty with honorable intentions, not aggressively, unpleasantly dirty. It's a fine line and one that Ivan, with his beautiful feet, trod perfectly.

My one-time boyfriend Gus Fallick had been the all-time master of dirty talk. His silver tongue didn't even need to touch your body: he could bring a girl to orgasm with verbal foreplay alone. It was lucky he was so good with words, as he lived in Glasgow and I was in London, so we hardly ever saw each other. I still look back on our time together as some of the best sex I've ever had. The relationship fizzled out when I went to Paris and out of earshot; phone calls were too expensive in those days. Last I'd heard he was married with kids, but I couldn't help hoping he'd set himself up in business with a sex chat line, his verbal mastery available to all. It would be a shame if all that talent were wasted on one ear alone.

Renewed sexual activity seemed to have reactivated my sexual memory and made me feel generous to lovers everywhere, I thought the next day, as I went down to the basement. The only sour note to an otherwise perfect morning was God's Gift's inky presence in my appointment book. He was my first patient. He leaned back in his chair, arms clasped behind the back of his head, legs stretched out in front of him. His goal, it seemed, was to occupy as much physical space as he could to assert his presence fully. He might just as well have peed in every corner of the room.

"Chloe," he said, his voice self-consciously low and husky, "how long are we going to go on fighting this thing?"

"Well, I think you're beginning to make a little progress. You just need to think more about what people are *actually* saying to you, rather than what you *think* they're saying—"

"No, no, no, Chloe, look at me." He leaned forward and fixed me with his eyes.

"Pardon?" I squirmed like a worm on a pin.

"We can't go on ignoring this heat between us." He tried to reach for my hand. "You're a very special lady." The trite phrase was delivered with what can only have been intended as a heavy-lidded smoldering glance but resembled instead the look of someone suffering from palsy.

"I am your therapist and this is not appropriate behavior," I said sharply.

God's Gift had sprung out of his chair and was now kneeling by mine and trying to kiss me, his wet mouth hoovering its way onto mine. I pulled away from the force of the suction, jumped up, and folded my arms across my chest. How I longed to knee him in the crotch.

"I'm afraid I don't think it's a good idea for you to come and see me any longer."

He nodded knowingly. "Yeah, babe, we need to get outside this room to see more of each other. Know what I'm saying? Come on, you know you want me."

"I really, really don't," I said. But there was no persuading him. This was a man with a device in his brain that translated whatever it was that people said to him into the words he wanted to hear. My only way out was to speak his language.

"We must fight this thing," I agreed. "It's better if we don't see each other anymore. We have to be strong." I promised to find him a new therapist and pushed him out the door.

Upstairs, I found Greg scrabbling through his underwear drawer looking for something, like a dog frantically sending earth in all directions in pursuit of a buried bone.

"Found it," he said triumphantly, holding aloft a small plastic Baggie.

He was wearing red-and-white spotted boxer shorts and a T-shirt. I looked at him appraisingly. He was a handsome man, still slim, with good legs, and that small muscular bum.

"What is it?"

"Hash. I confiscated it from Leo a few days ago. I'm making a hash cake."

"Why?"

"Sammy doesn't like smoking it since he's given up cigarettes, and John's coming over later." John was an old friend of Greg's from medical school. He'd been entirely unsuited to the profession: blood made him faint and when they were asked to dissect frogs or mice to reveal specific arteries and veins, in between passing out, he had simply diced them up as though mincing garlic. He'd left at the end of the second term and pursued a much more appropriate career as a bon vivant, the excesses of which had unfortunately resulted in a variety of health problems.

"You can't make a cake for John, you idiot, he's diabetic. It can't be good for your cholesterol either."

"Which is why I'm making a Low-fat Sugar-free Apple Hash Cake." Greg looked very pleased with himself. "Put that in your chicken soup pipe and smoke it," he added. Clearly, that defeat still stung.

"Hasn't it occurred to you that if everyone's given up smoking and is suffering from a range of diseases, it may be time to stop taking drugs?"

Greg looked incredulous. "You can't let a few minor medical problems stand in the way of a little recreational drug-taking. Anyhow, marijuana is medicinal. I recommend it to some of my patients to help them manage pain."

"So what pain do you, Sammy, and John need to manage?"

"The usual aches and pains of existential angst."

A wave of affection for his absurdity washed over me and I hugged him, savoring his familiar smell and the safe contours of his embrace. For once he didn't pull away; he hugged me back.

"You'll have to give me the recipe," I said.


H OW ABOUT TOMORROW BETWEEN 2 PM AND 4 PM? I was, it seemed, perfectly capable of feeling warm affection for my husband and setting up a rendezvous with my lover. I marveled at my own perfidy. This is how they do it, those men with double lives who maintain two families simultaneously. It was sociopathic compartmentalization: the ability to isolate portions of your life in separate boxes in your mind without letting the contents of any of the boxes spill into one another. I had never really believed it was possible to do this, and now I saw it was easy. I could lock the Greg box and open the Ivan one without breaking stride. CAN'T WAIT TO BE INSIDE YOU, Ivan texted back. It's strange how a man can be inside a woman's body but not inside her head, and how women can't be inside men at all.

Kitty and Leo were staying with friends for the night, and Greg, Sammy, and John had taken up residence around the kitchen table. They were halfway through having their hash cake and eating it and laughing uproariously at something only they could understand. Thighs were being slapped, tears were rolling down cheeks, and every time one of them tried to say anything, one of the others would hold his sides in a pantomime of mirth. I left them to it and was just getting ready to go out the door when FF phoned to tell me about the rapturous sex she and Jeremy had been having. Normally I would cover my ears, but on this occasion I listened, thinking, now that I was back in the saddle myself, I might pick up a few tips. She always appeared to be having better sex than anyone else. It made me feel like a fledgling musician plucking out my first few discordant notes on the violin, while she tucked the instrument confidently under her chin and swept her bow across the strings with the skill of a virtuoso.

"We were fucking, me on top; luckily, I'd tied my hair in a tight high ponytail—"

"Wait a minute, what's this ponytail business?"

"To stop your face from sagging when you lean over him, silly. You have to watch it past forty. When you face downward, your whole face drips off you, like overdone meat coming off a bone."

Ugh! Omigod (sometimes Kitty's lexicon is the only one up to the job)! Had I dripped my face all over Ivan? Thankfully, I seem to remember that I had buried my face in his shoulder out of shyness. What was I to do in the future, wear a swim cap in bed? Superglue my jowls behind my ears? The way ahead was strewn with dangerous obstacles. I ended the conversation as quickly as I could and hurried out to meet Dad.

Once a month, Dad and I would meet, just the two of us. It was a ritual we had started after Mum's death, when Sammy was in self-imposed exile. At first, we used to meet at his club, a disreputable, ramshackle old place in Bloomsbury frequented by actors and musicians. I found returning to the family home after Mum's death difficult. The memories were oppressive; the ghost of our former family life seemed to bounce off the walls and reverberate. Dad must have felt it too, because after a couple of years he sold up and moved into a light and airy flat in Primrose Hill with huge French windows, and we took to meeting there.

When I arrived, he was in his study, papers scattered everywhere, tea and coffee cups on all available surfaces. He was pacing up and down, his face an overgrown garden: hair standing on end and eyebrows trailing down to meet eyelashes halfway. He was seventy-eight, and today he looked his age. I experienced the sharp stab of fear I always felt whenever I contemplated the inevitable day when I would have to face life without him.

I looked at the untidy sheet music, covered with his signature blackbirds, and listened while he played me the new arrangement of one of his famous numbers. He was preparing for the gala performance of his most celebrated musical, based on Mark Twain's *The Prince and the Pauper,* which had been his favorite book as a child; he'd seen the film at the age of ten and been captivated by it. My mother was a fan of Errol Flynn, and Dad had taken her to see the film at the Everyman cinema in Hampstead three months after they first met in the spring of 1958. They met for tea and cakes in what was then Sherry's Patisserie on Heath Street; a few years before Louis the baker took over and renamed it eponymously. They sat in the back of the cinema as courting couples do, kissing and holding hands. As the end credits rolled, Dad got down on one knee in the aisle and asked her to marry him. Their most intimate moment made public, the auditorium had applauded them in rapturous delight. She'd rushed him to a telephone box to phone her family. "I just casually mentioned that we might perhaps get married one day, and the next thing I know, I'm on the phone to her parents and her aunts and uncles," Dad used to tease.

I loved to hear the tale of how my mother and father met; fell in love, and married; like all children, I felt the sole reason for their union was to make possible the miracle of my birth.

"Do you miss Mum?" It was a question I had always been afraid to ask. I felt in some curious way that my mother's death had liberated my father, given him a new lease on life and allowed him to reclaim his identity. I could only guess at the guilt that might accompany such a rebirth.

"I do sometimes. I miss sharing Kitty and Leo with her, and I often find myself talking to her photograph about them."

On the wall behind him was a photograph of my mother dancing Odette in *Swan Lake* the year before they met. She was on pointe and in arabesque, one exquisitely sculpted leg stretched out behind her, her body bent forward at an angle with her arms folded across her breast, her hands and fingers extended. Her face was framed by bird feathers and was full of that private pleasure unique to artists who are in their moment. There is little more alluring than seeing someone do something with excellence, and apart from her obvious beauty it was easy to see why he had fallen in love with her. On the piano below her was a photograph I had taken of Dad at Christmas five years ago. He was smiling as he watched Kitty and Leo open their Christmas presents, his expression one of great tenderness. It revealed all the sweetness of his personality and some of its humor and warmth.

Dad followed my eyes to the pictures that framed the room.

"When you're with someone for a long time, it's hard to stop from feeling like siblings or flat mates, isn't it?" he said.

I thought of Greg and how I knew his every nuance, the way he scratched an eyebrow when he was being serious, the way he nodded when he laughed, and how this familiarity, instead of engendering passion, bred a mixture of exasperation and affection.

"I wonder if that's the fate of every couple," I said.

"I think you have to work hard to avoid it. It's why Helga and I have conducted our relationship as a secret affair for all these years, long after it ceased to be necessary to do so. There's no good reason why we shouldn't live together, but no good reason why we should. We've both done marriage and children, and we don't want to make our relationship something we take for granted. The hellos and goodbyes keep it exciting and fresh; we're always so pleased to see each other."

"That must be nice. Whereas I feel that this is my life, forever and ever, the monotony of monogamy, amen. When you're young, the future belongs to you; as you age, it's only the past that does," I said.

"For God's sake, Chloe, you're still a young woman."

"I can't be an astronaut anymore."

"You've never shown the slightest interest in space travel."

"That's not the point, the point is I couldn't be one now even if I wanted to." I felt tears fill my eyes. "I couldn't be a pop star either," I added unreasonably.

"I know, darling. It's hard to come to terms with one's possibilities being limited. I'm still trying to work out what I'm going to be when I grow up." He drew me to him in a hug and my head took its little-girl place on his shoulder. I was shocked by how frail he felt.

"Have your affair if it will make you happy," he said, with the acuity of a parent who can always tell when a child has done something wrong. "But be careful; it means you have to keep the different areas of your life separate and make sure they don't spill into each other."

"You mean, compartmentalize?" I said. Dad nodded. "That's OK, I'm good at that."

"The thing is," he went on, "the secret compartments become like suburbs, areas outside your main area, which is where your life is with your family. It's easy to spend too much of your life in the lush green suburbs and ignore the main area, your inner city, which quickly becomes derelict because you're not doing the necessary maintenance."

"I see what you mean, but I'm so happy in my metaphorical deck chair in my sunny suburb at the moment. Can't I just enjoy that for a little bit, carpe diem and all that?" Part of me couldn't quite believe that I was discussing my extramarital affair with my father, but he was so nonjudgmental and wise it seemed perfectly natural.

Dad smiled. "Good and decent people sometimes do things themselves that they would censor in others. It's too easy to carry on your life in modest misery in order not to offend anyone, and of course one should do all one can not to hurt others, but as the cliché goes, life is short. Sometimes I catch sight of myself in the mirror and think *Who is that old man?* before I realize that it's me. There's nothing you can do about getting old." He put his arm around me and pulled me to him, stroking the back of my head. "You just have to remember that it's better than the alternative."

"Which is what?"

"Being dead."

Ah, yes. And that, I reasoned, is absolutely the reason why I should enjoy my time with Ivan while I could. *The grave's a fine and private place,/But none, I think, do there embrace.*

# Chapter 12

## Volodya's Mum's Poppy-seed Roll

. . . . . . . . . . . . . . . . .

FOR THE DOUGH

3½ cups flour

1 pinch salt

2 tablespoons superfine granulated sugar

2 teaspoons easy-blend dried yeast

¾ cup milk

Zest of 1 lemon

1 stick butter

1 egg yolk beaten with a little water for a glaze

FOR THE POPPY-SEED FILLING

⅔ cup poppy seeds plus 1 tablespoon

1 tablespoon sugar

2 tablespoons honey

1 teaspoon butter

Zest of 1 orange

Zest of 1 lemon

2 egg whites

For the dough, sift flour, salt, and sugar into a bowl. Mix in the easy-blend dried yeast. Make a well in the center. Meanwhile, heat milk and lemon zest in a pan with the butter until melted. Allow to cool a little, then add to the dry ingredients and mix to a dough. Knead the dough on a lightly floured surface for 10 minutes until smooth and elastic. Place in a clean bowl, cover with a damp tea towel, and leave in a warm place to rise until doubled in size (45 to 50 minutes) while you prepare the filling in the next step.

Grind ⅔ cup poppy seeds in a blender or processor. Melt butter in a pan and add ground poppy seeds, sugar, honey, and orange and lemon zests. Cook for 1 minute over high heat. Allow to cool. When cool, add the egg whites, blending well.

On a lightly floured surface, roll the dough into a long rectangle about 1 inch thick. Spread the filling evenly over the dough, stopping an inch from one long edge, and roll up, making sure that the filling is sealed inside. Place on a nonstick baking sheet, seam side down. Allow to rise for 30 minutes. Brush with the egg glaze and scatter the remaining tablespoon of poppy seeds on top. Bake in a preheated oven at 375°F for 35 to 40 minutes. Cool on wire rack before serving.

I was in the living room, texting Ivan to arrange what time we should meet, when I felt Greg coming up behind me. I reared up, a frightened horse into whose path a snake has strayed.

"Chloe, you're as white as a sheet."

"You gave me a fright," I said weakly.

"You seem a bit jumpy these days. Everything OK?" He gave me an odd look that made my heart beat fast with fear. Did he suspect something?

"Fine, just a bit tired, I think."

"Have you seen my stethoscope?"

"Isn't it in your bag?" He shook his head. "Greg, where have you hidden it?"

He hung his head sheepishly: a small boy caught out doing something he shouldn't.

"For God's sake, Greg, how am *I* supposed to know where you put it?"

He cast his eyes around the living room. Suddenly, they lit up and he strode confidently to the low table on which the television stood, threw himself to the ground, and reached an arm under it. "Got it," he said, with a delight worthy of Little Jack Horner pulling out his plum. Then he gave me a shrewd look. "I know your secret," he said.

My heart jumped and adrenaline coursed through my body. "What secret?"

How could he have found out about Ivan? I could barely breathe and had a clear vision of our lives collapsing: boxes packed; house sold; children in tears, all my own selfish fault.

"Blimey," he said, looking at me curiously. "I didn't know *you* cared about your chicken soup that much."

What was he talking about?

"It's that fat in the jar in the fridge, isn't it? That's your secret ingredient." He was waving a piece of paper in my face jubilantly.

I felt badly shaken and fought to return my breathing to normal and quell the anxious rise and fall of my chest. *Shmaltz!* His lab report had revealed the presence of chicken fat in the *knaydlach.* I counted myself lucky that he couldn't send me to a lab and have me tested for the presence of another man within me.

Later, Ivan and I were lying on the sofa in his living room. He was sleepy but I was wide awake. That's the difference between men and women; after orgasm, men seem to lose power and women to gain it. Becky was still away. I felt awful about sleeping with her husband in their house, but not quite awful enough not to do it. In any event, we had scrupulously avoided their bedroom, availing ourselves instead of the many other places and had even congratulated ourselves on our remarkable sensitivity. I brought up Dad's analysis of relationships: how people get too comfortable with each other, too much like siblings, and are then prevented by incest taboo from having sex. If I'm honest, I was really trying to find out if he and Becky still did it.

"There was a book written in Russia in the late nineteenth century that described a socialist utopia," he said. Just as Dad had a saying for every occasion, so Ivan had a book. It came down to the fact that there had been nothing to do in Soviet Russia except read. And have sex; he'd done quite a lot of that too. It was one of the few things that didn't get you into trouble with the authorities. On balance, I was pleased he had; it made him terribly good at it.

"That kind of book was very popular at that time," he went on. "Anyway, this one, by Chernyshevsky, was called *What Is to Be Done?*"

"I thought Lenin wrote that," I interrupted, keen to show off my erudition. I'd read Lenin's booklet during my brief student Communist phase, when I used to sell copies of *The Socialist Worker* on the streets of Camden Town. This unpaid labor was soon replaced by a weekend job as a waitress in a cavernous bistro, which funded my increasingly serious Miss Selfridge habit. My purchases were the fruits of my labor and therefore, I reasoned, in keeping with Marxist ideology. Not long after, I graduated from university and put a deposit on my first flat, thereby giving up all pretense of communism and wholeheartedly embracing capitalism as a fully paid-up member of the property-owning classes.

"He did, but it was Chernyshevsky's title first; Lenin deliberately used and echoed it later. Anyhow, it described a marriage of equality between a couple who agreed to respect each other's privacy. They only entered each other's rooms by invitation and reserved a third room for their meetings. I always thought there was something in that; it might be a way to preserve the mystery and sexual interest between two people and prevent them from taking each other for granted."

"Mmm, good idea, but you'd have to have a lot of rooms. What happened to them; did it work?"

"Well, it got a bit complicated. She fell in love with the husband's friend and they all lived together in a ménage à trois for a while. Then the husband staged his own death to allow his wife to marry his friend, as she loved him more."

"Very altruistic of him. I'm afraid I can't see Greg doing that for you, but then, you're not his friend." I thought for a moment. "I suppose that's one of the things that makes you and me so exciting, isn't it? The stolen moments and the separation from our everyday lives?"

"Maybe." He paused. We lay in silence for a minute; he ran his hand up and down my arm, making my flesh tingle. "You know, I should never have attended my children's births," he continued. "I found it difficult to think of Becky sexually after that. She became a mother in my eyes and the thought of having sex with her felt inappropriate."

"How can you say that? They were your babies too."

"I know, I'm simply being truthful and telling you how it made me feel. Not only that, it's all the *Where did you put the soap?* and *Why can't you put the cap back on the toothpaste?* stuff that erodes the mystery, isn't it? Do you know the Russian poet Mayakovsky?"

I nodded.

"He put it very well in one of his poems: *Liubovnaia lodka razbilas' o byt*—*Love's boat has crashed on the rocks of trivia.*"

I found it arousing when he spoke in Russian. "What about *our* boat?" I said, reaching between his legs.

"Our boat, my darling, is just setting sail," he said, drawing me to him and kissing me. "I can't get enough of you," he whispered, as he began to make love to me all over again.

I sat in the park café and watched a woman coyly eating some bacon and eggs, one hand placed in front of her mouth as she chewed, as if eating were a shameful habit that should be hidden from public view. Next to her sat a man in his sixties with thinning hair and a ponytail. It took every ounce of my self-control not to scream in his ear that he looked *ridiculous* before sawing his ponytail off with my nail scissors. I was feeling a little irritable. Ivan had had to cancel our next date as Becky had come home early, and my ill humor had spilled over into a stupid argument with Greg. Every couple dances their practiced moves of irritation and frustration in perfect step as they repeat the same argument time and time again. Ours had been of the *You're always grumpy and tired and never want to see anyone* and *You're always right and everyone else is wrong* variety. The end result was that I now hated everyone: Greg for being no fun, Ivan for canceling our date, and Becky for coming home unexpectedly and ruining my life by getting in the way of my having sex with her husband.

Through the window, I could see Sammy and the Pigeon Lady huddled on a bench together. I wondered what they found to talk about. Looking up, Sammy caught sight of me and gestured for me to join them. I wasn't sure I was in the mood, but then something caught my eye. It was Sammy's right hand, moving up and down. I looked more closely and saw he was playing a guitar. As far as I knew, he hadn't picked up a guitar, much less played one, since Mum died, and the sight of him holding one now signified a seismic shift that I found almost unbearably moving. I was drinking the last dregs of my coffee, and putting my coat on to hurry out to them, when my mobile rang. Was it Ivan phoning to tell me that we could meet after all? A flame of hope leaped in me, then quickly flickered and died. It was Gina, in a state of agitation.

"I'm going to tell Jim the wedding's off."

My attention was still focused on Sammy and his guitar. "Are you?" I said absently.

"How can I be with one man for the rest of my life?"

I shifted my attention to what she was saying. "Gina, wait until we meet. You need to think this through. This may be about fear."

"What do you mean?"

"Your fear of commitment and your resistance to allowing yourself to be happy. Let's discuss this properly at our session later today."

"Jim deserves someone better than me," she said.

Finally, she promised to do nothing until we'd met. As I was leaving the café, my phone rang again. It was FF.

"Is Jessie with you?" she asked. "I suddenly realized I haven't seen her for a while, so I thought I'd better just check that she's with you."

"She's fine, but it might be an idea for you to phone and talk to her."

"I will. I've just been so busy, darling, you know how it is. Come with me to Elton's White Tie and Tiara Ball? I've got an extra ticket; Jeremy can't come. It's so weird, I can't bear to be apart from him."

Being away from your daughter, however, causes you no problems, I thought but didn't say. "What is it you like so much about him?" I asked instead.

"He's terribly good at cunnilingus. You and Greg have to come for dinner soon and meet him. Must dash." She hung up.

I shuddered slightly at the image she'd stamped in my head, turned my phone off, and walked over to Sammy.

He was still sitting on the bench with the Pigeon Lady, playing "It Had to Be You" on his guitar. She was swaying and singing along, sweetly and in tune, with a pigeon perched on her shoulder:

*"For nobody else gave me a thrill,*
*With all your faults, I love you still."*

She sounded like a young woman when she sang, and I caught a glimpse of what she must once have been: a teenager, a child, someone's baby. Everyone was once someone's baby, pushed out into the world from a mother's womb. Now strange, solitary, and disconnected, she had become a generic madwoman who roamed the streets of Queen's Park talking to pigeons. What tricks had life played on her to bring her to this point? As I approached, she shooed away the pigeons that were crowding on the bench next to her to make space for me.

Sammy introduced us. "Chloe, this is Madge; Madge, Chloe." I'd seen her coming and going for the past ten years or so but had never gone to the trouble of finding out her name. I felt ashamed.

"Yes, yes," she said. "Chloe and I are old friends, aren't we, dear? But you're always so busy, busy, busy, we never have a moment for a proper conversation."

I looked at her closely for the first time. She had astonishingly clear green almond-shaped eyes in her careworn face. They were full of sadness and longing. She must have been in her late sixties, and something about her bearing suggested that she had once led a better, happier life. At her feet were the many carrier bags that always accompanied her. Some seemed to be full of pieces of cloth, like the ones that hung from the railings outside her flat; others carried crusts of bread for the pigeons.

"Madge used to be a textile designer," said Sammy.

Madge nodded, her hair flapping wildly. "I have children, you know," she said. "A lovely little boy and girl, just like you two."

"You're playing again," I said to Sammy, reaching out and touching the smooth wood of his guitar.

"Yes, it's time. Madge says everyone has a duty to do the thing they're meant to do." Madge patted Sammy's shoulder. He looked down at his fingers as though surprised to see them moving up and down the fret with such fluency after so long. "It feels like meeting an old friend after a long absence." He had tears in his eyes.

"Sammy's going to help me find my babies," Madge said.

I looked at him with mild alarm. My instinct was to recoil from people who needed my help unless they were paying for my services, in which case I could be in control and conduct the relationship on clearly defined professional terms. Sammy, on the other hand, was always open to waifs and strays. He couldn't walk past a beggar without giving him the price of a cup of tea and then accompanying him to drink it, throwing in a full English breakfast and making plans to meet the following day for good measure.

"Madge hasn't seen her children for thirty-five years," he explained.

Madge leaned back on the bench, closed her eyes in order to replay the past more clearly, and began to tell her story.

She told us how she had met her husband, Reg, when she was twenty; after a two-year courtship they had married in 1958. She was a textile designer working in a factory, he was the foreman. She was more educated than he, a grammar school girl who had gone on to art college to study design. "He was so handsome, all the girls wanted him. But he chose me," she said proudly. She had given up her job when she became pregnant with their first child, a girl, born in 1962, followed by a boy in 1964, the same years that Sammy and I were born. A parallel family, in the same city, living a parallel life. "We were happy at first," she explained. Reg was content in his role of breadwinner and father. They lived in a small terraced house in Kilburn, and she was happy enough to cook, clean, and raise the children. At first. When the children were both at school—Rosie was seven, Jimmy five—Madge became restless. "If Reg had just let me go back to work, it could all have been different," she said. But he was a working-class man who felt that a wife who worked was an indictment, a way of announcing to the world that he was not a proper man and couldn't provide for his family. Madge had too much time and too much energy. "I was lonely. Reg would come home from work and fall asleep on the sofa in front of the television. I was alone all day and then, after the children had gone to bed, all evening too. I needed someone to talk to." Armstrong (Armie), her lover, was that someone. Not only did he listen, he talked back too. They had met when Madge had slipped and fallen on an icy pavement in Kentish Town in the winter of 1969. He had helped her up, attended to her grazed knees, and taken her off for a cup of sweet tea to help with the shock. He was five years younger than she and a trained teacher, although he could only find work on the buses. Armie was from Jamaica, fresh off the boat and facing the disappointment of a country that had not lived up to its promise.

They fell in love and Madge's days became full once again, this time with secret meetings and stolen kisses. After a while, she told Reg that she was leaving him for another man and taking the children with her. When Reg found out that Armie was black, he said that no children of his were going to live with a nig-nog, thank you very much. "I don't know what happened then," said Madge sadly. "That's all I can remember. I think I was ill for a while and in hospital." She shook her head, as if trying to mine a memory she felt certain was inside but couldn't quite access.

She stood up abruptly. "I must get home. Jimmy and Rosie will be back for their tea soon." The temporary lucidity that had overtaken her and enabled her to tell her tale had evaporated, and Madge seemed disoriented again. She fussed with her carrier bags before hurrying away, scolding the pigeons as she went for making her late.

"Poor old thing," said Sammy. "I have to try and find out what happened to her children for her."

"She's about the same age as Mum would have been," I said.

The park was darkening. A Dalmatian and a Chihuahua ran happily alongside each other, pausing now and then to roll together in the grass. Their owners walked behind them in silence, an unlikely couple, forced into each other's company by their dogs' friendship. Elsewhere, a man wearing a neat red turban walked round and round the perimeter of the playground, as he did every day, his head bent in study over a holy book.

"You'd have thought he'd have finished that book by now," I whispered, as I nudged Sammy. We giggled like children before lapsing into silence; he strummed his guitar lovingly, at home once again.

"I'm thinking of moving back here," he said. "Is it OK if I stay till I find a place?"

I hugged him. "I'd love that. Stay as long as you like."

Madge's story had made me hum with anxiety, and I was suddenly eager to see Leo and Kitty. The house was quiet and empty when I got back. I felt an unexpected need to hear Greg's voice.

"The doctor is with a patient," said Marjorie, the surgery's receptionist, when I called.

She made no concession to the fact that Greg was my husband and often wouldn't even let me see him when I went to the surgery, saying, as she pursed her perfectly lipsticked mouth and pulled her cardigan over her neat and pointed bosom, "The doctor is busy. You'll have to take a seat and wait your turn." I'd tried everything: killing her with kindness, extravagant Christmas presents, homemade cakes, fierce hauteur, threats of emergency, violence. Nothing worked; she might as well have been the mother of one of Kitty's classmates.

"Marjorie, it's Chloe. Could you put me through to Greg, please." There must have been something in my voice, because for once she didn't argue and the next voice I heard was Greg's.

" 'It Had to Be You,' author and date?" I asked.

"Gus Kahn and Isham Jones, 1924."

"You really are marvelous."

"I know. Must go, darling, I've got a full list this afternoon."

The house seemed full of shadows. This is what it would feel like if we got divorced, an empty house on the days when the children were with their father. The aching loneliness of childless Wednesday nights and alternate weekends, and far worse for the divorced father who finds himself on his own most of the week. Either of us could bring about this fate for the other at any time. It takes two to have a relationship but only one to destroy it. However much one may want it to continue, if the other opts out, that's it, it's over.

The day was gray and a light drizzle was misting the air. Janet slipped through her cat flap and seemed to enjoy the slender ease with which she passed through it. Volodya's mother had left him copious amounts of her poppy-seed roll on her recent visit from Russia, and he'd given some to me as soon as she'd gone. He hated it, I loved it; it reminded me of Grandma Bella (who also used to make it) and of how she would use her handkerchief to wipe my sticky mouth, blackened by the sweet dark poppy-seed jam of the filling. I had no patients until six, so I cut myself a large slice and settled down with *Richard and Judy* for a little illicit afternoon TV. I watched their interplay with each other. They seemed so happily married; what was their secret? I wanted to write and ask them.

Dear Richard and Judy,
You live together and work together and although you sometimes bicker, you always seem so happy and are so nice to each other. How do you do it?
Very best, Chloe Zhivago, aged 43.
P.S.: How often do you have sex?

The doorbell pierced the quiet of my solitary afternoon. Ruthie was standing outside. She looked shrunken and had deep black shadows beneath her eyes.

"Is it open?" she asked.

"The Kvechatorium?"

She nodded.

"Always," I said.

"I hate my life," she said.

I pulled her inside, made her a cup of tea, and cut her some poppy seed roll. She'd lost a lot of weight and, although it may seem an oxymoron, she looked terrible.

"Which aspect of it?"

"I just can't bear going on with this feeling of waking up every morning and being unable to face what the day holds in store for me. I lie in bed and run through all the meetings I have, all the people I have to see, and the prospect of getting up, bathing, washing my hair, having breakfast, leaving the house, and driving to work feels insurmountable. Then, when I get there, there's that David Gibson wanker telling me *We're all on the same page* and I should *Get in the mix more.* I've been taking more and more days off, and I feel strung out, miserable, and depressed."

"Does Richard know how you're feeling?"

"No, he never notices anything unless it's an artifact from antiquity, which of course I soon will be if I go on like this. Anyhow, it doesn't matter anymore, they're making me redundant."

"How can they make you redundant? You're the editor."

"They're shifting responsibilities on the magazine and saying it's a different job. I could fight it, but I think it's a blessing in disguise, really, a sign it's time for me to change my life."

"You have to stop taking cocaine; that'll help you get back in control."

"Did I say, *Chloe, tell me like it is?* or *Chloe, give it to me straight?* No, I didn't, I came here to kvetch and for you to say *There, there* and *Poor you* in all the right places."

"Sorry, darling." Ruthie always retained her humor even in her darkest moments. "Screw tea, let's have a bottle of wine." I went to the fridge, where I found a bottle of champagne tucked out of sight behind some elderly vegetables. "Even better," I said, holding it aloft, "now we can be a couple of desperate but posh old lushes drinking in the afternoon. I wonder how long it would take us to get from here to a park bench—or to shouting at pigeons," I added, thinking of Madge.

"Poor her," said Ruthie, when I recounted Madge's story. "I feel awful that I've never taken the time to talk to her. What do you think happened?"

"It must have been something terrible for her not to remember."

We were quiet for a few moments, each of us trying to imagine what could have pushed Madge over the edge and onto the fringes of society.

"Can we go back to talking about me now?" Ruthie asked. I nodded and toasted her with my glass.

"I can't believe how hard I've worked all these years to become an editor and how little it means to me now," said Ruthie. "I mean, who gives a fuck whether we lead with a story of a woman who teaches other women how to marry a millionaire or the story of some soap star's battle against alcoholism." She poured herself another glass of champagne, relishing the irony. "I mean, in the great scheme of things, it's all tomorrow's chip paper. Well, actually, it isn't even that anymore; they use that white recycled stuff now, don't they?" She looked me up and down appraisingly. "You look great, Chloe. Maybe I should have an affair; as an addiction, it's clearly much better for your skin than cocaine."

"You really, really must stop."

"I'm going to, I promise. Tomorrow. I just need a little help getting used to this redundancy idea." Her phone beeped. "Oops, the eagle has landed. Just popping out to meet Carlos. See you later."

It was true, my growing obsession with Ivan was not so very different from Ruthie's cocaine habit; my affair was disturbing my equilibrium and turning me into a manic-depressive. You think you can handle it, but the addiction quickly starts to get out of hand and you begin to put satisfying your craving above other more important things in your life. I was irritable and withdrawn when I was away from Ivan and agitated and excited when I was with him.

I'M ACHING FOR YOU. I WILL FIND SOMEWHERE FOR US TO MEET.

My fix had arrived by mobile phone.

THE READING ON MY KISSOMETER IS DANGEROUSLY LOW, PLEASE HURRY I texted back. My mood immediately lightened and I danced my way down to the basement to meet Gina.

She started to speak before she'd even sat down. Her restless energy mirrored my own. I soon found out why.

"I've slept with someone else," she announced. "I decided I had to get it out of my system before I married Jim."

"So you *are* going to marry Jim?"

"Yes. Sorry about the panicky phone call earlier. I feel fine about it now. I realized I just needed to do this and then I'd be ready to settle down."

"How did it make you feel?"

Her face took on the misty expression of lust recollected. "Wonderful. I don't feel guilty about it either. I mean, not really. After all, Jim and I aren't married yet."

"Do you want to do it again?" I asked tentatively.

"No. . . . Yes. . . . Maybe once more." She looked troubled. "Damn, I do. I thought once would be it, but I do want to do it again. I'm a bad person, aren't I? You think I'm bad, I know you do."

I shook my head. "It doesn't matter what I think, Gina, it's what you think that matters," I said. "We're all good and bad, honest and dishonest, generous and mean. We're all of these things; it's how we live with it, how we manage it, that counts." I was aware I was talking as much to myself as to her.

Gina sat up in her chair, brightening. "I've got two months left before our wedding, so it won't count if I see the other guy again."

That was her way of justifying her *badness,* but she was merely another addict, rationalizing her next fix with the promise that it would be her last. We were all the same.

"He's someone I met ages ago. There was always this attraction between us, a feeling of unfinished business. I thought I'd better finish it—the business, I mean."

"What is it about him?"

"His newness, his untrammeled paths."

I nodded. I knew just what she meant.

"It'll be fine. I'll just get this out of the way and then I'll get married and have children and live happily ever after. Will you come to the wedding?"

It didn't feel right for me to do so, but Gina had been coming to see me for so long, and I wanted her to be happy, so I decided to break my unwritten rule. I agreed to attend the ceremony but not the reception.

*It's all your fault,* I thought unreasonably, as I looked at her lovely face. *If you hadn't planted the seed of betrayal in me, I wouldn't be sitting here in front of you, a woman with a lover and a secret life.*

*Did she hold a gun to your head?* asked an inner voice.

# Chapter 13

## Kitty's Vengeful Chocolate Cake

. . . . . . . . . . . . . . . . . .

**FOR THE CAKE**

*7½ ounces unsweetened chocolate*

*½ pound butter*

*1 cup superfine granulated sugar*

*7 eggs, separated*

*1 scant cup ground almonds*

Melt chocolate slowly. Cream butter and sugar. Add egg yolks and ground almonds. Add melted chocolate. Whisk egg whites until quite stiff, then fold into the chocolate mixture. Pour into buttered tin and bake for about 45 minutes in the middle of the oven at 350°F.

Now you have to make the chocolate icing.

FOR THE ICING

*5 ounces unsweetened chocolate*

*½ teaspoon vanilla extract*

*1 cup heavy cream*

Melt the chocolate in the top of a double boiler over medium heat. When chocolate is melted and smooth, stir in ½ teaspoon vanilla and the cream. Whisk until well blended and silky. Pour the icing over the cooled cake, letting it drip down the sides.

Lick the bowl. Yum.

I found Kitty lying on the stairs, crying. She was in her school uniform, a small black spider with her long thin limbs flung out around her in despair. She'd positioned herself so as to be able to observe her face in the mirror on the wall: sad princess crying at the injustices of life.

"What is it, baby?" I asked.

"Molly and Anna are being horrible to me. I hate them; they're such bitches."

"Don't say that. What happened?"

"Well, you know we went to Brent Cross after school?"

I nodded. This was what young girls did; they hung around shopping malls, grown-ups in miniature: drinking coffee and window-shopping. In my day, it was the High Street, which, I couldn't help feeling, had more soul than a mall. (What does that mean anyway, *in my day* as if your day only lasts until a certain point and then it's over and somebody else's begins? When was this magical point? At twenty? Thirty? Wasn't it still *my day*? I was still alive, after all. Surely it's your day for as long as you can draw breath?)

"Mum, *listen* to me," said Kitty, shaking my arm to bring my attention back to her. "OK, I was walking ahead of the others, and then when I turned round, they'd gone, yeah? They'd run away from me and I couldn't find them. I was, like, running everywhere looking for them, and then I tripped and grabbed on to this girl who was, like, passing to stop from falling over. She was a real chav—you know, big hoop earrings and trainers with cropped trousers. She stood in front of me and put her hands on her hips and said, 'Oi, don't touch me.' Then her friend saw me give her a dirty look, so she said to her, 'Ere, that girl just give you evils.' I thought I'd better run away from them after that before they beat me up."

Kitty had forgotten her sadness in her storytelling. She was playing every part, her voice, I was sure, a perfect mimicry of what she had heard. All of life was source material for her.

"So then what happened. Did you find the others?" I prompted.

"Oh, yes. Well, I did eventually, but I was like so upset."

I hugged her, remembering the cruelness of young girls to each other. And big girls could be just as bad, I thought, thinking about the way the mothers of these same girls behaved toward Ruthie and me.

"Everyone is always horrible to me and I've got no friends," Kitty sobbed, burying her head in my neck. I wanted to slap Molly and Anna.

"What about Sephy, darling?"

"Sephy doesn't count, she's like my sister."

"That's the point, sweetheart, if you've got one true friend, a real soul mate, the others don't count. They're not proper friends anyhow if they behave cruelly to you."

"But I want Molly and Anna to be my friends too."

One of the conditions of the girls going shopping by themselves was that they had to stay in a group. I never tired of reminding them of this. I phoned Molly's mother.

"This is Chloe, Kitty's mother."

"Oh, hello," she said, as if she couldn't quite recall who I was or whether we'd ever met.

I explained the situation. She gave a short, impatient laugh. "Well, girls will be girls. I can't see what you expect me to do about it."

The lioness within me stirred and growled. "As far as I'm concerned, this is bullying, and you should talk to Molly about it before it gets any worse."

"Whatever," she said, and hung up. If she'd been standing in front of me, I would have torn her head off with my Big Cat's teeth.

"Bitch," I muttered.

"Precisely," said Kitty, overhearing me. War had been declared. Bullying had broken out across two generations. Kitty and I discussed psychological warfare. It turned out that it was Molly's birthday the next day and girls always brought a cake in on their birthdays. Molly's mum was strictly Marks and Spencer; the only dish she was capable of preparing herself, when she wasn't too busy going to the gym, was a mountain out of a molehill. Jessie, who was two years above Kitty at school, had come home by now, so the three of us baked an exquisite chocolate cake for Kitty to take in. Kitty rehearsed her lines: "Oops, forgot it was Molly's birthday; we just felt like giving the class a treat." The custom was that bought cakes were always ignored in favor of homemade. We embroidered elaborate patterns in icing and wrote *Just Because It's Thursday* across the cake, delighted with our tactics.

"There, that should wind them up good and proper," I said, as I finished writing with a flourish.

Leo almost ruined our plan, as he bounced like a burglar, silently and on the balls of his feet, into the kitchen and prepared to sink a large knife into the cake to cut himself a generous slice. I had to throw myself across the kitchen and unplug him from his iPod to stop him in time.

"No need to shout," he said. "I just want a taste."

"It's for Kitty's school."

"As usual, everything for Kitty." He sighed.

I had to make him a sandwich in the shape of a gingerbread man to prove I loved him just as much. "Just a small one, though," I said. "We're going out for supper tonight, remember?"

We'd taken to going out for a meal on Wednesdays to escape Bea's sullen presence at the dinner table. For some reason, she was always at her worst mid-week. Since Zuzi's arrival and Bea's improved mood, this was no longer strictly necessary, but we'd continued anyhow and Zuzi and Bea had come to expect this weekly opportunity to have their own candlelit dinner à deux. The problem was that we were running out of neighborhood restaurants. Greg was not an easy customer and had defaced most of the restaurant listings in *Eating in Your Own Backyard*, our local restaurant guide, with a large red X, rather, I suspect, like those that marked the doors of sixteenth-century plague victims to indicate the presence of death within. Now and again a restaurant would be rehabilitated if it was under new management, but all too often it would go the way of its predecessor and a second X would be added to the first.

We seated ourselves in Jiminy Cricket, a new pizza joint on Willesden Lane that Ruthie and Richard had recommended. It had an irritatingly cheerful and overwritten menu: *Try our mouth-watering Cricket Pizza, oodles of melted cheese and spicy sausage, oozing with succulent flavor.*

"I don't want anything," said Kitty. "I keep thinking of crickets sitting on their pizza base getting roasted alive in a hot oven."

Greg was irritably miming a bread knife with which to butter his roll, denoting the absence of one on the table. I opted for Garden Salad: *crunchy, flavorsome vegetables lovingly laid out on crisp wholesome leaves.* They should have added *with a small gleaming jewel of a bug in their center,* because that's what I found when the salad arrived.

"Excuse me, waiter, could you call the chef over here, please," said Greg with the icy politeness he adopts when he's about to make a scene. I looked at the children and raised an eyebrow—well, both eyebrows actually, I've never been able to raise just the one—as if to say, *Here we go.* The chef arrived at our table, a young man with tendrils of untidy and not quite clean hair escaping from his chef's hat. His check trousers were tight and slightly grubby, his fingers covered in Band-Aids.

"Could you explain to me how you make your salad?" asked Greg.

The chef looked bemused. "Sorry?"

"You know, just talk me through the preparation of a salad."

"Well, chop the vegetables," he began slowly.

The children were shifting uncomfortably on their chairs in an agony of embarrassment. Greg raised his hand to warn them to remain silent. Jessie, who had come out with us, hadn't seen Greg in action before. She looked bemused.

"Yes." Greg nodded at the chef.

"Wash the lettuce."

"I beg your pardon?" said Greg, lifting his head and cocking his ears like an attentive hound that senses the fox is near.

"The lettuce," the chef repeated slowly, shaking his head.

"Yes, but what was the word that came before *lettuce?*"

The chef scratched his head in a pantomime of thought. "Um . . . *wash,* wash the lettuce."

"Quite," said Greg, holding up a finger for emphasis. "The very word, wash." He was now attentive dog turned wrathful master as he prepared to shove the chef's face into his mess and hit him on the back of his head with a rolled-up newspaper. "The washing is key, wouldn't you say?" Greg placed an unpleasant accent on the word *washing*. "So why, might I ask, is there a bug in my wife's salad?"

His erstwhile emphatic finger now swerved to point accusingly at the offending insect, curled up in its *flavorsome* bed, happily unaware of the trouble its quiet presence was causing. The chef whisked the dish away and strode off to the kitchen, muttering imprecations in an unfamiliar language and drawing a finger across his throat in a gesture of violence that needed no translation.

I insisted that we leave after Greg's "victory." My youthful profession as a waitress had taught me that the chef's humiliation was likely to find expression in spitting in our food or worse.

"Why you couldn't just tell the waiter there was a bug in the salad instead of going through that charade, I don't know," I said, as I hustled everyone out the door.

"They have to learn," answered the maniac to whom I had once so foolishly plighted my troth.

We returned home starving to find the fridge empty and Bea and Zuzi comfortably seated on the kitchen sofa, smacking their lips and patting their full bellies.

"That's it," I shouted at Greg. "I'm not going out to dinner with you ever again. From now on, all meals will be consumed on these premises."

Bea looked alarmed. "But not on the Wednesdays? This is the Bea and Zuzi night, no?"

I didn't trust myself to speak, so I followed Greg upstairs. He took down the restaurant guide and scored a large red X through Jiminy Cricket's entry before sitting down to compose a letter to *Eating in Your Own Backyard*. No doubt he would insist that they remove Jiminy Cricket's listing from their publication. Stalactites and stalagmites began to form in the air around me, as I stood frozen in glacial fury and watched him scratching away with the quill pen I now wished I'd never given him. I had become the ice maiden; it would take some days for the thaw to begin. "Oi, Dad, Mum just give you evils," Kitty said to him over her shoulder, as she skipped up to bed.

*Chapter 14*

## FF's Recipe for a Dinner Party

. . . . . . . . . . . . . . . . . .

Buy nuts and olives
Open and pour into bowls
Chill wine
Tell guests to prepare and bring the other courses

ecky's time away had convinced her that she and Ivan had to fight for their relationship and give it another chance. I was of two minds about this. It made me feel safer, since it helped keep my own relationship with him under control; but at the same time I felt unreasonably jealous. Her return to the marital home presented us with a problem. We had to find new venues for our meetings and resort to stolen hours in hotel bedrooms. Most hotels had strict rules about check-in times that didn't fit well with the needs of married lovers.

"Why aren't there any love hotels?" I asked Ivan. "We may have to go and live in Japan; apparently they've got lots of them there."

After a few disasters—clashes with candlewick bedspreads, not quite clean sheets, and furious, noisy humping in next-door rooms—Ivan had found a place in Bayswater aptly named Encounters that had become our own little love hotel. It was a pink double-fronted Georgian house run, appropriately, by Georgians from Tbilisi and set back in a side street off the Bayswater Road not too far from his house.

I would stock up on goodies from the exotic food shops that lined Queensway for our intermissions: hummus, falafel, nuts, olives, and bread—things we could eat easily with our fingers or lick off each other's. Sometimes we would spend a couple of hours there over lunchtime; now and again we managed to steal a whole afternoon. I was embarrassed by the behavior of Mgelika, the receptionist. He gave me significant gap-toothed smiles when we checked in and shook Ivan's hand a little too vigorously, as if to suggest what a virile son of a gun he was, fucking another man's wife. He had passed our room once as we were leaving and had looked openly at the crumpled sheets just visible through the gap in the door. I'd seen him smile wolfishly while giving me an appraising look, his eyes lingering too long on my breasts. It made me feel like a whore who rented rooms by the hour. Ivan had told me not to be silly and what did it matter what a stranger thought as long as we could be together?

"Don't forget Rule Four," Ruthie said, when I told her about our new love nest.

I looked at her quizzically.

"*Never pay by credit card.* It's such an easy way to get found out, and so many people are careless about it," she warned.

There was one unanticipated and unwelcome consequence to my renewed sexual activity, which was almost as damning as a carelessly guarded credit card bill: I had developed cystitis. None of the over-the-counter products helped me, and in desperation I made an appointment to see the nurse at Greg's practice. Risky, I know, but I couldn't think where else to go.

"Hello, Chloe, have you come to see Greg?" Marjorie asked me brightly as I attempted an inconspicuous entry into the surgery. She reached for the telephone. Naturally she had chosen today of all days to acknowledge that I was Greg's wife.

"No, no, please don't bother him, I'm sure he's very busy," I said. "I'm just popping in to ask the nurse something." She paused, her hand on the phone, and looked at me in a way that implied she could see right into my urinary tract, before switching into receptionist mode.

"If you'd just like to take a seat, the nurse will be with you shortly."

When my name was called, it sounded so loud I had to stop myself from saying *shush* to the intercom system. I tiptoed along the corridor, clinging to the walls lest Greg should catch sight of me.

"You wouldn't believe how many women in their forties come in with cystitis." The nurse seemed to shout, her voice determined to carry through the thin wall into Greg's surgery next door. "It's an epidemic. They're all divorced women who have rediscovered sex with a vengeance. The honeymoon disease, that's what they call it. Funny you've got it, though, you and Greg having been married for such ages and everything." She looked at me curiously and added, "Clearly, there's life in the old doctor yet. Lucky old you. Henry and I haven't had sex for at least a year." I laughed nervously and hastily scuttled out, clutching a prescription for antibiotics, terrified that she would say something to Greg.

There is nothing quite so pleasurable as lying in bed in the afternoon in the arms of a man you desire. It was a Friday, the sky was unusually blue for December, and the sun, observing its short winter working hours, was making a last brief appearance before retiring for the day. Ivan was sliding a hand up and down my back and I was nuzzled into his neck, inhaling him. His long legs were entwined in mine, and I could feel the heat of his thigh between my legs, an area that was still throbbing pleasurably after his expert ministrations. We were experiencing those last few precious moments before we had to get up and dress in order to return regretfully to our real lives when I'm afraid the *L* word reared its ugly head in strict contravention to Rule Five in Ruthie's book: *Never fall in love with your lover if you don't intend to leave your husband for him.*

"*Ia liubliu tebia,*" Ivan said.

"*Blu-blu blah-blah,* what's that mean?"

He laughed. "*Liubliu tebia.* I love you."

"*Blu-blu blah-blah* too," I said, before I could stop myself. Which wasn't the same as actually telling him that I loved him, I reasoned; I had merely spoken nonsense words to him in a language I didn't understand. Illogically, telling Ivan I loved him felt like more of a betrayal of Greg than having sex with Ivan did. Apparently, it was fine to allow another man and his penis to do what they wanted with me, but saying *I love you* would banish me to purgatory (although the likelihood of such a banishment was looking more and more like a foregone conclusion). I stopped further talk of love by kissing Ivan until it was time for us to part.

Was I falling in love? The thought terrified me. I could see why it was against Ruthie's rules, but beneath the terror was another feeling, one of tremendous well-being, and I found myself humming happily as I walked to my car. Couldn't I ignore the fact that I was a married woman for a little while and simply relive the past few hours I had spent with my lover? *My lover.* I turned the words around my tongue as one might a delicious sweetmeat and felt like an irresistible woman of the world, a Mata Hari, a temptress. Chloe Zhivago, thinner and more beautiful now than she's ever been. *Tra-la-la-la-la-la.* The last *la* seemed to stick in my throat as the words that haunt every Jew in the face of happiness or pleasure rang in my head: *It won't last.*

As I got into my car, my thoughts were interrupted by my mobile. *One more dance with you Momma*, it sang to me. Leo had replaced my ring tone with one of his hip-hop numbers; fortunately, it was more melodic and less violent than usual. (I panicked slightly at the thought that I must have left my phone unattended long enough for him to have been able to do so.) I thought it would be Ivan calling to say goodbye again; one of us was always sure to phone or text the other after we'd been together, eager to maintain contact.

"Hello," I said, my voice warm with the intimacy of our recent coupling.

"Just had FF on the phone," said Greg's voice, making me start. "She's summoned us to dinner at her place at eight o'clock next Tuesday to meet her new bloke. I tried to wriggle out of it but somehow found myself promising her that we'd both go. Ruthie and Richard are going, and so's that Russian chap, Ivan, and his wife. Apparently you're in charge of the starter, and Ruthie is doing the main course."

"And what about pudding?" I was so shocked, I couldn't think what else to say.

"She's buying a cake or something from the patisserie. You've got to hand it to her. No one else could get away with inviting people over and then getting them to bring their own dinner."

"Do we have to go?" I panicked.

"I can't win," said Greg, "You're the one who's always complaining I never go anywhere. She's your friend; I thought you'd want to."

"No, that's fine; of course we'll go."

Well, now, that would be a cozy scenario, my husband and my lover around the same dinner table. It was unconscionable, but since Greg had already committed us, I quickly texted Ivan to warn him not to accept. TOO LATE, he sent back, BECKY HAS JUST GOT OFF PHONE FROM TELLING HER WE'D LOVE TO GO.

I sat in the car in a state of alarm; phrases like *chickens coming home to roost* and *people getting their just desserts* came to mind. This last seemed rather appropriate in the circumstances, and I laughed hollowly at the idea that the dessert was the only thing that FF would be serving up herself.

"You'll just have to brazen it out," said Ruthie, when I phoned her in panic.

"Why does it feel so awful for me to be at a dinner table with my husband and my lover? I mean, I've just been in bed with my lover doing all manner of intimate things, and somehow that feels acceptable."

"I think it's because if your husband knew he was your lover and knew that others knew, it would be humiliating for him, as if you were taunting him with it in public. Whereas if you're discreet and your affair is kept separate from your everyday life, it's—not forgivable, exactly, but less unforgivable."

"It's a minefield, isn't it? The weird thing is that I'd be pleased if they liked each other."

"Be very careful, Chlo, you may give all sorts of stuff away without being aware of it. Body language, significant glances. . . . People can tell things about you; sometimes things you don't yet know yourself."

"Thanks for the reassurance," I said wryly.

I don't know what devil got into me, but I started to feel quite excited about the prospect; there was something about the danger of it all that made me feel alive. Suddenly I could understand why people took the risks they did: why Members of Parliament cavorted with known prostitutes, why celebrities took drugs in front of strangers. It fueled a dangerous need to heighten experience. It turned life into an exciting game of Russian roulette, and I was lucky enough to have my own real live Russian to play it with.

On the appointed day, I sifted through my many recipe books to find something to make for a starter. Ah: Buckwheat Blinis with Smoked Salmon, Sour Cream, and Caviar. Perfect. I went to the Volga for some ingredients. Volodya was in his customary pose, leaning back in his chair, feet up on a desk, reading *Doctor Zhivago* with an unlit cigarette clamped between his teeth. He looked up at the sound of the door.

"Which bit are you up to?" I asked.

"The part where Zhivago and Lara are having their affair and Tonya hasn't yet realized what's going on."

"That's what I've never quite understood," I said. "I mean, Zhivago loves Tonya so much and from such a young age; how come he falls in love with Lara?"

"It's possible to love two people at the same time." Volodya shrugged, looking at me pointedly.

And apparently to have dinner with them at the same time too. I avoided his gaze by busying myself with searching for something in my bag.

"More riddles?" he asked.

"No, today I have actually come to spend some money. I need buckwheat and caviar."

He sold me a tin of salmon caviar; bright orange balls that glistened, which he assured me were tastier than the usual black sturgeon eggs and much cheaper too.

"Russian love, *Russkaia liubov'*, it suits you," he said, his eyes searching my face. "*Sem'ia*, family, that's what's important, Chloe." He held me by my shoulders and turned me to him. "Be happy, enjoy yourself, but don't ever forget that."

It seemed no one could talk to me without urging caution or offering advice. He filled a little plastic bag with chocolates with squirrels on them and tucked them into my hand. "Here, take these *Belochki*, delicious with tea or coffee at the end of a meal, a little taste of home for your friend." Leaning behind me, he dipped his hand into a small wicker basket, took out a different chocolate, unwrapped it, and popped it in my mouth. It was delicious, a nut brittle covered in chocolate.

"It's called *Gril'iazh*, very popular in my country."

"What's Russian for *delicious?*"

"*Vkusno.*"

"*Vkusno,*" I repeated, storing it up for an intimate moment when I could offer it to Ivan like a gift, an endearment in his native tongue.

I got home, ready to roll up my sleeves and get cracking on the blinis, and found FF lying on my kitchen sofa. She was wearing a neck brace.

"What happened?" I asked.

"I cricked my neck shagging Jeremy. I was on top and trying to keep my face from sagging, so I arched my back and my neck really far up to keep everything taut. I must have been a little over-enthusiastic."

"Perhaps we *femmes d'un certain age* should stick to the missionary position," I said, trying not to laugh.

"It doesn't matter what *you* look like," said FF. "I mean, it's only Greg; you don't have to impress him."

"Yes. Yes, of course," I replied, flustered. "But still, I have to keep him from straying off with some firm-faced young thing." I'd nearly given myself away; I would have to be more careful. "Why did you ask Ivan and Becky to dinner?" I asked, in what I hoped was a casual tone.

"They're my new best friends and I want him to do the drawings for my new book. I thought sexy cartoons of people making love would work well. Now, I really have to dash." FF got up to go as if I were detaining her. "I have to nip down to Saigon and get my nails done." (This was her moniker for the proliferating nail bars that were run by the Vietnamese. She called Stoke Newington *Istanbul* as a result of all the Turkish shops there, Acton was *Tokyo,* and Southall, *New Delhi.*) "Those girls in Saigon have impossibly small bottoms," she added. "They make me feel enormous. Still, it's very restful and silent there. Each of us is completely unintelligible to the other, so there's no point talking—just what I need before tonight." She blew me a kiss. "See you later."

"Can't wait," I muttered, as I closed the door behind her.

FF lived in a large double-fronted house in an area she called West Hampstead and Greg insisted should really be called East Kilburn. It had recently become popular with the arty, muso, bohemian set who couldn't quite manage Notting Hill Gate or Primrose Hill prices. Just before we'd set out, she'd rung up and asked us to pick up dessert on our way, as she had too much to do. Going into her pristine cement-topped kitchen (cement was the current dernier cri in work surfaces apparently), it was hard to tell what it was that had kept her so busy. The only signs that she was expecting guests were a few bowls of olives and nuts.

"I'm furious," she announced. "Jeremy phoned literally five minutes ago to say he can't come. He's had to go to Cardiff; one of his producers was arrested for assaulting someone and he has to sort it out. Honestly, the whole point of this evening was so you could all finally get to meet him."

I was busy comforting her, sitting her down and pouring her a drink, when Ivan and Becky arrived. Becky was smaller and prettier than her photograph had suggested, but there was a slight wetness about her mouth that made you want to dab her with a tissue. It wasn't the moistness of sexual promise; rather a prelude to overly wet kisses. I was able to overlook this minor flaw since I wasn't planning to kiss her, and I found that I took to her immediately, a possibility I hadn't considered.

"Ivan and I are barely speaking," she said. "We got lost on the way here; as usual, he wouldn't stop to ask anyone the way."

"Greg's just the same," I said. "He would rather drive round and round for hours than face the ignominy of asking for help. Does testosterone render men incapable of asking for directions?"

"It drives me insane, and the kids too," Becky said. "When they were younger, they'd lean out of the car window and wave at passersby, shouting, *We're lost, but our dad won't stop and ask for directions.*"

"Did it work?"

"No, it made Ivan more determined than ever to keep going; he just drove faster."

We laughed, women united by the foibles of men. Becky was friendly and funny. I'd have been furious on her behalf about her husband playing away from home if it hadn't been me he was playing with. It was a shame I couldn't just ask her if I could borrow him, as a child borrows a toy from a friend. Could I have a go at her husband? I'd promise to give him back when I was finished. *"Come on, Becky, don't be mean, give me a turn."* That's what swinging is, I suppose: having a turn on other people's husbands and wives and giving them back nicely when you've finished.

FF was so busy behaving like a guest that Ruthie and I had to take charge or we'd never have been fed.

"What do you think?" I whispered to Ruthie, as she helped me serve the first course. She swayed slightly as she slapped pieces of smoked salmon haphazardly on blinis. She had been DOA (drunk on arrival).

"He's gorgeous," she said. "His wife's nice too," she added dryly.

FF's one concession to playing host was to organize the seating, and she had placed Ivan next to me. It took every ounce of self-control to stop myself from intertwining calves and ankles with him under the table. Greg was sitting next to Becky, and they seemed to be getting on famously.

Ruthie threw me meaningful looks over the table. She followed me as I cleared the plates.

"Rule Number six," she said. *"Deny and lie."* I looked at her quizzically. "Unless you are actually caught in flagrante, deny everything." I nodded obediently. "Mind you," she added, "the way you two are looking at each other, I wouldn't be surprised if you treated everyone to a live sex show a little later."

"Is it really that obvious?"

"To me, yes. But then, this is one of my special subjects."

"You don't think Greg or Becky suspects?"

"No." She paused before adding, "Not yet."

FF spent most of the evening either in another room on the phone to Jeremy or at the table in conversation with Richard about the sexual practices of the ancient world, in case there was anything she could plunder for use in her new book. The rest of us were pretty much left to fend for ourselves. After her main course (grilled halibut with black bean sauce and wild rice), Ruthie started a discussion about marriage. She'd added a few more glasses of wine to the quantity she'd already drunk, in addition, no doubt, to a few little visits with her Colombian friend, if frequent trips to the bathroom were anything to judge by. Richard was watching her, twisting his lower lip between thumb and forefinger as he always does when anxious. I knew I'd have to have a serious talk with him sooner or later and betray Ruthie's secret. I couldn't see her getting back on track without his help.

"The thing is," she was saying, "marriages aren't meant to last as long as all of ours have. Ten years used to be about the normal length of time for a marriage. By then we women would have died in childbirth and you lot"—she waved an arm vaguely in the direction of the men around the table—"you lot would all have died in a duel or something."

"Perhaps I should challenge Ivan to one," said Greg, as he opened another bottle of wine. I choked on the mouthful of food I'd just taken. "Fishbone," I gasped, when I could speak again.

"Why me?" said Ivan calmly.

"Why not? I'm sure we could find something to fight over," said Greg. I held my breath nervously. "Let's see," Greg continued. "What, for instance, are your views on the countryside?" I relaxed and took a soothing gulp of wine from my glass; the danger had passed.

This was one of Greg's pet subjects and he loved to spar. "Life is so dull when everyone agrees with each other all the time," he would say.

"I love the countryside," said Ivan.

"No, I mean foxhunting," Greg persisted. Here we go, I thought wearily.

"Very useful way of applying Darwinian theory," said Ivan, his eyes meeting Greg's. "The foxes that get caught are the old and the sick."

Off they went, back and forth. Greg held forth on the disgrace of killing for sport; Ivan waxed lyrical on the joys of the hunt.

Becky tried to make herself heard. "I'm the only one here who is country born and bred." But the men weren't interested in anyone who had real experience of the subject, and their voices merely grew louder and drowned us out. Ivan interrupted Becky every time she tried to say something, just as Greg did me. She and I looked at each other and shrugged. Our husbands were more similar than I had first thought, although, on balance, as I observed Ivan's relationship with Becky, I couldn't help feeling that Greg was nicer to me than he was to her. When she spoke, he looked impatient and rarely met her eyes with his own.

"It's an important part of the economic and social fabric of rural living. I'm not talking about—what do you call them—*toffs*, but about the ordinary men and women whose livelihood has been connected with foxhunting for generations," Ivan was saying.

"All this stuff about how many jobs will be lost is beside the point," countered Greg. "The by-product of progress is sometimes the loss of jobs. The people affected will just have to find another way to earn a living. You have to do what's right, and foxhunting isn't right."

"Foxes are pests. Anyhow, hunting only eliminates three percent of the fox population," said Ivan.

"Well, why not sanction murder while you're at it; you could shoot a few human beings and say that it only eliminates a very small percentage of the human population. A death is a death," answered Greg.

"Look," said Ivan, pointing at FF's Siamese cat, which was curled up on a doormat, neatly illustrating that early reading sentence, *The cat sat on the mat.* "People keep cats, and they take care of mice infestations."

"Actually," I interrupted, "our cat doesn't. She's anorexic."

"Oh, who cares, foxes, shmoxes," Ruthie said loudly, and started to cry in great gulping sobs that astounded us all. "It's all so fucking irrelevant," she said, staggering to her feet. Richard looked at me helplessly; he's not usually much good in a crisis. So I quickly hustled her out of the room and up to FF's bedroom so she could lie down.

"Sorry, Chlo, bit pissed," she said, as she turned over and passed out.

Ivan cornered me on the stairs on my way back down.

"Someone will see us," I said, alarmed.

He pulled me to him and I could feel him, warm against my thigh, a reminder of pleasure shared. It was almost unbearably exciting. Forget Russian roulette, this was akin to outright suicide. He put his hand down the front of my trousers and caressed me before pulling it out and slowly sucking the finger that had touched me, while holding my eyes with his own. I flushed with a mixture of shock and arousal. If anyone saw us, Rule six would be useless. Summoning all the self-control I could muster, I pushed past him and ran back down the stairs. FF's face appeared round the doorjamb, looking quizzical. "What have I missed?" she asked.

I shrugged casually. "Just showing Ivan where the upstairs loo is."

As we were driving home, Greg said, "Ivan and Becky are quite nice. I mean, Ivan's a bit fond of himself, but he's an interesting bloke. I might go out for a drink with him."

I tried to hide my unease and busied myself with looking for the latest weather forecast on the car radio to deflect Greg's attention. That's all I needed, my husband and my lover, out for a cozy little drink together. Perhaps they'd like to discuss my performance in bed.

"Ruthie's not in great shape," I said, changing the subject.

"Probably perimenopausal," said Greg, in that infuriating way men have of discounting women's emotions by attributing any upset to hormonal fluctuations.

"She's only forty-three, for God's sake."

"Lots of women start getting symptoms at your and Ruthie's age."

"Good. Well, I'll look forward to them, shall I?" I said crisply.

I'd been so aroused by Ivan that I contemplated seducing Greg when he came to bed, even though it didn't seem right for Greg to finish the job that Ivan had started on the stairs. I know I wouldn't have been the first woman nor the last who has thought of another man while making love to her husband. While I was wrestling with my conscience, the sound of Greg's heavy snoring made the decision for me. I'd always thought of myself as a decent and honorable person, but

I seemed to have developed a natural talent for wickedness. Was this what happened once one's toes inched over the invisible boundary that separates good behavior from bad? The first step was not the final one, merely the beginning of the inevitable path to ruin, one's own and everyone else's. I lay awake for some time, searching with my treacherous boundary-crossing feet for smooth cool spaces in the sheets to soothe me to sleep.

I'm so sorry!" Ruthie wailed on the phone the next morning. "I woke up in such a spiral of shame. That's it, no more, I promise. I've erased Carlos's phone number from my mobile, my Palm Pilot, and my computer."

"Yes, that's all very well, but what about from your head?" Ruthie has an extraordinary facility for storing phone numbers. She can still recall Benny Tart's number, the first boy she kissed. (Everyone's first love seems to have a ridiculous name like Amanda Blow or Jimmy Quick.)

"I will boil my head in a vat of oil to make it disappear from there too," said Ruthie, full of contrition. "I was a bit overwrought and drank three glasses of wine before I even got there last night. I had had such a vile day, setting goals for all the people who work for me. It took hours, and David Gibfuck insisted that they all had to be done and signed by the end of the day, even though I'm leaving. It's such time-wasting nonsense. 'What's your objective?' 'To do my job well.' 'Oh, that's a surprise, most people put 'To do my job really badly.' It's all such bollocks; thank God I haven't got long to go. Then, when I came home, Atlas was crying and when I asked him what was wrong he told me he thinks he's gay."

"It's probably just a phase; most boys go through it at about his age," I said, in an attempt to comfort her. "Anyway, it could be quite nice if he were, he'd coordinate your accessories for you; you wouldn't be losing a son, you'd be gaining a daughter."

"That's true." She laughed. "I know I'm not meant to mind, and of course in theory I don't, but all I could think when he told me was that he might get AIDS, he wouldn't ever give me any grandchildren, and one day he might be a lonely old man with no one to care for him."

"Oh, darling, you should have told me. There's no insurance for any of us against a lonely old age, straight or gay. Anyhow, even if he is gay, he could still father children. Look at that gay couple in Manchester who've got two sets of surrogate twins. I'm so sorry, I've been so obsessed with all this Ivan business, I should have seen that something was wrong."

"I'll be fine. By the way, Ivan is very sexy, but you need to watch it."

"I know, I'm so relieved the evening's over; it was terribly nerve-racking but also exciting, which made it even more worrying."

"I'm not sure whose addiction is more dangerous, yours or mine," she said.

# Chapter 15

## Chloe Zhivago's Recipe for Falafel

*1 pound chickpeas, cooked and drained*
*1 large onion, finely chopped*
*2 tablespoons finely chopped parsley*
*1 egg, beaten*
*1 teaspoon ground cumin*
*½ teaspoon ground coriander (or use fresh)*
*2 cloves crushed garlic*
*1 teaspoon salt*
*½ cup bread crumbs*
*Olive oil for frying*

Combine chickpeas, onion, parsley, egg, and spices. Mix in blender. Place in a bowl and add bread crumbs until mixture forms a small ball without sticking to your hands. Form this dough into small balls about 1 inch in diameter. Flatten balls slightly and fry in olive oil until golden brown on both sides; drain on paper towels. Serve in pita bread with chopped tomato, cucumber, lettuce, and onion and some tahini or chili sauce.

How's the girlfriend hunt going?" I asked Leo. He was at that stage of adolescent development known as *self-imposed-solitary-confinement-in-bedroom*. His room looked like it had been constructed as a film set for the bedroom of a teenage boy. The director wouldn't have needed to change a thing. There were dirty clothes in piles on the floor, bowls with the dried crusted remnants of cereal, empty cups, and socks on every surface. The atmosphere was pervaded with a stale doggy smell, *eau de teenage boy*. On Leo's rare appearances in other parts of the house, his ears were usually stoppered up by headphones, which rendered him inaccessible. My head had also been stoppered up recently, with the imaginings of my own secret life. When not actually with Ivan, my mind was usually replaying the time we had spent together on a loop. As a result, I realized I hadn't talked to Leo properly for weeks. I had become dissociated from my everyday life and spent all my time in my adulterous leafy suburbs, just as Dad had predicted. I had become, in short, a bad wife and mother and was in danger of turning into a bad psychotherapist too. I was seeking to make amends, but my opening gambit was badly judged.

"Who told you I wanted a girlfriend? It was Kitty, wasn't it? Bitch, I told her to keep quiet about it. I'm going to get her for this." He got up to find her and turn his threat into reality.

"No, no." I backtracked. Damn, now I'd betrayed a confidence. "I just thought you were probably at that age."

"Oh, yeah, right. Look, Mum, I really can't talk to you about this sort of stuff," he said.

"Why not? I'm a girl. I know about these things."

He looked at me disbelievingly. "Yeah, right. Look, it's not like it was, in your day."

"This is still my day," I muttered through clenched teeth.

Leo laughed shortly. "Yeah, right."

If he said that again, I might have to hit him. Affecting a casual tone, I said, "But it *is* girls that you like, isn't it?"

"What do you mean?"

"I mean, girls rather than boys. It's fine if it *is* boys, I just thought we should have a chat about it."

"Look Mum, I know Atlas thinks he's a poof and good luck to him. That's fine if he is, I don't care, he's just Atlas and he's my mate whatever. But it's girls for me, OK? End of."

I was ashamed at how relieved I felt.

"Now, if you don't mind," Leo said, "I'd like to carry on reading my porn mags and smoking crack in peace." I looked horrified. "I'm joking," he said. "I'm going round to see Grandpa to get some advice." As I was leaving, he looked up and said quietly, "It's not easy being fifteen, you know."

"I know, sweetheart." I came back in and kissed him. He allowed me to hug him and rested his head on my shoulder for a moment.

"It's quite hard being forty-three too," I said quietly, as I closed the door.

I hadn't seen much of Sammy recently; his determined sleuthing on Madge's behalf had been taking up most of his time. I think he'd been seeing quite a bit of a Spanish girl who worked in the Tapas Bar round the corner too. He'd always been secretive about his love life. I found him now on the stairs, with a tearstained face and a tattered yellow newspaper cutting in his hand. Our staircase, it seemed, had become the designated crying area. I sat down next to him and put my arm around his shoulders. I didn't say anything; he would speak when he felt able to. As it turned out, I didn't need him to say a word, because when I looked at the newspaper it told me everything I needed to know.

FATHER AND CHILDREN SUFFOCATE IN CAR.

*Reg Jackson, 31, and his two children, Rosie, 7, and Jimmy, 5, were found dead in their car from carbon monoxide poisoning early on Monday morning. "It looked like they were all asleep," said Joyce Hinkin, 35, who lived next door to the tragic family. The car, a white Ford Cortina, was parked in a quiet*

*alleyway near the house. "I was taking a shortcut back home with my shop-*
*ping when I saw them," said Mrs. Hinkin. "They seemed such a nice family.*
*What could make someone do such a terrible thing?" Reg's wife and mother of*
*the children, Madge Jackson, had gone out for the day, leaving her two chil-*
*dren in their father's care. She is being comforted by friends in the hospital,*
*where she is being treated for shock.*

I carefully took the cutting from Sammy's hand. It was dated
December 12, 1969.

"Where did you find this?" I asked.

"It was in Madge's flat. I've been tracing them, going to various
authorities, looking for birth certificates, and I was getting close. But
then today I was at Madge's having a cup of tea and I saw it pinned to
the wall with lots of other pieces of paper. It turns out she's known all
along—well, some part of her has. But she must find it too painful to
believe, so most of the time she forgets and thinks they're still alive."

"How awful. Can you imagine?" I felt like crying. "What about
Armie?"

"I'm still trying to find out what happened to him," said Sammy.

Ruthie called round to apologize once again for her behavior the
night before. "I've just bumped into Lou," she said. "She's got a new
man and she looks fabulous."

"Really, who?" I was balanced precariously on a chair, looking for a
vase on the top of the cupboard. I'd found a lot of dust instead and a
broken hash water pipe. Whose was it, Greg's? Leo's?

"Someone she met on ushag.com, an Internet dating site."

"Is it really called that?"

"It might as well be." Ruthie laughed.

"Blimey," I said. "The Internet is the most successful pimp of all time.
The number of people who subscribe to those things is amazing."

"Anyhow, it seems this chap knows you; he's called Les Fallick."

"Les?" I paused, tracing a pattern in the dust with a finger. "I used to know a *Gus* Fallick."

"That's right, Lou said he'd changed his name."

I couldn't help feeling that, if I were him, it wouldn't have been my first name I'd have changed.

"Last I heard, he was living in Glasgow and was married with kids."

"Yes, well, he's divorced now. There seems to be a general recycling of husbands going on at the moment," said Ruthie dryly.

"That can only be good for the environment, surely?"

"Mmm. I might put Richard outside the front door in a green box and see what happens. Apparently Les is still living in Glasgow, so they only see each other on weekends. Lou goes up there when James has the kids and Les comes down when she has them. Meanwhile, during the week they have constant Internet sex."

Of course! The Internet would be the perfect tool for his silver tongue. I was delighted that he was still putting his remarkable talent to good use and doubtless, thanks to the Net, had been able to give pleasure to thousands of women around the globe.

Ruthie was feeling a little better about her cocaine habit. She'd discovered that it was a recognized syndrome; she was a MICCA: Middle Class Cocaine Abuser.

"It makes me feel much more comfortable to know I'm a statistic and I've got a name," she said. "Apparently there are loads of us. FF first got me started on this cocaine thing, you know, even before the girls in the office; it was when she was writing her celibacy book. You know how she thinks she's a twenty-first-century philosopher?"

I nodded wearily.

"Well, she was experimenting with cocaine for her art, doing her Timothy Leary explorer-of-the-mind thing. She found it tremendously useful for understanding the inner workings of her psyche or some such crap. Anyhow, she's given it up now she's back in the saddle. It's no good for orgasms: makes it hard to have one, she tells me, which is good for boys but not so good for girls."

Ruthie pushed her hair out of her eyes and realigned her pleats; her Issey Miyake was looking crumpled, the outward manifestation of her inner state, the disintegration of a uniform she would soon no longer need.

"I really am going to stop now, Chlo. I've been reading up on it, and so many people die in Colombia in drug wars that it feels immoral to be taking it. Apparently, for every gram of cocaine that makes its way onto a dinner-party table, one person dies. I've made myself visualize each line as a trail of blood I'm snorting up my nose. It's really put me off."

"Be a good magazine article: Cocaine Housewives," I said.

"That's a great idea. In fact, I might write it myself as a freelance for a rival magazine, now that my mag's dumped me." Ruthie looked cheerier than she had for weeks.

"Why did you get so into it?" I asked.

"It was fun and I needed some fun."

"It didn't look as though you were having much fun last night."

"In actual fact, it was only fun in the beginning. It quickly got sad and desperate. I'll have to think of another way to have fun."

"I hope my way of having fun doesn't get sad and desperate too quickly," I said.

Ivan and I were lying in bed in Encounters, eating falafel in pita with chili sauce. A little of the sauce had run down Ivan's chin, and I was licking it off. Mgelika was making me feel increasingly uncomfortable. He'd taken to kissing me wetly on each cheek in greeting as if we were old friends and had just knocked on the door for the third time, entering with his passkey before we'd had time to answer, on the flimsy pretext that he thought we had called him. Luckily we'd been pausing for breath each time and not actually at it. Encounters was history. We needed a new venue.

"Becky really liked you," Ivan said.

"Greg liked you too."

"Maybe he will stage his own death à la Chernyshevsky after all, and then we can get married," Ivan said. (Could I really imagine myself married to Ivan, a man who was not the father of my children?) We discussed whether or not our spouses' liking for each other made us feel more or less guilty. There was a part of me that was pleased Greg liked Ivan. It was a curious validation of my own good taste. It would have been worse somehow if the man with whom I was cuckolding him were someone he didn't respect; I needed his approval, even if he was unaware of giving it. Objectively, it was terribly immoral to have a relationship with each other's spouses, but it felt strangely natural to want the people who were important to us to like and even approve of each other.

"I want to spend the night with you," Ivan said, drawing my head onto his chest.

"Me too," I said.


It was becoming harder and harder to get up and dress and reenter our married lives. I drove toward home, feeling melancholy. WHY AREN'T YOU MY WIFE? Ivan texted me. I WAS JUST WONDERING THE SAME THING, I texted back. WE HAVE TO GET AWAY FOR A FEW DAYS TOGETHER, he replied. Even now my skin bore the memory of his touch; it was as if he touched me still. I clutched my mobile phone; it had become the umbilical cord that bound me to Ivan when we couldn't be together, permitting us the luxury of contact at any time. Textual intercourse, the next best thing. I guarded my phone jealously, never letting it out of my sight; it was the source both of my pleasure and, should it fall into the wrong hands, my potential downfall.

I phoned Dad.

"Who is this, please?"

I laughed; he always had the ability to cheer me up. "Why do I feel so sad after I've been with my lover?"

"A common phenomenon," he said.

"How can I even be discussing this with you? You're my father."

"You must have been very badly brought up. It's postcoital tristesse. Surely you know about that; it's a recognized syndrome, there's a French word for it and everything."

"That makes me feel better. One thing, Dad. Why am I bothered by Ivan's slight coldness toward his wife?" I told him about our dinner at FF's.

"Is that so surprising? He is having an affair with another woman, after all, so his marriage must hardly be perfect."

"True. It just worried me for some reason."

"There's a saying: You can know a man by how he is in his cups, how he is with money, and in his anger. Perhaps it should add: how he is with his wife."

"Yes. Well, that's what concerns me, although I suppose he could think the same thing about how I am with Greg."

"You're not planning on running away with him, are you?" Dad asked. I could hear a note of concern in his voice.

"No, of course not." Was I?

"Good. See you later then, darling." He was coming for supper.

How long could I go on like this? I lost myself in a reverie of possibilities. What if I were to divorce Greg? I didn't think I could bear those lonely Wednesday nights and alternate weekends assigned to fathers. What was that joke: *What does a woman think when she meets a man? Is that the man I want my children to spend every other weekend with?* I wasn't like that; as a Jewish mother, I was programmed to keep the family together at all costs. What if Greg were to disappear instead? You read stories like that in the papers all the time, quoting bewildered and abandoned wives, "He only popped out for a pint of milk, said he'd be gone ten minutes, and that was the last time I saw him; it's been seven months now." It was what his own father had done, after all. Perhaps such behavior was genetic. I was horrified by my disloyalty but comforted myself with the knowledge that I wasn't nearly as bad as Camus, who wrote that all normal people sometimes wished their loved ones were dead. I didn't want that, I had merely fleetingly wished for Greg to disappear. Of course I didn't really mean it, and these black thoughts were merely a sign that I loved Greg, weren't they? The thing was, I just wasn't *in* love with him anymore. I absentmindedly sang along to the car radio that Kitty always kept tuned to a pop station. It was a song about being a bitch and a lover, a sinner and a saint. I was in trouble; pop songs had become pregnant with meaning for me once again. The words summed up exactly what it was I'd been trying to tell Gina at her last session: a fundamentally good person is capable of bad behavior. It was an analysis that applied perfectly to me too.

As I turned into our road, I spotted Sammy helping Madge tie more rags to the railings outside her flat.

"I hang these here so Jimmy and Rosie will be able to find my house," Madge said. "They love all my silks and satins, they call them their treasure." She ran her fingers up and down the rich golds, reds, and purples of the fabrics, shimmering like flags in the breeze.

I put an arm around her shoulders, and was aware of her bony lack of flesh. I held her for a brief moment, surprised that she smelled fresh and clean, like rosewater. She lifted her head and looked at me with her clear green gaze.

"Be careful what you wish for, Chloe," she said at last.

Was she inside my head? I didn't really wish it, and anyway I'm not as bad as Albert Camus, I almost blurted back. Had she wished for a similar thing herself all those years before? Could she once have hoped that Reg would vanish and leave her free to love Armie?

She smoothed my hair out of my eyes with her soft hand. She looked old, her expression heavy with the sorrow of hiding from a truth for so many years by taking refuge in madness. The passage of time means nothing to memory, which brings events closer to us or pushes them farther away at its whim. Time is elastic, a thing of our imagining, and has meaning only in subjective experience. Seconds, minutes, hours, days, weeks, months, and years signified nothing to Madge. Her children's death was an event that had just occurred. Thirty-five years, the time that had elapsed since then, had done nothing to diminish either her pain or her loss. She was no more able to face reality now than she had been all those years before.

Madge took me by the hand and led me inside her flat. It was cleaner and neater than I expected: one big room with a bathroom off it. Papers and clothes were stacked neatly in piles, and a lonely cup and plate were draining next to the sink in the kitchen area. A tea towel celebrating a faded summer long ago in Bognor Regis hung neatly from a hook on the wall. A small single bed, a sign that all hope of intimacy had been abandoned, stood beneath the window. It had been carefully made and was covered with a threadbare blue and yellow patchwork quilt. By the bed was a small framed photograph. From where I was standing, I could just make out the smiling faces of two children, neatly dressed in round-collared coats. An ironing board occupied the center of the room; on it stood two piles of white knickers, one ironed, the other waiting its turn. Madge followed my eyes.

"It's very important to be clean. Very important. Children need a clean home."

Out of the corner of my eye I saw a movement; it seemed to mirror the pure white of Madge's laundry. It was a dove.

"He's got a message for me," said Madge. The dove flew over to her and settled on her shoulder; she stroked the back of its head with a forefinger and its chest puffed out with pleasure. Twitching its small black-eyed head from side to side, it emitted deep-throated cooing sounds.

"What's it saying?" I asked.

"Can't you hear?" she answered quietly. "He's saying *find Armie.*"

I looked at Sammy, who had come in quietly and was looking out of the window, holding himself very still and quiet in that Buddhist way of his. I was beginning to feel I had stepped into a remake of *Mary Poppins* with all this talking birds business and was half surprised not to see Dick Van Dyke come whooshing down the chimney to emerge sooty-faced from the fireplace, clicking his heels and singing in his mockney accent, but who knows, perhaps the birds really did talk to Madge.

Sammy and I left her with the promise that we would help her find Armie and set off arm in arm down the road together. As we walked, we quietly chanted one of Dad's old army marching rhymes to keep us in step.

*Left, left, I had a good job and I left.*
*Right, right, it serves me jolly well right.*

It occurred to me that I should have taught Ruthie this before she behaved in a manner that had led to her redundancy. Unfortunately, it was too late now.

"Can we invite Madge for Christmas lunch?" asked Sammy.

I'd barely thought about Christmas, and it was just over a week away. I'd have to go into whirling dervish mode to organize presents and food in time.

"Yes," I said, "of course. Let's just check with the others first."

We had a family confab at supper that night and everyone agreed that Christmas was a time for waifs and strays and Madge should be invited.

"What shall we eat this year?" asked Dad, as he did every year. "A goose?"

"Yuck, no thanks," said Leo.

"Too fatty," said Greg.

"In my country we always to have the carp fish on the night before the Christmas," said Bea.

I shuddered, recalling the oily carp that swarmed like piranha tearing at flesh in the reservoir near Sammy's tepee in Spain. It was a local sport, throwing stale bread into the water and watching the carps' feeding frenzy.

"If we're going to be such Jews for Jesus, why don't we go the whole hog, so to speak, and have roast suckling pig," Dad said.

"Very funny. No, we'll have turkey as usual, but I'll roast a ham too if it'll make you feel more irreverent," I said.

"And I make the carp fish for the night before," said Bea firmly.

I usually enjoyed Christmas, but I wasn't looking forward to it this year, as it would mean that Ivan and I wouldn't be able to see each other for at least a week. We'd be too firmly in the bosoms of our respective families. His son, in his final year at university, and daughter, who worked in Paris, were both coming home.

In the event, Madge didn't come. She told Sammy she had to stay in her flat in case Jimmy and Rosie came home, and he couldn't persuade her otherwise. After lunch (turkey and roast ham with all the trimmings), while the others lay bloated in front of the living room TV, I crept back to the kitchen to call Ivan.

"I want to hold you in my arms," he said.

"Me too. I'm really missing you."

"Come and meet me now, just for an hour," he said.

"It's impossible. It would look far too suspicious."

A noise behind me made me jump. It was Greg.

"OK then. Happy Christmas, talk to you soon," I said, far too brightly, and hung up.

"Who were you talking to?" asked Greg.

I could feel the color drain from my face and I was trying not to shake. I had to think fast.

"When? Oh, you mean just then? That was only FF calling to say hello."

"What would look too suspicious?" Greg said.

"What do you mean?" I feigned ignorance.

"I heard you say, *It would look too suspicious.*" He wasn't going to let this go.

"Did I? Oh, yeah. Um, she said why didn't I get some Botox for the New Year to look younger, so I said I couldn't because you'd be far too suspicious and notice immediately."

Not perfect, I grant you, since Greg rarely noticed anything about my appearance, but it seemed to appease him. He shrugged and put the kettle on for tea.

Can I go and stay in your tepee in Spain?" I asked Sammy later that evening, while I was making cold turkey sandwiches. He was playing the same few notes over and over on a small wooden pipe. He paused, took it out of his mouth, and ran his thumb up its smoothness.

"Mango wood," he said. "It's sacred to Hindus because Prajapati, the Lord of Creatures, was changed into a mango tree."

"Really," I said impatiently. I wasn't in the mood for Eastern mysticism.

"When Hindu believers die, their bodies are burned on pyres, and the firewood of choice is mango wood because it is supposed to have an everlasting heat."

"Lovely." I looked at him expectantly. "Well, can I go and stay?"

"Of course," he answered, raising his eyes to meet mine. "Alone?"

"Don't ask," I said. "It's much better if you don't know."

# Chapter 16

## GEM LETTUCE WITH GARLIC AND WALNUTS
### *Serves 2 as an appetizer*

*2 heads gem lettuce*
*10 cloves garlic*
*Olive oil*
*Balsamic vinegar*
*Walnut pieces*
*Salt and pepper to taste*

Wash and dry two heads of gem lettuce.

Roast ten unpeeled cloves of garlic in oven with olive oil (allow to cool).

Take a generous handful of walnut pieces.

Arrange lettuce in a bowl, squeeze garlic out of their skins and into the bowl, add the walnuts, and dress with olive oil and balsamic vinegar, salt, and pepper.

Especially delicious when each feeds the other by hand.

The light played on the Alpujarras mountains, transforming them into a giant's eiderdown, which rested in soft billows beneath the sky. Eight white windmills seemed to graze the horizon as they turned gracefully in the breeze, generating power for the valley below. The sky was a deep cloudless blue, and ripe oranges and lemons hung heavily on the trees that proliferated on the hillside. Ivan and I had met at the airport that morning, and now at last we were alone together. It had been easier to escape than I'd anticipated; I'd broached the subject of my going away to Greg while he was busy exchanging e-mails with his parking-fine chums. I explained I needed peace and quiet to finish a paper I was writing. He'd waved me away, saying, "Fine, fine, whatever you want. Can't you see I'm busy?" I'd chosen a week when Kitty would be away on a school field trip and Jessie was back with FF. Since the boys could manage very well on their own for a few days, it had caused minimal disruption to all. The lying was hard, although Greg's indifference had helped to alleviate my guilt. And, as Ruthie said, it was all part of Rule Seven: *Make sure you're strong enough to bear the guilt of deception.*

In the distance, the snowy peaks of the highest mountains were visible as Ivan and I wound our way up in our small rental car. Conversation had been temporarily suspended, and I watched his profile as he drove. "I can't talk when I'm driving," he had said. For, just like Greg and all the other men I have ever known, he could do only one thing at a time. (Like most women, I can drive, talk, shout at squabbling children in the backseat, balance a ball on my nose, and clap my flippers all at once.) Unlike Greg, however, he did permit me to touch him while he drove, and so I first stroked the back of his head, that warm place where the top of his spine meets the base of his skull, and then ran my hand along his long trouser-clad thigh, bringing it to rest at the top just by his crotch. It lingered there, heavy and warm with possibility. Ivan turned to look at me and wordlessly pulled over into a small space by the side of the road. He took my hand and pulled me up a mountain path and, after removing only as many clothes as strictly necessary, he made love to me right there and then against a tree. It was quick, urgent, and exciting: a tasty hors d'oeuvre before the more sensual main course that we would serve up for each other later.

That wasn't like Greg at all. I couldn't remember the last time he and I had had sex anywhere other than in our bed at night with the lights off. We never started fully dressed anymore. I remembered our first couple of years together, the hurried trail of clothes along corridors and stairs leading to the bedroom. Often we didn't get that far and would make love on the stairway, my back pressed against the sharpness of a step, Greg's knees covered in telltale carpet burns; we bore the marks of passion on our bodies with pride—our love-battle scars. With an extramarital lover, of course, Rule Eight applied: *Do not leave any visible marks.* Biting and scratching had to be kept to a minimum, lest their traces betray your secret.

Ivan and I arrived in Bubion and made our way up a steep hill on the edge of the village to the land where Sammy's tepee stood. The windows, of which Sammy was so proud, gave out onto a view of snow-capped mountains. The valley beneath us was green and lush in the benign Spanish winter, and a river was just visible below, languidly making its way toward the Mediterranean coast some 25 miles away. From the side of a rock, a small waterfall hurried to join it, filling the air with the hypnotic sound of rushing water. Ivan stood beside me, his arm around my waist, and hugged me to him. I loved the way his tallness dwarfed me. I felt delicate and fragile in his arms. We ran down the hill, arms flailing with the unself-consciousness of children, to the village shop. I felt suddenly embarrassed when I saw Jorge, the shopkeeper. What would he think, seeing me with this strange man? He'd seen me with Greg and the children on numerous visits and knew me as Sammy's sister. In my schoolgirl Spanish, I introduced Ivan as a colleague and explained that we had some business here for a few days. Jorge nodded and smiled, talking rapidly in his strong Andalusian accent, where the endings of words can only be guessed at. Comprehension was made even more difficult by the fact that Jorge had only two teeth in his gray-haired head, albeit incongruously white shiny ones, and always had a cigarette clamped firmly between his lips. His trousers were belted high on his waist; as his one concession to winter, he wore a cardigan over his customary short-sleeved shirt. His shop was an Aladdin's cave: balls of string jostled for space on shelves next to plastic toy dinosaurs, frying pans, spicy sausages, and fragrant cheeses. He had never disappointed us. If what you wanted wasn't available in the shop itself, he would disappear into his *almacén*, the adjacent storeroom, and produce what you needed from there, a magician conjuring a coin from behind an ear. We bought *jamon serrano*, bread, cheeses, and honey with nuts and, like squirrels readying themselves for winter, scurried back with them to our nest.

The inside of the tepee was cold but colorful. Mexican rugs and blankets covered the floor, and a soft fur rug engulfed the large double mattress that occupied the center. Ivan efficiently lit the small kerosene stove and the gas lamp, and we huddled beneath the blankets fully dressed, slowly removing our clothing as the joint heat of the fire and our mutual desire warmed us.

"Can I call you Givan?" I said. "It's just that my boyfriends' names have always begun with *G*."

Ivan laughed. "You can call me whatever you like, as long as you go on making me feel like I'm feeling now."

We lay feeding each other hunks of bread, cheese, and sausage and sipping strong red Rioja.

"When I was a teenager," Ivan said, "I read a novella by a nineteenth-century writer called Reshetnikov. It was about a peasant boy's love for his girlfriend. When she died prematurely, his sorrow and anguish at his loss was so great that he wanted to dig her body from the grave and bite the nose off her face. It sounds barbaric but understandable, this need to consume someone you love. I always wondered if I would ever find someone I felt like that about, and now I have." He leaned over me and kissed my nose, grazing it playfully with his teeth.

I knew what he meant. I too had the desire to possess him entirely. Ivan was so delicious, I wanted to eat him up and so I did, defiantly contravening one of the rules of the book according to Ruthie in the process, Rule Nine pertaining to fellatio: *Only swallow the first time and then you never have to again, but they always think you might.* I wanted to know everything about him, to make him mine and to belong to him too.

After we'd made love, Ivan drew my head onto his chest and told me how he and his family had lived in a crumbling prerevolutionary building a few streets away from Nevsky Prospekt in the heart of St. Petersburg. It was a communal flat, which they shared with another family. Listening to him made me feel I was living in the pages of an epic Russian novel. There were eight of them and one bathroom. He described their rooms, which still bore the marks of a former era, the faded glamour of Czarist times visible in its high windows and ceilings with their curlicued borders. It was on the third floor, and through the window you could see one of the many canals that had earned St. Petersburg the title of Venice of the North. Ivan's father was an artist, and the rooms they occupied smelled strongly of oil paints, a smell he would forever associate with childhood. Jars with brushes and smudged pieces of rag covered every surface in the kitchen, incurring the wrath of the disagreeable neighbors with whom they had to share it. I found it hard to contemplate sharing your home life with another family.

"We used to go to a small dacha in the country whenever we could," said Ivan. "It was just a simple wooden shack, but it gave us some privacy and meant we could make noise without fear of complaint. We would make a fire and cook shashlik in the open air."

"Let's do it here," I said sleepily.

He wanted to get up and start collecting pieces of wood and kindling to build his fire immediately, but I pulled him back to me and distracted him with kisses, reminding him of a different hunger. Afterward we lay together and I started to tell him about the holidays I had had with my parents and Sammy as a child, but after a few moments I realized from his breathing that he had fallen asleep.

For the next two days, I was on holiday from my life. Ivan and I walked through orange groves, kissing, and skidded stones over passing brooks. I watched the rise and fall of his breath as we slept entwined or spooned into each other's bodies, his hand moving between my legs in the middle of the night and rousing me to continue the lovemaking that sleep had briefly interrupted. In the morning, we awoke to the peremptory horn of the bread van as it made its way through the village selling freshly baked loaves, and in the evening we walked through the streets of nearby Granada and sat together by candlelight in the small tiled dining room of Los Manueles, feeding each other gem lettuce with garlic and walnuts.

"We could be so happy together, Chloe," Ivan said, feeding me a walnut with his fingers.

"I know, but think of how much hurt we'd cause."

"Lots of people get divorced."

"But I have this thing about families staying together. I think parents owe their children that."

"Don't you owe it to yourself to be happy too? I would devote myself to making you happy." He ran his hand down the side of my body, just barely touching my breast. Could I imagine myself living with Ivan? I was beginning to, but when I thought what would need to happen to make that possible, I felt a big lump of sorrow in my throat. Greg's and my lives, woven together over the course of the past seventeen years, would have to be dismantled, our house sold, possessions divided. I could imagine my ghastly forced jollity as I tried to sell the idea to the children of how much fun it would be for them to have two bedrooms, two houses . . .

On the fourth day I woke abruptly with a sense of unease in the pale light of dawn. I thought I'd heard someone calling my name, but Ivan was still fast asleep beside me. I curled into his body and tried to go back to sleep. I could hear the sounds of early morning: a cock crowing, ubiquitous Spanish dogs barking, a woman calling to her child: *"Gracia, ven acqui."* The bells of a nearby church chimed. It was seven o'clock. I got up quietly, picked up my mobile phone, and went outside, shivering in the morning air.

"Dad."

"That's funny, darling, I was just thinking about you and how much I'd like to hear your voice."

"What are you doing?"

"Pootling on the piano."

"Why do you think Mum died, Dad?"

"As you know, they never really found the reason. I know it sounds odd, but I think she simply didn't want to go on living any longer. She had a terrible and unreasonable fear of aging. It's such a waste. She missed so much of you and Sammy and, of course, her grandchildren."

"Do you think you'd have stayed together?"

"Hard to say, darling. I think so. Difficult as she was, I did love her, I just loved Helga too. Greedy of me, I know. That's the trouble with you and me, we want it all."

Ivan's face appeared at the entrance to the tepee. He looked like a schoolboy as he stood there yawning and rubbing his eyes, his hair standing on end.

"I've got to go, Dad. I'll be back tomorrow. Love you."

Ivan chased me back to bed, where we remained all morning, playing happily with each other's bodies before drifting off into the delicious doze of sated lovers.

Later that day, as we dressed, and I watched Ivan perform his bizarre ritual of stretching his socks before pulling them on (he didn't like the sensation of tight fabric around his feet and ankles), the thought flashed that this was precisely the sort of mannerism that could, with time, become irritating. We drove down to the coast at Salobreña and stopped for a drink at La Roca, a bar perched on a rock in the sea. The rock was a reclining centurion in profile, lying in the water, chest curving out beneath him, nose patrician.

"Can you see him, my rock man?" I asked Ivan.

"No. I see a crocodile on a log."

He described it to me, and I, in turn, outlined my prone soldier with a finger. We watched the sun, a fiery orange ball, as it sank below the horizon and disappeared from sight. To the right, a small fishing boat stood motionless, silhouetted in its vanishing glow; two figures, distant pin men, were visible on board. We were a romantic couple on a seaside postcard made flesh. Ivan took my hand over the table. "I love you," he said.

"Me too."

"Say it."

"*Liubliu tebia.*"

"*Po-angliiski.* Say it in English."

I opened my mouth to speak and paused, fearful, as if uttering these words might invoke a thunderbolt. I did love him, of course I did. I stroked his cheek with a finger and bent forward to kiss him by way of a reply. He held my face with both his hands and looked at me intently.

"Say it," he repeated.

*I love you,* I mouthed soundlessly. And I crossed the fingers of one hand behind my back, in the hope that this unique combination would ward off any impending thunderbolts.

# Chapter 17

## ƐDIE'S SPECIAL ƔUNA ƇASSEROLE

### *Serves 4*

. . . . . . . . . . . . . . . . . .

*One can of Campbell's cream of mushroom soup*
*⅓ cup milk*
*1 six-ounce can of tuna (packed in oil), drained and flaked*
*2 sliced hard-boiled eggs*
*1 cup cooked peas*
*1 cup potato chips (slightly crumbled)*

Preheat oven to 350°F. Blend soup and milk in a 1-quart casserole. Stir in tuna, eggs, and peas. Bake 20 minutes. Top with chips and bake 10 minutes longer.

When I arrived home, Greg was asleep on the living room sofa with the television blaring. Irritation rippled through me, each wave breaking farther up my body with the rising cadence of his snores. Notwithstanding the fact that I'd been away with another man, I'd somehow wanted him to be waiting to welcome me home, to save me from myself and the path I seemed intent on taking. I closed the door quietly and found Dad in the hall, pacing to and fro and shouting at someone on the telephone. It was the day before the Albert Hall performance of his *Prince and the Pauper* musical and, according to him, the identical twins playing the lead roles couldn't even sing in tune. On the hall table, I noticed a small glass with the sticky remains of something sweet in it. I picked it up and sniffed it suspiciously. It was Baileys, which could mean only one thing: Edie McTernan was *in da house.* This explained why Greg was asleep at 5 P.M., early even by his standards. I had forgotten she was coming for Dad's gala. I contemplated bolting straight out the front door, finding Ivan, and making him run back to Spain with me, far, far from all this, but Dad finished his call and led me firmly off to the kitchen, a jailer dragging a recalcitrant prisoner into a cell.

Edie was standing by the kitchen table, wearing an apron. She never traveled without at least two identical ones, freshly laundered and ironed. They were always decorated with miniature shamrocks to show her allegiance to the motherland, a country where she had never spent more than a few days at any one time. She would take off her coat and tie one tightly around her waist and get to work on some area of dirt that had offended her, muttering, "They live in filth," loudly enough for us all to hear. Leo was next to her, seated at the table, his head leaning back and his eyes closed. Edie was holding a pair of scissors near his eyes.

"What are you doing?" I screamed.

"Trimming his eyelashes," said Edie.

I snatched the scissors from Edie and, with difficulty, resisted the temptation to snip vengeful bald patches into her bottle-black hair.

"They make him look like a girl," said Edie huffily.

"Leo, what on earth were you thinking?"

Leo shrugged. "I thought if I looked more masculine, it might help me get a girlfriend."

"They're wasted on him. He looks like one of those what-do-you-call-thems, transvestials. In my day, men were men." Edie sniffed.

"This is still your day," I said.

Dad, seeking to calm matters, poured some more Baileys into Edie's glass, which made her giggle. It was a pleasure to watch Dad at work; he brought out the flirt in every woman he came in contact with, whatever her age. He loved the company of women, and they sank back into his easy charm as though into a warm scented bath.

"You should have a glass yourself, Bertie," Edie said coquettishly, downing hers in one. "No alcohol, you know."

I kissed Leo and hugged him to me, seeking to anchor myself home after my absence.

"Any presents?" he asked, as he has done since the age of two whenever I arrive home after an absence of more than a day. His eyes quickly registered the small bag in my hand bearing a slogan much beloved of my children, El Mundo de los Caramelos.

"Only the usual Spanish sweets, darling, I didn't have time for anything else."

Sammy walked into the room, spotted Edie, and kept right on walking, out through the French doors and into the garden to hide in his tent.

"No one told me you were home." Kitty's reproachful voice spun me round as she ran into the room to hurl herself into my arms.

"How was the field trip? Did you have fun? Were you warm enough? What was the food like?" The questions rushed from my lips as I held her to me.

"Fun-ish, but Molly was a bitch as usual and whispered about me on the coach on the way back. I'm glad I'm home. You look really pretty, Mummy. What did you do in Spain?"

I felt a stab of guilt, and an image flickered of Ivan, naked and intent above me.

"Nothing much. Tell me about your trip."

Kitty started to answer but was quickly interrupted by Edie, who launched into a long story about her neighbors Barbara and Derek and the minutiae of their lives. It seemed Derek had back problems and Barbara was finding it hard work coping with all the lifting and carrying that life necessitates, and last Tuesday, or was it Wednesday, just after the milkman had called for his money and before the washing machine man had arrived to have a look at her Hotpoint, a 1970s model that was playing up—and it's no use telling her to get a new one, these things should last forever—Barbara had come round for a cup of tea and to pour out her troubles to Edie, and Edie had told her it was all right for her, at least she had a man around the house, unlike Edie, who had been left on her own all those years ago.

"Go and wake your father," I hissed at Leo. I didn't see why I had to play the dutiful daughter-in-law while he shirked his responsibilities.

"Let the poor boy sleep," said Edie, patting my hand. "He looks exhausted, running the house on his own all week. He's got an awful cold too; has he been wearing his vest? You really ought to look after him better."

Like a salamander catching flies on its sticky tongue, I only just managed to catch the words *fuck, right,* and *off* as they were about to fly from my lips. Edie continued her monologue and the room emptied around her: first Leo, then Kitty, and then Dad, just barely suppressing a yawn. Finally, I stole away too, leaving Edie's incessant chatter to fall on the bewildered ears of Bea and Zuzi, who continued to sit at the table as though frozen.

"Promise me you will have me put down if I ever get like that," Dad whispered, as we ran away, sniggering like naughty schoolchildren bunking assembly.

I crashed noisily through the living room door.

"Lo for thy kingdom lies yonder, sayeth he," Greg announced, as he jumped and sat bolt upright.

"Oops! Sorry, darling, didn't know you were asleep." He tried to turn over, so I sat on him.

"Where is my mother?" Greg asked fearfully. I half expected him to get on a chair and cower, a man afraid of a mouse.

"Holding forth in the kitchen. Come on, we have to go in there."

He groaned. "I can't, it will kill me."

I hit him. Quite hard. "By the way," I said, climbing off him. "Hello. I'm back."

"Does that mean *I* can go away now?" he asked, flicking a fearful look in the direction of his mother's voice, which carried from the kitchen, a long, continuous, enervating hum. Then he looked at me appraisingly. "You look well. Nice time?"

"Yes, a good break. I mean, I got lots of writing done," I said, recalling the reason I'd given for going away.

He kissed me, a quick dry dutiful kiss, near but not quite on my mouth. This reminder of our chaste existence went some small way toward relieving the guilt that had threatened to overpower me after my reunion with my children. We went to the kitchen.

"On the Thursday—no, it can't have been Thursday, because that was the day I went into the town center and had a cup of tea with old Mr. Yates, who used to do the flower beds. Oh, there you are, Greg, you remember Mr. Yates?" Edie hailed us as we entered the room. "He's got five grandchildren now: Benny, David, Colin, Georgina, and—oh, what was the other one . . . tip of my tongue, tip of my tongue; it'll come to me in a minute. I was just telling these two about Barbara and Derek." Edie was still in full flow. Bea and Zuzi were both wearing the glazed look of a boxer who has been punched repeatedly in the face and is unsure how he has managed to remain standing. Dad had made a brave effort to return to the front line but was already looking around wildly for some means of escape.

"Has Dad told you about what's happening at the gala?" I asked Edie, trying to shut her up by passing the conversational baton to him.

"Yes and it reminds me of the father of a boy in Greg's class. This was a few years B.E."

Here her voice dipped to a hushed whisper as she alluded to Greg's father and his disappearance. "There was a boy in his class—Dickie was his name, I think—and his father. . . ."

A small cry of despair involuntarily escaped Greg's lips. He sounded just like Janet when I locked her up in the cat box to take her to the vet, trapped and desperate, unsure whether she would ever be free again.

Our arrival had the effect of breaking Edie's stultifying spell over Bea and Zuzi and jolting them back to life. They took in their surroundings like Rip Van Winkle awaking from his long sleep. Bea looked at Zuzi and brushed a strand of hair from her eyes with a tender finger.

"We have the news to announce," she said.

Edie opened her mouth to continue, but Greg held a hand up in front of her and said assertively, "Wait. Let's hear Bea's news." Bea was visibly nourished by the attention. She waited until we were all seated around the table and there was silence.

"Me and the Zuzi are getting married, and we would like all you for to come to wedding." Bea took her betrothed's hand and flourished the ring that glinted on her wedding finger. Zuzi flushed prettily, her eyes cast down, the fair maiden whose hand has been won fair and square.

"That's nice, dears," said Edie. "I hope you've both found nice young men. Are you having a double wedding?"

"They're marrying each other, Mother," said Greg.

"Don't be silly," said Edie, "they're both girls. Honestly, Greg, you do talk the most terrible nonsense sometimes. Did you know," she went on, without pausing for breath, "these days, most marriages end in divorce?"

Greg opened his mouth to speak again, but I gave him a look to silence him. What was the point?

"This calls for champagne." I interrupted Edie's divorce statistics and foraged in the fridge. "You and Zuzi will obviously be wanting to find a nice place of your own now," I continued, circumstances making an opportunist of me. "I'll help you find something." I avoided their eyes as I unscrewed the wire hood and removed the foil.

"You do not want us for to stay here?" Bea asked.

Kitty rushed over to Bea and sat on her lap. "She's only joking, aren't you, Mummy?" Kitty said. "She knows I couldn't bear it if you left us *ever*. When I'm grown up you can move in with me and take care of my children."

I lost control of the pop, and the cork hit the ceiling instead of exhaling, as it should, with a faint hiss in my hand.

"We stay," Bea reassured Kitty, stroking her hair. "Is our home where we have shared the happy times and the love."

She and Zuzi exchanged an intimate, fond look. I know I should have stood firm, but as with most working mothers, the fragile stability of my life revolved around the unsteady axis of paid help. Furthermore, I was aware of the potential damage, not only to Kitty but to Leo and Greg too, that my recent behavior, if discovered, would cause, and I didn't want to do anything further to upset the balance.

*Well, we'll see,* I thought with frustration, retreating in defeat from my attempt to oust Bea and Zuzi. *Let's see what happens after you get married, I wonder how* happily ever after *you two will live.* Would it be any different for same-sex couples? Same sex, different sex; the truth is, I suspected, after marriage there's precious little sex. Unless, of course, it's with other people. Would their love boat crash on the rock of daily trivia? I wondered sadly.

"I've made my tuna casserole," said Edie, pulling a foul-smelling dish from the oven. It was her specialty, a culinary delight from *her day*, the 1950s: canned tuna cooked in concentrated mushroom soup with potato chips crumbled over the top. Kitty and Leo gagged slightly as Edie laid a generous steaming portion in front of each of them. For Dad, Edie's culinary efforts were the final straw, and he made a great show of checking his watch, registering extreme surprise at the time, and hurriedly putting his coat on.

"Have something to eat before you go," I said mischievously.

"Wish I could, darling, but I've got to meet the director." He deftly parried my thrust and kissed me triumphantly. "See you all tomorrow, six-thirty; don't be late."

"We have to go too," said Leo. He and Kitty jumped up. "We said we'd help Grandpa."

"But I've just got back," I complained.

"You'll see them in the morning; sorry, but we arranged this weeks ago." Dad quickly whisked them to the tuna-free safety of the world beyond. Bea and Zuzi succeeded in cutting and running amid the general goodbyes. Of Sammy there was no trace.

"That's a shame. Never mind, Greggie, you can have theirs too," said Edie, setting Kitty and Leo's portions in front of him. Greg valiantly forced down a few mouthfuls. If Janet had been any kind of normal cat, he would have been able to decant food slyly into her bowl, where she would have gobbled it up gratefully, but she wasn't and so, when Edie wasn't looking and with the dexterity that comes of years of practice, he scooped most of it onto a napkin in his lap.

"Not for me, Edie," I said firmly. "I'm on a diet."

"Ooh, you have to take care after forty, Chloe," Edie said. "If you're too thin, you'll look scraggy; we older women have to stay a bit plumper for the sake of our faces. You know what they say: *visage* or *derrière?*" She nodded her head with pleasure as though inviting appreciation of her mastery of foreign words. Her pronunciation of *derrière* rhymed with *terrier*, but considering that Southern Ireland was the farthest she had traveled abroad, it was a wonder that she knew any French at all. Edie despised foreigners but liked to mimic some of their ways, thinking this lent her an air of sophistication and, as she would put it, *savvy fair.*

I resented being lumped into a group of older women with Edie and sharing the first person plural pronoun with her. I did not belong there; I belonged with the *we* of twenty-five- to forty-year-olds. That was my set. Or did you, after forty, automatically join an amorphous gang of forty- to eighty-year-olds?

"I'm really not feeling well," said Greg. He took his own health far more seriously than he did that of any of his paying customers, and now he looked as if he might be about to cry, but I suspected this was less to do with his physical state than with the sheer misery caused by his mother's presence.

"You go and lie down, dear. Chloe and I will clear up and have a nice long chat."

I looked at Greg as he left the room; he winked at me, a wink of victory. If my eyes had been capable of it, they would have fired poison-tipped arrows straight into his scheming heart.

I have always understood the word *chat* to imply a convivial exchange of news and views. This is not what happened next. Certainly there were news and views; but the exchange thereof was absent. Instead, I was the sole recipient of a barrage of information. The words that left Edie's mouth came at me in a steady stream; I felt whipped as by driving rain; whichever way I turned, more were waiting to lash me. I found my means of survival in the sending and receiving of surreptitious text messages to and from Ivan. "Sorry about this," I said to Edie as I tapped. "One of my patients." So, as Edie talked, Ivan and I engaged in textual intercourse and as a consequence of our increasingly sexually charged messages—the last of which, from him, had read I KEEP SEEING YOUR FACE AS YOU CAME WHEN WE MADE LOVE IN THE TEPEE THIS MORNING—Ivan and I agreed to meet in fifteen minutes. You wouldn't have thought it was possible to sit opposite your mother-in-law and have an erotic exchange with the man for whom you were betraying her son, but apparently it was not only possible, it was happening. I WANT YOU NOW, wrote Ivan. Our time away together had merely served to increase our appetite for each other.

"I'm so sorry, Edie," I said, getting up. "I have to go and see this patient. He's in a state of some agitation and can't wait until tomorrow." It was all perfectly true, except for the patient part.

Ivan's car was parked on the edge of the park at the entrance farthest from our house. He stood, a tall misty silhouette, haloed by the phosphorescent glow of a streetlamp.

"Did you know," I said, as I went into his arms, "it's illegal to tie a giraffe to either a lamppost or a telegraph pole in Georgia?"

"What about a beautiful woman you want to make love to? Can you tie her to one?" He smiled.

"Only if she lets you."

I burrowed into his coat and inhaled his scent of intimacy and desire.

"I want to be with you, Chloe. I want us to be together."

How had we arrived at this point so quickly? I said nothing but pressed my body into his. He kissed me. I loved these kisses, how our lips meshed together and our tongues lost themselves in each other's mouths in a way that was simultaneously a journey and a homecoming. I loved the feel and smell of him and the excitement of our bodies together. But could I sacrifice everything for this? His mobile rang. It was Becky.

"Yes?" he asked her, his voice cold. "What is it? . . . I told you where I put it." He hung up abruptly, without saying goodbye; he closed his eyes for a moment as though to clear himself of irritation and turned to me. He must have noticed my expression, for he said, "I would never speak to you like that, Chloe. You don't know what she's like; you don't know what it's like to live with her."

I felt uncomfortable. A sudden twist of the lens had brought into focus an image of him that fractured the Hollywood movie of our affair; a side of Ivan had been revealed that I would prefer never to see or know. We sat in his car, and as he kissed and caressed me my discomfort ebbed away. He was right, I didn't know what she was really like; no one *could* ever know what went on between two people. In the distance, through the car window, I could see Madge's familiar form walking along the park railing. I could just make out the white dove that she carried, cradled in her arms like a baby.

Ivan drove to a secluded spot, a dark mews that bustled with the trade of its garages by day and gave shelter to lovers by night. We made love in his car like teenagers, keeping most of our clothes on for warmth and discretion. There was no doubt about it; an illicit affair was a time machine that restored you to your youth—or at any rate gave you the illusion that it did. When we made love, I wanted to do it again before we had even finished doing it the first time, with all the greediness of a chocolate fanatic who craves a second bar while her mouth is still busy with the first.

"We'd be so good together, Chloe," Ivan whispered in my ear. "Just think about it."

"It's too soon for all this," I said tearfully.

"It's OK, it's OK." He stroked my hair and wiped my sudden tears away with a finger. "We can go on like this. Just promise me you'll think about it."

I felt afraid, as if I had swum into deep and unfamiliar waters, leaving the safe dry land of my normal life too far behind. It was as if I could see Greg, Leo, and Kitty waving to me from the remote shore and hear their increasingly thin cries entreating me to return as their figures grew ever smaller and I shrank to nothing more than a distant spot on their horizon. I struggled to return but was caught up in a current so strong that, try as I might, I couldn't swim back to them. The vision made me ache with misery. What I wanted was everything, no more and no less, my husband *and* my lover. Was it really so greedy of me to want them both? After all, isn't it unrealistic to assume you can find everything you need from life in one person? In France, extramarital affairs are an accepted part of life, with *cinq à sept* (*sinka cept*, as Edie would doubtless say, to rhyme with *except*) the hours set aside for the daily meeting of lovers, an institution. But I couldn't move us all to Paris and become French, and it was already some hours after seven and time I returned home.

"Heart, mind, and body," said Ivan, as I was getting out of his car. "Those are the areas where you need to fit each other. You tick all three boxes for me, Chloe." I was flattered, but I couldn't help feeling that this need to categorize and draw up lists was a uniquely male tendency: the way that men referred to a beautiful and desirable woman as a ten and always wanted to know your top five records or books or your favorite film. What would happen if the tick in one of Ivan's boxes grew fainter with the passing of years, leaving a dark smudge before ultimately morphing into a large black **X**?

"Didn't Becky once tick all your boxes?" I asked.

"Never really the heart box," he answered. He looked at me and rubbed his thumb over my mouth in a way that was both tender and a promissory note to be held on account until our next sexual encounter.

"I'll see you tomorrow night," he said, "at your father's gala." *The Times* was sending him to *cartoon* the event. I felt that newly familiar thrill of excitement and fear that occurred when my two lives collided.

I walked quickly home, searching in my pocket for my mobile phone to send Ivan some sweet punctuation to our tryst. I couldn't find it. I closed my eyes and saw at once, with shocking clarity, where I had left it: in plain view on the kitchen table with all of Ivan's earlier messages intact and ticking like a time bomb should anyone think to open them. I felt panic rising in me, keeping pace with the accelerating click of my every step. Greg was asleep; he had escaped his mother by going to bed. Edie wouldn't know how to access messages. It's all right, it's all right, no one will have seen it, I repeated to myself like a mantra. I ran the remaining fifty yards home.

"Is that you, Chloe?" Greg's voice came up from the kitchen to greet me with all the reassurance of a siren shrieking. I took my coat off slowly and looked at myself in the mirror. Did I look like a woman who'd just had sex? Guilt seemed etched in my every pore: my eyes shone, my hair was sticking up at the back as it always did after the friction of enthusiastic intercourse. I brushed it down, straightened my clothes, took a deep breath, and went downstairs.

*Please let him not have looked at my phone and I promise I'll never do it again,* I lied to the God in whom I didn't believe. Greg was sitting at the table with Sammy. My phone lay on the table between them; it throbbed there radioactively, malignly, mockingly. *Really,* it seemed to say. *Page one: Keep your phone with you at all times. How hard is that?*

Greg's eyes seemed full of a silent question, but perhaps that was simply my guilt. "Where have you been?" he asked. Was there an edge to his voice?

"Had to talk a patient down from the ledge," I said. "She's freaking out because she's getting married." I was talking too much and too fast. I resisted the temptation to clamp my lips together with my fingers and with an effort of will forced myself to shut up.

"Not like you to make a house call," Greg said. Was he suspicious? Had he read my messages?

"It was either that or stay here listening to your mother," I retorted. He couldn't argue with that.

Sammy went off into the garden to his tent. His face told me that he knew exactly what I'd been up to. No doubt he felt his continued presence implied a collusion he was unwilling to enter into.

"Oh, here, you left your phone." Greg handed it to me.

"Thanks," I said carelessly, using all my self-control to keep my breathing steady. "I'm off to bed. Coming?"

"I'll be up in a minute."

It was far too suspicious to take a shower in our bathroom, and with Edie asleep in the bedroom next to my consulting room the basement bathroom was off limits too. I had to make do with washing myself as thoroughly as a face flannel would allow, a *flannie wash*, Kitty used to call it, when she was little and didn't want a bath. Her childish phrase rang in my head incongruously. I felt whorish, a working girl between tricks, out of a car with one man and into bed with another. Still, I reasoned, at least one thing was certain; Greg wouldn't want to have sex.


Greg rubbed his foot up and down my calf; he reached for me and took me in his arms. Tonight of all nights, and after more than a year. I wish I could say I found it difficult to make love to my husband after having left the arms of my lover. But even after all this time it felt like a perfectly natural thing to do. Was Greg reclaiming his territory? Was he spraying his scent over me in the hope of keeping me for his own? Whatever the reason, it was comforting to be in his arms. Why couldn't I just stay there and be happy instead of wanting something more or

# Chapter 18

## ZHIVAGO'S REVENGE RECIPE

........................

½ ounce Stolichnaya Pepper Vodka
½ ounce cinnamon schnapps
3 drops Tabasco

Pour ingredients in order into a chilled shot glass and stir. Best served ice-cold.

something different? *If one were to look on life as a si*
*perhaps be less exacting.*

"Are you happy, Chlo?" Greg asked, as we lay in
afterward.

I wanted to ask him why we hadn't had sex for so
vous of where the conversation might lead. Did he ki
up to earlier and that I hadn't gone to Spain alone?

"Happy-ish," I said. "I just wish we could be lik
beginning, full of the wonder of each other. What al
happy?"

"I'm fine. This is what life is. It can't all be breath
every turn."

I looked into his familiar blue eyes, inhaled the (
nodded, and fell asleep in his arms. I was only allowe
a few minutes before he began his usual nighttime
aloud and invoking unseen deities.

*A strange thing*, I thought, as I spooned him, *but mine*

We posed by the front door on our way out to Dad's gala and, pressing a camera into his hands, asked a passing stranger to record for posterity the tableau of our première finery.

"You're still a very attractive man, Greg," Edie said, looking him up and down as we walked to the car. "You'd better keep your eye on him, Chloe. I remember when he was just sixteen. This was quite a few years A.E., of course. . . ."

The rest of her reminiscences were drowned out by Kitty and Leo, who began squabbling over who should sit where. Sammy's face wore an absent, detached look, the result, perhaps, of too many words engulfing him with the force of a tidal wave.

"You've got your mountain face on," I said.

"The peace of the Alpujarras," he said. "I'm missing my tepee."

"I'm missing your tepee too."

"Yes, but I suspect your reasons are rather different from mine," he said.

We'd barely rounded the corner by the park when Kitty leaned over me from the backseat. I thought she was going to stroke my hair as she used to when she was little and sat behind me in the car.

"You're skirt's too short at the back, Mum," she said. "It's disgusting. I can nearly see your bum."

Hmm, maybe I should have worn long after all. The knowledge that Ivan would be there was making me feel nervous enough as it was. But there is nothing like the disapproval of a twelve-year-old for destroying the fragile confidence of the older woman.

Dad was standing outside the foyer when we arrived, seal sleek in black tie, his silver hair combed back. Only the hair of his eyebrows, escaping wildly in all directions, gave an indication of how he was feeling. Helga, tall, elegant, and newly arrived from Berlin, stood by his side. She was still beautiful in her seventies and shone with a self-assurance born of a lifetime of admiration. For my own sake, I wished Dad had brought her into our lives more; I would have liked a mother figure, having been prematurely deprived of one. But this wasn't about me, and her absence from the humdrum routine of daily life was precisely the point. Tonight was the first time she had appeared on his arm at a public event, and the sight of them together made me hang back. I had never seen my father partnered with anyone but my mother. He looked more at ease beside Helga, not poised for flight as he had always seemed next to Girlie, fearful of the fluctuating emotional weather she brought with her, which caught all who came near in its unpredictable downpours or sudden bursts of sunshine. Helga had a steadiness to her, discernible in her soothing hand on my father's arm and the absorbed inclination of her head toward his.

The paparazzi were out in force, ladders clutched competitively to their sides, heads swiveling hungrily as they sought their prey. Tickets for the event had sold out the first day they went on sale, and the presence of London's celebocracy was eagerly anticipated.

I was moving toward Dad and Helga when I heard an irritated voice behind me. "Isn't that Kitty McTernan's mother? What on earth is *she* doing here?" I turned to see Mr. and Mrs. Fractions, Molly's parents. My presence seemed to affront them, as if in some way it diminished their own appearance at this fashionable event. No doubt Mrs. Fractions was still smarting from Kitty's and my Chocolate Cake coup.

"Phil's bank are sponsoring the event," she told me, before I could say anything, implying an ownership of the occasion and tacitly inviting me to explain my presence. She glanced around the growing crowd as though seeking someone more worthy of her attention. "But then I've always followed Bertie Zhivago's work. I'm a huge fan. As a matter of fact, I've met him several times."

Very occasionally life affords you the perfect opportunity for revenge. All those years of feeling scorned on the playground had been worth it for this: an unusually warm January evening in London's Shaftesbury Avenue, when I was able to savor the moment before saying these five simple words: "Bertie Zhivago is my father."

Mrs. Fractions looked me up and down as though seeing me for the first time. "I didn't know that."

"Yes, well, it's hard to make the connection," I said caustically, "what with there being so many Zhivagos around these days. Although," I allowed grudgingly, "since Kitty's surname is McTernan, you probably didn't know that mine is still Zhivago."

I was about to warn her to take better care in the future to determine whom it was that she was snubbing but that was when Dad arrived by my side. He put his arms around me, turned me to Helga, and said, "Here's my beautiful daughter, Chloe."

Out of the corner of my eye, I could see the Fractions opening and closing their mouths like goldfish.

"Dad, Helga, this is Phil and Jane, they're parents of a girl in Kitty's class." (I was so used to thinking of them as Mr. and Mrs. Fractions, I couldn't remember their actual surname.)

"How lovely to meet you both and how kind of you to come," Dad said. It was quite clear that he had never met them before or, if he had, had no memory of any such meeting.

Jane looked as though she might faint with gratitude and shame and although my act of generosity in introducing them had initially been intended as a vengeful rubbing of their noses in the excrement of their own discourtesy, I was pleased that I had done it. Their noses were about to be rubbed further anyhow, I realized, as I heard Dad shout, "Ruthie, over here, my darling! Let me kiss you; you look wonderful." Jane watched, horrified, as Dad hugged Ruthie, whom she had also deemed unworthy of her attention, looked at us both, and said, "You two are as beautiful as when you were eighteen." Ruthie did indeed look radiant in a tight red dress that clung to her curves, Richard, Atlas, and Sephy by her side.

"Just saying no to the Colombian marching powder seems to be doing you a world of good," I whispered, as I kissed her. She squeezed my hand, took in the Fractions, whose gaping mouths were reduced to perfectly round zeros, and greeted them as magnanimously as a queen might her loyal subjects. Revenge was sweet. We swished past them to make our way down the red carpet and into the foyer, to the flashes and calls of the paparazzi.

Leo, a man/boy in a tuxedo, willing slave to the great god iPodicus, walked the walk of the home boy on his native streets of Harlem to a rhythm only he could hear. Kitty pulled my skirt down from behind. "Honestly, Mum, you're so embarrassing." Family patterns repeat themselves unavoidably, however much you may try to escape them: Like my mother before me, I simply didn't dress as a mother should. Or perhaps no mother can ever dress or behave in a way that will satisfy her daughter. I looked at Kitty, enjoying the sight of her earnest little face; she seemed caught motionless, briefly suspended between childhood and womanhood; I could see simultaneously the baby she had been and the beautiful woman she would soon become. A familiar profile caught my attention. (In truth, I'd been surreptitiously on the lookout for it ever since we'd arrived.) Kitty followed my gaze and gave me a brief hard look, at once knowing and quizzical, a woman's look. It was Ivan. I felt my breath quicken, as much with the fear of what Kitty might know or suspect as with the pleasure I always felt at seeing him.

I found myself standing between my husband and my lover as they shook hands and engaged in the sort of gruff confrontational joshing that men enjoy.

"I see, like me, you can still safely wear your shirt tucked into your trousers," said Ivan, patting his own crisp flat white shirt.

"Not many of us left. I weigh the same as I did twenty years ago," Greg answered smugly.

"You're on a tightrope with no safety net, Chloe," Ruthie murmured beside me. "Just keep your nerve and don't look down."

The evening was a curious confluence of the many parts of my life: my husband and children at my side; my father and his hitherto hidden mistress; my mother-in-law; my brother; my best friend with her family; my lover and his wife; the school bully's hateful parents; and now, in a rising crescendo of whistles and cries of *Over here! Lizzie, look this way!*, and *Just one more!* I could see my Famous Friend making her way toward us as flashbulbs exploded and voracious photographers captured her image on cameras thrust at her like weapons. FF was in her element, the attention a welcome sun that warmed her upturned face; her eyes were half closed, her lips parted as though in ecstasy. This was to be her first public outing with Jeremy, and she wore sexual fulfillment on the easy swing of her hips as she declared to the world that her celibacy was a thing of the past. She might just as well have arrived as Lady Godiva, naked on a horse to advertise being back in the saddle. Jessie trailed behind them, her eyes searching the pavement as if she might find some meaning to her own neglected existence in the cracks between the flagstones.

"He's even stolen my name," she told me, as they joined us. "She calls him Jezzie."

"Hello, darling," said FF, kissing the air around my head.

"I see you've had time for another little procedure," I murmured.

"Lipodissolve. It literally dissolves the fat away. They don't do it here yet; I had to pop over to Paris for the day. It's brilliant, you can do it in your lunch hour and go straight back to work." She glanced at Jeremy, who had his back to us, and added, "or to play. You should try it on your sticky-out tum."

"What tum?" I said complacently.

"What happened to it?" FF narrowed her eyes and studied me closely.

Jeremy turned around. I took a proper look at him and gasped. He was none other than God's Gift; I'd forgotten his real name was Jeremy.

"Oh, yes," said FF, following my gaze. "Jezzie told me earlier that you two know each other." She leaned forward and whispered in my ear. "He thinks you've got a bit of a thing for him, actually. Where did you meet?"

In the distance I could hear a car alarm, an irritating repetitive shriek that seemed to herald either an end or a beginning of something. It filled me with a sense of apprehension.

I took my seat and breathed in the heightened aroma peculiar to a large important event. The string section was tuning up and the orchestra shifted in their seats like restless circus horses pawing the earth; best

224 · Olivia Lichtenstein

frocks in peacock-bright colors rustled, and people called to one another in voices that were accustomed to being heard. We were right in front and I was holding Dad's right hand. He nervously counted my fingers in a ritual game we'd played together ever since I was a child. After each counting, I would hide another finger until none remained. He would first feign astonishment, at the disappearance of all my fingers, and then relief as, one by one, I made them reappear.

His hands were warm and dry, instruments he had always used to play the steady notes of parental love. As a child they had soothed me to sleep, wiped away my tears, and expressed his love; I had never seen them raised in anger, toward me or anyone else. But for tonight I was the reassuring parent whose hands soothed.

"Remind me never to do this ever again," he murmured. "It's bound to be a complete disaster."

"You always say that, Dad, and it's always a huge success," I said, kissing his cheek. I caught Helga's eye as she pressed his left hand to her lips from where she sat on his other side. We looked at each other and smiled shyly. Helga leaned across Dad and squeezed my arm.

"Bertie talks about you all the time, Chloe," she said. "He's so proud of you." She was so warm that I felt a sudden urge to cry and explain my complicated life to her and ask for her guidance.

"You and Helga should get to know each other better," said Dad. I smiled and nodded, thinking uneasily that if I did get to know her I might like her more than I had my mother.

I turned around and saw Ivan looking at me from the row behind. Becky was sitting next to him, her face pinched and miserable, her body kept carefully separate from his as if physical contact could wound her.

"He's not very nice to her," Kitty said suddenly.

"Who isn't?" I turned to her beside me; she had been watching me watch them.

"That Russian man you keep looking at. He's not very nice to his wife."

I affected casual indifference. "Mmm, really, darling."

"He told her she was like a heavy wet towel round his neck. I heard him."

"You're right, that isn't very nice," I said. The same dissonant note that always played when I observed Ivan with Becky sounded loudly in my head. Could he really be so nasty?

"I think he fancies you," said Kitty. "He keeps looking at you in a funny way. You're not going to have an affair, are you?"

"Don't be silly, darling." The reassuring warm chuckle I had intended came out all wrong and sounded like glass breaking.

"Only Lucy Gray's mum had an affair and her dad found out so her parents got divorced and now she never knows where any of her things are because she has to live in two different houses."

I hugged her so she couldn't see my face and was saved from replying by the curtain's going up. A clash of cymbals signaled the overture and awakened me for the first time to the full enormity of my actions. I was risking the happiness of my husband and children for a man who wasn't very nice to his wife. How long would it be before he started being not very nice to me? If Kitty suspected me, what must Greg think? I looked at Greg, seated next to Kitty. Despite our rare intimacy of the night before, he had the distant familiarity of an often-seen stranger, like the man you might pass each morning on the way to the bus.

The audience's applause brought me back to the present and I turned my attention to the stage. It was divided into two halves: one half was a royal court, rejoicing at the birth of a baby prince; the other a pauper's home where the family was ruing the unwanted arrival of yet another mouth to feed. The contrast between the opulence of the one household and the poverty of the other was exquisitely realized; all plush velvets, candles, and sumptuous clothes on one side and dirty barren squalor on the other. It seemed to reflect my life, or at least the way I perceived it: the sensuous plushness of my relationship with Ivan contrasted with my increasingly impoverished relationship with my husband. I was poor little Tom Canty, my nose pressed up against the bars of the palace gate longing for a life of plenty, only to gain it and find it brought nothing but trouble. Like Tom, I had found that the thing I had wished for was not quite as I had dreamed it. I longed for the simplicity of my former life, where I'd had no need to tiptoe in secret shadows, ever fearful of the glare of imminent discovery.

Dad had been clutching my hand tightly, and now seemed to relax a little as he sensed the warmth of the audience's response.

"It may still be touch and go, but so far it looks like it's not going to be a total fuckup after all," he whispered.

"When will you realize it never is?" I said.

"When I'm dead."

"Stop it, Dad, don't say that."

I lost myself in the music and movement. It was a relief to throw myself into the story on stage and escape my own.

At the interval, we all crowded into a VIP room for Zhivago's Revenge, lethal and aptly named cocktails. God's Gift was standing by the entrance and gave me the sort of knowing smirk that suggested we had unfinished business while simultaneously admiring his own reflection in the pane of glass behind me. What on earth could FF see in him beyond physical gratification? Although, given his self-absorption, it was hard to imagine he could be a generous lover. A young journalist was standing next to FF, translating every word she uttered into spidery shorthand soon to be immortalized in print. She nodded earnestly like a woodpecker and gave an excited little acquiescent "Mmm" with each peck. FF was holding forth about her yet-to-be-written next book.

"Sex," she was saying, "is very important for a person's energy. It is our fuel; just as a full tank of petrol allows a car to travel a certain number of miles, so too satisfying sex gives us the energy to live our busy lives. Like a car, a human being has to refill regularly to run optimally."

"But wasn't your last book about celibacy?" the journalist asked.

"Yes, but that is the first part of the process, a cleansing of the person—or of the engine, if you will—at the end of one relationship, where you learn to love yourself again before taking on the fuel of the next new relationship."

"I don't think it's like that at all," I interjected. "Sex doesn't fuel you for ages like petrol does a car, quite the reverse. I think it's like eating a huge meal and thinking you can never eat again, and then waking up the next morning to find you are absolutely ravenous. The more sex you have the more you want." FF was looking at me as if I were the pope pontificating on the joys of sexual union.

"Anyhow," I added hastily, "what do I know? I've been married to the same man for a hundred years and have so little sex I'm probably technically a virgin again."

FF was still looking at me curiously: if sexual fulfillment oozed from her every pore, who was to say that it didn't from mine? I could see Ivan a few yards away. He brushed past me and pushed a note into my hand.

*Meet me in the box two doors down.*

"What's that?" asked Kitty, creeping up on me.

"Nothing, a bit of paper, that's all."

"*He* gave it to you, didn't he?"

"Will you stop it?" I said, with the defensive anger so familiar to the rightfully accused when caught red-handed.

"Where are you going?" said Kitty as I moved away.

"To the Ladies."

"I'll come with you."

Kitty insisted on walking right behind me to the Ladies, ostensibly to keep my skirt pulled down so that it covered my bottom, but it felt more like being under police escort. I was ashamed that her anxiety made her scared to let me out of her sight. I closed the door of my cubicle and heard an odd snuffling noise from the one next to it. Bending down to look under the partition, I was met with the sight of a nose with a straw up it sniffing up something from the floor. The ring on the finger holding the straw looked familiar.

"Ruthie, what are you doing?"

The nose and the finger jerked out of view. I stood on the lavatory seat and looked over into the next cubicle. Ruthie was on her hands and knees, caught in flagrante as she tried to sweep up scattered white powder onto a square of paper.

"What the fuck are you doing?"

"Chloe! You frightened the life out of me. Look, I was just having a little sharpener and dropped the fucking stuff all over the floor. It seemed safest to simply hoover it up with my nose."

"You promised me you'd stopped."

"I have, really. I haven't had one for ages. It was just one teensy little line to go with my glass of champagne."

"We'll talk about this later." I glanced over to the washbasin area where Kitty was drying her hands. Sephy came in, and a few moments later the two of them skipped out together, Kitty's surveillance of me temporarily forgotten.

As I made my way to the box to meet Ivan, I couldn't help but feel that my life had veered dangerously out of control. How could I even like myself, a woman whose own child suspected her of having a lover? That felt far worse than deceiving a husband. The understanding of how my actions were affecting those I loved, combined with Greg's repossession of me the night before, had finally brought me to my senses. It seemed portentous that Ivan's note inviting me to the box was the first one he had ever written me in English, and I knew with sudden clarity what I had to do—and do immediately—before I lost my nerve.

I sensed him before I saw him; standing to one side in shadow, and for a moment I wanted nothing more than to float in the scent of him. He stepped forward to touch me and I pulled myself back with an effort.

"This can't go on, Ivan," I said. "I just can't do this anymore."

"Shh, shh," he said, stroking my face.

"Don't," I said. "Please. We must stop."

"I want you, Chloe," he said, as he tried to pull me against him. "I want you all the time."

"It's over," I said, folding my arms in front of me. "I can't see you anymore, I just can't. It's different for me. Your children have left home, but mine haven't. They need their mother and father; they need to be part of a proper family. I can't do this to them; it's just not fair. Please understand."

Ivan looked at me. He shut his eyes tightly, and when he opened them again something had closed in his face.

"I am not a man who likes to beg," he said. I looked at him, and it was as though we had suddenly become strangers to each other. He took a step away from me, and I turned and ran from the box, fat messy tears gouging muddy footprints through my makeup. All I had wanted, I thought self-pityingly, was to live a little, and now misery was unpacking its bags and settling in for a lengthy stay in my gut. I ducked behind a pillar at the sound of Greg's voice. He was explaining the story of *The Prince and the Pauper* to Edie with the sort of controlled patience that is barely contained exasperation.

"It's a case of mistaken identity. Tom's not doing it deliberately. He tried to tell everyone that he wasn't the prince, but they refused to believe him and now he's trapped."

"But can't they see he's not him?"

"No. He and the prince look identical."

"Oh. Is that why the palace guard made the real prince leave the palace, because in Tom's rags he looked like Tom?"

"That's it, Mother, now you've got it."

"I had wondered about that. It didn't seem like a very wise thing for the guard to do."

I remained hidden until after the bell and made my way back to my seat in that brief interval of darkness between the lights coming down and the curtain going up.

"We were looking for you, darling," Dad whispered.

I squeezed his hand and then took it and made his fingers start to count my own. . . .

When the closing number of *The Prince and Pauper* rang out, I sneaked a look at Ivan. He was rigid, staring resolutely ahead, his sketchbook gripped in his hand. The illusory palace of my languorous lovemaking was lost to me, a flicker of light receding to a pinpoint before vanishing altogether. I was back with Tom Canty in Offal Court, destined for a life of emotional starvation and sensory deprivation. Well, that may be putting it a bit strongly, but even though I knew I'd done the right thing, that's what it felt like.

The twin boys playing the future Edward VI and Tom Canty took the stage hand in hand and sang:

*"Never judge a book by its cover,*
*Never say you see what's not there,*
*Never give your heart to another,*
*Never eat a crust you can't share."*

They sang in perfect harmony; Dad's earlier fears about their talent had been unwarranted. The house thundered with applause as the curtain came down and Dad went up on stage to take his bow.

"Thank you, everyone," he said. "I must admit, when I was first told there was to be this gala performance to mark my fifty years in musical theater, I thought, My God, they must all know something I don't."

He paused. The audience looked up at him, their faces full of affection.

"You must all have noticed," Dad continued, "that any recognition or celebration of a lifetime achievement in showbiz is a prequel to death. I'm sorry to disappoint you all, but I plan to stick around for quite a few years to come."

The audience roared with laughter, applauded, and stood up. I looked at the small figure of my father standing alone on the big stage and shivered. I put my arm around Greg. "Stop it," he said, shrugging me off. "That tickles."

# Chapter 19

## HELGA'S QUICK AND EASY APFELSTRUDEL

*1 pound sweet apples, peeled, cored, and thinly sliced*
*¼ cup golden raisins*
*¼ cup dried currants*
*½ teaspoon ground cinnamon*
*2 tablespoons superfine granulated sugar*
*2 slices stale brown bread, crumbled into bread crumbs*
*1 4-ounce package filo pastry dough (life is too short to make*
  *your own)*
*¼ cup butter, melted*

In a bowl, combine apples, raisins, currants, cinnamon, sugar, and bread crumbs; stir well. Spread several sheets of pastry dough generously with melted butter and lay them on top of one another on a baking sheet. Spread the fruit mixture evenly over the top sheet, then roll up the sheets to form a log. Brush the top with melted butter. Bake in oven preheated to 380°F for 30 minutes, until pastry is golden brown and fruit is tender.

I must have drunk at least two bottles of champagne at the after-show party. Greg and the children had left almost immediately, dragging a reluctant Edie behind them. She was knocking back Baileys with wanton delight and was on her fifth or sixth; one more and she would have been singing "Danny Boy." She had pinned a woman against the wall and was showering her with inconsequential chatter. The woman's eyes were darting around desperately.

"Stay," I'd said to Greg, as he went to the woman's aid.

"I've seen Bertie and congratulated him. I can't be bothered with the rest of them, a bunch of self-obsessed luvvies all doing the moi-moi-moi thing. I want to go home and write to the council about their proposed plan to increase speed bumps in the area. The way they're going, we might as well give up cars and become bloody show jumpers instead."

"Hey, you're a fun guy."

"Just because you want to stay doesn't mean I have to want to."

"No, you never do anything you don't want to do. God forbid you should do anything to please someone else."

"For God's sake, Chloe, are you looking for a fight?"

"It might be nice if I could occasionally be at a party with my husband instead of always on my own. I might as well not be married at all," I'd said, my voice getting a little too loud.

"I'm really not in the mood for this. I'll see you in the morning." He'd turned away from me and left.

Ivan hadn't come to the party at all; we'd exchanged a last lingering pain-filled look in the theater foyer. He'd pushed his body up against me in a way that felt full both of longing and reproach as he bustled Becky out.

"I thought we were going to the party," I heard her say.

"You go. I'm not in the mood."

"No, no, I'll come home with you, darling."

I'd seen him smile tightly and turn away from her. Poor Becky, she tried so hard and got so little back. And yet, they must once have been happy, lost in each other, drowning happily in kisses and caresses and whispered words of love just as Greg and I had been. How corrosive time was to a relationship, slowly nibbling away at affection and desire until all that remained was habit and obligation. Was it a question of having married the wrong person? Or would you end up feeling detached from whomever it was you had married?

At the party, I saw Lou in a corner with a bald man. It was Gus Fallick, or should I say Les. He'd had hair when we were together and I would never have known him, but for the familiarity of the way his neck inclined toward Lou. Our brains store intimate memories of a lover's gait and movement, the way he laughs and kisses, long after the intimacy has expired. What would I remember most about Ivan? I wondered. The way he urgently took possession of me, his smile after we'd made love, the intentness of his gaze when he talked to me? Les was whispering in Lou's ear, and she flushed as he spoke, her chest rising and falling quickly. I was about to go over and find out if he recognized me when I saw Lou leave the room, followed almost immediately by him. They were on a mission; his verbal gifts were obviously still working their magic. Memory told me he must have laid the groundwork in whisper form and now completion would follow urgently in some dark and discreet corner. What if I'd married him? Would that have been any better or worse than marrying Greg? But then of course I wouldn't have Kitty and Leo, so for that reason alone, I could never regret marrying Greg. I thought of Ivan and how we'd parted earlier that evening. I clenched my fists, digging my nails into the palms of my hands in an attempt both to externalize the pain and to stop myself from crying. I had condemned myself to my marriage.

"What is the point of husbands?" I asked Ruthie, as she walked past.

"That's a tough one, I'll have to get back to you."

I gulped the rest of my champagne, helped myself to another glass, and took a canapé of bread and dripping from a waiter dressed in rags. All the Prince canapés, the caviar on small black squares of pumpernickel, had been gobbled up, and now all that remained were the Pauper ones.

I went over to Dad, who was surrounded by a crowd of well-wishers.

"It was wonderful, Dad, I'm so proud of you." I hugged him and then quickly took the opportunity to slip away when someone came up to talk to him, fearful of disgracing myself by bursting into drunken tears and ruining his finest hour. There are times when you can't expect your parents to kiss you and make everything better.

"Come on," said Ruthie, who had spotted me swaying toward the exit. "I'll take you home."

"The thing is, Ruthie, people often decide it's time for them to get married, and they marry whoever they happen to be with at that moment," I said, as though we were already in the middle of a conversation. "So you don't necessarily marry the right person, you just marry the person who's there. You know, the one you might be going out with at the moment you decide it's time to get married."

I was not only repeating myself but also slurring my words slightly and hiccuping.

"I mean, you could just as well have married the person you'd been going out with before, but you weren't thinking of getting married then, so you didn't. But now, suddenly, you decide it's time to get married, so you do; you just marry the person you happen to be going out with at that moment."

Ruthie kindly pretended that I was talking sense. "There's some truth in that. I think everyone does reach a time when they decide they should settle down, but unless you're unlucky enough to choose a violent or mad partner, you probably have just as much chance of finding happiness with one person as you do with another, which is why arranged marriages aren't necessarily a bad thing. You know, I've come to the conclusion that it doesn't much matter whom you marry as long as they're from an appropriate pool of people." She looked at me keenly. "We'll be all right, Chloe, really we will. We're both having a bit of a crisis; it's just a blip. Carry on seeing Ivan if it helps you get through it, but be discreet."

"But I finished it with him. I told him I didn't want to see him anymore, and now I feel so sad. I've spoiled everything, and I'll never be happy ever again." I started crying in great noisy gulps.

I'm not entirely sure what happened after that, but Ruthie must have got me home somehow. I woke up the next morning, a Sunday, alone in an empty house. I phoned her to fill in some gaps.

"Do you have any idea where my husband might be?"

"He's in the park with Richard, all the kids, and his mother, looking like one of those stone statues on Easter Island."

"Stern, immovable, and permanent?"

"That's the one."

"Would you say that this stonelike demeanor is a result of his mother's presence or of his wife's behavior?"

"I would think a little bit of both."

"Fuck. I might have to run away from home."

I got up and drifted around. The kitchen was spotless—a silent reproach. Edie had been hard at work in her apron. I didn't know what to do with myself in this unusually silent weekend house, so I crawled back into bed and flicked through the Sunday papers. Ivan's cartoon of Dad stared out at me from the pages of the *Sunday Times*. He'd drawn him dressed in ermine seated on a throne in the theater's royal box: *Bertie Zhivago's long reign as king of the West End musical* read the caption. Something caught my eye; I looked more closely and could see that Ivan had drawn the silhouette of a couple standing together in a neighboring box, an homage to our parting.

Sometime later, Sammy came in and sat on the edge of my bed.

"Is everyone back?"

He nodded. "Yes. The kids are doing their homework, and Greg's taking Edie to the station."

"I didn't say goodbye to her."

"It's OK. Greg told her you weren't feeling well."

"What did she say?"

"She snorted disbelievingly and reminded Greg of his old girlfriend, Mary O'Grady, a *nice strong girl* who's got six children, the last of whom she delivered herself at home before going and collecting the others from school and making her husband his dinner. Fish pie, I think she said it was."

Greg and I moved around each other warily for the rest of the day, avoiding eye contact and conversation. I felt miserable and ached to think I wouldn't see Ivan again. But I couldn't very well confide my sadness at the loss of my lover to my husband or children. That was the trouble with secret lives; they had to remain secret and you had to bear the consequences. Forced to suffer grief silently, I found it easier simply to be angry with Greg.

By the following evening, the silence between us was growing oppressive.

"What exactly are my crimes, apart from sleeping for most of Sunday?" I asked Greg, when I had come back upstairs after an exhausting day of dealing with other people's psyches. I wasn't much up to the task; keeping my own in order seemed to be taking all my efforts these days. Greg was sitting in an armchair in the living room, his body curved away from me, just as Becky's had been from Ivan the night of the gala. But with Greg it was as if proximity to me might infect him with disease. He held the newspaper up like a shield. Beneath its lower edges, I could just make out his mouth, pursed tightly. Without lowering the paper, he said, "If you don't know, there's not much point in my telling you."

OK, so I'd been a little drunk and had raised my voice at him in public. It seemed to me he was overreacting. Greg had a thing about not washing one's dirty linen in public; he liked to present a picture of family harmony to the world. I thought it was rather bourgeois of him, but then I came from a long line of shouty let-it-all-hang-out Jews. Of course, before I worked myself up into a state of righteous indignation at what I considered to be his unwarranted anger, I should remember that I had been conducting an extramarital affair for the past four months, thus forfeiting any right to indignation. As I sat there under Greg's silent reprimand, I felt like a scolded adolescent.

"So as usual you're not going to talk about it? You'll just ignore me instead?" It made me feel better to go on the offensive.

He didn't answer.

I was worn down—by him, by the house, by our lives. The residue of Edie's floral perfume still hung in the air hours after her departure. I felt imprisoned by Greg's mood in the same way that my mother's moods had once held me captive as she lay disappointed in her darkened bedroom. I needed air.

"Fine," I said. "I'm going out."

"Do what you want, you always do anyway," Greg said.

I slammed the living room door as I left.

"Where are you going?" asked Kitty, as I took my coat off the hook by the door.

"Out."

"You're always going out. You're never here anymore. I may as well not have a mother." She looked me up and down. "And you're dressed like one of those women who's trying to look like a teenager again, like divorced women dress when they're looking for a new husband."

"Oh, darling." I knelt down and took her in my arms. Her small body was stiff and unyielding.

"Are you and Daddy friends yet?" she asked.

"Nearly. But sweetheart, it's normal for people to argue; it doesn't mean they don't love each other." Although, I thought, I wasn't sure I *did* love Greg anymore. I seemed to have succeeded in ruining everything.

"Come with me, let's pop over and see Grandpa. It'll cheer us both up."


It was a relief to leave the house and run home to Daddy. Everyone needs a sanctuary, and mine had always been wherever my father or Ruthie was. Helga had extended her stay, and after greeting me warmly she whisked Kitty off for an apple strudel lesson, leaving Dad and me alone in his music room. I told him I'd ended my affair. He didn't say anything; he simply hugged me and sat down at his piano.

I watched his hands as he played one of his songs and thought about Ivan and the way his hands had played my body. I must have let out a moan of anguish because Dad stopped playing and turned to look at me.

"Are you all right, Chlo?"

"I just wish I could have another go at everything."

"What do you mean?"

"My life. I want to rub it out and start again; I seem to have made an awful mess of this one. Do you think I'm having a nervous breakdown? Jung had one, you know. He called it a confrontation with the unconscious. I think mine is more of a collision with the conscious; I just can't seem to stand my life anymore."

"Everything has a purpose. Even illness can be creative," said Dad, "although I can see that may be hard to appreciate now."


Greg and I didn't seem able to say anything to each other without one of us taking it as a rebuke or a criticism. Consequently, we spent the next week baring our teeth like animals forced to share the same cage. The marital scoreboard might just as well have been hanging up in full view, all of our respective misdemeanors over the past seventeen years illuminated in neon lights.

I found myself calculating how many days remained until Kitty left school (five and a half years; 5 multiplied by 365 equals 1,825 plus half a year, 182, equals 1,997; call it 2,000). In about two thousand days I could leave him, and my children's home would be broken only after they'd left it; but by then I'd be forty-nine, Ivan would have forgotten me, and no one else would want me.

Greg spent his time busying himself with his various battles with the council, correcting the misdemeanors of everyone he encountered—fellow drivers and shopkeepers alike—and shouting at the children. Now and again I would catch him watching me thoughtfully as if contemplating speech. Was he planning to confront me? I replayed my memories of the times with Ivan over and over. Not surprisingly, everyone felt the tension. Bea and Zuzi kept their distance, and even Jessie chose to stay home with her mother.

# Chapter 20

## ABE'S POTATO LATKES
## WITH JAMAICAN HOT SAUCE

FOR THE LATKES
*1 lemon*
*Bowl of ice water*
*1½ pounds russet potatoes*
*1 onion, grated*
*1 egg, beaten*
*2 tablespoons flour*
*2 teaspoons baking powder*
*Good pinch salt*
*Pinch pepper*
*Vegetable oil or shmaltz for frying*

Preheat oven to 285°F. Squeeze the lemon and add the juice to a large bowl of ice water. Peel the potatoes and grate them roughly into the bowl; let stand for half an hour. Drain the potatoes well, squeezing dry with a kitchen towel. Place the grated potato in a large bowl and add onion, egg, flour, baking powder, and salt and pepper. Place a few tablespoons of vegetable oil in a heavy-duty frying pan and heat over medium flame. Scoop 1 tablespoon of the potato mixture into the skillet for each latke, cooking four of them at a time. Cook until golden and puffy, about 1 minute. Turn and brown the other side for about 30 seconds. Place on a rack and keep them warm in the oven. Add a bit more oil to pan for each batch.

FOR THE SAUCE

*½ pound red habanero chilies, seeds and stems removed*

*1 white onion, chopped*

*2 cloves garlic, chopped*

*1 medium papaya, boiled until tender; peeled, seeded, and finely chopped*

*1 tomato, finely chopped*

*½ cup cider vinegar*

*½ cup lime (or lemon) juice*

*2 tablespoons water*

*1 teaspoon thyme*

*1 teaspoon basil*

*½ teaspoon ground nutmeg*

*2 tablespoons dry mustard*

*½ teaspoon turmeric*

Combine the chilies, onion, garlic, papaya, and tomato in a food processor and puree (you may have to do this in batches). Remove to a shallow bowl. Combine the vinegar, lime juice, and water in a saucepan and heat until it reaches a slight boil, then sprinkle the thyme, basil, nutmeg, mustard, and turmeric. Pour heated mixture over the reserved puree and mix thoroughly. It will keep up to eight weeks in the refrigerator.

It was ten o'clock. Sammy was out and so were the au pairs; everyone else was in bed and asleep except me. It had been four weeks since Dad's gala, four weeks since I'd seen or spoken to Ivan, and I still couldn't stop thinking about him.

"What do you expect?" Ruthie had said that afternoon in the park café. "It's only been twenty-eight days. You aren't allowed to call him or see him for sixty days; that's the rule."

"What rule? You mean there are more rules?"

"Yes, lots. These are the rules pertaining to breakups, don't you remember? No phoning, no writing, no meeting. And if you feel yourself weakening, you have to phone me so I can protect you from yourself."

"What am I, a teenager?"

Ruthie didn't answer, she just gave a sort of expressive snort instead. It was true; I might as well have been a sixteen-year-old.

My fingers were itching to text him and ask him to meet me immediately. I walked through the sleeping house and went down to the kitchen, where I poured a glass of wine, hoping either to give myself the courage to call him or to knock myself out so I couldn't. I rarely drink alone. I rested my head against the window and looked out into the garden. The bare branches of the cherry tree we'd planted for Mum were just visible in the moonlight. I caught sight of a reflection in the glass and, for a moment, thought I saw my mother's face but soon realized it was my own. I was looking more and more like her as I grew older. Mum had only been twelve years older than I was now when she died. None of us know how long we have to live; what would I do if I knew I had only twelve years left? How would I choose to live out the remainder of my life? I reached for the phone to call Ivan, but it started to ring as soon as I touched it.

"Ruthie, thank God! I was just about to call him."

"Come over. Now," she ordered.

On my way out, I saw a small envelope lying on the floor by the front door. It was addressed to me and had been hand-delivered. It was from Ivan, as though my longing for him had reeled him in to me. I opened it up to find a cartoon of him and me. I was sitting in my shrink's chair listening to him talking. He was holding his hands out toward me. Underneath he had captioned it in Russian: *Ne mogu bez tebia. Davai budem, kak my byli v nachale. Ia tak tebia liubliu.*

How could he have taken the risk of pushing it through the letter box? I walked with it resolutely to the trash bin, but at the last moment I stuck it in my coat pocket instead.

Ruthie and I sat in her kitchen, where she watched me drink another large glass of wine very fast before bursting messily into tears. I'd never mastered the art of crying prettily: a lone tear, a quiet sniff, a lace handkerchief pressed to the eye. No, I was an untidy, puffy-eyed, red-nosed weeper. Ruthie made a surreptitious trip to the loo, so I guessed she had some cocaine. I could see it in her face anyhow. What a state we were both in.

"I wouldn't normally push drugs," she said, "but would you like a line of coke? It might cheer you up."

I was still crying noisily, wiping my nose on my sleeve, hiccuping and gulping. I shook my head.

"No, thanks, when I tried it years ago it made me cry, and I seem to be managing that perfectly well at the moment without any help."

I poured myself a shot of vodka instead and followed Ruthie to the safety of the bathroom, where she dried the marble next to the sink and laid out a fat line of white powder. As she deftly sniffed up her cocaine, I knocked back my shot of vodka. The vodka seemed to have the same effect on me as the coke did on her; we both perked up enormously.

"I feel marvelous, never felt better, I really feel wonderful," I said. "Come on, let's get out of here and find somewhere to go and dance. Where shall we go? I know, let's go to Abe's all-night deli and see if his brother Herbie's band is playing. Come on, hurry up, let's go."

"God, you're like a demented teenager. What was in that vodka?" Ruthie muttered as she restrained me long enough to dab Touche Eclat all over my tearstained face before following me out.

Abraham "Abe" Green was a six-foot four-inch Rastafarian with waist-length dreadlocks who ran an all-night Jewish delicatessen just a few doors down from the Volga. He wore a rainbow-colored crocheted skullcap, a mini-version of a Rasta hat. Abe insisted he was a nice Jewish boy whose Portuguese-Spanish forefathers had arrived in Jamaica in the sixteenth century, and, indeed, his pale green eyes suggested complicated ancestry. His speech was littered with *oy vays* and *ai-ai-ais* and "please Gods." In his spare time, he was studying to be a rabbi, and the breadth of his knowledge of Jewish texts, coupled with the authenticity and deliciousness of his cuisine, had led quickly to him being clasped to the collective bosom of the local Jewish community. ("He may be a *shvartzer* with hair too long, but he's our *shvartzer*.")

"Well, well, well," he greeted us, as we walked through the door, "to what do I owe the unexpected pleasure? You don't phone, you don't write, you found somewhere better that you haven't been here for so long?" He could certainly do guilt like a Jew.

"How's business," I asked.

"Gefilte fish! Feh! How should it be?"

Abe had an endearing habit of using the names of Jewish dishes as expletives in the place of swearwords. Ruthie and I sat down. I felt restless and couldn't keep still. Why had I brought us here? The last thing I wanted was food. I was drunk and wanted to be drunker. The room was full of elderly Jews, all having a little snack before going home to bed (God forbid they should die of hunger before they reached their own fridges), and Rastas with the munchies. Abe was berating a couple who, their meal long over, still lingered at their table, "You want to sit, go home and sit, you want to eat, stay and eat." Hard wooden chairs, a studied lack of ambience, and stark Formica tables all reinforced the rule of the house: No loitering. Eat and go! Abe liked *turnover*. He brought a plate of pickled cucumbers and chopped liver to our table.

"I'm sorry, but I'm just not hungry, Abe. Have you got any booze?" I asked.

"Booze? What do we Jews know from alcohol? Sheesh, what is it with you people, all sitting and no eating. What am I, a park bench?" He paused. "A little Israeli Sabbath wine, I got."

Ruthie and I looked at each other. Just how desperate were we? "Is it dry?"

Abe shrugged, lifted his hands, palms turned up toward the heavens, and pulled his face into an expression familiar to Jews since time immemorial. It was the sort of look that said, *What do you want, a miracle?*

"Me, I'm thinking you don't so much need alcohol; you look edgy. What you need is a little smoke, to calm you down and bring back your appetite, and then a little snack."

We went to the back room with him and watched as he expertly rolled a one-skin joint with some grass.

"In this matter, your Rasta genes clearly supersede your Jewish ones," I said.

"Genes, shmeens, they're complementary, two halves that make a perfect whole: Rasta grass to give you an appetite, Jewish food to feed your munchies. Yin and yang, you should pardon the expression. The Rastafarian Jew is the most highly evolved human being on the planet," Abe said smugly.

Ruthie and I nodded at his wisdom, which struck us with added force after the sixth toke on the little joint.

I played idly with one of Abe's snow globes; he had a collection of some two hundred, tumbling dustily from book-crammed shelves. My favorite was of two Hasidic Jews, bent against the wind in their long black overcoats and black hats. Their long beards and forelocks seemed to sway in an imaginary wind. Now, as I looked at it, I felt I was being sucked into the small glass dome and into the eighteenth-century Polish shtetl that was their home. Was that why I had felt so at home with Ivan, I wondered, because of the Eastern European connection, an indelible race memory that was my birthright? There seemed to be something so familiar about him, a cultural sense of belonging that I didn't have with Greg. I pressed the globe to my face, feeling the cool of the glass. I'd never noticed before how slowly each little silvery snowflake fell, almost in slow motion really. Everything had been going too fast moments before, and now it had all become so very s . . . l . . . o . . . w.

"When are you going to bring me some more of your chicken soup, Chloe?" Abe's voice asked. It sounded like he was speaking from the bottom of a very deep well.

"Soon, I promise." My answer seemed to come sometime later, as if the sounds could only be heard a long time after they had left my mouth. Or was it my mouth? It felt like my mouth, but what did *my* really mean? And what, after all, was a mouth, when you came down to it?

(*You smoked Abe's grass?* Greg asked me the next day. *You smoked Abe's grass?* he repeated, shaking his head in disbelief, *Are you insane? I would never take more than two tokes on an Abe joint and I'm a master. You're lucky you didn't get locked-in syndrome. What do you mean? I said. When you can't move or speak at all. Jesus, Chloe, what's the matter with you?*)

"Greg was here yesterday." Abe's eyes were shut and he was swaying slightly, as though he were praying. "He was talking to Moishe in the kitchen and asking how much *shmaltz* he put in his *knaydlach*. Moishe's aren't as good as yours, though." He slapped his hand to his forehead, "*Tsimmes!* What a shmuck! I was supposed to keep that a secret."

"Safe with me. I'm the Queen of Secrets," I said.

Abe looked at me quizzically as he put a CD into a ghetto blaster. "Listen to this. Herbie's done a new mix of the Shema."

We tapped our feet to Herbie's reggae version of the Jewish prayer. I got up and started dancing, and I have a faint but terrifying memory of leading the other two out into the restaurant in a sort of conga line, our right hands covering our eyes as is customary when saying this particular prayer, while we sang *Shma Yisrael Adonai Elohaynu Adonai Echad*. The mood seemed to catch everyone, and the rest of the customers joined in. Never let it be said that we Jews don't know how to have fun. By then, Ruthie and I had become ravenously hungry, so we sat back down and fell on the familiar food of our forefathers: salt beef, chopped egg, bagels, and—Abe's variation on an old favorite—potato latkes with Jamaican hot sauce, all washed down with sweet Israeli Sabbath wine.

"Have they settled the terms of your redundancy?" I asked, chopped liver escaping from my mouth.

I heard the hiss of a collective intake of breath. Everyone around us froze in a pantomime of shock. Forks stopped on their journey to mouths, glasses failed to reach their final destinations, and here and there a couple of people could be seen spitting three times over their left shoulders to ward off the evil eye.

"What? What? What did I say?" I asked the room at large.

A smartly dressed man in a business suit leaned forward from the next table and gripped me tightly by the arm. "You should forgive me, but you think that's a word we want to hear when we're eating?"

"What, redundancy?"

The room gasped again and turned away from us. I saw Volodya coming through the door and waved. I'd secretly texted him when Ruthie wasn't looking and asked him to meet me here. He had a coat on over his pajamas and was carrying his tattered copy of *Doctor Zhivago.*

"Which bit are you up to?"

"Lara's gone off to the station and Yuri's said he'll follow and meet her there."

"Do you really not know what happens?"

"No, shush, don't spoil it."

"How can you be Russian and not know?"

"What can I say? I was out of school that day."

I emptied my pockets. Dirty tissues, fluffy pieces of unchewed gum, coins, a screwed-up parking ticket. . . . Finally, I found it, the card from Ivan.

"What does it say?"

Volodya looked around. The couple at the next table were watching with some interest. I got up, took Volodya by the arm, and led him outside. He held the card up to the light of a streetlamp and screwed up his eyes so he could make out the words.

"It says, *I can't bear it without you. Let's be like we were in the beginning. I love you so much.*"

I started crying again. Quite prettily this time, just a couple of tears tracing a dignified path down my cheeks.

"Don't be like Yuri Zhivago, Chloe. Go to the *vokzal*, the railway station; don't throw away your chance of happiness."

"You liar, you do know what happens." I hit him on the shoulder.

Volodya shrugged noncommittally.

"Anyhow, what happened to all that *be careful* stuff?" I said.

"Sometimes you just can't stand in the way of love."

"I love Russians," I said, throwing my arms around him. "You're so irresistibly passionate and romantic."

Well, I reasoned to myself, it hadn't done Yuri Zhivago much good, had it, ignoring his love for Lara in the end? He'd ended up without Tonya and without Lara, dying alone and lonely in Moscow. It seemed like a sign, as though the universe were showing me the way forward. I kissed Volodya and went back inside the restaurant.

"*Nu*, what did the piece of paper say?" asked the heavily made-up matron who'd been sitting next to me as she passed on her way out.

"Not telling," I said.

She waved a hand at me in disgust. "Spoilsport."

"Come on, Ruthie," I said, sweeping her up and paying Abe. He pressed a small plastic bag into my hand, containing some of his grass.

"For Greg," he said.

I blew him a kiss as I led Ruthie off down the road. "Let's go to your house. You can have a little more of that white powder of yours, while I smoke Greg's grass."

"You've turned into an animal," she said, "a wild drug-guzzling beast."

It was all a bit of a blur after that, although I seem to recall lying on the floor of Ruthie's kitchen, smoking a joint and watching her sniff a line of cocaine that circumvented one of the table legs.

"Who says they have to be straight lines?" Ruthie had said. "Boring, boring, boring. I want to live a little, to make squiggles, circles, squares, inventing whole new shapes for cocaine and the snorting thereof."

God but we were clever, creative, interesting, witty, and marvelous, and we had such a lot to talk about. Pity I can't really remember much of what we said, but I think we solved quite a lot of problems, our own and other people's.

"That's it!" Ruthie had exclaimed at one point. "I'll squirt Super Glue into the locks of David Gibfuck's car. That'll teach him to make me redundant. The bastard! He won't look so clever when he can't get into his snazzy Saab and has to walk or take public transport like the rest of us, who are unemployed because of him and who also don't have jobs because of him." And she stabbed the air with a finger for emphasis.

I have a disturbing memory of composing a very long text message to Ivan, which may or may not have said something along the lines of

*I'm so sorry about our parting, you must know that you are very important to me and that you have awakened my spirit in the past few months. I feel that we are soul mates with a unique connection. You have made me feel again, touched my senses in a way that they haven't been touched for years, opened my heart, and . . .*

"The essence of the text is brevity," Ruthie had said, as I tapped away.

"Yes, yes, but I just have to tell him a few things. It's very, very important; I can see it all so clearly now." My finger had taken on a life of its own.

*I felt a little overwhelmed by everything that was happening between us and thought it would be best for both of us if I ended our relationship. I see now that this was a terrible mistake. Ever since, I have felt deep despair and sorrow. I so want to see you, my darling, and to feel your arms around me.*

Just before I tried to press SEND, I added, in a dope-fueled rush of lust:

*I also want to feel you moving inside me once more so that we can soar high together on the plains of carnal bliss.*

It made me blush to think of it the next morning. *In vino veritas?* Perhaps. *In narcotics nonsensicus?* Clearly.

Now I lay in bed flushed with shame and reached out a tentative hand to pat the bed next to me. Empty. I looked at my watch: one o'clock. What did that mean? What sort of one o'clock, 1 A.M. or 1 P.M.? I could see light filtering through the still-closed curtains. Oh, God, I'd slept half the day away. What time had I come home? I could remember Ruthie opening yet another bottle of wine at seven-thirty in the morning, before sending Sephy, who had just got up, round the corner to buy newspapers and cigarettes. (We'd both decided in the course of the night that smoking was a very grown-up thing to do.)

"How come they sold you cigarettes?" Ruthie asked, when she returned.

"Easy," she answered. "I just told them my mum was too drunk to come and get them herself."

This had the effect of sobering us up immediately, and I'd somehow made my way across the park, which appeared to be hosting an early morning convention for park-bench drunks. They lolled wordlessly, clutching beer cans like security blankets. For once, I knew just how they felt; I was among my people. I stood in the chill dawn of a winter Sunday and looked at my front door. I had forgotten my keys and, after standing in a numb bemused state for some minutes, threw a pebble in the direction of our bedroom window. It missed, but the loud and indignant squawk of the pigeon it hit (one of Madge's flock?) brought Greg to the window, mute and grim-faced. He came down and let me in without saying a word.

Now I lay in bed; my mouth was dry, I had pins and needles in my arms and legs, and my brain felt bruised. The house was silent. I found the phone and pulled it into my den of disgrace beneath the covers as I dialed.

"Ruthie?" I whispered hoarsely.

"I'm so sorry," Ruthie said. "I'm afraid your friend Ruthie is dead. A drug overdose, I believe. I am merely her walking corpse."

"God, Ruthie, I'm so sorry about last night."

"Actually, I'm not," she said. "I'm pleased. It was the big bang I needed to end on, you know? The enough-no-more point I needed to reach. After you left, I sat and thought about how it wasn't big or funny or even very clever. I tipped the rest of the stuff down the loo, confessed to Richard, and went to a Narcotics Anonymous meeting in Notting Hill Gate."

"See anyone we know?"

"My lips are sealed; I have taken the NA oath."

"You're no fun."

I felt full of shame that I had encouraged Ruthie to do coke when I had been trying so hard to wean her off it. It made nonsense of the discreet conversation I'd had with Richard only the week before. I'd gone over there one afternoon when I'd known Ruthie would be out. Richard was in his study, buried in a book about Ancient Greek writings inscribed in stone. I'd explained to him that Ruthie was in trouble and had a coke habit. He'd looked rather bewildered. I realized I would need to frame it in a context that he could understand.

"Cocaine's been around for centuries," I said. "Perhaps the Ancient Greeks were just as partial to the white powder as the Ancient Egyptians?"

"Yes, indeed," said Richard, brightening up at once and pinching the bridge of his nose as he always did when he was about to explain something. "During the ancient Olympic Games, there is evidence that the earliest athletes found all sorts of ways to enhance their performance: alcohol, stimulants, and opiates that they probably chewed. As you know, of course, the ancient games stopped for good in A.D. 395 and Olympia was vandalized beyond repair."

I didn't know that, but I nodded anyhow. He paused for a moment, shaking his head sorrowfully as if the destruction of Olympia were a breaking news story.

"When the Olympics in their current incarnation were reborn in Athens in 1896," he went on, "some competitors did use cocaine and other stimulants to give them an extra edge." He carefully put his book down, first marking his place with a leather bookmark, and walked over to his desk. On it stood his silver gleaming concession to the modern world: an Apple laptop computer. He entered the words *cocaine abuse* into the search engine. "Thank you for telling me, Chloe," he said. "I know Ruthie hasn't been happy recently." I'd asked him not to shop me but I'm not sure whether he was listening, and I'd left him researching the subject of drug addiction and making meticulous notes in the slim black notebook he always carried with him.

"What did Richard say?" I asked Ruthie nervously, coming back to the present and wondering if Richard had grassed on me.

"He seemed relieved I'd finally come clean about why I've been such a madwoman for the past few months. He hugged me and told me he loved me and would do whatever was needed to help me sort myself out."

"So there may be a point to husbands after all?"

"Well, let's not get carried away. Although I may have to concede that mine is not entirely without purpose at this precise moment."

"God," I said, as memory of the previous night flooded me. "You're so lucky you're already dead. I want to die too."

I retrieved my mobile phone from the safety of a locked drawer, where, out of a sense of self-preservation and notwithstanding my drunken, stoned state, I had hidden it. There were my messages to Ivan, intact and mercifully saved in *drafts*. Thank God I hadn't sent them! I had woken up with new resolve and knew I mustn't contact him. My affair with Ivan was over. Finished. The End. The phone beeped in my hand, making me jump. Ivan? No, a message from Greg: *TEXT WHEN YOU DEIGN TO GET UP.* Oops, it was clear I was firmly in the doghouse. I texted him back: *I AM AWAKE.*

I had never before seen the woman who looked back at me from the bathroom mirror; she was a stranger, older than me by some years.

Eyes encompassed by dark circles glimmered with desperation, and hair hung greasily around a ravaged, puffy face in which the traces of any previous beauty appeared to have been all but extinguished. I ran a bath, made my way through the empty house (whose every brick seemed to scream reproach), and collected an array of vegetables and cold wet tea bags that I placed carefully along the edge of the tub. Cucumber on its own wasn't enough; in my current condition I needed a fuller selection of crudités to soothe my swollen eyes. I added essential oils to the water, got in, lay down, and prayed that natural remedies could counteract the damage wrought by alcohol and drug abuse. It was all very well, your mind thinking you were still a teenager, but your body was there to tell you that you were a middle-aged woman and simply couldn't take the pace any longer. Nothing seemed to help. I felt agitated and unwell and needed a doctor, but I doubted whether my own personal physician would be sympathetic to my plight. Perhaps FF was right; sex was like petrol and I was running on empty, soon to splutter, gasp, and die.

# Chapter 21

## CHLOE ZHIVAGO'S HUMBLE PIE

*The expression* humble pie *dates back to William the Conqueror's time, when the lord of the manor dined on the flesh of the deer while the servants had to content themselves with the heart, liver, kidney, and other innards, known as nombles or umbles. Since then, eating humble pie has come to connote a voluntary acceptance of low status or humiliating treatment. I am not an offal fan—in my opinion, one rarely needs to be quite that humble—so I cheat and use beef instead, making my own particular humble pie more fit for a prince than for a pauper.*

FOR THE FILLING

1 tablespoon flour, seasoned with salt, pepper, and a teaspoon
   of cinnamon

1½ pounds good stewing steak cut into cubes

1 tablespoon olive oil

1 medium onion, chopped

4 or 5 carrots, cut into chunks (I use Chantenay carrots)

1 cup water

1 cup red wine

1 teaspoon Marigold vegetable bouillon or an Oxo cube

½ cup flour

4 tablespoons water

Several tears of apology

Mix tablespoon of flour with seasonings in a plastic bag; add beef, and shake to coat evenly. Heat a little oil in a pressure cooker and brown beef with the chopped onion. Add carrots, 1 cup water, and the wine. Add Marigold bouillon (or, if you prefer a darker look, use Oxo cube). Cook on high until cooker comes up to pressure, then reduce to medium and time for 10 minutes. Add 4 tablespoons cold water and tears of apology to flour and mix to a smooth paste; add carefully to beef and carrots and stir well.

FOR THE PASTRY
*3 ounces butter*
*1½ cups flour*
*salt*
*1 egg yolk*
*cold water*
*1 beaten egg to glaze*

While beef is cooking, cube the butter and rub into flour and salt with your fingertips until it resembles bread crumbs. Add egg yolk and enough water to bind the mixture. Cut in half, roll first half out on a floured surface, and place in a 9-inch greased pie dish, trimming excess edges. Pour in beef and carrot mixture, roll out remaining pastry dough, and cover. Brush with beaten egg, cut vents with a sharp knife. Bake at 350°F for 30 minutes.

Needless to say, my most recent transgression didn't endear me to my husband. I couldn't blame him, really. In spite of my repeated attempts to apologize, he stopped talking to me altogether.

One evening I found Kitty in her room, packing a bag. She handed me a letter addressed to Greg and me, written in purple ink:

Dear Mum and Dad,
    I cannot take this any longer. I don't know when I will be back. Why are you fighting? Two people who have been together for so long should grow closer, not farther apart. This is why I must love you and leave you.
Love from your daughter xxx Kitty xxx

Even Greg was chastened by Kitty's attempt to run away from home. Her grasp of our situation highlighted the childishness of our behavior. It was ironic; Kitty had been the trigger for my ending my affair with Ivan, but it hadn't improved matters; if anything, Greg's and my relationship had worsened. In a curious way, having an affair had maintained a sort of equilibrium in my marriage.

That same evening, Leo came in drunk and vomited on the hall floor. He staggered toward me, tears streaming down his face, and hiccuped.

"I hate myself," he slurred. "I really, really love you, but I hate myself."

"What have you been drinking?"

"Vodka," he said. He hugged me before lying down on the floor, where he passed out, only to rouse moments later as he started to vomit again.

"We can't let him go to sleep," I said to Greg, as I turned him on his side into the recovery position. "He'll choke."

Greg and I helped him into the shower. I hadn't seen Leo naked for years, not since before puberty, when he'd still had a little boy's body. It's true what they say: Oaks do grow from acorns. I was so shocked I couldn't help staring. Where was my baby boy? I remembered the moment he was laid in my arms for the first time, a tightly wrapped bundle proffered by the midwife. "Take your son," she had said and I swelled with pride, unable to believe that my female body could have created this small and perfect male creature; it was quite simply the cleverest thing I had ever done in my life. Now, in the blink of an eye, here he was, a drunk vomiting naked man. But, for all that, he was still defenseless, still in need of my protection, still my baby boy.

"I jus' had a few drinks, Mum."

"His sugar levels will be all over the place," said Greg. "He'll need to go to hospital."

"I'll take him," I said. "You stay here with Kitty."

In the hospital, Leo vomited on a stranger's shoes before falling onto the hard cold floor. This was too much even for the hardened, wounded brawlers who frequented the emergency room. They all looked at me reproachfully. What kind of a mother lets her son get so drunk?

"I imagine you must be pleased about this," the staff nurse said, as she led Leo briskly to a bed and put him on a drip to stabilize his blood sugar.

"Yes," I agreed wryly. "I'm absolutely delighted."

I sat at my child's bedside through the night and watched as old drunks were brought off the streets and into safety. One of them in particular caught my eye, a tall man in a suit, which, although shabby, had a faded elegance about it. He was well-spoken and courteous to the nursing staff, speaking in the measured tones of someone pretending to be sober. I watched as he smoothed back his silver hair and laid his hat down carefully on the end of his bed in an action that was at once fastidious and familiar; it was clear he was no stranger to the hospital, and indeed, a moment later, a smiling nurse walked past him, gave him a mock salute, and said, "Evening, Major." I couldn't help wondering what his story was and what had led him to this. A lifetime of heavy drinking that had begun as an adolescent foible and somewhere along the way had unwittingly become a career decision? I turned to Leo and saw in his eyes that shame was beginning to replace inebriation. He was watching the drunk man too. I didn't need to say anything; I could see he was learning the lesson for himself. Sometimes you need a crisis to move on to a new phase in your life. Perhaps I had needed my affair with Ivan to enable Greg and me to move forward. I wasn't sure how, but as I sat there listening to my son's steady breathing, I resolved more than ever to put Ivan in the past and focus on a future with Greg.

Life in Grumpy Towers remained difficult nevertheless, and my tentative attempts to inch my nose and paws out of the *maison du chien* and win back Greg's favor had so far fallen on deaf ears. Greg pretended everything was fine when the children were around, but when we were on our own he spoke to me in the distant tones of a not altogether friendly acquaintance.

"How are things at home?" Ruthie asked me in the café one morning.

"Bad."

"Sex?"

"None."

"Don't you think you should talk to him about it? I mean, after all, you are Mrs. Talking Cure; it's what you do for a living."

"I know, but the trouble is I feel I forfeited that right by having an affair," I said sadly.

It was hard to feel indignant with Greg for not doing with me what I'd so readily done with someone else. It was also hard not to long for Ivan and his kisses. Over the past few days, he'd started sending me text messages again. So far I'd managed not to text him back, although I had to confess that, whatever my resolutions, I still wanted to.

There was nothing for it, I'd have to woo my husband back, and the first step was to eat humble pie; both literally and metaphorically. And make some for Greg to eat too. The way to a man's heart is not, as one all too often wishes, with a knife through his chest but through his stomach.

"What are you up to, Mum?" Kitty asked me, as I peeled vegetables.

"What do you mean? I'm cooking supper."

"You've got your faraway face on," she said unhappily. "I thought it had gone, but it's come back."

She'd caught me thinking about Ivan. Kitty might just as well have still been in my womb, sharing my emotions through the umbilical cord that had once bound us; she can always sense emotional change in me. I was saved from further scrutiny by her phone beeping. Her face softened as she read the message.

She held the phone up for me to read: I WISH I COULD SEE YOU.

"Who's that from?" I asked.

"Max. I'm going out with him."

"Since when?"

"Yesterday."

It was all so marvelously simple; Max had phoned Kitty up and asked her to go out. She'd told him to hang on while she dumped Joe, who had been her boyfriend for the past fortnight, and now Kitty and Max were going out, although they didn't actually seem to *go* anywhere. In a few days or weeks, one of them would dump the other, usually by text or phone, and start going out with someone else, perhaps the dumped boyfriend's best friend. It was a useful training slope for relationships. What a pity it got so complicated as the years went on. Perhaps I should just tell Greg he was dumped and go off with Ivan. Judging by the regularity with which Kitty and her friends dumped boys and took up with new ones, was it any wonder that no one seemed to expect relationships to last and that the pattern for so many these days was serial monogamy? If only it were that straightforward and relationships could be like light bulbs: simply replaced when they burned out.

My phone beeped. It was Ivan: I WISH I COULD SEE YOU.

"Let's see," said Kitty, holding her hand out.

I hid the phone in my hand.

"I showed you mine," she said.

"Sorry, darling, it's a patient," I lied.

Kitty gave a disbelieving snort and left the room, bumping into Leo as he came in.

"Fuck off, Leo," she said, shoving him.

"Fuckoffyourselfyoulittlebitchwhatdoyouthinkyouarefuckingdoing don'ttellmetofuckoff." I looked at him, astonished less by the violence of his response than by the extreme rapidity with which it was delivered.

"HelloMumwhat'stheproblemwhyareyoulookingatmethatway?"

"Don't talk to your sister like that. What's going on? You have been a man of few words these last two years, and now it's like listening to a machine-gun volley."

"YeswellthatsbecauseI'mgoingtobethewhiteTwista,he'stheman,the-numberonerapacrobatthefastestrapperintheworldandI'mgoingtobethe whiteenglishversionsoI'mpracticingtalkingasfastasIcan."

"God help us," I muttered.

"I can't win," Leo said, with exaggerated slowness. "You go on about me grunting, and now when I talk you complain about that as well. You just don't understand anything. I've finally found the one thing I want to do with my life." He stormed out, slamming the door as he left.

The scene was set for a peaceful and conciliatory family dinner. Greg and the children sat wordlessly around the table while I served supper. For once it was just us four, which only served to highlight the tensions between us. Greg started the meal with his nose in the paper, tetchily scolding the children for chewing too loudly and not using their knives and forks properly. Without the distraction of talk and laughter, it was all too easy to be irritated by one another's table manners. Sensing this, the children quickly gobbled their food and left as soon as they could, while Greg and I continued to eat in silence. But as the pie began to work its magic, he relaxed, put the paper aside, and met my eyes for the first time in what felt like ages. I paused, a full forkful of pie on its way to my mouth.

"You know how I love watching you eat humble pie," he said.

I laughed, got up to get him another helping, and, passing it to him, said, "Not as much as I enjoy making you eat it." I reached out a tentative hand toward him. "Let's try being kinder to each other," I said, and later I reached for him in bed, rubbing up against him, hoping we could find our way back to each other physically as well.

"Too tired," he said, moving away and turning over with his back to me.

I lay awake for some time, listening to the wind and rain outside and watching the fluorescent hands of the alarm clock as they inched toward 2 A.M. Sometimes you can feel far lonelier with someone beside you than you ever would on your own.

On Thursday morning there were three messages from Gina on my practice answering machine. Each one was more hysterical than the last, the cries of a bride panicking in the final hours before her journey to the altar. She was getting married that afternoon. I sighed and called her back.

"Do you think it's possible to be happily married, Chloe?" she asked, in a voice tight with fear.

"I think the thing is not to expect too much and to take note of the good times, not just the bad."

"I'm not sure I can go through with this."

"I never thought I'd cite Dolly Parton as the font of all knowledge," I said, "but I once heard her interviewed about how she managed to remain cheerful when she'd had so many bad things happen to her, and she said, 'I decided to choose happiness.' It can be as easy as that. So Gina, choose happiness. You have a lovely man, you love him, and he loves you. I'll see you at the wedding."

Gina was getting married in her parents' home, which turned out to be a grand mansion on the edge of Holland Park. The clean white lines of more than a hundred arum lilies flanked the stairway that led to the front door. A uniformed maid took my coat at the door, and I joined the throng for a glass of champagne. I wasn't feeling well, and the boom of well-bred voices threatened to deafen me. I was also dying for a pee and made my way up the stairs. As I was pausing to decide which of the many doors facing me might lead to a lavatory, I heard voices and the sound of a door opening. Gina appeared in a froth of white lace, laughing as she tamed a few curls that threatened to escape from her wedding hairdo. Behind her, I could make out the figure of a man tucking his shirt into his trousers.

"Don't you know it's bad luck for the groom to see you before the wedding?" I asked, smiling. She looked at me in silence. The penny dropped.

"Ah, that's not the groom," I said. "I see."

"We were just saying goodbye. I'm not actually married yet."

I held a hand up to stem the flow of her explanations. It wasn't the moment for therapy, so I wished her luck and told her she looked beautiful. That's what you're meant to say to brides, and in this case it was the truth: She radiated that singular beauty of a woman who has just been sexually satisfied.

I found the bathroom and scrutinized my face in the mirror. I wasn't looking my best. I sat on the edge of the lavatory, dampened one of the many appliquéd guest towels that are the trademark of the middle classes acting posh, and held it against my forehead. Shakily I made my way downstairs, where the ceremony was about to begin. The drawing room must have been over thirty feet long; at one end, tall French windows opened onto a large garden where trees were just beginning to come back to life. Here and there among their still-bare branches, tender green leaves were emerging, and early daffodils were celebrating in the flower beds. Chairs had been laid out on either side of the room, with an aisle down the middle. More lilies crowded the space, and I realized their aroma was making me feel nauseated. Gina stood waiting on her father's arm, ethereally bathed in the early spring sunlight that poured in from the window behind her. I smiled at her reassuringly as I took my seat. She appeared as if she might be about to cry. She was looking not at the handsome groom, who turned to watch her as she walked down the aisle, but at the man I had glimpsed earlier, who was seated halfway down. When she passed him, her body seemed to lean toward him as though magneti-cally drawn by their attraction to each other. She faltered for a moment, recovered herself, and, squaring her shoulders, walked resolutely on. As her father handed her to her groom, she reminded me of nothing so much as a prisoner who, having just received her sentence, turns from the dock to be led into custody by the jailers who await her. I knew then what she hadn't yet understood: Her affair with the shirt-tucking man, now brooding in his seat, was far from over. It is so much easier to see the truth about someone else's situation than it is about one's own. This flash of clarity about Gina and her lover made me realize that the same was true of Ivan and me. I had to see him again.

Later, as I was trying to slip away unnoticed, a sharp-featured woman in a fuchsia suit hurried up to me and laid a hand on my arm.

"You must be Chloe Zhivago," she said. "I'm Gina's mother. Thank you so much for everything you've done for her. I don't think we'd ever have got her up the aisle without your help."

She looked over at Gina, who was standing next to her new husband and smiling for the photographer. Photographs are not emotionally reliable. They show only what can be seen on the surface; they can and do lie. This one would smile out down the years from a well-thumbed wedding album, a captured moment of fraudulent newly wedded bliss; it wouldn't hint that the bride had been in the arms of another man less than an hour before the ceremony. Even as I watched, I could see Gina's eyes slide away and rest on the dark figure of her lover, who was lean-ing against a door and watching her closely.

"I hope they'll be very happy together," I said to Gina's mother. I felt an impostor in this particular fairy tale, the bad fairy who placed the curse on Sleeping Beauty that made her prick her finger on the spin-ning wheel. It was as though my helping Gina into a life of matrimony was an act not of giving but of taking away.

The scent from the lilies followed me down the stairs and I stood on the street for a moment, feeling dizzy. My phone, which I'd switched to silent, vibrated in my pocket, an angry insect intent on attracting my attention. I ignored it, walked into Holland Park Gardens, and found a bench in the Japanese Gardens; I needed a moment alone. Whatever my relationship with Ivan meant for the future of my marriage, I knew I had to see him again. I sat and watched the still water of the Japanese pond in front of me, from which a white rock rose and stood sentry: the gatekeeper, perhaps, to a more contemplative and spiritual way of being. My phone vibrated again, drawing me back to the present. It was Ivan.

"Come and meet me, Chloe," he said. "Just let me have one whole night with you. I've missed you so much."

"I know, me too." His voice warmed me. I wanted nothing more than for him to hold me in his arms and tell me his stories of Russia. That was what I had loved the most, even more than the lovemaking, that feeling of being transported out of my own world and into another where life once again vibrated with possibility.

As I turned the car into our street, I saw Madge hurrying along the pavement, laughing and talking to herself. What sort of a sanctuary was madness from the unbearable sadness of her reality? There are, I reflected, some things it is impossible to recover from: the death of a marriage, yes; the death of your children, never.

Fortunately, the house was empty, and within twenty minutes I was washed, changed, made up, and back out, on my way to meet Ivan in a country hotel. Ruthie had tut-tutted at me down the phone but had conceded defeat and agreed to have Kitty and Leo stay the night with her.

"It's classic," she said, "the one last fix of the addict who's gone cold turkey. Just make sure it's not an overdose."

I'd left a message on Greg's voice mail, burbling some nonsense about staying on at Gina's reception after all and explaining I wouldn't be back until morning as it was out of town.

I traveled by train to our meeting place, an Oxfordshire pub with a Michelin star. Ivan was waiting for me, lying naked in a four-poster bed in a bedroom designed for lovers. I turned away from him as I undressed, made shy by our absence from each other, and slipped quickly between the sheets and into his arms. I nuzzled up against him like a cat that wants to be stroked; it felt so wonderful to be touched again that it was all I could do to stop myself from purring out loud.

"I've missed you so much," he murmured, after we'd made love.

"Me too," I answered, although the truth was that now, after the act, I felt detached; the high from my fix of him was not as intense as I'd remembered. Sex had left me feeling strangely empty, and I wanted to chat in order to find closeness with him again.

"Tell me a story about Russia," I said. But I could tell from his breathing that he'd fallen asleep.

I got up, walked over to the window, and looked out into the night. It was much darker and quieter than I was accustomed to; I could hear Ivan's breathing as he slept. In the distance the forlorn yipping bark of a lone fox calling for its mate broke the silence. I got back into bed and turned my phone on. It rang almost immediately. It was Greg, and his next words were the thunderbolt I'd always feared was waiting to strike me.

"Chloe, I've got some bad news."

"What's happened? Are the children all right? What is it?"

"It's your dad; he's had a heart attack. It's OK, he's in hospital and his condition is stable."

"Oh, God, and I'm not there with him."

This was it, my punishment, the outcome of my wickedness. The price of my pleasure in the man beside me had to be paid for with the illness of my father and my absence from his side. I told Greg I'd be back as soon as I could and woke Ivan to explain.

"I'm sure he'll be fine," he said sleepily.

Waves of dread coursed through me, starting in the pit of my stomach and traveling throughout my body until fear throbbed in my fingertips and at the ends of my toes. Ever since I was a child I have lived with the terror of my father's mortality. I wanted to rush to him, to be in my own home, to see my children and my husband. What was I doing in a hotel room with someone else's husband?

"I have to go home now," I said.

"It's late," he said. "We'll go back first thing in the morning; Greg said he was stable. Let's enjoy our night together. You promised me a night." He took my hand and tried to pull me back into bed with him.

"I can't. I have to go and see my dad now; he needs me." The soft bed with its warm sheets was a cruel contradiction to the dark well of fear that threatened to overwhelm me.

"I need you too, Chloe." Ivan sighed heavily, the sigh of a man who doesn't like to have his fun spoiled. Real life and illicit love affairs were uneasy bedfellows.

"Sorry darling." I took his hand. "You do understand, don't you?"

With obvious effort, Ivan smiled tightly. "Of course. Come on, the last train's gone. I'll drive you back."

As we drove, something curious struck me; earlier, while we had been making love, I'd been thinking of my husband.

# Chapter 22

It was late by the time I arrived at the hospital. At the entrance, a couple of patients stood smoking cigarettes, undeterred either by the drizzling cold or by the drip stands that stood guard beside them. Clinging to life even as they sought their own destruction, they pulled fiercely on their cigarettes until the ends burned hot, long and red. You'd have thought they were trying to suck new life out of them rather than accelerate their own demise. How ill did you have to be before the threat of death overcame addiction? I wondered. I watched an amputee in a wheelchair as he lit a fresh cigarette from the butt of an old one. He had the emaciated frailty of the lifelong smoker and was literally on his last leg. He caught my eye and gave an apologetic what-can-you-do? kind of shrug.

The lights were dim on the floor; behind the desk, a nurse whose breasts threatened to spring out from her tightly buttoned uniform talked quietly on the phone. She looked more like an actress from a TV hospital drama than a trained medical professional. Anxiety, I thought, doesn't prevent one from observing detail; it simply renders it absurd.

"Where can I find Bertie Zhivago?" I asked.

"Visiting hours are over," she answered, looking pointedly at the upside-down watch pinned onto her fugitive bosom.

"I'm his daughter."

She flicked her eyes over me as though searching for any distin-guishing characteristics that might support my assertion.

"Do you want a bloody birth certificate?" I snapped, fear overcoming decorum.

"Bed number twelve," she said, pretending not to hear me as she busied herself with files. "Don't stay long."

The patients were grouped in fours in the bays, most of them lying inert. I peered into the first bay, and someone gave a throaty, mucus-filled cough. The odor of sickness combined with that of the anxious offerings of flowers and fresh fruit to create a cloying aroma of misery and despair: illness's frequent companions. I felt nauseated and dizzy. Helga was dozing in a chair next to Dad's bed, her chest rising and falling in unison with his own. He looked small and frail and his skin appeared gray against the white of the hospital sheets. I went to take his hand, but it was punctured with intravenous needles that pumped drugs into him. Wires were taped to his chest, leading to a monitor whose screen flickered with the graph of his heart's labored workings.

He stirred and opened his eyes. Dad has always seemed able to sense my presence; we share that invisible bond that only a mother is supposed to have with her child.

"I'm sorry, darling," he said. "I'm being a bit of a nuisance."

"Yes, it's all me, me, me with you." I smiled as I squeezed his shoulder. I was shocked by how thin he felt. I wanted to fling myself onto his chest so he could comfort me for being upset because he was ill. But he needed my comfort, so I kept on joking, talking with difficulty through the hard lump that had formed in my throat.

"What happened?"

"I was sitting in the study just starting to get the birds down for a new tune when a great big horse kicked me in the chest—at least that's what it felt like. Next thing I knew I was in here, all wired up."

"Thank God Helga was with you," I said. If he'd been alone, how long would he have lain there unaided while I was out of town with a man who was neither my husband nor my children's father? Helga opened her eyes and smiled at us.

"I'll leave you two alone together for a bit," she said, in the brisk, cheerful tone that people adopt when they're trying to pretend there's nothing to worry about.

"I'm feeling much better," Dad said, "now that I've got my two favorite grown-up women here." Helga patted Dad's cheek, hugged me, and went in search of air.

"I really like her, Dad," I said. "She's so loving."

"She likes you too. I'm very pleased; it's important to me that the two women I love should get along."

"Where's Sammy?"

"He and Greg left about an hour ago," Dad said.

"Did Greg talk to the doctor?" I asked.

"I'm not sure I've actually seen a doctor. A twelve-year-old girl in a white coat came and took my pulse and said something about keeping me over the weekend. Greg had a little chat with her."

I marched over to the desk. Soap Star Nurse was still on the phone, and, judging from the way she was toying with the top button of her uniform, she was probably talking to her boyfriend. I stood in her eye line and stared her down.

"I'll call you back in a minute, I have a possible FAR situation," she said and hung up.

"Fucking Awkward Relative," I said. She blushed. How could she know I'd done my clinical practice in a hospital, had a doctor for a husband, and was familiar with the many acronyms hospital staff were so fond of using. I was pleased to have her off guard.

"Has my father seen a doctor?"

"Yes, Dr. Ashby saw him earlier. She's the cardiology resident on duty."

The twelve-year-old, clearly.

"What about the consultant?"

"He's not here on the weekend."

"Is Dr. Ashby still here?"

"No, she's off now, but she's on call. She was happy with his progress."

"I see. If he needed a doctor, how quickly could he see one?"

"Well, it's the weekend now, so it would usually take a few hours to get a doctor, I should think." I felt a sudden rush of blood to my head, a rage precipitated by her pitying smile, which seemed to suggest that she knew how to deal with difficult people like me.

"You say that as though a weekend were an unexpected event: oh, goodness me, a weekend is upon us, what a surprise," I said. "You do know this is something that happens every week?"

She moved objects around the desk, taking particular care to ensure that the telephone was perpendicular to a plastic tower of in-trays from which human lives in the form of patients' folders spilled untidily. Perhaps she hoped that her methodical organization of inanimate objects would soothe me.

"I'm not sure that illness knows it should take Saturday and Sunday off and only trouble its victims from Monday to Friday." I wasn't yet ready to relinquish my point.

"I'm sorry, that's how the hospital works," she said. "Your father is quite comfortable at the moment."

I leaned forward over the counter. "How would you feel if it was *your* father lying in a hospital bed having just suffered a heart attack? This isn't just some old man that no one cares about, you know, someone who's had a good innings. Everyone deserves the best care, but this is my father, a very loved man, with friends and family, and if anything happens to him on your watch I will hold you personally responsible."

My eyes had filled with tears and I was on the point of losing control, but I could see by her expression that I'd got through to her. Dad was no longer just another patient in her eyes, he had become a real person with a life; he had become, in short, an individual.

She leaned forward and put her hand on mine. "Don't worry, we'll look after him."

"Thank you. I'm sorry for my FARish behavior."

We were united now, both daughters of fathers, so she smiled and said, "I'm sure I'd be just the same if I were you."

Dad was reading the newspaper and looking quite chirpy by the time I returned to his bedside. "How was your trip to the suburbs?" he asked.

"Ha-ha, very funny. Am I really so transparent?"

"You're my daughter."

"I'm not sure. It was strange to see him, and you're right about what happens to your inner city; mine's in danger of becoming so derelict it may soon have a demolition order slapped on it. Crumbling apartment houses, smashed windows, the lot. I mean, look at recent events: Son ends up in hospital with alcohol poisoning, husband wages one-man war against local government, daughter is most probably only moments away from teenage pregnancy, and father has heart attack."

"I don't think you can be held responsible for my heart attack or Greg's eccentricity, although obviously Leo and Kitty's misdemeanors are your fault by virtue of the fact that you are their parent." He took my hand and stroked it. "Greg is a good man, Chloe, and he loves you. You know what Simone Signoret said?"

I shook my head.

"'Chains do not hold a marriage together. It is threads, hundreds of tiny threads, which sew people together through the years. That is what makes a marriage last, more than passion or even sex!' I think she's right. That's what bound me to your mother and binds me now to Helga."

Helga came back just then with a plastic cup of some tasteless, brownish liquid that had the audacity to pass itself off as tea.

"You are looking better, Bertie. I think Chloe may be the best medicine."

Dad smiled and patted my hand. "I'm going to sleep now," he said, "so why don't you two girls go home and get some rest as well?"

Helga and I looked at each other. I could see she didn't want to usurp my place, but it was also clear that she didn't want to leave Dad.

"You stay, but phone me if you need to," I said.

She smiled gratefully. "I'll feel much happier sleeping next to him in this chair."

It wasn't easy relinquishing Dad's care to another woman. I was used to having him to myself. But I was needed at home.

I turned my phone back on as I left the hospital, and it immediately beeped.

PHONE ME, CHUDO. IVAN XX

I had the distinct sensation that Ivan was slipping away from me. His face and voice, usually sharp and present in my head, felt blurred. It was as though I'd had a long fever and it had finally burned out, leaving me weak and exhausted. He seemed remote and strangely irrelevant, as if he belonged to some other half-forgotten life. I called him.

"How is he?"

"He doesn't seem too bad, rather pale and weak but very much himself," I said.

"Go back to the country with me." His voice became low and husky. "I'll tie you up and make you come in five different ways."

"Um, yes—well, I really need to be near my father." Sex talk didn't go with hospitals somehow, or with parental heart attacks, come to that. "Look, I've got to go, let's speak tomorrow."

My tryst with Ivan had almost been that fatal overdose after all, but with my father the victim, not me.

I experienced a rush of affection when I saw Greg. It was well past midnight, and he was sitting on the sofa in the flickering light of the television screen. The children were asleep on either side of him, their arms flung out with the carelessness of babies. Seeing the three of them huddled together brought tears to my eyes. Greg stood up, taking care not to wake them. We looked at each other; he sighed and pulled me to him. I wept on his shoulder, silent sobs of fear for my father and of sadness and regret for what had happened to Greg and me.

"It's all right, darling," said Greg, stroking the back of my head. "They said it was a minor heart attack and he'll be fine with rest."

"He just looked so thin and frail. I can't bear the thought of losing him."

"I know, darling, I know." He held my chin and tilted my face up to his. "But the children and I will always be here to look after you. It's true what you said; we do need to be nicer to each other."

I was crying now, as much for Greg and me as for my father.

"Everyone goes through rough patches; that's just how life is," he went on. "It doesn't mean it's the end, sometimes it's just the middle, a point along the journey."

He was so much more grown up than I, I realized, remembering that this was one of the things about him that had first made me love him. And I had loved him so much. When we'd first started living together, I would rush home, excited when I saw his car parked outside, happy that he was home and waiting for me. I was the one who was trained to understand human behavior and yet Greg, despite his foibles, was so much steadier.

First Kitty, and then Leo stirred and sat up. Kitty pushed Greg and me closer together.

"Kiss each other," she said.

"Ugh," said Leo. "Must they?"

"Why not? You did; you pulled in the park," Kitty said.

Leo kicked her.

"What does that mean exactly?" I asked.

"He kissed a girl."

"We used to call that *getting off* with someone."

"Yeah,wellthingshavechanged,it'snotlikeitwasinyourday," said Leo, lapsing into fastest-white-rapper-in-the-world speak as he glared threateningly at Kitty.

We looked at one another and smiled. I began to feel that some of the madness of the previous months was ebbing away.

"I'm sorry, Greg," I said.

"What for?"

"Everything."

Our family idyll was disturbed by the sound of Janet the cat being sick in a corner and the distant strains of raised voices from the top floor of the house. Bea and Zuzi were clearly having words.

The next day dawned crisp and bright. Bea was angrily buttering bread for sandwiches in the kitchen, her thick brows knitted in a mixture of irritation and concentration. Kitty was standing on a chair behind her, brushing her hair and coaching her in marriage vows formulated for same-sex couples.

"Where did you find that?" I asked, indicating the typewritten pages in her hand.

"Special Website, Mrs&Mrs.com," she answered, with the technological savvy of a twenty-first-century child. "I looked it up for them so they'd know what to do." She turned back to Bea. "You say, *I, Bea Havlova, take you, Zuzi Palakhova, to be my lawful partner.*"

Although it was months before their happy day, the preparations for what had become known to us as the Lesbitian Wedding were occupying more and more of everyone's time. (Leo, learning to carve wood with Sammy while I was cooking supper one evening, had constructed a fantasy where Bea and Zuzi were not from the Czech Republic after all but were natives of the isle of Lesbos and should henceforth be known as Lesbitians. "Nopointlettingallmyclassical-educationgotowasteMum," he'd said. "It makes it sound like they're Martians," I'd protested. "Welltheyaretomewhatawasteofpussy," he'd said, shocking me.)

Leo entered the kitchen and reached blindly into the fridge for some orange juice. I don't think I'd ever seen him up so early on a Saturday morning before.

"You are very bad boy," Bea complained, "standing on chair looking into our room through glass at top when we are in the bed."

Leo smirked with discomfort but said nothing.

"You didn't!" I said.

He shrugged noncommittally. "WellmaybeIdidandmaybeIdidn'tthat's-formetoknowandnotreallyanyoneelse'sbusinessbutmyown. It'scertainly-notthesortofthingasonwantstodiscusswithhismother."

"He and Atlas also are looking all the time in the telescope from the Ruthie's roof into the window at us," Bea said, jabbing her knife in Leo's direction.

Oh, dear, it was all very well being wishy-washy liberals, but I suppose we really should draw the line at staging live home girl-on-girl sex shows for our adolescent son and his friends. Although, in Atlas's case it had clearly been therapeutic, since, Ruthie had told me only a few days before, he'd recently been considering that he might be heterosexual after all.

I escaped the embarrassment of my son's burgeoning sexuality by seeking shelter in the living room. I found Zuzi there, her hands clasped around a cup of tea as though she needed to draw every drop of warmth from it she could. A closed copy of *Doctor Zhivago* was on the table beside her. She'd finished it at last. She was looking ahead bleakly in a glassy-eyed sort of way.

"Marriage for me is always seem like fairy tale. My Bea, she love me now, but do she love me enough? What if she find other girl? What if I am not, for her, her Lara?"

"That's a risk everyone has to take. Choose to be happy." Once again, the gospel according to Dolly Parton was proving a useful counseling tool.

She put her cup down and began twisting the sapphire engagement ring on her finger. Sapphire rings for Sapphic brides.

"In Czech we have different saying: *Do not always expect good to happen, but do not let evil take you by surprise.*"

I could see I was going to have a problem with the Czech psyche as far as Dolly and my little *be happy* mantra were concerned. Eastern Europeans were like Jews when it came to living on the brink of disaster and expecting the worst.

"Have you ever been with a man, Zuzi?" I asked.

"Few time, but for me is horrible. It make me sick how they smell."
She wrinkled her freckled nose in disgust.

That was what I loved the most about men, their smell. Not all of
them, just the ones you were attracted to. There'd been a lot of research
into pheromones recently, and I'd been following it in an attempt to
blame something other than my faithless heart for my affair with Ivan;
perhaps he'd been leading me by the nose. What was it about the olfactory systems of gay men and lesbian women that made them attracted
to the same sex? I should tell Ruthie to get Atlas to sniff both men and
women and see which he preferred. That way he'd work out once and
for all where his sexual proclivities lay. I began to get quite excited as I
thought about this; it would make a good paper for *Psychological Review*.
For the first time in ages, I felt stimulated by my work.

Zuzi was still looking glum.

"You see, Yuri Zhivago, in beginning, he love the Tonya, the one he
make for his wife, and then he go to the war and fall for the Lara and
he hurt the Tonya so bad. Maybe I am the Tonya and not the Lara, and
when Bea find the Lara she leave me behind."

"There's a Jewish saying too," I said, quoting one of Dad's many
aphorisms. "*Do not ask questions of fairy tales.*"

For some reason, this made her face brighten and she went downstairs to see Bea. Everyone, it seems, needs to believe in a happily ever
after.


Dad was wide awake and scratching blackbirds onto a sheet of
manuscript when Sammy and I went in to see him later that morning.
Helga told us the doctor had said he could go home in a few days. She
looked exhausted. Wisps of hair were escaping in all directions and
her clothes were creased; not even her recently applied lipstick could
hide her fatigue. We sent her home to change and rest.

"Helga's going to move in with me," Dad said. "She says she wants
to look after me. I don't need looking after, but I'd like her to stay, for

276 · Olivia Lichtenstein

us to be together properly. Aristotle said, *No one would choose a friendless existence on condition of having all the other things in the world.* He's right. In the end, the minor irritations of day-to-day cohabitation are more than compensated for by the love and companionship you find in each other's company. If nothing else, this heart attack has taught me that."

"I'm pleased," I said. "We really like her, don't we, Sammy?"

"Yes," he agreed, but I could tell, from the way his eyes wouldn't meet mine, that even after all these years he felt we were being unfaithful to Mum.

"It's about time you found someone yourself, Sammy," Dad said.

"I am seeing someone, a Spanish girl. She's called Nieves."

"Good," Dad said. "I don't like to think of you being lonely."

At the other side of the room I could see the pretty nurse I'd lashed with my tongue the day before. She caught my eye and smiled. I went over to her.

"Thank you," I said. "He's so much better."

"He's a pleasure to look after. I wish everyone was like him," she said, as a man in a nearby bed called out irritably, "Nurse, nurse, nurse!" his voice growing louder with each summons.

I went back to Dad. In the bed next to him lay an old man, pale and unmoving. His family was seated solemnly around his bed as they prepared to face the worst. I watched the face of one of them, a woman of about my own age who must have been his daughter. She looked up as though my gaze had touched her, and as our eyes met we gave each other a shy smile of recognition. We were both daughters who shared a special bond with their fathers. I wanted to get Dad out of here as quickly as possible and to the safety of the outside world as if her father's obvious fate were contagious.

"I'm going to have a sleep now and you two must have lots to do, so off you go," Dad said, giving us both his signature triple kiss.

On the way downstairs, Sammy said, "I traced Madge's Armie."

"And?"

"He went back to Jamaica."

"What will you do now?"

"I'm not sure what I *can* do. I suppose I'll see if I can get information from the Jamaican authorities and tell Madge I'm still searching."

The smokers continued their silent vigil by the hospital entrance, wrapped tightly against the chill in dressing gowns topped with sweaters. As we passed them, my phone rang. It was Ruthie.

"Bea's just phoned me; Zuzi's vanished," she said.

"What do you mean?"

"She left a note telling Bea to meet her at the railway station and saying something about testing the strength of her love. She didn't say which station, though."

It was *Doctor Zhivago* come to life: Lara going on ahead and Yuri Zhivago promising to follow her. Or, perhaps she was intending to throw herself in front of a train like Anna Karenina instead?

"Oh for fuck's sake," I said, "hang on a minute. Let me think." Station. *Vokzal*, I remembered. Once in that cosy postcoital exchange of stories that Ivan and I so enjoyed, he had told me that the Russian word for railway station derived from Vauxhall Station. The story goes that Czar Nicholas I was on a state visit to London in 1844 and was taken to see the trains at Vauxhall. He mistakenly assumed that "Vauxhall" (*vokzal* in Russian) was the generic term for a railway station. It was a guess, but it felt like a good one in the context of the Russian literature that the Russo-Czech Club of the Books had been reading over the past few months.

"I'll go," I told Ruthie, once again caught up in keeping Bea happy. "I think I know where she'll be. Put Bea in a taxi and tell the driver to take her to Vauxhall Station."


As I hurried up the street to the station, I saw Bea getting out of a cab and running inside. I hung back; this was their story, not mine. While I waited, I phoned the hospital to check on Dad and was told he was asleep. Soon, Bea and Zuzi emerged from the station's archway. They had their arms around each other and were laughing and crying at the same time. A monkey's wedding, that's what Sammy and I used to say when we were children and it rained while the sun shone.

"How did you know she'd be here?" Bea asked me.

"*Vokzal*," I answered, with a shrug.

POB, passengers on board, I texted Ruthie, as I swung out into the midday traffic against the murmur of backseat sweet nothings in Czech.

"I am tell her she too sensitive for Russian literature, she take it too much to the heart; all the emotions, it is too much for her and make her to run away," said Bea, from where she and Zuzi sat behind me, "but this is why I love her, for the tender heart."

I glanced at them in the rearview mirror. Zuzi had her head on Bea's shoulder and Bea was stroking her arm.

"I am her Lara," said Zuzi. Their innocent belief that love was enough made me want to cry; it takes so much more than love to get through a life in partnership with someone else.

I pulled up at traffic lights and looked in my mirror again. I could see Bea placing her hand proprietarily over the slight flare of Zuzi's belly. *Was Zuzi pregnant?* I wondered. *But where had they got the sperm?* I had a disturbing vision of them robbing Leo of his nightly emissions as he slept. As the lights changed, I realized with frightening clarity that it was I who was pregnant, not Zuzi. No wonder I'd been feeling queasy. I mentally counted back and remembered that my last period had been ten days before I had slept with both my lover and my husband on the same night. I hadn't used contraception with either of them. That made me two months pregnant, and I couldn't be certain who the father was.

You all right?" Greg asked, when I opened the front door. "You're looking very pale."

I couldn't talk to him about it now, I needed time to think. How could I have another baby? How could I go back to the beginning and start again? The sleepless nights, the nappies, the twenty-four-hour police surveillance required of the toddler's parent. Back to never finishing a sentence or reading a book. But then, I remembered the sweet milky smells, the small creature stretching and pulling funny baby faces, the short little arms stretched straight upward that only reached as far as the top of its head. The arrival of a new person, whole and complete. You shouldn't have a baby to save a relationship, but at the same time I knew it could be another chance for Greg and me. Except it might not be his child. In which case, it would be an end and not a beginning at all. I'd said to Dad that I wanted another go, wanted to rub this life out and start again, so was this a sign that I should start a new life with Ivan? Could we have a child and live happily ever after? What was that Jewish proverb? *When two divorced people marry, four people get into bed.* More like eight if you count the children, or nine, if you were to count the new baby too.

FF was sitting in the living room holding forth to the assembled company about the importance of sex in a relationship. There was quite a party going on. FF looked beautiful despite a preposterous pink-and-white hat that looked like an upside-down ice cream cone. Jeremy sat on one side of her, while Jessie appeared frozen to her seat on the other. He was smirking in an *I'm a hell of a guy* sort of way as FF alluded to his sexual prowess, and Jessie looked as though she had forced her mind out of her body to escape her exquisite embarrassment. Three Eastern European lesbians, summoned earlier by Bea in her hour of need, were hanging on FF's every word, particularly at the point where she began a detailed discourse on how few men really understood women's bodies and how if it weren't for the fact that she liked being fucked, she'd be a lesbian herself. A tall serious-looking woman with short bleached-blond hair scribbled something on a piece of paper and passed it to FF right under Jeremy's nose, saying, "If you are changing your mind about this, please to phone me."

Trust FF to pull a lesbian. I could just see what her next book might be: *Sapphic Love: The True Female Orgasm.* Jeremy's confident smile wavered for a moment, and Jessie, looking as though she might be sick, finally found the strength to get up and leave the room.

"Jezzie and I are going to get married," FF whispered to me. "I think I'll announce it to everyone now." She raised a fork to chime it against the side of her glass to get everyone's attention.

"Don't do it now," I said, my hand staying hers as I looked over at Bea and Zuzi sitting closely together with their arms around each other. "Let Bea and Zuzi have their moment."

FF paused and looked at me. "You're right," she said. "I am horribly self-centered sometimes, aren't I? I don't know why you put up with me."

I didn't know why I did either, but perhaps it was because while I was with her I couldn't help but be entertained. The fact that sometimes even she knew when she'd overstepped the mark also redeemed her. Everyone should have an absurdly beautiful friend; it was like having a work of art: whatever the difficulties involved in acquiring and keeping it, nothing ultimately can detract from the pleasure of contemplating it.

FF looked at me now and said quietly, "It's over, isn't it?"

"What?"

"Your affair with Ivan."

"I don't know what you mean."

"Come on, Chlo, you know I have witchy powers. I suspected for ages and then the night of Bertie's gala I knew for sure. But it's finished now, I can see."

Was it finally over? Perhaps it was. What was it that Ruthie had said? Sometimes other people can tell things about you that you don't yet know yourself.

"Are you really going to marry Jeremy?" I asked, changing the subject.

"Yes. The beginning of a marriage is such heaven, isn't it?"

"I don't know," I answered. "I've only had one and I'm still having it."

I knew what she meant, though; the first part of a relationship *was* heavenly. That's what I had loved about my affair with Ivan. But the sad truth is that there was no guarantee that it would go on like that, and more likely than not we would have slid inevitably into that state somewhere between contentment and indifference that is the fate of most married couples.

Greg came toward me, his face solemn. Had he decided to confront me about Ivan?

"Chloe, Helga just called. Bertie's had another heart attack. He's in intensive care."

# Chapter 23

D ad's face was barely visible beneath the oxygen mask. Helga stood at the foot of his bed in conversation with a doctor. I was pleased to see that he was over forty and looked like a consultant. He turned as Greg, Sammy, and I approached, his expression grave.

"This is Mr. Zhivago's son, daughter, and son-in-law," Helga explained, coming to stand next to me. "Mr. McTernan is also a doctor," she added, placing a hand on Greg's arm.

The doctor gave Greg a tight smile, the smile of a professional who knows he can tell it like it is to a colleague.

"Mr. Zhivago has suffered a severe myocardial infarction and is very weak," he said. "We're treating him with medication; he's on a GTM infusion and has a hyperium IV. We're monitoring his blood for oxygen levels and carrying out serial ECGs."

"What about surgery?" Greg asked.

"His arteries are not suitable for a bypass, I'm afraid, and he's too old for a transplant. We'll have to watch and wait."

More than his words, I didn't like what I saw in the doctor's expression. Neither did Greg; he drew me to him. It was dark outside, and the room was quiet save for the sound of Dad's breathing. A nurse moved around him, taking his blood pressure and monitoring his various drips. She didn't meet our eyes.

We sat through the night, the four of us, and watched the labored rise and fall of Dad's chest. I think we all knew it would be his last night and didn't want to miss a moment of it. We didn't talk much, just held one another's hands and wiped our tears away. We took turns holding Dad's hands too, moving silently around the bed, swapping a foot for a hand; it was as though by touching him we were tethering him to life. Helga sang softly:

*Bertie is from England,*
*Zhivago is his name,*
*Lives in Temple Fortune*
*On High Market Lane,*
*Building number twenty,*
*The doorbell's just the same.*

It was the verse Jürgen had memorized so he could find Dad after the war.

At one point in that still, dark, and timeless night, I sat vigil alone for a few minutes. I took Dad's hand and stroked it, held it to my face and kissed it. There was so much I wanted to tell him. I wanted to beg him not to leave us, I wanted to laugh with him one more time, to enjoy his warmth, wisdom, and humor, and to thank him for the love he'd given me all my life. But I couldn't do any of those things; I didn't want him to know he was dying. So I said the only thing I could, words that didn't seem up to the job of expressing how I felt about him.

"I love you, Dad."

He stirred and suddenly pulled his oxygen mask from his face. "I love you too," he said. He looked at me and added, "You know what I'm proudest of?"

I didn't trust myself to speak, so I shook my head.

"My family: being a father and a grandfather." His voice sounded surprisingly normal. He smiled at me so sweetly, patted my hand, and closed his eyes. I replaced the oxygen mask gently and smoothed the soft silver hair on his clever witty head, which was packed so full of knowledge and sayings, music and blackbirds. Where would it all go? Surely it had to go somewhere. It couldn't just be extinguished like a light at the flick of a switch. Helga came back and sat on his other side. Our hands met as we stroked his head.

I thought of him, a young man far from home, in an Italian forest with an enemy soldier's gun at his head, his life still ahead of him yet fearing death was upon him. I thought of all the vicissitudes of the path that had led to this point, with that same German soldier's widow beside him, loving him to the end, when death finally did look certain. How curious it would be if we knew at the start how our lives would play out. I sat there, with a new life that would soon begin to stir within me, the first flutterings of a baby popping like bubbles within me. All my life I had dreaded the loss of my father, and now it appeared as though there could be no escape. All the chicken wishbones I'd pulled, the dandelions I had blown, the salt I had thrown over my left shoulder while I incanted *Please let Daddy live to be ninety-four in perfect health,* an age I had plucked from the air because it seemed so impossibly old and distant. None of it had worked. Why was I always pregnant when one of my parents was dying? It was a cruel reminder of the inevitable cycle of life, each birth paid for with a death. When Mum died, Kitty was growing inside me and I used to think about how having her would mean a rebirth of part of my mother. I had the raw material, the DNA, to re-create my mother in some way, although not to replace her, for there can be no replacing. Now, as Dad lay fading in front of us, I was growing another new life inside me, a new member of my family who would have something of my father in him or her. I knew then that whatever happened I would have this baby, whoever the father was. I also knew it would be a boy.

The consultant returned early the next morning. He took Sammy and me aside.

"I want you to realize how serious your father's condition is," he said. I think until that point I'd been praying that our love for him would be enough to keep Dad with us. Sammy and I hugged each other as we wept.

"We have to get the children here," I said to Greg.

"Won't it be too upsetting for them?" Helga asked.

"They'd never forgive us if we didn't let them see him."

I'd asked Ruthie to stay at our house with the children and I went outside to call her, my voice breaking as I told her the news. I walked back along the corridor; the hospital was coming to life. Here and there, nurses and doctors were chatting and laughing; I was offended by their normality. *How will I bear this?* I thought, the question repeating itself in my head. I could understand now why Madge had chosen madness; grief is so painful it can chase you to a different place.

Ruthie arrived with Kitty and Leo, their faces weighted with a sorrow they seemed too young to support. They were bravely trying not to cry. We stood there, all of us around him, watching and waiting, as the consultant had advised, but each knowing that we were saying goodbye. Suddenly, Dad sat up and removed his mask completely. He looked around at us.

"Hello, everybody," he said. He was delighted to see us all and sounded like he had just opened a door to welcome us in. For an instant I dared to hope that he was recovering; then I remembered hearing about those moments of lucidity that often precede death. Dad looked at each of us in turn, as though memorizing our faces, lay back, closed his eyes, and breathed out, a long sigh of letting go. He had left us. In the end, his passing reflected his being; it was dignified and quiet.

I don't know what made me go in search of some scissors so I could cut off small locks of Dad's silver hair as a keepsake. The same need to hold on, to possess a piece of the loved one that had fueled the peasant boy's desire from Ivan's Russian tale to bite off the nose of the dead girl he loved? I held Leo and Kitty to me. In that moment, apart from the unbearable sorrow of losing my father, a grief that threatened to crush me forever, I knew that I would stay with Greg and that my affair with Ivan was, as FF had observed, quite over.

*Chapter 24*

I did see Ivan once more. It was some weeks after the funeral, after the initial searing pain of loss had settled into a dull and continuous ache. Each morning, when I woke up, I had a brief moment of normality before I remembered that I was waking up to a world that no longer contained my father. Then the familiar ache would settle in for the rest of the day. We'd held the funeral two days after Dad's death, Sammy and my Jewishness kicking in atavistically. Jews bury their dead as soon as possible. I used to think it was due to the heat of the desert, but in fact, Ruthie had explained to me, it's because once a person's soul has returned to God, it's considered shameful to allow the body to linger in the land of the living.

"Births, marriages, and deaths, that's when religion comes into its own," Sammy had said, as we sat in Dad's flat a few days after he'd died. We'd all gone there from the hospital; it had felt like the obvious place to be, as if it were a way of remaining in his presence and keeping him alive. The flat still smelled of him and the piano was open, as he had left it, motes of dust dancing in the rays of a spring sunshine that insolently shone on our sorrow. The room was quiet, as if the piano knew that my father's hands would never make it sing again. We'd stayed in the flat much of the time since the funeral, sitting shiva as was customary. Ruthie had brought food and looked after us as we sat and cried and shared memories of Bertie.

"Jews do some things well," Sammy went on. "I mean, you can see why they tear their clothes. It helps to have an external expression of your inner state. That's just how I feel: torn. Don't you?" In accordance with Jewish custom in times of mourning, Sammy was unshaven and wearing a ripped shirt. He looked like I felt: bereft, an orphan. It doesn't matter how old or grown-up you are when your parents die, you still feel abandoned and alone. When they die, part of you dies with them, your younger self, your childhood. There's no one left to tell you what you were like as a baby, what your first words were or what your favorite toy was. All those memories are buried with them. I was no longer somebody's daughter. The safety net had gone; no generation lay between Sammy and me and the grave.

At the end of that terrible first week, Helga had left for Germany, leaving us orphaned and bereft all over again. "You do understand, don't you?" she'd explained. "I need to be with my children in Germany. But I will come and visit you often; we will always be a part of each other's lives."

A few weeks later, Sammy and I went to the flat to begin the business of sifting, sorting, and packing away in boxes a life that was now over. I found some of our childhood there, hidden in drawers in the shape of old yellowing school reports and little nonsense notes of love that I'd written to Dad and he to me. He'd kept them all, tucked away in a wooden box in the back of a cupboard. Daughters, if they're lucky, learn the business of loving from their fathers. The notes almost undid me; they made me realize all over again how much I had lost.

"You should be really grateful for all those years you had a dad," FF had said to me the day before. She stood in my kitchen, holding out her hand for me to admire the engagement ring Jeremy had given her. "I didn't have any of that." FF's father died when she was ten. "Here, I've got you something to cheer you up." She handed me an envelope. Inside was a voucher for a session with Rasa Rastumfari, the legendary colonic irrigator. I suppose she meant well, but did she honestly think a clean colon could remedy the loss of a beloved father?

Sammy found me in the bedroom, weeping over a photograph I had found. It was a picture of me at fourteen sitting next to Dad, my head resting on his shoulder. He was smiling, half turned toward me. I remembered the day it was taken, the day after Grandma Bella's funeral. Just moments before, Dad and I had been weeping in each other's arms. Sammy was carrying a cardboard box he'd found in the same cupboard, portentously labeled MY YOUTH. He sat beside me and ran his own past through his fingers.

"Ginny Best's vagina," he said suddenly, holding something up.

"I beg your pardon?"

"These photos. I took them of her vagina. Actually, strictly speaking they're of her vulva, not her vagina. Must have been when we were both about nineteen. Not bad," he said, bringing the photo closer to him.

"The vagina or the photo?"

"Both. I was a good photographer."

He used to spend hours in the bathroom, which he'd turned into a darkroom, with me hammering impatiently on the door.

"What should I do with them?" he asked me now.

"Send them to her?" I suggested. "Throw them away?"

"Do you want to see them before I do?"

"I think not, OK?"

The vagina/vulva episode lightened our mood, so that when Ivan texted me a few moments later, asking if he could see me, I told him to meet me in a café round the corner.


It is death and not love that changes everything. How handsome Ivan looked when he arrived, a handsome stranger. I could see why I had wanted him, though the connection between us now felt quite broken. At first, we didn't openly acknowledge that we were saying goodbye: We didn't have to; we both knew. I sat opposite him and ran my little finger along the scar in his eyebrow, reading the Braille of his face with my hands to memorize it.

"Becky and I are getting divorced," he told me. "I hate the way I am with her; she deserves better."

"Is she all right?"

"I think she's relieved."

We sat in silence for a few moments.

"I'm so sorry about Bertie—" he began.

My eyes filled with tears. "I have to go," I said. "Sammy is waiting for me."

"If you need me or things change . . ." he said, as I was leaving.

I put a finger to his lips before replacing it with my mouth as I kissed him, as he had once done to me when all of this began.

At the door, he handed me a piece of paper. A verse was typewritten on it in Russian.

"One more note," he said, with a sad smile. "Forgive me for borrowing someone else's words to tell you how I feel. These are the words of the greatest Russian poet, Aleksandr Pushkin."

He held me to him one last time, turned, and left.

*Ia vas liubil: liubov' eshche, byt' mozhet,*
*V dushe moei ugasla ne sovsem;*
*No pust' ona vas bol'she ne trevozhit;*
*Ia ne khochu pechalit' vas ni chem.*
*Ia vas liubil bezmolvno, beznadezhno,*
*To robost'iu, to revnost'iu tomim;*
*Ia vas liubil tak iskrenno, tak nezhno,*
*Kak dai vam bog liubimoi byt' drugim.*

This time, I wasn't going to ask Volodya to translate. Instinctively, I knew that this was both too private and too sad. Instead, I logged on to Dad's computer back at his flat and found a translation myself on the Internet:

*I loved you: it may be that love has not completely died in my soul; but let it trouble you no longer; I do not wish to sadden you in any way. I loved you silently, hopelessly, tormented now by shyness and now by jealousy; I loved you so sincerely, so tenderly, as God grant you may be loved by another.*

Pushkin had written it in 1829. Nothing's new in love, it seems, There is some comfort in that.

I didn't see Ivan again after that. I couldn't. The knowledge that the new life growing inside me might belong in part to him made it impossible for me to see him. The only way I could cope was to compartmentalize: to deny his existence and tell myself that none of it had happened and I was nothing more than a married woman, pregnant with her third child.

Should I tell Greg about Ivan?" I asked Ruthie, one afternoon on the phone.

"Rule Two, remember?" she said. "*Never confess. If you can't do the time, don't do the crime.*"

"But I do have to tell him that I'm pregnant."

"Yes, that you do have to do."

That evening, Greg came through the front door looking very pleased with himself and waving a piece of paper. "Read this," he said.

Dear Sir or Madam,

With regard to your Penalty Charge for entering the Congestion Charge Zone without paying the fee.

I was careful to await the time of 18:30 before entering the Congestion Charge Zone.

In your letter you inform me that your system is synchronized to the Rugby Atomic Clock. I made sure to note that 18:30 was the time recorded on both my watch and my car clock before entering the zone. Your first letter claims that I entered two minutes and forty-six seconds before 18:30—presumably according to the Rugby Atomic Clock. I must say that I have always regarded myself as a highly punctual individual and have always considered it very important to ensure that my various timepieces are accurate. I shall be sure in the future to check my watch against the speaking clock before setting out on a journey into central London's Congestion Charge Zone in the evening.

However, I made two other two points in my letter:

[1] I believe a difference of less than three minutes to be within the limits of acceptable variation between chronometers.

[2] If Transport for London wish motorists to adhere to the Congestion Charging times as accurately as the Rugby Atomic Clock, then I believe clocks recording the accurate time should be in place at every road junction within the Congestion Charge zone.

Therefore, I again respectfully request, in view of the two points that I have presented above, that you cancel this Penalty Charge Notice.

Yours sincerely,

Greg McTernan

"Very good, darling," I said. "I'm pregnant." (Well, when *is* the right moment to tell someone that?)

"That'll give them something to think . . . what?"

"I'm pregnant."

He looked at me, a long hard calculating look. "But we've hardly had sex recently and you used your cap, didn't you?"

"You're a doctor, you should know it only takes one go. And no, I didn't use my cap. Don't you remember, it was among the many items you hid that neither of us have been able to find."

"Oh, yes," he said sheepishly. "You could have gone and got a new one."

"It hardly seemed worth it," I said, a little more smartly than I'd intended.

292 · *Olivia Lichtenstein*

He seemed about to say something but changed his mind. "What do you want to do, Chlo?"

We were standing in the kitchen. Greg was leaning against the fridge, next to the photograph of us all taken outside the house as we set off for Dad's gala. Dad had been right after all; it had been a life-time achievement award for a life that was almost over. Next to it was the order of service from his funeral. It had the photo of him that had hung above his piano, the one where he was so fondly watching Leo and Kitty as they opened their presents. Who could have known that this photograph, taken so spontaneously at a time of joy, would one day come to symbolize the sorrow we felt at losing him?

I turned to Greg. "Did Dad ever talk to you about dying?"

"Not so much about dying," he answered quietly, "as about after he was dead."

"What did he say?"

Greg paused, turned on the kettle, and busied himself with getting mugs out to make tea. "He loved you, and he was worried about how you would cope. He told me to look after you, and I told him I would always look after you, because I love you too."

I looked into his eyes and recognized the expression in them. It was the way he used to look at me when we were first together.

"I remember you," I said, poking him playfully to chase away the tears that were filling my eyes. "You're my boyfriend Greg, that boy I fell in love with all those years ago. I feel like I haven't seen you for ages."

"I'm the same person and so are you. Nothing's changed," he said, stroking my face.

If only that were true.

"What do *you* want?" I asked Greg, running a hand over the as yet barely perceptible swelling of my stomach.

"I want you to be happy; I want us to be happy. I want you to under-stand that I love you." He put his hands on my shoulders and drew me toward him. "I want whatever you want."

"I want to have the baby."

"Then we will, even though it means we'll have to go on working until we're seventy."

Kitty and Leo were excited by the news, once they'd got over the disgusting fact that their parents still had sex. I wasn't sure how I was going to tell Jessie that I'd need her room back for the baby. She was back to spending every weekend with us and frequently a night or two in the week. When I tried to broach the subject with FF she waved her arm dismissively and said, "Don't worry, darling, she can bunk in with Kitty." She was far more concerned with telling me that it was extremely unlikely I'd ever get my figure back this time, after a third child and at my advanced age.

"You should have a caesarean and a tummy tuck at the same time," she said. "That's what everyone is doing these days."

Perversely, I was almost more afraid of telling Bea I was pregnant than I had been about telling Greg. As it turned out, my concern was well-founded.

I found her standing in front of the hall mirror, plucking her eyebrows.

"I do not look after the babies," she said firmly.

Perhaps it was for the best. We couldn't go on having both her and Zuzi in the house; it would finally give me the perfect way out and the opportunity to find someone new who might actually do some work.

"This is not my job," Bea continued, turning from her scowling image to face me. "For this you need my Zuzi. This is the work she done in Czech Republic; she is the trained baby nurse." Before I could respond, she'd called Zuzi down and, far from getting rid of them, I found myself agreeing to employ them both: Bea for Kitty, Leo, and, of course, Jessie, and Zuzi for the baby. Now I would have two people to pay instead of one and an extra child in the house—two, in fact, if you counted Jessie.

"One hundred," Greg said, when I told him.

"One hundred what?"

"Now we'll have to work until we're one hundred, not seventy."

Only to Ruthie could I sometimes confess my sadness at losing Ivan and the anxiety about my baby's paternity that kept me awake most nights.

"You wouldn't be the first, Chlo," she said, trying to comfort me as we lay on the sofa in my living room one afternoon several months later. I was seven months pregnant and she was now officially and happily unemployed, relaxing until she decided what she would do next. We'd taken to having an afternoon rest together, slavishly watching *Richard and Judy.*

"I did a piece on DNA paternity testing for *Smart* once," she went on. "Did you know that roughly thirty percent of men taking the tests discover that they are not the biological fathers of the children they've been bringing up as their own? Rule Number Ten, by the way: *Never agree to a DNA test.*"

"It amazes me," I said, "how some people change partners so effortlessly. You read about these women who get divorced and then a second later they're shacked up with someone else and having their baby. They all seem to do it so lightly."

"Who are these women?" Ruthie said, looking at me a little more pointedly than I would have liked. After all, I had chosen the path of righteousness, sacrificing my lover for my husband.

"Oh, you know, they're in all those magazines: *Wigga Weekly,* or whatever they're called."

"Maybe they don't have that family thing we have—you know, the compulsion to preserve the unit whatever the cost."

"Mmm, I suppose that's a good thing though, isn't it? What else is there really that's as important as family?"

"Are you and Greg having sex again?" Ruthie asked.

"Constant," I answered. "It's so weird; it's as if nothing happened."

She gave me a shrewd look. "Once a week?"

I nodded.

"That's about right," she agreed. "For marital sex, that *is* pretty constant. What was all the abstention about, then?"

"I don't know. Greg says it was just a stage in our lives before we moved on. I told you about the GrayAway I found in the bathroom, didn't I?"

Ruthie nodded. "He's stopped using it, hasn't he? I like his graying temples."

"Me too," I said. "Strangely, that frosting was one of the things I found so attractive in Ivan."

"Do you think you'd ever have another affair?"

"Never say never," I quipped.

Ruthie sat up and looked at me in horror.

"Only kidding, next time it's your turn," I said.

We sat for a few moments in silence, enjoying the laziness of the afternoon until the doorbell interrupted us.

It was Madge with a bunch of roses she'd picked in her small garden, tied with a strip of gold satin from her fabric collection. Their rich scent made you want to bury your nose deep in the petals.

"I want to thank you for helping me," she said.

"It wasn't me, it was Sammy," I said.

"Well, both of you have made me feel better."

"Sammy's still trying to find Armie for you."

She nodded and we looked at each other for a few moments. I invited her in, but she shook her head and turned to go. I watched her walk across the road and into the park, where she was at once surrounded by a small flock of pigeons.

"I miss Bertie," said Ruthie, when I came back in.

"Yes," I answered quietly. "Sometimes it's the smallest things that undo me. I was on the tube yesterday and there was an elderly man opposite me. The sight of his hands made me cry; they reminded me of Dad's."

Old man's hands that symbolized love, parental hands that soothed brows and stroked cheeks.

We sat together silently, playing our own memories of my father in our heads.

I looked at her. She appeared healthy again, her cocaine addiction in the past. Between us, Richard and I had barely let her out of our sight for the past few months.

"Do you remember the box?" I asked. "I wonder whether anyone ever found it." A tartan biscuit tin buried in a garden more than thirty years ago. It had been a rainy Saturday afternoon in July, and we'd spent most of it getting ready to get ready (the best part) for a birthday party that night. As the rain fell, we'd sat inside and discussed what we wanted from life. Who could have known then what living happily ever after would come to mean? It certainly wasn't quite what either of us had envisaged at the time.

Now, all these years later, it was time to bury something else, something unbearably sad that marked the end of an era: Dad's ashes. On a gray cloudy day, on what would have been his seventy-ninth birthday, we gathered in the garden by the cherry tree where Mum's ashes were already buried. Helga had come over from Germany. She'd been thrilled that I was pregnant, and I'd asked her to be an honorary grandmother.

"That means a great deal to me, Chloe," she'd said.

We squeezed each other's hands, unable to say more. She stood tall and erect with her arms around Kitty and Leo. She'd become their grandmother too. Kitty sang one of Dad's songs, and Leo read a poem he had written specially. They looked so sad and broken, stumbling on their words as tears ran down their young faces. It seemed unfair that they should have to know this sorrow at such a young age, and yet this was life's inevitable cycle of love and death. One day, as for all children, if the natural order of events were observed, they would have to bury Greg and me. I looked at Greg, slim and handsome, his blue eyes rimmed red as he stood solemnly beside me. The passage I'd chosen to read was about fathers and daughters, but it applied to all of us in relation to Dad. It was from a novel I'd read recently, *Decorations in a Ruined Cemetery* by John Gregory Brown:

> *There's something like a line of gold thread running through a man's words when he talks to his daughter, and gradually over the years it gets to be long enough for you to pick up in your hands and weave into a cloth that feels like love itself.*

Ruthie reached for my hand. Sammy opened the urn and poured the ashes into the earth, and as they fell an unexpected ray of sunlight shone through the clouds and illuminated the ground. A blackbird alighted on a branch of the cherry tree, its head twitching inquisitively from side to side. It opened its mouth and sang; one long high ringing note as though a call to wake us up. Janet, who still ate only rarely, eyed it hungrily, and Sammy looked up and scanned the clouds.

"I thought I saw Dad's face there for a moment," he said sadly. "Wouldn't it be great if he were watching us?"

Perhaps in some curious sense he was. What if a relationship does not end with death after all and can continue even if someone is no longer physically present? For a moment, I had a brief glimpse into some other world not as seemingly absolute as the one we inhabited. Dad's voice was still in my head, and sometimes I felt his presence beside me. The baby kicked me under my ribs, making me cry out. Greg and the kids put their hands on my stomach. We knew we'd never get over our loss, but that time with its inexorable passage would, possibly, one day make it a little more bearable.

## CHLOE ZHIVAGO'S THAI GREEN
## PLACENTA CURRY
### (NOT FOR THE SQUEAMISH)

*Serves 6*

. . . . . . . . . . . . . . . . . .

2 teaspoons coriander seeds

1 teaspoon black peppercorns

2 fresh green chilies, seeded and chopped

1 inch-long piece of ginger, finely chopped

3 tablespoons chopped coriander leaves and stems

2 large cloves of garlic

3 tablespoons chopped spring onions

1 lemon grass root, roughly chopped

2 tablespoons vegetable oil

1½ cups coconut milk

4 kaffir lime leaves, destemmed and deveined

1½ lbs fresh placenta

1 cup water

1 small bunch fresh basil leaves, chopped

1 tablespoon fish sauce

Grind the coriander and peppercorns to a powder in a coffee grinder or mortar. Add the chilies, ginger, coriander leaves, garlic, spring onions, and lemon grass and grind to a paste. (If you want to cheat, you can buy Thai green curry paste readymade from an oriental supermarket and skip this step.) Fry this seasoning paste in a saucepan with the vegetable oil for a couple of minutes. Add the coconut milk and lime leaves and simmer for 10 minutes. Cut the placenta into bite-sized cubes. Add to the sauce with a cup of water and simmer until tender (about 20 minutes).

Add chopped basil leaves and fish sauce to the curry to taste. Serve with rice.

Chloe Zhivago, age forty-four, cradled her newborn third child, a boy, in her arms. "Can we call him Bertie?" she said, looking at her husband, Greg. He nodded, leaned toward the baby, and pulled back the blanket to reveal a tiny foot. The little toe lay crookedly on top of the fourth. Greg kissed the baby's foot, covered it up, and said to his wife, "I'm not sure I could have borne it if he hadn't been mine." The baby stared at his parents with all the wisdom of an old man in the body of a freshly minted infant. Chloe seemed about to say something, but Greg silenced her with a kiss. "Here, eat this," he said, feeding her with a spoon. It was chicken soup with knaydlach. "Delicious, darling," Chloe said. "It's got the secret ingredient, hasn't it? My shmaltz? It's perfect." In truth, it wasn't absolutely perfect, but pretty damn near.

# AUTHOR'S NOTE

Ivan would, of course, have used the Cyrillic alphabet when writing his notes to Chloe, as did Pushkin when he wrote his poem. I decided it would be best for all the Russian in this novel to be transliterated into the Latin alphabet so that the non-Russian speaking reader would be able to get a sense of the music of the language. I have used the Library of Congress (without diacritics) system of transliteration.

ACKNOWLEDGMENTS

I would like to thank my brother, Conrad Lichtenstein, and dear
friend Claire Ladsky, who were the first to read the manuscript of this
book and who offered so much valuable help and encouragement. My
friends, who sustained me while I was writing it: Simon Booker (who
kindly explained to me that writing isn't just typing, it's all the hours
away from the keyboard too), Lola Borg, Richard Denton, Neil Grant,
Alla Svirinskaya, and Colleen Toomey. Thanks also to Tania Ab-
dulezer, Jochen Encke, Marc Faupel, and Neil Geraghty, who kept my
body and soul functioning, and to Amy Jenkins and Philip McGrade
for valuable writing insights. I'd also like to thank many people named
Gill—Gill Morgan, Jill Robinson and her Wimpole Street workshop,
and Annabel Giles (not Gill exactly, but a Gile thing going on in her
surname), who were there at the beginning of this; Gillian Gordon for
her inspirational dream-writing workshop; and Gill Hudson, who
gave me an office in which to write. Thanks too to Henrietta Morri-
son for the generous use of her office on Poland Street, where much of
this book was written. I am grateful to heart surgeon Mr. Shyam
Kolvekar for his advice. Enormous thanks are due to my agent, Clare
Alexander, who guided me with a steady, wise hand throughout, and
to my editors, Jane Wood and Anika Streitfeld—I couldn't have had
better women on my team. And to Sally Riley, who has sold Chloe
Zhivago and her gang all over the place. A great debt of gratitude

to my husband, Simon Humphreys, and my children, Oscar and Francesca, without whom I would be nothing. And to Edwin Lichtenstein, my darling Dad, who read the first three chapters—all that I had then written—before he died and told me I should carry on. I hope he would have been proud.

ABOUT THE AUTHOR

OLIVIA LICHTENSTEIN is an award-winning documentary film-maker who had a distinguished career at BBC Television before becoming a freelance documentary and drama producer/director and journalist. She lives in unalloyed bliss with her husband—who does not hide everyday objects in obscure places—and their two children in West London.

ABOUT THE TYPE

This book was set in Weiss, a typeface designed by a German artist, Emil Rudolf Weiss (1875–1942). The designs of the roman and italic were completed in 1928 and 1931 respectively. The Weiss types are rich, well-balanced and even in color, and they reflect the subtle skill of a fine calligrapher.

ABOUT THE TYPE

This book was set in Weiss, a typeface designed by a German artist, Emil Rudolf Weiss (1875–1942). The designs of the roman and italic were completed in 1928 and 1931 respectively. The Weiss types are rich, well-balanced and even in color, and they reflect the subtle skill of a fine calligrapher.